P9-DBP-693

# OUT OF THE SHADOWS

Cyd walked briskly to the shack where her mother had plied her trade. Brush tore at her clothing and skin, just as fear pricked her emotions. Something scurried away and rustled the underbrush. Birds, waiting for full light and disturbed by Cyd's passing, flew into the sky, and the rapid beat of their wings echoed that of her heart.

What had happened to her twenty-five years ago? Cyd wondered again. How could a six-year-old remain frightened inside a woman's mind? What lay trapped within her, screaming to come out with every nightmare?

Vines crawled over the windowless two-room shack, the roof and porch sagging. She remembered how this shack had once echoed with drunken laughter and primitive sounds and scents. Cyd closed her eyes against the burning tears.

When she forced them open, the shadow of a big man moved through the mist toward her. She opened her lips to scream—because the man was real, coming for her in the dim light and shadows . . .

## By Cait London

WHAT MEMORIES REMAIN
WITH HER LAST BREATH
WHEN NIGHT FALLS
LEAVING LONELY TOWN
IT HAPPENED AT MIDNIGHT
SLEEPLESS IN MONTANA
THREE KISSES

**ATTENTION: ORGANIZATIONS AND CORPORATIONS**
Most Avon Books paperbacks are available at special quantity discounts for bulk purchases for sales promotions, premiums, or fund-raising. For information, please call or write:

**Special Markets Department, HarperCollins Publishers, Inc.,** 10 East 53rd Street, New York, N.Y. 10022-5299. Telephone: (212) 207-7528.   Fax: (212) 207-7222.

# CAIT LONDON

## What Memories Remain

AVON BOOKS
*An Imprint of HarperCollinsPublishers*

This is a work of fiction. Names, characters, places, and incidents are products of the author's imagination or are used fictitiously and are not to be construed as real. Any resemblance to actual events, locales, organizations, or persons, living or dead, is entirely coincidental.

AVON BOOKS
*An Imprint of* HarperCollins*Publishers*
10 East 53rd Street
New York, New York 10022-5299

Copyright © 2004 by Lois E. Kleinsasser
ISBN: 0-06-055588-2
www.avonromance.com

All rights reserved. No part of this book may be used or reproduced in any manner whatsoever without written permission, except in the case of brief quotations embodied in critical articles and reviews. For information address Avon Books, an Imprint of HarperCollins Publishers.

First Avon Books paperback printing: May 2004

Avon Trademark Reg. U.S. Pat. Off. and in Other Countries, Marca Registrada, Hecho en U.S.A.
HarperCollins® is a registered trademark of HarperCollins Publishers Inc.

Printed in the U.S.A.

10 9 8 7 6 5 4 3 2 1

If you purchased this book without a cover, you should be aware that this book is stolen property. It was reported as "unsold and destroyed" to the publisher, and neither the author nor the publisher has received any payment for this "stripped book."

# Prologue

Ewan Lochlain stepped back into the night's shadows of the wharf near Boston. He lifted his face to mid-March's chilly Atlantic wind and thought about Fairy Cove, a small peaceful town on Lake Michigan's shores. Ewan lifted his pea coat's collar and tugged down his knitted cap, bracing himself against the stinging rain—and the bitterness that came when he thought of that town.

This time he was coming back to Fairy Cove, not only to visit and check on his sister, Hallie, but to stay and settle the mystery of his parents' boating accident.

This time, he wasn't an eighteen-year-old boy who had to leave Hallie, then fourteen, in the care of someone he trusted.

This time, his maternal aunt had to deal with a man set on untangling her lies and finding the truth. The thought of her name brought bitterness churning inside him—*Dear Aunt Angela*.

Ewan impatiently wiped away the rain blurring his vision of the harbor and the schooner he'd been commissioned to bring there safely. He could have moved deeper into the shelter of the large crates, but he preferred the stark weather, which mirrored his bitterness.

He and Hallie had only been children when their parents died, and Angela had been appointed the executrix of his parents' estate and their guardian.

Guardian? Was that the right word for her heartless treatment?

Ewan released the breath he'd been holding. At least he'd been able to wrench Hallie from Angela's control with a neat bit of blackmail.

Was it blackmail for a boy to protect his sister?

Ewan forced himself to breathe slowly, fighting memories of Angela's mistreatment, of the reason he had to leave Fairy Cove—to make enough money to come back and battle Angela, to prove that his father did not try to murder his mother. Yet somehow, both of his parents had died on the lake that day. . . .

Just as the wind and rain changed, battering him from another direction, his emotions shifted and stirred. They settled on a girl who had taunted him years ago.

"Only cowards run away," Cyd Callahan had said, when he left Fairy Cove that first time. At sixteen, she'd been a long-legged, red-haired firebrand, and a good friend of Hallie's.

*Cyd.* A woman now, Cyd remained Hallie's best friend, and a damned fascinating, irritating one at that, Ewan decided darkly. Half of him couldn't wait to taunt her, as he did on his visits to Fairy Cove, to watch those brilliant blue eyes narrow dangerously and flame seem to leap in her red hair. But the other half, Ewan's protective side, knew that she'd had enough trouble in her childhood to scar her forever.

Sweet little Molly Claire's mother had made her living in a little house, outside the city limits of Fairy Cove. How often had Ewan held Molly Claire, the child, giving her comfort?

When she was ten, he'd helped her choose a brand-new spiffy name to tuck away the frightened child. And Molly Claire had become Cyd Callahan, now a tough business-woman and one who made clear her low opinion of him.

And, of course, because of the Irish in his blood, he'd had to taunt her with her old name to bring her temper churning to the surface—

Ewan smiled briefly as the swells crashed against the piers. He licked a snowflake from his lips. At eighteen, he'd given Cyd a kiss, steeped with a man's desire and raw enough to keep her from her mother's profession.

And for fifteen years, that kiss still simmered, unfinished, inside him where he could not erase it with other women.

With a shrug to push himself free of that kiss and the dark memories that coming home to Fairy Cove brought, Ewan decided to call his sister. Though he'd see her in just two weeks, he'd needed to hear Hallie's voice, to know that she was safe.

He moved into the cold night with one warming thought: He couldn't wait to see Cyd ignite when he used her child-hood name, Molly Claire. . . .

# Chapter 1

"*Leave Molly Claire alone!*" *her mother screamed.*

*Outside the shack, thunder raged, and rain slashed the windows. Lightning's silver flash painted the face of the man leering down at Molly Claire. She was only a child, too small to fight him as he held her hands with one of his, his other prowling in places she didn't want him to touch.*

*"Don't you touch my Molly Claire," her mother was yelling, hitting the man. He shoved her away. Another man pushed open the door. He stood outlined by a bolt of lightning, the wind tearing at his hair. Then the storm was inside the shack, mixed with terrible, primitive grunts of two big men fighting savagely. Her mother clawed Molly Claire into a corner and huddled protectively over her.*

*One man staggered and slumped and the other kept hitting and kicking him.*

*The man, who said he'd come back for her, turned; he came toward Molly Claire and her mother. He'd hurt her mother before, and now her face was bruised and swollen. But Linda Callahan wasn't afraid now, standing to push her child behind her. "You're the one who's been telling her those horrible things, aren't you? You told her that the Night*

*Man would get her if she didn't do what you wanted. You told her you'd come back for her. You were going to—"*

*Suddenly the man crouched, the gun in his hand pointed at the fallen man. Molly Claire's mother didn't hesitate. She hit the bad man with her iron.*

*He fell in slow motion, cursing her. Then his blood crept toward her feet, sucking at the soles.*

*Terrified and screaming, Molly Claire edged back from the red liquid fingers reaching out to her. Unblinking, his eyes locked upon her. . . .*

*His lips were closed, but she understood his silent promise, "I'm the Night Man, and I'll be back for you. . . ."*

Cyd's scream awoke her, even as she lurched upright from her tangled, sweat-damp sheets. She forced air into her lungs, fighting fiercely for the reality that she was now an adult, safe in her own home with its locks and alarms.

She wasn't Molly Claire, the child who longed for the green-eyed father her mother wouldn't name. As Cyd, she'd changed her name and her life.

She rubbed her face with her hands and discovered tears. She rubbed them away on her sheets. "I'm a woman, damn it, not a child. I've built a life for myself . . . I should be able to get a night's sleep."

But she couldn't, because bits and pieces of a child's confused memory soon leaped to life, haunting her.

On her feet, Cyd paced her bedroom, furious with herself. Whatever had happened to her as a child had roots set so deep that she couldn't forget—or entirely recall—a man's face. The blurred images were of a weathered face, broad and fierce, so fierce his eyes blazed, his expression filled with rage.

Cyd shook as she forced herself away from the man who always haunted her.

She'd made desperate attempts to resolve the fears that

rose in her each night, which caused her to lock herself into her home at sundown. Away from Fairy Cove, she'd sought a number of psychiatrists and delved into the past—but the cause of her nightmares was buried too deep and maybe too dangerous to be freed.

As a drug-addicted prostitute's daughter, Cyd was very careful to keep private her forays into the dark realms of her mind. She wouldn't want the town's queen bee—Angela Greer—to know that Cyd could have her mother's addictions or her insanity. She wouldn't give Angela, a woman who had made Cyd's mother's life miserable, that edge.

Resolved not to waste the remainder of the night, Cyd settled herself at her desk. In her living room, the desk was small and neat, just like the house—her very safe house, with shutters, locks, and alarms.

She'd chosen the house carefully, a nice bit of a bungalow-style house that she'd renovated herself. It stood away from her summer rentals and was next door to a friend and the police chief, Marvin Kendrick.

A successful real estate agent, Cyd ran through her notes on the cost of renovating a small house she'd just purchased and the profit she could make selling it. She was good at making money, *because she was never going back to being poor again.* Cyd's goal was obsessive—to rise above contempt and pity.

A stirring of the wind, and just a tiny noise turned her head to the window and something—someone moved outside the glass. She saw the man's face, the one in her nightmares. She hurled herself at the windows, closing the blinds she'd forgotten to pull.

She leaned against the wall and tried to stop shaking, terror chilling her . . . because she knew the man well. It was the man from her nightmares. . . .

The town called him the Night Man and fostered stories to sell tourists ball caps and cups. At times, the businesses hired a man to act the part, roaming at night and fascinating tourists; dressed in tatters, the actor would plop a shaggy wig on his head and paint shadows beneath his eyes.

But Cyd had known the real Night Man since she was little Molly Claire and afraid, listening to his whispered threats—"Don't tell, or you know what will happen. To your mother, too. You have to do what I say. I'll come back for you, because our game isn't ended. You haven't done what I wanted. . . . Don't tell . . . don't tell. . . ."

Molly Claire had given him nothing, wouldn't let him touch her, and the game wasn't finished. Cyd pushed back the panic and the shudder that came with it. She ached for the comfort of her friend, Hallie, who knew of Cyd's terror.

But Hallie didn't know of the tiny carved reminders that the Night Man had left.

Hallie had had enough of her own fears, and Cyd wasn't giving her more. . . .

Or was the Night Man just in Cyd's mind? Was she losing her mind as her mother had?

The collection of little sweet carved fairies and ugly leering gnomes that he sometimes left on her doorstep after an appearance said he hadn't forgotten her—that one day he would be coming for her. . . .

And she knew that the Night Man wanted her. . . .


"So he's coming back, is he? Ewan Lochlain has finally decided to return to Fairy Cove and show his hand. He's the reason Finlay has been able to keep the old Lochlain Boat Shop. Ewan has been helping Finlay pay the bills for ten years, and now he's coming back to buy it outright and take possession from Finlay—over my dead body. That's a choice piece of real estate, and I intend to make a hefty profit from its sale."

In her contemporary-style real estate office on Main Street, Cyd Callahan tapped her sleek black pen—the one that she used especially for moneymaking deals and nice juicy real estate contracts.

After fifteen years, Ewan Lochlain was coming back to stay—and not just a sometimes quarterly drop-in visit to check on Hallie, either.

Cyd studied the weathered building at the end of a wooden pier jutting out into the small harbor. Across Lake Michigan's big black waves lay Three Ravens Island, easily seen on a clear day. Those with imagination, and perhaps a little Scotch-Irish blood in their veins, said that Three Ravens Island had been torn from the Michigan shoreline, creating the harbor.

If Finlay, an elderly man, would sell the old Lochlain Boat Shop to McGruder's restaurant chain, Cyd's real estate agent commission would be enough to buy a sweet little house. It was perfect for a summer rental cottage, and she could lease it at a nice price to tourists.

McGruder's chain location and development team had contacted her with an offer for the owner of the boat shop. All Cyd had to do was to talk Finlay into selling.

Over the crisp early-April air, Fairy Cove's gossip flew across the streets and alleys and across the small Lake Michigan harbor. The whys and the wherefores came alive once more: Old man Finlay had played a good game of poker fifteen years ago. He'd won the boat shop from Paddy O'Connor, who had bought it for a pittance from Angela.

And the first thing Finlay had done when the deed lay safely in his gnarled hand was to put up the old weathered sign, LOCHLAIN BOAT SHOP. Finlay, an aged friend of Ewan and Hallie's deceased parents, had barely managed to keep the boat shop by doing small motor repairs.

Then about ten years ago, he seemed to have an easier time of it. He'd said that a rich friend had helped him out a bit.

Finlay had balked at selling the boat shop to a restaurant chain, dismissing Cyd's wrangling. When people asked why he didn't, especially with a hefty profit involved, Finlay's thin lips had closed. But now, everyone knew the reason Finlay wouldn't sell—he had saved the shop for Tom Lochlain's son, Ewan Lochlain.

Cyd placed the pen neatly on her gleaming desk. Out of habit, and deeply in thought, she put aside the expensive calculator on her desk and scooped a smaller version from her designer wool suit. With expert speed, she jabbed in the percentage she would make from handling the sale of Lochlain's Boat Shop to the trendy restaurant chain.

Impatient to close a simple deal—but for Ewan's interference—Cyd stood and walked to the window.

Fairy Cove was perfect for McGruder's restaurant chain. Though the day was grim, brewing a storm, in warmer weather the harbor's water could sparkle blue and enchanting, the brown sand fine and perfect for tourists.

Across the huge rolling waves were Three Ravens Island and the resort designed for honeymooners to escape the world. Everything was perfect to spike business income in Fairy Cove, and Cyd intended to get her share.

Only a small indentation on Lake Michigan's western shore, with a small community wrapped around it, Fairy Cove was where Cyd intended to be someone—other than a prostitute's daughter.

If McGruder's bought the boat shop, the visitors to Fairy Cove would need a place to stay, and Cyd had spotted the perfect place—a beautiful old house on Elfindale Street. The elderly occupants would move soon, and the house would be for sale. With a little renovation, it would be perfect for a bed-and-breakfast.

She intended to be the person who brought Angela Greer to her knees, to make that old crone apologize to her, and to Hallie.

Cyd pushed away the simmering dark emotions and concentrated on Fairy Cove and the possibilities that she could develop—out of Angela's grasp.

And everything hung on the sale of Lochlain's Boat Shop

to McGruder's. "It will be a long time before a chance like this comes around again."

The tourist shops on Main Street overlooked the tiny harbor, separated only by a stretch of sandy beach, parking places, a street, and a sidewalk with benches. Eastward, behind it, lay the streets fingering up and away from the water, bordered by houses—mostly small, practical homes, and a few small cabins that were empty of the "summer people" now.

From her office on Fairy Cove's Main Street, which ran parallel to the horseshoe-shaped harbor, Cyd's gaze skimmed over the pier, with its boat stalls and docks, and over the waterfront buildings, to the prize she wanted—a huge, weathered, gray building, a long wooden pier spiking out onto the tiny harbor. "Lochlain Boat Shop is barely standing, an eyesore. It's a wonder it hasn't been condemned."

In the airy cluttered building, Finlay had installed himself and wouldn't hear of selling to McGruder's chain; the old man was horrified that a restaurant could replace the boat shop. With a smirk and a spit, old Finlay had laid Cyd low— "'Tis only a building. But one with life that Tom Lochlain gave her. It's fine boats he built, and fine boats that should be built here—dinghies and dories, the handcrafted kind that few know how to build nowadays," he'd sniffed in a superior tone.

Cyd had often slid a platter of Finlay's favorite cookies in front of him, and had set about to win him. "History is one thing. Money is another. There's not much money in handcrafting wooden boats now, not as much as in selling this place. Think of what you'd be doing for Fairy Cove, the tourists McGruder's could bring here. You could retire in fine style, Finlay."

Again, Finlay had issued the superior sniff of a man who had his mind set. But he had reached a gnarled hand to take a cookie, munching on it thoughtfully. He scanned the clear blue day and the great dark waves with whitecaps riding their crests. After a sip of tea, he had his final say. "'Tis rightful this place goes to Tom Lochlain's son, and that is why I'm selling to Ewan. 'Tis already arranged. He's coming home to stay, as he should, to where he was born. What's that? The price he'd pay? None of your bargaining guile, girl. Tom Lochlain's son is as good as his word. A gentleman Ewan is, and we'll finish the deal when he comes."

Brooding in her office, Cyd pushed back the desk chair and lurched to her feet. She stalked the length, never losing sight of the boat shop, while chewing on Finlay's refusal, the percentage she'd lose by being cut out of a sale, and the return of Ewan Lochlain.

*Ewan Lochlain.* When Cyd was just four or so, the first thing she could remember was Tom Lochlain's strong, safe arms, his soothing Irish lilt. He'd given her to his son to hold and cuddle, and for a time life was bright and good, and she was Ewan's "fairy-girl."

Only later, in her early teens—long after Ewan's parents had died—did she know that there was something inside him that no one but his sister, Hallie, could reach. Bitter and cold, it nestled in his heart, so unforgiving that sometimes Cyd could almost taste it. Or maybe it was a hunger that no woman could feed.

Every time Ewan came back to Fairy Cove, just for brief visits with Hallie, the hardness crept more surely on his face and glittered in his cold gray eyes.

Cyd prowled the sleek office, flipped through her appointment book, the list of rental payments due, and checked her message machine one last time. With that dark mood ruling her, she punched in the code for her security alarm system and turned on the video camera.

In another minute, Cyd was striding down Fairy Cove's Main Street, her high heels clicking as she hurried to Hallie's Fairy Bin. Cyd ignored the chilly wind tugging open her long black all-weather coat to reveal her gray slacks; she had her temper to keep her warm.

She smoothed her hair, disdaining the dampness that could change its carefully straightened length into layers of long, dark, red curls. She'd spent a fortune on beauty shops, chemically straightening her hair, and had settled for what she could do herself with gels and brushes and blowers.

Cyd glanced out at the harbor, the clutter of boats riding the swells, fishermen busy with their poles and lines. Dressed in knit caps and winter jackets, they worked to keep their fingers and faces warm. From the sandy shoreline, wooden piers poked through the cove's dark water as stark as Fairy Cove's financial bones, waiting to be fleshed out with the tourist trade.

Cyd glanced at the prize she wanted desperately—Lochlain Boat Shop. Big and airy, it would be perfect for Mc-Gruder's. She could almost see McGruder's neon lights reflecting in the harbor, taste the sandwiches and chowder, hear the music floating across the water, and the tourists' laughter inside—more business and more money for Fairy Cove, and for her. There would be land and lots needed, houses to be sold and renovated, and rental property incomes.

She should have made her move long ago, gathering that choice piece of property under her wing to market and profit. Only her affection for Finlay kept her from pushing through the deal, from using her influence to condemn the building.

In daylight, the Lochlain Boat Shop stood on its own wooden pier and mocked her—gray with weather, a painted sign cracked and peeling, a disgusting clutter of boards and rubbish piled against the side, broken windows sealed by plastic, a thin line of smoke from an old heating stove rising into the overcast sky.

Cyd had crawled from nothing, pasted together a life and bank balance that she tended with every breath, and Ewan

Lochlain wasn't taking a small fortune in commission away from her.

She almost heard the hiss of her own indrawn breath as Angela Greer's big, black Lincoln Town Car glided down the street. Behind the wheel, her husband's face was in shadow, like his life. A retired attorney, and always a quiet man, Fred now tended only to his wife's needs.

Swathed in her mink coat, and sitting on the passenger side of the car, Angela's face was also shadowed. Then, as though she sensed someone watching her, Angela turned. A witch's senses would pick up a challenger for her realm, Cyd decided, acknowledging that a good portion of herself rode on instinct.

"Too bad, old woman. You hold the deeds on all the prime shops on Main Street—except my office and Hallie's Fairy Bin, and that really rubs you raw, doesn't it? You forgot the loopholes in the clauses, didn't you? The shopkeepers were tired of your badgering, ready to move away. I snatched up those leases right under your nose. The day their leases were up and the purchase price you demanded paid, they were mine," Cyd muttered. "You were too slow that day, Angela. You didn't know that anonymous buyer was me, did you?"

For a moment, Angela's eyes locked with Cyd's, then she turned away, the haughty dame dismissing the upstart, the commoner businesswoman.

The daughter of a prostitute. The girl who didn't know her father's name.

For years, Angela and her cronies had ruled Fairy Cove, gathering at the Greers' two-story mansion for their tea parties and plotting. That one sneer from Angela was meant to insult Cyd, to remind her of her lowly roots—her mother had never named Cyd's father. He could have been any passing man with money in his pocket.

"He had the most beautiful green eyes, and I felt like a queen when we waltzed," Linda Callahan had said. "I loved only him, and he gave me you."

Cyd watched the Greers' car glide down Main Street. At the end, it would move upward on the knoll overlooking Fairy Cove to Greer House—where Angela could overlook the streets and lives in her kingdom.

"You old biddy. I'm getting McGruder's to locate in Fairy Cove."

With her fingers into politics and lives, Angela wasn't likely to want anything changed in Fairy Cove; she'd fight progress, power taken from her grasp.

All those years ago, what was it that Ewan knew? Just how had he kept Angela from Hallie, releasing her guardianship to the Donovans?

*Ewan.* Cyd had known him all her life, Hallie's older brother. Cyd had half worshiped him, half hated him for that cocksure, tough attitude, no matter how bad things got. At eighteen and on his way into life outside Fairy Cove, he'd been tall, rangy, and tough, his body already seasoned by hard work on the docks—because he'd take nothing from Angela or anyone.

Back then, that he'd lived in a shack behind her mansion only added to young Cyd's fascination for him.

Years ago, he had that simmering raw edge women craved, yet wanted to tame. He looked as if he belonged in a storm, fighting and loving it, riding the wild waves, and could belong to no one but himself. When he walked, it was with self-assured magic, the command that said he knew who and what he was. With a shaggy mass of black hair, smoky gray eyes, a chiseled hard face, and a way of looking at a woman as if he could see right through her clothes, Ewan had never been interested in dating one girl too long, and he could tempt a girl past what was right. He'd done just that, a legend with women, kissing with fire and magic.

And damn him, he was the only man Cyd knew she could trust.

Damn him. He'd taken her first kiss and held it captive on

those hard lips, because she could give it to no other—the honesty of a girl's first love. And he knew it each time he came home. It was there in his gray eyes, in the knowing set of a man's body.

Cyd pushed herself into the wind, careless of its tearing at her long, willful hair, pushing her slacks against her legs, legs long enough to make men stop and drool. At five feet nine inches, lean and fit, Cyd knew the power of her body. Her legs could distract a man from negotiating a tight business deal and let her grasp the upper hand—that much Cyd had learned from her mother.

But the rest, who actually touched her body, was for her to say; she ruled her own heart and her body.

Safety of mind and body was Cyd's highest priority. But money was a close second, and right now Ewan Lochlain could endanger a hefty profit from the sale of the old boat shop.

A big, beefy man suddenly stepped to block Cyd's path. Wearing seaman's garb and a leer, Paddy O'Connor looked her up and down. "In a hurry now, sweetheart? No time for old Paddy?"

He'd been after her for years. Lust glistened in his small eyes, and it told Cyd that he'd sampled her mother and wanted to do the same with the daughter. He rubbed one hand with the other, covering the scar she'd given him with her knife years ago. The stab had been meant to warn him, because Cyd wasn't letting Paddy touch her, then or now.

"Out of my way, Paddy, or you'll be picking yourself up off the sidewalk."

Lust changed to rage as Paddy growled, "That knee trick won't work again, girlie."

She tilted her head and eyed him. "I don't have time for you. Instead, I'll just raise your rent. You may have a hard time finding another place with tourists coming and rental houses in demand."

With a look that said he wasn't done with her, Paddy stepped back, and Cyd felt his eyes following her as she walked away. She'd handled men like him before, men waiting for her to make her mother's mistake, but money and resolve made the difference.

She'd made enemies along the way, and Paddy was definitely one of them . . . along with Hallie's ex-husband and a few more. Cyd straightened her back; she'd grown used to snide remarks and threats from those who didn't like her clawing her way up from poverty.

Cyd steamed full speed ahead to Hallie's Fairy Bin, to her best friend and Ewan's little sister—the sweetest, most innocent and giving woman in the world, the bright spot in Cyd's life—Hallie.

Because Hallie could read her emotions too well, Cyd pushed them aside as she entered the Fairy Bin. The familiar little bell tinkled over her head, and from behind the counter, Hallie smiled warmly at Cyd.

Dressed in a warm blue sweater and worn bib overalls, Hallie seemed almost as delicate as the fairy gifts that surrounded her. Fairies of every kind seemed to tumble about the shop, delicate little wings catching the light on those that hovered from the ceiling. Across the shelves, fairy queens of all sizes and poses ranged amid pixies and elves, and good-natured gnomes. Hanging near the window, the cut-glass fairies caught the sunlight and shot tiny spears of brightness into the shop.

Fairies seemed to dance around the shop, resting on handcrafted pot holders and shawls and quilts from local craftsmen.

The shop was perfect for Hallie: small, easy to heat and cool, with an apartment in the rear. Cyd had arranged the sale to Hallie, held the mortgage, and not for one moment had she thought of a real estate agent's percentage. Cyd simply wanted Hallie happy and safe.

The sweet scents of cinnamon seduced Cyd, easing the

tension and anger in her. Hallie was just putting the finishing touches—a raffia bow—on a fat Christmas candle with three wicks, circled by upright cinnamon sticks and decorated with a sprig of pine needles and tiny cones.

A feminine version of Ewan, Hallie's gray eyes were soft with welcome and laughter, her black hair carelessly caught by a band and bobbing on top of her head. "You're in a mood," she said with a smile, as Cyd took off her coat. "Would you like a cup of tea? I've just baked your favorite cookies—oatmeal with raisins and lots of cinnamon."

With the familiarity of a close friend, Cyd hung her coat on the stand by the door. "I've always loved your 'fairy-food' tea parties. When did they start? When you were two and I was four?"

Hallie laughed softly. "Probably before that. Come back to the kitchen."

Cyd's need for money warred against her love of Hallie; she wouldn't use her friend, not even to wrench the boat shop from Ewan's grasp.

She settled into Hallie's kitchen chair and kicked off her high heels, propping her feet on another chair as she watched her friend fill a kettle. Graceful and vulnerable and sweet, Hallie did not look as though she'd survived an abusive marriage. But Cyd would never forget how Hallie had looked that day she arrived back in Fairy Cove—battered and badly frightened.

Cyd had given Hallie her promise not to tell Ewan—to protect him from assault charges. Because Ewan would have surely sought Allan out and repaid Hallie's bruises twice over.

Cyd munched on an oatmeal cookie and didn't enjoy it as she thought about protecting and emotionally supporting Hallie through her divorce. When Hallie's story came out, Cyd had been furious that she hadn't been told before. But she recognized Hallie's shame and had kept her frustration to herself.

"I love you, you know," Cyd stated fiercely, emotion erupting in her. "You're my best friend. You've always been. No matter what anyone said about me or my mother, you never let that stand between us. You never asked."

"I know you love me. And I love you. I know how good you are. Even when you're mad, like you are now." Hallie dropped the silver loose tea holder into the Brown Betty pot, secured the chain, and poured in the boiling water. She placed the teapot on the table, expertly wrapped a quilted cosy around it, and sat.

Hallie looked at Cyd, and years of knowing each other tangled between them. "Stay with me tonight. We'll give each other pedicures and gossip till midnight."

Cyd shook her head; her best friend knew her fear of the coming storm, of the nightmares it could bring, and had offered her shelter. "Some other time, okay? I've got plotting to do against your brother."

"Call if you change your mind. I'll keep watch at the door. I'm looking for Ewan to come in tonight or tomorrow, anyway—I don't know exactly when. Or I'll stay at your place, Cyd. I'll leave a note for him to call me there."

"Thanks, honey, but I'll be okay." How could anyone bear to hurt someone so gentle and sweet, so perfect and loving? Cyd wondered, as Hallie delicately poured tea into cups. "You have your mother's eyes, Hallie. As soft and gray as your own. I remember her very well. She was very loving. Back then, I wished she was my mother."

Hallie also resembled her aunt Angela in the color of her hair and eyes and facial features. But then, Angela's identical twin had been Hallie's mother, with none of the tender love that Mary gave so freely.

Hallie sipped her tea, then said, "You're brooding about Ewan coming home to stay, aren't you? It's been two weeks since he called me, and you've been in a dark mood ever since. You're after Finlay, and he's enjoying the tussle—and the bribery that comes with it."

Cyd shot her a look. "If your father's boat shop doesn't mean that much to you, I don't know why it would to Ewan. I don't know why he has to have it and talk a poor old man into keeping it for him."

Hallie's eyes were soft and knowing. "Because Ewan is a man. Because he worked with our father and because he remembers more. His blood has stirred, wanting his home. He only left because he couldn't take the gossip anymore—the rumors that our father planned Mother's drowning death for insurance money, and accidentally got caught in his own trap."

"Things haven't changed. There is still that gossip. It's simmering again, now that Ewan is coming back. And I never believed any of it for a minute."

Hallie's gray eyes darkened, and her words shot fiercely into the small feminine kitchen. "I don't care what Aunt Angela and her friends say. My father was a gentle . . . man. He wasn't a drunk or a wife beater. You know it, too. So does Ewan."

Cyd smiled gently and eased aside the image of a tiny fairy picking up a battle sword to defend her own. She linked her hand with Hallie's. "I know. Your father was the nearest thing I'd ever had to my own."

Hallie's hand reached to hold Cyd's. "In her way, your mother loved you. Linda did the best she could."

"No, she didn't."

Cyd forced away the darkness and turned herself to making money. She had already tested Hallie's emotional ties to the boat shop and found none. "I'm going to get that property. Ewan isn't standing in my way. My percentage off the sale to McGruder's will pay for a house I've got my eye on. With a little fixing up, I can sell that jewel at a profit."

Hallie's expression changed to an impish grin. "Well, then, I guess it's between you and Ewan."

Cyd's finger circled her teacup as she leveled a look at Hallie and lifted a warning eyebrow. "It could be war. After childhood, we were never exactly friendly. I don't want you hurt."

Hallie sniffed delicately, and pride lifted her head. Her eyes upon Cyd were clear and level. "I'm stronger than you think."

"You're sweet and good and kind." Cyd munched on a cookie and licked the cinnamon taste from her lips. "I don't want to lose you. You could call me off, and only you. You haven't. Why not?"

With a knowing smile, Hallie asked, "More tea?"

That gentle smile nagged at Cyd as she went back to her office. She punched in the safety codes, went in, and hurled her coat onto the nearest chair. A check at the video camera told her that no one had entered the office.

Sunlight skipped through the window, and she reached out her hand, letting the narrow gold shaft warm her palm.

She'd keep that with her for luck, she thought, capturing the warmth in her palm and shoving it in her pocket.

Because a storm was brewing, expected to hit tonight, and she feared both—the night and the storm.

And just maybe she feared the nightmares that came crawling over her, a mix of rage and faces and men fighting in the storm, bone crashing against bone, lightning framed their struggling bodies, and the man's face as he reached for her. . . .

Tonight, when the storm came, she'd be safe in her small house, behind her locks and bolts, the curtains and shutters closed against the face that could appear—

Cyd shivered and pushed the images that were never far from her away; they were certain to come on the storm tonight, but she didn't need to give them her days, too.

Ewan was just business, Cyd told herself briskly as she settled down to her accounts, the rental payments to be collected, investments that needed shuffling. She could handle Ewan Lochlain.

# Chapter 2

"I've kept out of your way because of Hallie. I didn't want to stir you up while I was away. But I'm home to stay now, dear auntie. Let's see you run me out this time." He was alone, but yet he needed to say the words.

It was an hour past midnight, and an early-April storm was brewing on Lake Michigan. As Ewan stood on the pier in front of the Lochlain Boat Shop, a familiar mist lay upon his face. He drew the scent of home into him, letting it sweeten the bitter aches of his life.

All he had to show for his life away from Fairy Cove was the clothing he wore, the duffel bag propped against the shop, and enough money to start a dream. . . .

His parents had lost their lives in the lake between Fairy Cove and Three Ravens Island. They'd gone for a day's sailing and never came back. . . .

Then his aunt, Angela, had taken over Ewan's and Hallie's care. Angela's words had carried over and over again through the years—"Your father wanted to murder my sister for that insurance policy money and got caught in his own doing. You're no better than he was."

He'd heard Angela's voice in his nightmares, and it challenged him to succeed, and now he would. Thanks to Andrew Larkin.

Ewan had helped make a dying man's wish come true, to sail the "Seven Seas in an 1812 replica schooner." And for acting as Andrew Larkin's right-hand man and his friend, Ewan had received a large final paycheck—enough to make a last payment to Finlay and more.

Handcrafting wooden boats was one thing, but making a profit was another. Instead of crafting boats himself, one at a time, Ewan planned to make that profit by mass-marketing and promoting kits and instructions to the home "do-it-yourselfer." While Ewan's bank account looked hefty for the moment, the machines required to make wooden boat kits would be pricey, and advertising for a new business wouldn't come cheap.

But he needed to heal, to craft with his hands and tear the pain out of him. Ewan had to find peace, before the bitterness of the past ate away his future.

The wooden pier creaked beneath Ewan's feet as the cruiser that had brought him to Fairy Cove motored out of the harbor, leaving a white thread in the black water. The high fee to bring Ewan to Fairy Cove at night was worth it. He preferred the cover of darkness, where no one could see the emotions storming him.

He could fail, and lose everything, including his pride.

This time he wasn't leaving until he'd cleared his father's name. He'd tear the truth out of Fairy Cove and set aside his aunt's cruel jabs and rumors: Tom Lochlain had not set out to murder his wife for insurance money twenty-one years ago; he'd only wanted to enjoy the clear, fine day boating on the lake with his love.

Or was Tom Lochlain's innocence the dream of a boy, held dear by a grown man of thirty-three? Was it possible that Ewan's father was guilty?

"Either way, I intend to find out." At two o'clock in the

morning, the past clawed at him as he paced the boardwalk in front of the boat shop.

Though he couldn't see Angela's house, Ewan knew the two-story nineteenth-century white house loomed on the highest knoll, looking down upon the town that his aunt had ruled.

According to Hallie, there was a newcomer or two who challenged her now, but most people still trod lightly when Angela Greer was involved. She knew too many secrets and had the money to back up her dislikes.

Cyd Callahan had sworn that she would bring Angela to her knees. That one day, Angela would come begging to her.

Ewan smiled briefly. Cyd was a fighter and probably a good match for Angela. If ever witches clashed over a cauldron, it would be those two.

So he was home, and his Irish was upon him, the stories handed down from his paternal grandfather stirring in his mind. Ewan lifted his face to the cold damp wind signaling a storm. Great waves pushed against the creaking pier, the sound of trouble waiting for him.

Above him, the metal roof's ice gleamed like silver spears. On the pier, icy spots ran smooth and dangerous across the worn boards. The wind tore at the ancient plastic covering the boat shop's second-story window. Its flapping noise sounded as dark and evil as the beating of Angela's heart.

But he knew what she feared most: With proof in his keeping, Ewan could unravel her high-and-mighty grip on Fairy Cove. Amid a tangle of potential legalities, what Angela feared most was losing respect and power. The information Ewan held could damage her business and private associations— they would back away from controversy. Angela's precious charity balls and fancy garden teas would suffer; her calls to arrange business deals might not be answered.

The private war between them had more to do with pride and revenge than with money—at least for Ewan. To be honest, his dark side enjoyed his aunt's discomfort, that he held the power to expose and destroy her. In his bargain to keep Hallie safe, he didn't stir the pot that could damage what Angela loved most—her position of power and influence in Fairy Cove.

Ewan actually didn't want to expose her, to damage the Lochlain name more than it had been. Hallie had had enough gossip to last her a lifetime, and with a forgiving heart, her feelings toward family were tender.

Ewan hitched up the collar on his seaman's navy pea coat, but the chill he felt was in his heart, not in his flesh and bones. He remembered the day his mother's body had washed ashore. He'd been only twelve and Hallie eight when Angela forced them to come see their mother—not a pretty sight amid the canvas sail and ropes. His father's body was never found.

Ewan gave himself to the darkness, prowling through a past he could not change.

Angela had fostered a worse storm than nature could conceive—she'd accepted the Lochlain estate, the guardianship of Hallie and Ewan, and the insurance money due them . . . then, when it was safe to raise questions, she'd started the rumors.

*Tom Lochlain was a drunk. . . . He'd mistreated his wife, Mary. . . . He'd planned to kill her, and his plans had backfired, killing him, too.*

Ewan settled back into the shadows cast by the boat shop, the interior as familiar to him as his own big, broad, callused hands.

Across the short distance of water from the pier on which Ewan stood to Fairy Cove, Main Street's store lights seemed to glow, dimmed by the cold mist that clung to his skin and beard. He was familiar with most of the stores and the people running them. He wouldn't be the outsider asking questions; Ewan intended to make himself at home.

The soft light in Hallie's shop window reached out to ease the chill in his heart, but Ewan decided against waking her. He stroked his beard, just four days' growth since the last time he'd shaved. There were too many people in Fairy Cove who peered out their windows at night, wary of a man walking the streets, and Ewan didn't want to rouse the town before he was ready.

Ewan let the familiar smells waft around him—the clean freshness of the lake, the musty scent of damp wood.

Finlay had said that Angela and her cronies' grip on the town was still strong, and Cyd Callahan was circling the boat shop. She was attempting to seduce Finlay into selling with a Brown Betty teapot—just like his Irish mother's—good whiskey and home-cooked dinners. Finlay suspected that Cyd didn't cook those dinners, but the old man wouldn't muck up a good thing by questioning her motives.

While Finlay liked to "tip a pint and enjoy a good nip," he remembered Tom Lochlain as only "Partaking lightly, you see. Your father wasn't the drunk and wife beater that they say. You have my word on it. Never was there a kinder man, nor one who loved his wife more. They lied, boy. He wasn't drunk the day he took your mother out for that sail, and the only thing he'd tasted was her sweet kiss."

It would take time, but Ewan would unravel the mystery of his parents' deaths. He'd get the proof he needed to clear his father's name, or he'd find truth in the rumors. . . .

Clouds seemed to roll from the lake, enveloping Ewan. Sleet cut at his face, and the wind lifted his hair. But wrapped in his thoughts, he didn't notice.

Ewan ran his hand over the wide double doors through which his father's boats had been carried. On the inside, a sturdy plank and floor wedges stopped entry; the smaller door to one side served as an individual's access.

With a weary sigh, Ewan hefted his duffel bag onto his

shoulder, slid the old key into Finlay's padlock, and opened
the smaller door to the boat shop.

A flip of the light switch said the bulb wasn't cooperating
tonight. Touched by a draft, it swayed high above him.

He closed the door against the storm and found the lantern
by the door, lighting it. The eerie glow spread over the huge,
cluttered room, fishing poles and tackle ready at the door,
boards stacked along a wall, a half-finished dory resting on its
side. Old gallons of varnish, epoxy, and sealers, some empty
and rusted, were stacked in a corner. The sight of a workbench, cluttered with tools and musty magazines and paper
plates spread across one end of the building, caused Ewan's
breath to catch—because he remembered being a child, and
his father's neat habits, caring for his tools and brushes.

Ewan circled the flat-bottomed skiff he'd started on his
last visit, unfinished and still in the center of the shop. A
touch of his hand stripped through the layers of dust. On his
brief visits home, Ewan had needed the feel of tools in his
hand, the smell of wood. His work was crude in comparison
to his father's, but had served to settle Ewan's emotions.

Now, the fierce desire to reclaim everything he'd lost long
ago burned in Ewan.

"A man's family and his honor should be the dearest in his
heart. He should fight for them, if need be," Tom Lochlain
had told his son many, many times. "Above all, protect those
you love, give your heart to them, and hold your honor and
pride second."

Ewan intended to retrieve the Lochlain name from the
muck Angela had created with her rumors. Finlay's offer to
sell to Ewan had provided the path to that goal.

At eighty, Finlay was past hard work, tending more to
spin tales of the fine boats he and Tom Lochlain had once
made. Each day, he made his way to the shop, to fish and
protect the shop for Tom's son—and probably enjoyed
Cyd's visits, harvesting his dinners and desserts.

Ewan smiled slightly. Cyd wasn't one to spend money, and she couldn't cook. That meant she wanted the shop badly.

The building creaked in the wind's blast, and sleet hit the plastic covering the windows as Ewan stood very still, remembering. He could almost hear his father's voice, with that lilt of Irish on his tongue and tales of fairies and gnomes and tiny kingdoms that lay beneath the grass and toadstools.

Then, because miles of road and water and time dragged at his bones, Ewan placed the lantern on the counter. He reached for the bottle hidden in the dusty cupboard, expertly wiped the top, and lifted it to his lips. Finlay's Irish whiskey burned a trail down Ewan's throat. He waited for the liquid fire to warm him, then toasted Andrew Larkin, a good man, with a second drink.

Ewan took a miniature skiff from his bag, the one Cyd had studied years ago. He placed it on the dusty countertop and eased into a rickety chair to consider the ugly past, the truth he would have.

Was it possible that Tom Lochlain had murdered his wife and gotten caught in his own wrongdoing?

The question had kept him awake too many nights, wondering if a boy's love blurred the memory of a man who could kill his wife . . . wondering why his father's body hadn't been found . . .

The whiskey was curling warmth into Ewan's bones, sleep dragging at him. With a sigh, he rose stiffly, stretched, and set about finding a place to rest. From the look of the shop, it would be difficult, but here was where he wanted to stay this first night, where he'd built wooden boats with his father, and life had been good.

He was home to stay, not just for a visit to check on Hallie or the boat shop. And Angela would have to swallow that bitter brew . . . that after roaming the world, home had called to Tom Lochlain's son.

* * *

Angela Greer sipped her morning tea and, from her home above Fairy Cove, watched the morning fog curl around the streets below.

Trouble was afoot, and Angela had read it in Hallie's face. Amazing how an innocently placed question could yield answers from the girl's expression. "Have you heard from Ewan lately?"

Hallie had been evasive, her eyes looking away from Angela's, and that usually meant that Ewan would visit.

As long as he had stayed away, brief visits were permitted. The gossip that he was coming home to stay was just that—gossip, Angela decided briskly as she placed the flower-and-gold-embellished china cup on its saucer. She stood by her study window, one hand over the other, her fingers stroking the tiny ring. Only cheap silver filigree and a small black onyx, it was meant for a courting gift—from Tom Lochlain to Angela's identical twin, Mary.

Angela's fingers squeezed the ring. And it should have been Angela's. Now it was, just as Tom should have been hers.

She glanced at her husband, seated in his leather chair; Fred's balding head showed above the edges of his morning newspaper. Second best, that's what he was. But he did the job she required, an attorney who served up contracts and investments in her empire.

When they'd first married, Fred's income as a local attorney hadn't been enough, but Angela had pushed him to agreeing to the house of her dreams—elegant enough for a rich woman.

And all the while her twin, Mary, was building a family with Tom Lochlain.

Angela could have helped Tom build that struggling boat shop into a fine business, those could have been her children. But they weren't. They were Mary's. Hallie had the same dull innocence as her mother, and the boy—well, the boy looked like Tom, a reminder of the man Angela had really wanted.

She heard her breath hiss around the thick drapes and carpeting and forced her bitterness back into its concealing depths.

Everything was in place as it should be.

Any slight disturbance that Ewan would arouse during his visit would soon settle when he left Fairy Cove.

Angela circled the problem of Bertha Linnea's missing brooch. It was only a cheap, sentimental piece, but Angela wanted it. Her longtime friend, Bertha Linnea, had died six months ago from a heart attack. Fred had carefully sculpted the will, and, as Bertha's beneficiary, Angela had inherited the widow's small bankroll. The sale of her friend's house would bring Angela a tidy sum.

But that brooch was missing, one that had once been Mary's. Years ago, Angela had given it to Bertha, and now it was gone. Where was it?

Was the banging in the room or in his head?

Ewan managed to push one eyelid open, and found Cyd frowning over him, a frosty bite in her sky-blue eyes. He focused and forced open his other eye to admire the wild fire of her hair, the layered spirals framing her pale face and spilling onto her shoulders.

In the years since she'd been a child, she'd tamed that silky mass of curls, and Ewan had missed them.

There were years and probably lovers between them now. They had clashed each time he visited. The woman bending over him was set for war, and his need to torment her was at the ready.

"So you've found me," he managed through a dry mouth and a thick tongue. "I knew it was only a matter of time before you'd come after me, darling-mine."

He'd grabbed a roll of canvas, shook out most of the dust and spiders, and eased it into the unfinished twelve-footer rowing skiff. Still lacking the center storage seat, the boat's frame and canvas had been enough to keep the drafts from him. He'd slept in worse places and had used his duffel bag as softness against the wood.

Now, after a few hours of sleep, his bones had settled into the canvas and wood, his muscles stiff. Above him was Cyd, ready to torture him just as he'd been at sixteen, wrapped in his woes and his first drinking binge—ready to pull out all the guilt drawer and wag his sweet little sister's name, shaming him. . . .

There was Cyd, all fired up; her thick, dark red mane seemed to have a life of its own, tossed by the wind howling outside. Set in a pale, edgy face, her eyes shot pure hatred at him as she ripped away the canvas fully away, and an icy draft hit his face. Then she smiled coldly, knowingly. "Having a bit of a hangover, are we?"

She banged the side of the boat again, and the echo rattled like a cannon blast inside his brain. But he forced himself to show his teeth, and his whole face hurt, even his beard. "You're in a fine mood. Glad to see me, darling?"

"I didn't come to see you, you egotist. I came to see Finlay. Where is he?" She banged whatever she held against the side of the boat nearest his head, and Ewan winced with the throbbing pain.

"He's at the inn, sleeping in, I imagine. He knew I was coming in late. Jesus, have mercy, Cyd. Stop it," he whispered rawly, as she hit the side of the boat once more. This time, he managed to get both eyes open. The boat shop was big, cold, and dimly lighted by the gray sky outside. The rafters above him were strung with cobwebs, shifting in the drafts.

She looked as if she would reach in and tug him out of the boat. For a moment, Ewan toyed with the idea of Cyd's ripe woman's body warming him. She smelled like a woman, too—exotic, tantalizing. With a deep rich need to capture those soft glossy lips, feel the sensual heat of a woman, he reached for the fringed shawl around her throat.

And saw the oar she'd been banging the boat with lift threateningly above him.

This was the real Cyd—all revved and ready to battle. Half witch and all woman, she was tough and bristling and made his primitive instincts stir.

Ewan released the shawl; he wasn't up to Cyd's taunts just yet, but here she was, ready to start in on him. There had been no gentle truce through the years, the silences foretelling a storm of nasty accusations—that looked as if they were about to start again.

On his feet and rested, he might enjoy taunting her; Cyd's flash fire temper was something to see. But at the moment, facing Cyd in a temper would make a brave man shudder. Ewan needed to even the odds, because Finlay had said she was on the prowl, pushing for the sale of the boat shop and none too happy about the sale to Ewan. "Is that cinnamon rolls and coffee I smell, darling-mine?"

The teasing words came easily to his lips, for if there was one joy Cyd could give him as no other woman could, it was to see her light up with temper.

"Don't you 'darling' me, Ewan Lochlain. The cinnamon rolls are for Finlay. You and I need to talk. You should have gone straight to Hallie's last night. Instead, I find you snoring away under this canvas." She used the oar to push the canvas aside from his body.

"You're not going away, are you?" he asked with a groan, still hoping for mercy.

"No. Get up, you great big baby. It smells like a brewery in there."

"Only if you lay out my breakfast, darling. Pour me a cup, will you?" he asked, and enjoyed Cyd's furious scowl over

him, before he heard her footsteps clicking away from his
boat.

Ewan silenced his groan and placed his hand over the
thunder in his forehead. So she thought he was comfortable,
did she? When every bone ached, and he felt as if he'd
crawled a thousand miles to come home? He eased out of
the boat carefully and wrapped his own dark mood around
him as he walked toward the coffee she had poured from a
thermos.

He took his time settling in, getting a good hot drink in
him, and clearing his mind before tackling Cyd. Ewan
opened the paper bag she'd brought, sniffed and reached for
a fat cinnamon roll, then settled down to enjoy himself—
which he knew only annoyed her more. It wouldn't take
much to push her over the edge—

He wondered briefly about the men she knew and if any
had touched that flame, the very heart of her—but then Cyd
was likely to love a man, not for his heart, but for his money.

Those blue eyes, filled with disgust, ripped down him.
"You could make a fire."

"I'm busy. Make it for me will you, darling? Then we'll
talk. You can tell me about your love life."

The hiss of her indrawn breath said his taunt had scored,
and Ewan decided that things were looking better, despite
his fatigue and the pounding of his head. He again sipped the
coffee she'd brought and admired Cyd's fine temper, barely
held in check. Her eyes locked with his, and Ewan lifted an
eyebrow, which he knew would torment her more.

Cyd reached for a stack of newspapers. She crumpled one,
shoving it into the enormous old woodstove. From the bin
beside it, she tossed in wood scraps, expertly struck a match,
and lit the fire.

She was a fine-looking woman, Ewan decided critically.
The soft green cowl collar framed her face and matched her
slacks. Over them she wore an expensive black raincoat.

Like sequins, raindrops glittered softly on her coat and jeweled her hair—and Ewan's fist clenched slowly, needing the feel of that heavy, rich mane.

Her high-heeled boots only lengthened her legs, and Ewan resented thinking that he'd like to see all that white skin in nothing but those black leather boots.

But this was Cyd—with a past as dark as his own and Hallie's. Cyd had a calculator for a heart and had used that quick mind to scramble out of her mother's gutter.

They both loved Hallie, and that was why they'd kept their clashes away from her—but if Cyd pushed him too hard now, Ewan wouldn't back away.

He intended to stay. Too much was at stake—his chance to reclaim his father's good name—and Ewan's own pride, of course. Angela had marked him to fail, and that he wouldn't do—not because of Cyd's evil moods.

She was gathering her forces, impatiently pushing back the tendrils around her face with long, pale fingers. Ewan wondered how a strand would feel, wrapped around his hand.

He sipped the steaming coffee as he looked at the stove's growing flames and waited for the first volley.

Cyd sailed it across the airy, dusty space to him. "This place hasn't been on a paying basis for years. There is no reason why you should want it. McGruder's could put Fairy Cove on the map, bring in a different crowd."

She started to walk around the building, her black coat flying around her like a cape, inspecting the shop for potential.

Ewan knew what he saw in the rough wooden planks, the view of the harbor with its choppy waves and whitecaps—possibilities and dollar signs, a hefty profit to tuck in her money bags. Too bad, he thought, as a bit of sunlight seeped through the dark clouds and murky windows, coming to light on her hair. She turned to him suddenly, and the different lengths of the silky strands caught fire. Ewan wondered then if there was ever a woman whose hair he wanted to touch so badly—to hold as he sank into her.

He took another burning sip of coffee to remind him that this was Cyd. She had a pocketbook for a heart—unless it came to Hallie. The two women shared a secret, and they had been keeping it from him for the past few years. But he'd caught the knowing glances at each other.

What ran between them, other than growing up together in Fairy Cove?

Whatever it was, Cyd was fiercely protective of Hallie's soft heart and gentle ways. And in return, Hallie had given Cyd an unshakable love that ran true and deep.

With a deep breath, Ewan decided that it was time to get on with business—the sorting out with Cyd. He headed straight for the heart of Cyd's early-morning visit.

He placed his cup aside and crossed his arms, leaning back against the countertop littered with tools that had seen better days.

Yet they had most likely been his father's, and now they were his, dear to his hands and heart. "McGruder's or any other business isn't getting this place—and neither are you, Cyd. I'm home to stay."

She turned and pinned him with a stare. "I checked—Finlay still legally owns this place—it hasn't transferred to you yet. Whatever agreement you've made with him can be canceled easily. He needs money, Ewan, not the dreams of Tom Lochlain's son running this place. And the capital that it would take to get this place going isn't small. . . . A handcrafter's boat shop is slow money and takes time to build. You'll be under before you've cleared red ink. You're home to make trouble, Ewan. Don't say that you aren't. Whatever burned you as a boy is still in there, smoldering and waiting to make trouble. Do you honestly think that Hallie can take a second helping of the past?"

"Leave my sister to me," he warned softly, too aware that

he'd left Hallie on her own long ago—but he'd done the best he could to protect her by putting her into the care of the Donovans.

He took a long, steadying breath. When Cyd came to battle, she didn't spare the soft, inner edges, but hit him on all fronts.

Cyd's slender hands balled into fists at her sides. "When you walked away from Fairy Cove, you tore her heart in two. You didn't see the pieces, how she struggled to live."

But Ewan already knew this bit of unwelcome information. When he had called, he'd heard the need in Hallie's voice. When he visited, he saw it in her eyes. The call of her heart had been difficult to ignore, but a return to Fairy Cove too soon could have meant financial failure—and he wasn't giving that to Angela. She'd already done enough damage to the Lochlain name.

His anger curled crisp and biting around him; Cyd knew exactly how to hit the soft underbelly of his pride. "Hallie was safe enough with the Donovans. I made certain of that."

"'You made certain of that.' You may have kept Angela from Hallie, from hurting her, but she needed you, Ewan Lochlain. *She needed you, a part of her family.*"

"Back off, Cyd. We've been down this slash-and-cut road before."

She trembled with rage and, despite himself, Ewan let her temper warm him. Honest in her mood, he had a better chance to fight her. He wondered, then, what would happen if Cyd ever softened to him—who would win the game then?

She leveled a dark look at him, her words soft and bitter. "So you came back every few months at first, then only twice a year, and lately just once a year. Meanwhile, she bled, Ewan, wondering where you were and if you'd come back again. After all, she'd seen her mother and father sail off onto the lake that day, and they didn't come back."

Pain sailed into him again, fresh and ugly. He'd never forget Hallie's frantic cries as she recognized the body of her mother. "Don't forget, Cyd, they were my mother and father, too."

"You . . . ran," she stated boldly, slashing at him, and Ewan fought to keep his arms crossed, his hands from shaking her.

"I was a boy, and I'd fought all that I could. With Angela and her biddies in control, I couldn't get a real start here."

"You said that the wind was calling your name, that it was time to go," Cyd recalled in a bitter tone, again thrusting the words at him, branding him as a coward. "So you think you can just waltz back in here and take over your father's boat shop?"

Ewan shrugged lightly; he'd waited for years to do just that. The wind calling his name was a statement that a boy would make to cover his fears. "There's nothing—no one to stop me."

"You could have helped Hallie with a better life. Instead, you started making payments on this . . . this run-down piece of—"

He saw no reason to justify the balance of his investments—yet he'd sent Hallie regular allotments. "If you want it, it's worth something."

"I wondered how Finlay could manage keeping up this place to pass town requirements. It was you, wasn't it? You sent him money you could have sent Hallie."

Ewan knew his own temper, and Cyd was stoking it, hitting all the sore spots—his return to Fairy Cove had taken longer than he thought. Andrew Larkin's sickness wasn't kind, his journey into death slow and needful of a good friend.

In another minute, he'd be tossing Cyd out of the shop. That wouldn't sit well with Hallie. "I did what I could on both fronts. I know that you maneuvered Hallie into the

Fairy Bin, a perfect place for her. How long is this . . . gutting me going to take?"

"I can make quite the profit on this place. Set a price, and we'll do business. I'll arrange the paperwork from Finlay to you. I'll see that he's taken care of—"

"No."

"How long do you think it will be before Angela starts making life difficult for you, and for Hallie, too?"

Ewan pushed away from the work counter and started to walk past Cyd on his way to his duffel bag. "Speaking of my sister. She's expecting me this morning. Try not to upset her, will you, Cyd? Because there isn't going to be a McGruder's deal, just one from Finlay to me. Close the door on your way out."

Then, with temper heating him and coffee clearing his mind, Ewan caught her arm. He'd caught a glimpse of something she hadn't shielded, and he would have more of it. He tugged her to him, framing her face, lifting it for his inspection.

"There are circles under your eyes, Cyd. Your face is pale beneath that makeup. You had a bad night, did you? The storm still frightens you, doesn't it?"

The soft flare of fear in those deep blue eyes and the stillness in her body told him the truth. He spoke it quietly, what he knew of Cyd's fears. "Just as his father before him and his father before him, Dad used to tell stories of the Night Man, the *Dooinney-Oie* who howled in the storm but would never hurt us. The wind howled last night, and thunder and lightning crossed the sky. You always were afraid of storms at night, the howling of the wind, and you didn't sleep, did you? That's why you're in such a fine mood, isn't it?"

Ewan noted his thumb was cruising Cyd's pale cheek, and the tender sight startled him enough to jerk his hand away. For a heartbeat, he ached for the girl she'd been, barely noted by her mother, finding gentleness with his family.

The darkness came prowling, gathering its fury, because fear had leaped again—just by the touch of his hand.

*Boy, take care not to make fun of the girl's fear,* his father had once said. *She's been badly frightened by more than one man, if you can call them that. Give her shelter and patience when you can, for you've a magical touch about you that soothes—when you want. But as a boy, you've got the devil in you, too, and tormenting the girl comes naturally—but don't. She needs a kind hand.*

Cyd whirled away from him and stood looking out the windows to the waves tossing in the harbor. Her hands tightly gripped the dark, expensive material of her coat.

Ewan noted the snag of sensual heat in his body, and pushed it away. This was a money-hungry woman set on taking his property, his dream. This wasn't little Molly Claire, a girl needing safety in the night while her mother took men to her bed, the girl who had crossed the night from her mother's house outside the city limits, who had come climbing in Hallie's window, shaking with fear.

As a boy, he'd pushed aside his disdain for girls and held Cyd on his lap, rocking her as he would Hallie, especially on the nights that it stormed. He had given that Cyd what he could, the same stories of fairies and brownies and pixies and tenderhearted gnomes that his father had told

But it wouldn't do, not with her woman's scent and softness, snaring him to feel anything for Cyd—she'd use it to lay him open and get the boat shop.

Her back was to him, and Ewan didn't need to see her face to know her fear. Her hand trembled as it lifted to smooth her hair. Then she turned slowly to him, and those dark blue eyes held the lash of anger.

"Getting worked up for a royal fight, are you, darling?" he asked rawly, remembering the tomboy who had hurt him once or twice.

To cover his unsteady emotions and needing to put distance between the child and the woman, Ewan eased off his pea coat. He removed his sweatshirt and T-shirt beneath it, tossing them into the skiff. He walked to the stove, to the kettle of water heating there, and poured it into a basin. Finlay had left him clean towels and soap, and, still ignoring Cyd, Ewan roughly washed and dried his face and beard.

He reached for a clean sweatshirt, pulled it over his head, and when he looked at the cracked, dusty mirror, he saw Cyd. In the window's shaft of gray light, she hadn't moved, her eyes huge in her pale, thin face, and the softness he'd felt for the girl came dancing back.

Though she'd become a woman, someone with a dark heart had long ago placed a dreadful seed inside Mollie Claire that hadn't gone away.

"Fairy Cove's Night Man is only a legend, Cyd. It's good for tourist business, nothing more," he said more gently than he'd planned, and noted the shudder rippling through her body. Fear danced across her face before she shoved it away.

"You're going to stir up Angela. She'll start in on Hallie again, and it will be your fault."

"Angela be damned," he said curtly, meaning it. He swiped his hand across the old mirror, felt the grit on his palm and in his heart, and leveled a look at Cyd. "If it has to be war, then she'll deal with a man this time, not a boy."

"You can't take back the past, Ewan," she whispered, soft enough to chill him once more with the truth.

"Can't I? What about the honor of a family name, of a good man's name?" This time, his eyes met his own, making a silent promise.

In the old mirror, Ewan watched her walk stiffly to the door, open it, and pause as the wind howled around her, lifting that bright hair and opening her coat as if it were a cape. She closed the door behind her, leaving Ewan with his guilt—he'd seen inside Cyd's glossy protective shell to the childish fear still ruling her after all these years.

Fairy Cove's Night Man had scared more than one child in the last few years, but a grown woman should recognize the difference between fable and the reality of businesses promoting tourist trade.

Ewan ran his hands through the shaggy length of his hair and rubbed his beard. The mirror caught his image, and he could have matched Fairy Cove's bogeyman, a big man with shaggy hair roaming the streets at night, peering in windows.

He tilted his head to listen to the howling cold wind and knew that it would not call him again, not until he'd done what he had to do. . . .

# Chapter 3

After battling with Ewan, Cyd was too restless to settle down to managing her investments and business, and it was only eight o'clock in the morning.

Shaken by the unexpected sight of Ewan, Cyd had raced from the boat shop to Main Street, then hurried up the sidewalk on Delaney Street to her small, safe home.

Cyd automatically checked the bolts and locks of her house, and the electronic alarms. She sat in a big overstuffed chair to brood. She'd known it had been Tom Lochlain's chair the moment Mrs. Eddy's estate auction goods had been placed on her front yard. Ordinarily Cyd would never bid so high, but she did that day, just to have Tom Lochlain near her once again.

She snuggled down into the chair and immediately imagined that Tom's big strong arms were around her. As a child, he'd kept her fear of the Night Man away with his stories of fairies and elves—always sweet and charming, soothing away the "nasties."

Sometimes, she felt like a child again, terrified by the storm and by the man who had come after her—big and strong with thick wild hair and a black beard—the Night

Man who still peered in her windows and left carved fairies, to remind her that he'd come back for her. The man who still came to her window, rapping, rapping . . .

"I'll be back for you, lovely," he'd said in the howling of the wind long ago, and her mother had ordered that she couldn't tell anyone.

The first little carved gnome had appeared after her eighteenth birthday—just after her first glimpse of the Night Man in her window.

Through the years, his carvings came less frequently, and only once in the last year—still, deep inside, she knew that he waited to kill her, just as she had seen him do in her nightmares—with blood on his hands and rage in his eyes.

As she fought her panic, Cyd's fingernails bit into the chair's arms.

She had herself to protect. As her mother's daughter, Cyd had had enough of sly looks and gossip, and if she told anyone of her fears, they'd question her and whisper. Her hidden terror of the Night Man wouldn't be used against her; because if Angela discovered Cyd's weakness, she'd use it. After all, Cyd's mother was mentally unstable but easily managed in a "retirement" home.

"Like mother, like daughter," Angela would say.

Cyd forced herself from any thoughts that she was losing her mind; she wouldn't tell anyone of the man who peered in her window or the tiny carved fairies and gnomes.

And damn him, hangover or not, Ewan had been keen enough to notice her lack of sleep and the emergence of her childhood fear.

Cyd lurched to her feet. She resented Ewan for what he knew, for the nightmares he saw still holding her—and her, a grown woman, who should know better.

Still, when the wind howled and the storms came, so did her fears.

Cyd hated Ewan for the tenderness he could call from her,

the memory of his father and young Ewan, giving Cyd-the-child shelter with his wonderful stories and strong arms.

She hated Ewan-the-man for his careless stripping away of his clothing, that hard, tanned body rippling with power and sensuality, that arrogant tilt of his head as he challenged her, a man set on his course.

"So he thinks he can step back in that easily, does he?" she said aloud. "We'll see, Ewan. You gave up the right to Fairy Cove when you ran away. And this town isn't big enough for the two of us."

Then Cyd punched in Hallie's number, returning the call on her answering machine. After a storm, Hallie always called, just to check on her. "Hi, Hallie. I'm fine, but I'm not coming in for my scone this morning. I found your brother sleeping in the boat shop, so he'll probably drop in today. I'd rather keep my distance."

Cyd replaced the telephone. In another minute Cyd had tugged on her coat, set the alarms, and sailed out into the wind to find Finlay. Ewan was likely to go to Hallie's first, so until the boat shop's papers were officially signed and registered, Cyd still had time.

"Ewan!" Hallie hurried toward him, her eyes glistening with tears. He closed the shop's door behind him, and the bell that had announced his arrival slowly stopped tinkling.

With the soft gray eyes of his mother and thick black hair that matched his own, she was all Ewan had left. The darkness that had seemed to wrap around him vanished into one big happy glow. Within her shop, which was stuffed with filled baskets of candy, candles, and fairies, Hallie wore her hair in a ponytail and loose denim bib overalls over her sweatshirt. She looked fresh and young and happy.

He'd done *this* at least, Ewan thought, given his sister the down payment and mortgage payments for her dream—this shop.

He dropped his bag of dirty laundry, placed his shaving kit on the upraised hands of a large fairy statue, and opened his arms to her. "Hi, Scamp. Did you miss me?"

"What a question!" Hallie hurled herself into his arms, and he lifted her tight against him, careful of the cramped shop that suited her so well. Maybe he floated a bit, groggy with happiness as she took his face in her hands and began kissing it all over.

His chest tightened with emotion, and Ewan held her tightly, wishing he could have saved her all those years ago. "Hey, now, little sister. I'm needing a shower and a shave, so you might want to save your hugs and kisses."

Her arms tightened around his waist, and Hallie shook her head. "Never. Oh, I'm so glad you're here, Ewan. I've missed you so much."

Still sweet, he thought, ready to love and to hope. At least he'd kept her safe from the darker side of life, a reaffirmation that at eighteen he'd done one right thing.

When he let her down, Hallie tugged on his beard. She looped her arm around his waist and, with her other hand, took his shaving kit from the fairy. "Come into the kitchen. I'll fix breakfast. Cyd said you were home. From the sound of her voice, you two have already tangled."

Ewan hefted the bag of his dirty laundry. "She was on me before I had time to wake up. She's not getting the boat shop."

"Well, she's set to make a fat profit, and you'll be taking the prize from her. You're probably in for a hard time."

"She gave me that already. The woman has a cash register for a heart." He tugged Hallie's ponytail lightly. "I don't suppose I'd have time for a quick shower before breakfast, would I?"

Hallie giggled as they entered the small, neat apartment at the back of her shop. She tossed his shaving kit to him and took the cloth sack of dirty laundry. "Oh, I'm so glad you're home, Ewan. You've come so far. And now, with the money

Andrew Larkin left you, you've got enough to buy the boat shop and get a good start in business."

"It will be a while before there's a profit, and a lot of work to do."

"But you'll be building wooden boats? Like Dad did?"

"For a start. I'll use his patterns, build a few and test them, maybe starting with a skiff. And then I'm making kits—"

"Kits?"

"Kits for the amateur boatbuilder, a do-it-yourselfer's pre-cut wood with instructions. It will be a hard go before I'm set to launch sales. I'll start with a skiff first, using Dad's as a first pattern, just a neat little fishing boat or one for tendering around the docks. I thought to maybe offer a dinghy design, but later for the adventurers, a canoe for the rivers, and a sea kayak. . . . I'll need tools—power equipment—and advertising, but first of all, I need to feel the wood run beneath my hand and settle in a bit. I figure I've got enough to make it for two years, buy some reconditioned power tools, and . . . and it's chancy at best."

Hallie's eyes rounded. "More," she whispered. "You're planning even more than Dad."

"And chancy," he repeated. "Andrew Larkin paid me well, and there's money for the dream—if nothing goes wrong. It will cost a pretty penny to put the shop in shape, and the pier needs work, too."

"You'll make it work. I know you will. Oh, how wonderful! And Andrew was truly lucky to have you see him through, to make his dreams come true and stay with him in his pain, tending him."

The memory of Andrew Larkin's painful, slow exit from life caused Ewan to tug Hallie into his arms, holding her close.

When Hallie hugged him, Ewan rested his chin on her head and closed his eyes. Now that Ewan was actually in Fairy Cove, fear curled around him, the reality that he could fail. If he failed, not only his pride would sink, but Angela would be proven right, that he was "worthless and would never amount to anything."

Hallie was already moving toward her stove, a woman familiar with the use of pots and pans. When he didn't move, captured by the sight of his sister, a grown woman, gracefully moving within her own kitchen, Hallie turned to him and smiled. "I know. It's a rich feeling, the two of us together, a family again," she said softly. "I love you, Ewan. Welcome home."

He felt awkward, unable to speak as his heart wanted. But he gave her what he knew she wanted to hear. "I'm not leaving this time, Hallie. I'll never leave you again."

Hallie could have cried at the sight of her brother—fatigue lines etched on his face, his hair uncut and to his shoulders, the thick growth of black beard. His pea coat had been mended, the collar and cuffs frayed, a mismatched button replacing one that had been lost or broken. His boots should have been replaced long ago. Ewan looked as if he'd come through a lifetime, not miles across land and sea.

When he took off his coat and slowly, methodically hung it over the back of a kitchen chair, her heart squeezed just that bit more. He moved like a tired old man. His sweatshirt was worn, the denim of his loose-fitting pants had been patched several times.

She understood Ewan's fear of failure and knew that he'd fought and saved desperately to make his dream come true.

Hallie turned to the stove, shielding her face and the emotions that showed too readily. She forced cheer into her voice, as she said, "I've laid out your clean clothes in the bathroom. Breakfast will be ready when you come out."

When he moved toward her tiny bathroom, Hallie almost cried at his slow, weary movements—but Ewan might see pity instead of love, and that wouldn't do at all—not if she wanted to win him over to her plan.

Hallie braced herself, because Ewan wouldn't like what she had done, or rather that she hadn't followed his orders—he wouldn't like it at all. She sniffed and tilted her head, because she would have her way, older brother or not.

While the bacon sizzled, and the coffee perked, Hallie knew she had to take her moment—before Ewan saw and that bitter look of guilt came back to his face. He'd done what he had to do, a boy facing too many hardships and needing a start in life. Ewan had gotten her to the Donovans and safety, then he'd gone—

While Ewan showered, Hallie sat in a kitchen chair and placed a napkin over her eyes and silently freed her tears. She wouldn't let him see any of it, the twenty-year-old girl filled with dreams of a marriage that would equal her parents' love—the girl who lost all illusions on her wedding night.

With a hard effort, she pried her way from the past, because she didn't want Ewan to know that darkest part of her life. She hurried to stuff his clothes into the washer, and almost cried again at the sight of them—worn, filled with holes and patches over patches, the stitches neater than most, socks darned and thin.

He'd sent her money and skimped on himself.

Ewan had always put her before his own needs, and it was time he got the start in life that he deserved—she would have nothing else.

As she poured coffee and filled his plate, Hallie pushed away the guilty ache and set her mind to her first battle with Ewan. She didn't doubt that she would have plenty more clashes.

When the shower stopped, Hallie braced herself, then walked quickly to the shop door and turned the sign to CLOSED. She wanted nothing to interfere with what she had to tell Ewan, her very stubborn, proud brother.

He opened the bathroom door and steam rolled around his body. Ewan frowned at Hallie and smoothed the arm of his long-sleeved knit shirt. "These aren't my things. They're new. I don't want you buying me anything, Hallie. I told you—"

The navy shirt suited him well, and so did the new, loose-fitting jeans. Women would be after her brother soon enough, a few of them remembering the boy with the "hot lips." "So you did. Now come eat."

She loved Ewan's surly scowl, the little-boy look on a craggy, weathered face that had women sighing dreamily. There was the seaman's swagger, the callused hands jerking back a chair, the arrogant sprawl of a man's body as he glared at her, ignoring the plate of food in front of him.

Well, it was time to let Ewan know that she could take care of herself, Hallie told herself as she kissed his forehead.

Her brother was overprotective, and to learn what she had done was certain to raise his temper.

Too bad. It was time. Hallie sat and Ewan's frown deepened. "You've got that prim, sweet look," he stated warily. "The one you have just before you tell me something you know I won't like."

She pushed his plate toward him. "Eat first. You're always much sweeter when you've got a full belly."

Ewan ran his finger around the rim of his plain, cheap, sturdy cup. "Still no china for you, Fairy-Girl?"

A dark memory lurked nearby, shared by both, and Hallie pushed it away. "These do fine. Complaining, are you?"

"Not a bit."

Hallie ached for how quickly Ewan ate, hunger driving him. She sipped her peppermint tea and waited until he pushed his plate aside, leaning back to inhale the scent of coffee with a dreamy look on his face. He sipped and smiled at her. "So now you have me fed. Are you telling me you're getting married again?"

"I've been married, Ewan. It didn't work. Six years ago, Allan went his way, and I came back to Fairy Cove. I took back the Lochlain name. We live in different towns, and it's not like I see him on the street every day. I like my life as it is. I'm really happy." That was one lie Hallie didn't regret telling Ewan. If she told him about the three years of abuse and beatings that had ended six years ago, he'd be calling out her ex-husband, and that wouldn't do—Ewan needed a fresh start, not more trouble.

"Three years is a short marriage. Your message was late in getting to me, or I would have been here for the wedding. You were married before I could get here from Larkin's schooner in Africa. When I did meet Allan, you seemed happy enough. But I was hoping for Sean Donovan."

"Stop brooding over Sean. He's a friend, almost a brother. I see him often enough. He knows you're coming home to stay." Hallie sipped her tea, then added quietly, "So does Aunt Angela. Finlay had a pint or two in him when he told her off, and let go of that fact."

"I'm not worried about Angela. She's kept her hands off you, and that is good enough."

"She still holds the town, Ewan . . . she and her cronies. One of them died just six months ago—Mrs. Linnea, of a heart attack."

"How many does that leave now? Of the witches she kept around her back then?"

Her brother's bitterness curled through his words. Hallie ached for him; Ewan had taken the brunt of Angela's sharp tongue, and those emotional scars remained deep.

"She's lost a few friends. One moved away, another died year before last, a couple others come in the shop now and then and seem nice enough—they're careful to let me know that they aren't that close to her anymore. Mrs. Linnea died, so that would leave two, I guess."

"And Fred, dear Uncle Fred?"

The image of Ewan-the-boy furious with their uncle for not protecting them, for not interfering with Angela's spiteful tactics, slid across Hallie's mind. "Uncle Fred comes in here sometimes. I like him. He tries to soften the edges a bit, and when I hug him, I can tell he's very touched. He's almost grateful. He just couldn't stand up to Angela, Ewan. He didn't have it in him. It would be wrong to ask more of him than he can give. But I think he admired you then, for the courage to speak your piece and hold up for us."

Ewan's dark expression and his grunt said that a man should stand up for what was right.

Hallie knew the courage it took to confront a bully; she'd failed miserably at facing her own problems alone. It had taken Cyd to help her.

Ewan nodded, but she knew that his mind was set. He took another sip and leveled a look at her. "I'll be fine, Hallie. I don't expect an invitation to Angela's tea parties or a grand family reunion. . . . You're chattering on, and when you do that, you're up to something. And you don't think I'll like it. . . . I'll pay you for the clothes."

"You'll pay me by sitting still, Ewan Lochlain. I'll be right back." Hallie hurried to her upstairs bedroom closet, where she kept her brother's things. She decided against bringing out the stacks of other new clothes and instead reached for a very special shoe box. The savings account booklet with Ewan's name on it rested on top of a pair of new work boots. She'd taken care to do business away from Fairy Cove, and sent the deposits—checks from Ewan and endorsed by her, through the mail. Computer banking eliminated the need for mail at the local post office, and the account was her own very private secret—not even Cyd knew.

Hallie made her brother wait while she cleaned the table, then slid the box in front of him and sat down to wait out the storm.

It was soon in coming. Ewan flipped through the savings

book, his scowl deepening. "You did not use the money I sent you."

"Yes, I did. I cashed one check right here in Fairy Cove, and I used it. What's left is in that box. You can't go around Fairy Cove looking like you did on your other visits, all patches and worn clothing. You're a businessman now, Ewan, or will be. I will not have my brother looking as if no one loves him."

The familiar lock of Ewan's freshly shaven jaw said he didn't agree. "This—" He slapped the booklet on the table and glared at her. "Is why Cyd doesn't think I sent money home. I was making good money, and my sister was scrimping and slaving."

His pride had been bruised, and that wasn't what Hallie wanted. "Ewan. Be reasonable. I did well enough. Cyd is my friend, but if she knew that—"

He was up on his stocking feet, pacing the small kitchen. Hallie sat very still and quiet, just as she had learned to do when Angela's temper was brewing.

Living with the rowdy big Donovan family, Hallie had learned to hold her ground. But this was her brother. He was filled with fierce pride, and it would take time for him to come around—if he did. "You gave that money to me to do as I wished—that's what you said, to do with it as I wanted. Well, I am. I have my pride, the same as you. I need to make my mark, the same as you. I'm doing exactly what I want, and you aren't going to take that away from me, Ewan Lochlain—doing what I want. You'll have to sign that paperwork to withdraw money, and don't be stubborn about it."

No one was ever going to take anything from Hallie again—that she didn't want to give, she thought furiously. Nor was anyone going to force her into taking anything she didn't want—not even her brother.

Ewan suddenly glanced at the window facing the alley, jerked open the back door, and nodded grimly to Sean

Donovan. Entering the tiny kitchen from the back porch, Sean instantly bumped his shoulder against Ewan's in a friendly male-to-male bonding. When the play wasn't returned and Ewan turned to look out of the window, Sean closed the door behind him.

Tall, rugged, and blond, Sean looked from Ewan's scowl to Hallie's set expression. "I heard you were back, Ewan. Cyd is trying to roust out Finlay at the inn, and he wants to sleep a bit more. Poor old man. She's been after him day and night about the boat shop. Glad you're back to take it over. Old Finlay has been waiting long enough. I don't know that he could have held her off much longer. I think she was getting ready to propose."

Despite her mood, Hallie couldn't help but admire the men standing side by side. A match in height and build, all broad shoulders and strength, they contrasted in color and mood—Ewan with his shaggy long black hair, searing frown, and gray eyes, and Sean with curling blond hair, neatly cut, and those teasing blue eyes. Both men's complexions bore the weather. But Ewan's ran darker, the bones broader and more defined, while Sean had a Viking's fair looks, creased by laughter.

Sean took off his plaid wool coat and tossed it into the living room, only a few steps from the kitchen. He studied Ewan's frown at Hallie, and asked, "Is there an extra cup of that coffee? Or should I leave? Your brother doesn't seem to be in a good mood."

"He's only making adjustments to a situation that he can do nothing about."

"She's skimped on herself—for me. I sent money she didn't use—she saved it. Women," Ewan stated darkly, as if the one plague on earth was female.

"God love 'em," Sean said with a grin as he walked to waggle Hallie's head, just as her brother did at other times—when he was less in a mood.

A woman used to making others comfortable, Hallie automatically stood and reached for a sturdy mug from the cupboard. She placed it on the table, poured coffee into it, and set the fairy cookie jar on the table. Because Ewan was brooding was no reason for her to forget that she was a woman in her own kitchen and Sean Donovan was a good friend. "Where's your son?"

Sean sat and looked at Ewan, who was still standing, his arms crossed, looking out of the window. Sean's look at Hallie said he knew there was trouble and added a silent question if he could help.

She shook her head. He'd helped her enough through the years, a protective pseudo big brother. But Sean didn't know about the abuse that six years ago brought her back to Fairy Cove and under Cyd's protection.

Hallie wanted no one to know her shame, how she had been victimized, and that she couldn't hold her own in life back then.

She loved them all—Ewan, Cyd, and Sean. But she was learning to stand on her own, and she would keep her independence without Ewan's money.

"My son is at Mom's amid a gang of his cousins. Timmy won the block-building contest, and now they're watching television."

"How's Three Raven Island and your resort?" Ewan asked, but his tone said his mind was brooding about the money Hallie had saved for him.

"Closed now. We'll open in late May, and we've got honeymooner reservations for the summer. When school is out, Timmy will come when he wants, to stay with me at the resort. It's working out—in off-season we live with my parents, and I boat back and forth to work at the resort. Then during the busy season, I stay at the island, and he comes out for a few days now and then. Norma Johnson is still housekeeping for me, and she keeps an eye on him when I can't.

The passenger boat could use some repairs—think you might do that?"

"For a friend, I might. Your grandfather picked a good one to inherit that island and his resort." Ewan continued to look out of the window, and Hallie knew his mind was still on the money she'd saved for him.

Sean reached for a cookie, dunked it in his coffee, and ate with a look of a man who had found heaven. "That's not much of a view from the window, Ewan. Only a bit of the back alley, some garbage cans, and bricks. One end leads to Main Street, and the other to that overgrown lot behind where the kids sometimes play Frisbee or ball."

Ewan turned to look at Hallie. "My sister stuffed the money I sent into a bank account for me, and all the time I thought I was helping her. Now the interest on it is enough to choke a horse."

"Oh, that's a pity, now," Sean teased. "Money is such a burden. Especially money that grows into a fat wad."

"I did so use your money, Ewan," Hallie shot back and stood, clearing the table. "I bought those new clothes you needed so badly. And there's more in the closet."

He turned to her, her older brother-imperial-lord-protector. "Take them back. Get a refund and use that money I sent."

Brother or not, Hallie was not taking those orders. "I did."

"On me, not yourself. If you didn't use that money, how the hell did you get this place up and running?"

Hallie refused to answer. She'd worked until she dropped, and had made tiny payments to repay Cyd, who never complained if they were late. Hallie would account for her actions to no one now—not even her brother. It was her struggle, her right to find herself as a woman who could take care of herself.

Sean glanced at Hallie, then at Ewan. When Sean opened his mouth with the predictable peacemaking comment, Hallie slid him a warning. "Stay out of it, Donovan. We're only settling my brother's stiff pride. I bought him a few clothes and saved his money, and he sees that as a bad thing—but I did as I saw fit."

Sean reached for another cookie and munched on it in the heavy silence. He took a handful more and rose to his feet. "She's got a bit of a temper now, Ewan. I'd go easy if I were you. And a few people have been asking when you're ready to start taking orders for new boats and if you'll do repairs, too. Should I send them around?"

"You can, but I'm not opening for regular business. I've got a long way to go before then. But I'll be in the shop first thing tomorrow morning. This morning, Finlay and I are doing legal business, and I'll be fixing up that old storage room in the shop later on. It will be ready enough tonight. I'll be living there."

"I'll be over to help—" Sean began.

Hallie dropped the dishes she'd been clearing into the sink's sudsy water. "You're staying here, Ewan. Don't even think of somewhere else."

When Ewan's eyebrows rose at the order, Sean grinned. "She's a bossy little thing, isn't she? Got to go. I'll be over with some of my brothers to help later. Meanwhile, I've kept a few of your favorite things safe."

Ewan nodded and met Sean's meaningful look.

Hallie caught that look and crossed her arms. She frowned at both men. "Cards and a poker game, no doubt. He's staying here, Sean. Don't you dare help him fix up that old storeroom. And don't—"

"Too late, love. Mom is happily tearing up the house, washing sheets and towels for him, stuffing old pots and pans in a box. She's filled a stack of boxes right now, and she's making a pot of good Irish stew to fill him. There's nothing she likes best than a homecoming for one of Fairy Cove's own, especially your brother. She told me to make sure you both come to dinner tonight. She's saving a whole pie just for Ewan."

Hallie braced herself to make her point. Sean had a good-natured way of making her lose focus. "My brother is *not* staying at the boat shop. It's drafty and cold and—"

"It'll be warm soon enough. There's nothing better than wood heat to take the dampness of the sea out of a man's bones."

"But—"

"He's still feeling the sea in his bones, and he'd miss the sound of the waves nearby. For the past few years, they've rocked him to sleep in Larkin's fancy sailing toy." Sean's arms were around her before Hallie could move. He lifted her off her feet, turned, and set her out of his way. He tilted his head and studied her with clear blue eyes. "It's a bit small in here, love. Ewan is going to need his space. There will be women calling for him, you know. And then there is Cyd. You wouldn't want all your fairy inventory slaughtered when the two of them fight, would you?"

Sean's scenario wasn't that far-fetched. Cyd wasn't going to make Ewan's life easy, and Ewan wasn't a man to push. "She's my best friend, and he's my brother. They'll just have to get along."

Sean kissed Hallie's nose and grinned. "But they won't. Not ever. Cyd is ready for war. She's probably stocking up on bullets and grenades right now. Let the man have a fighting chance, sweetheart, because she's sure to come after him. She wasn't happy that he scooped the boat shop sale out from under her nose. See you."

On his way out of the door, Sean reached for Ewan's hand, shook it, and said solemnly, "I'm glad you're back. Hallie has been floating on air since she found out almost a year ago."

"I had to see a good man leave life, or I would have been here sooner."

"I would have done the same."

Ewan nodded and matched Sean's boyish grin. They turned to consider Hallie. "Ah, she's a darling little fairy-girl, my sister is," Ewan said in the lilt that came from their father.

"She's a beauty, all right. The fairest of the fair."

Hallie couldn't help smiling at the two big men in her kitchen, arms looped around each other's broad shoulders, grinning at her. As boys, they stood the same way, teasing her, and now they were together again—her brother had finally come home. Because she was truly happy, she pirouetted and curtsied to them, just as she had done as a girl.

"It's a pretty thing she is, my little sister," Ewan said softly.

"She is that." Sean's voice was unsteady, and for a moment Ewan studied him closely.

"Don't you two try to sweet-talk me. You've just ignored what I want—Ewan to stay here until he finds a place of his own."

"Oh, now, would we do that?" Sean asked softly.

Hallie looked away from Sean, because the longing of a man for a woman was there, frightening her. "You'll wear those new boots, Ewan, or nothing at all. I know they fit, because you've had others just like them. You paid for them, and the sale is long past. There's no taking anything back, so you'll just have to stuff that pride of yours somewhere else," she said firmly, though her hands trembled as she plunged them into the dishwater.

When Ewan left for his appointment to transfer the shop from Finlay to himself, and she was alone, Hallie sat down at her kitchen table. She needed to think and to quiet her nerves with a cup of tea in her hand. Ewan was one thing—headstrong and yet beloved and vulnerable. Sean was another matter—a big man, almost a brother, whom she'd known all her life. His eyes said he now wanted her as a man wants a woman—and she couldn't have that. She couldn't bear to hurt him, nor to let another man touch her as a lover would—she'd struggled too hard to be independent.

Then back to Ewan—her brother's parting argument hadn't been sweet, and it had taken everything she had to withstand his demand that she take his money—she wouldn't. Her brother wasn't done arguing, and he was certain to clash with Cyd and worse—Angela.

Angela with her cutting words and raised hand— Hallie pushed the childhood image from her. Staying with the Donovans' large happy brood had wiped most of the memories away. . . .

Except for that last day, when Ewan was eighteen and had just returned from working on the docks after school.

From habit, when that dark scene came upon her, Hallie's finger circled the plain cheap cup. Angela had been in a rage over fifteen years ago, furious that Hallie had broken a china cup. Hallie's welts were burning when, unannounced, Ewan had entered the parlor.

He'd been so quietly cold as he removed the belt from Angela's grasp and placed Hallie behind him. "You promised, Angela," he'd said so softly that the room shook with his words.

At eighteen, Ewan had been tall and powerful, and fear had leaped to Angela's face. "Don't you hurt me, Ewan. Hallie was only getting what she deserved. She broke a cup of my best china."

Ewan had ignored her and turned to Hallie, inspecting the fresh bruise along her face. "She made you promise not to tell me that she was still hurting you, didn't she?" he'd asked even softer. "What did she say?"

Hallie had shaken her head, fearing to tell him, fearful of what Angela would do to Ewan—maybe having him put in jail, accusing him of thievery and—and incest that wasn't true. At fourteen years old, Hallie knew Angela's capabilities and power.

"You've done nothing wrong, Hallie," Ewan had said. "Go along now and start packing your things. You're going to stay with the Donovans from now on. You'd like that, wouldn't you? I want to talk with Angela, then I'll come get you, Hallie."

What had he told Angela all those years ago that had caused her to agree to the Donovans as Hallie's guardians?

What secret did Ewan hoard so close that not even his sister would know?

# Chapter 4

After dinner at the Donovans, Hallie and Ewan walked toward their old home on Fairy Lane. On Ewan's brief visits, the walk had become a ritual, a return to the house that brought back happy memories—the echoes of their father's laughter, the love of their parents. Brother and sister locked hands, just as they had all those years ago when they had first entered Angela's house to live. Wrapped in memories, Ewan and Hallie ignored the bite of April's cold wind.

Ewan turned his body slightly to protect his sister from the wind. They paused only for him to adjust Hallie's knit cap, to tuck it more closely around her face, just as he had when they were children, caring for her. But this time, she turned to him, her eyes soft and brimming with tears, her hand on his cheek. "I'm so glad you're home, Ewan," she whispered. "Everything is going to be fine now. You'll see."

This time, it was Hallie comforting him, because she understood Ewan's fears—that he might fail. "You couldn't have helped what happened, Ewan. You were only a boy. You're a man now, and, most of all, you're a Lochlain."

He ignored her tease. "Someone should have helped, Hallie. They didn't."

Hallie's expression slid from tenderness to earnest concern. "They were afraid for their jobs. You can't blame them for that. Angela and her friends could reach into their lives and destroy them. The Donovans and others tried, though, but they couldn't match her power and money—"

"They didn't try hard enough. She made us ashamed to tell anyone how we were being treated. She took the money from our parents' insurance and the sale of the house and everything in it."

"And used it on us."

When Ewan stared at her and didn't speak, Hallie shook her head. "That was a long time ago, Ewan. A lifetime. We both have new lives. Let it go."

"Dad did *not* plan Mother's death," he stated fiercely to the person who most understood his pain.

"Of course not. Those were just rumors."

"Rumors Angela and her cronies started."

Hallie's lack of bitterness never failed to startle Ewan, nor her abrupt defiance. "I refuse to be a victim any longer, Ewan. Looking back at the past makes me feel like one. I'm a different person now. So are you."

"You forgive Angela, then?" he prodded too sharply, and immediately regretted the slip. It labeled his sister as a defector.

Hallie took his hand, and they began walking again. "She's so alone, Ewan. Money hasn't brought her happiness. And there is poor Fred."

" 'Poor Fred' should have helped us. Instead, he cowered while she mistreated us and sold everything that meant anything to us."

"Hush, now, Ewan," Hallie said, reminding him once again of his mother's soothing voice. " 'Tis time for the fairies to come out, to sit atop the toadstools and polish their wings."

He couldn't help smiling at his father's bit of whimsy on

Hallie's lips, teasing him away from the past. "There it is—home."

"Cyd lived here for a time, you know. But she said that it deserved children, and she's decided family life isn't for her. And she said the Night Man came here too much."

"Profit has a way of making Cyd's decisions, not some bogeyman."

"She's still afraid at night, Ewan. She was only a child when someone fed her those awful stories. It isn't for us to make light of her fears. You won't, will you? She's always home before dark, and no one else knows about how terrified she is at night. She's terribly proud, and I won't have you teasing her."

"I won't. I remember her as a child, how scared she was. I'd hoped for the best, that her fear had passed."

Arms around each other's waists, they stood on the sidewalk as childhood memories curled around them.

Amid other houses of the same age, all different colors and sizes of working-class families, the house was well kept, bordered by a white picket fence. A tricycle had been left on the sidewalk leading up to the wooden porch, where long ago Ewan had suffered his sister's "pretend" tea parties. Moved a little by the wind, a rocking chair nudged a toy dump truck, and it came rolling out of the shadows.

"In the summer, there's a plastic pool in front, with boats floating in it—plastic, not the wooden boats Dad made for you. I do so wish those could be found. Angela says she doesn't know where they are. . . . The Simmons own the house now, and they're good people. She works at the dime store, and he's on the city's maintenance crew. There's an old tire swing in the backyard, like we used to have. The owners before them remodeled a bit, but it still has that warm feeling . . . especially when the scent of Mary's fresh baked cookies is in the air. The children—they saw me passing by one day and invited me in to watch Annie hold her nose underwater. I . . . didn't. I'm afraid to get too close."

Ewan nodded, but couldn't speak, his emotions running too full. Then he asked, "You could have your own, easy enough. Sean is in love with you. I can see it in his eyes. Why haven't you given him a chance in all these years?"

"It wouldn't be fair. Don't ask anymore, Ewan. There are things you don't want me to know—like how you got Angela to agree to me staying at the Donovans—and I have my secrets, too. And don't be playing matchmaker between Sean and me."

"That savings account would make a nice dowry," he returned, teasing her away from the secret that had held Angela at bay. Through the years, Hallie had often asked how Ewan had arranged the Donovans as her guardians; Ewan had avoided the truth—it was as dark as Angela's heart.

Hallie's elbow in his ribs was light enough to stop his teasing. "Let's not argue about that tonight, Ewan. Not tonight. It's too good now, with you home at last."

At Hallie's back porch, she reached to frame his face with her hands. "Everything is going to be fine now, Ewan."

"Is it?" he asked, unafraid to show his fears to her—the bald, scraping fears that he might fail and Angela's predictions would come true.

The time had come. . . . The whole foundation of the business Ewan wanted lay beneath the shop's flooring. . . . If they weren't there, after all these years . . . If something had happened to them . . .

He'd waited for this moment, fearing what he would find. Ewan held his breath and knelt, using a crowbar to lift the worn floorboard beneath the cluttered workbench. His father had tramped back and forth in front of the workbench often enough, and the boards were worn.

Until he'd left at eighteen, Ewan had often managed to

slip inside the shop and check on the big box that now held
his dreams. Each time he came back, Ewan ritualistically
cared for his father's creations, tiny boats, a handcrafter's
scale models. For the long months when Ewan was away,
Sean had managed their care, replacing the charcoal and
drying them carefully. He'd asked often enough if he could
put them in another place, but Ewan felt the scale models belonged where they had been created.

Earlier, the boisterous Donovan family had helped Ewan
clean the boat shop of clutter and dirt. The workbench was
heaped with things Ewan had to sort, and it would be a
long job. The storage room had been cleared and the makings of a one-room apartment had been roughed out. Repairs to the drafty windows and damaged boards would
take time, and Ewan could cure the sad disrepair of Tom
Lochlain's tools.

In the quiet of his first full night in Fairy Cove, his body
was tired, but Ewan's mind flew through the fears of starting
a new business—and the potential failure.

His hands shook as they sought the opening to the airtight
box and the tiny treasures inside and the notebook of a good
boatbuilder's secrets—

Ewan's jerk tore one end of the board free, and he carefully pried it away. Inside the shadowy depths, beneath a
light film of dust and cobwebs, was the metal box. Hurrying,
Ewan pried away three more boards.

A rusty nail scratched his palm, and still Ewan worked,
bending to lift the heavy box that had strained two twelve-
year-old boys' strength. Somehow he'd managed all those
years ago, to hurry with Sean, protecting what Tom Lochlain
held dear from Angela's grasp.

Ewan stood, hefting the box onto the workbench. His
hands shook as he carefully used a putty knife, edging it
through the mold and new rust that melded the lid to the box.
Then he carefully lifted the lid, placing it aside.

Ewan stepped back, rubbing his hands on his jeans to dry the anxious sweat from them.

"A good boat man can't go wrong when he has these," Tom Lochlain had told his son, and now Ewan repeated the words, which echoed in the airy, cold space. Taking a deep breath, Ewan stepped toward the bench. He brushed aside the charcoal lying on top of the bag. A slow, delicate slide of his pocketknife opened the bag.

One by one, he eased the small boats from the bag, carefully placing them on the workbench, on the towel he had prepared. From inside each boat, Ewan lifted away the tiny bags of silica gel, a drying agent.

Mildew would come off with light sanding, but each of the six was in good shape. Tom Lochlain built things to last, and instead of using light basswood or birch for the models, he'd chosen the more time-consuming and sturdier cherry. By using a scale to enlarge the models' designs, Tom Lochlain's skiffs and dinghies and other boats could once more become real.

Ewan ran a fingertip over a tiny boat, admiring his father's work.

He stepped back again and, prepared for the worst, took care in lifting the old notebook free. Despite the packets of desiccant tucked inside the covers, it still held the dampness, and Ewan decided to give it time before opening. Inside were his father's notes, a handcrafter who wanted his son to follow in his footsteps.

Ewan scrubbed his hands over his face; he was still stunned—even after all the years that he'd checked—that the treasures had waited for him, from his father to him.

When his hands came away, the glitter of gold next to the old notebook on the workbench caused him to frown. He reached for the brooch that had never been there before, and recognized it as his mother's.

Small and perfect and gold, inlaid with bits of emeralds

and tiny pearls, it lay in his hand, a gift from Tom Lochlain to his wife. To Ewan, the relatively inexpensive brooch's value lay in sentiment.

Sally Donovan had probably kept it for Ewan. Sean had likely placed it where it could be found after he'd left—one man wary of another breaking down to cry.

The telephone rang and, taking care, Ewan tore a piece of toweling and wrapped his mother's brooch inside, tucking it in his shirt pocket.

"Ewan Lochlain," he answered briskly.

Cyd's husky tone slid across the line, "So you're really staying there."

"Why, yes, I am," Ewan said, settling in to nudge Cyd's glorious temper and that hot, luscious mouth—one that he ached to try and wouldn't. "You're invited, anytime. I'm not open for business now, just for friends who drop by. Do drop by, Cyd. Bring me coffee in the morning, and something to eat, will you?"

"I heard the Donovans were over there, helping to ready the place. McGruder's chain would take it as it is, without the repair that's needed."

Ewan smiled because there was nothing like a cat-and-mouse game with Cyd to tear him from the past. "I'm staying put, love. Why don't you come over now?"

He regretted the invitation immediately. Cyd's fear of the Night Man would prevent her from going out at night, and Ewan was mindful of others' fears. He'd had enough of his own, and Cyd had had a rougher start in life than he. As a child, her blue eyes had filled most of that pixie face, and she'd come to tell him what one of her mother's customers had said, tormenting a helpless child with a bogeyman story.

"Tomorrow will be good enough," Ewan amended. He knew what drove Cyd, her bottomless need for money—a childhood she was lucky to survive. Linda Callahan had tended her customers and forgotten her child. And yet, Cyd now paid for Linda's care in the retirement home in another town. The grown child had banished the careless parent to live fifty miles away, and that was light enough revenge.

"It will take years to put that place on a paying basis. I'll see if McGruder's won't up the offer, and we'll talk. The price is more than fair now, but if you're going to be difficult, they just might go up. This is big money, Ewan. You can set up a new place somewhere else—away from Fairy Cove."

He picked up a tiny boat, studying the smooth running lines. "And out of your way, Cyd?"

"Something like that."

The electronic click and the buzz of an empty line said she had hung up. Ewan replaced the telephone firmly and reached for a bottle of antiseptic, pouring it over his hand and the nail's wound. "Like hell we'll talk about selling this place."

When the telephone rang again, Ewan reached for a thick slice of Mrs. Donovan's carrot cake. He took a good bite of it before lifting the receiver and patiently listening for Cyd's next argument—even in a temper, there was something about Cyd's husky voice now that could reach inside his gut and warm his need for a woman's soft body.

Instead, Angela's shrill voice came across the lines. "So you've come back, Ewan Lochlain."

The carrot cake suddenly lost its flavor, and Ewan placed the rest on a paper plate. He leaned back against the work counter and pictured Angela standing in her ornate study, the high-backed red velvet chair from where she issued her high-and-mighty orders. Her call was no surprise, nor the threat that was certain to come. "Hello, Angela. Fred has already reported the news to you, has he?"

They hadn't spoken in years, and he recognized her hesitation as an adjustment to the dawning reality that this wasn't a visit—he intended to make his home in Fairy Cove. Or perhaps her mind flew back through time, to another man who married her twin sister, when Angela would have had him for her own. Perhaps that was why Angela hated Tom Lochlain so much, because he had loved his Mary deeply and faithfully.

"Don't go stirring up anything you can't finish, boy. I know you for what you are, your father's son, a worthless—"

"I *am* my father's son, Angela, and proud of it." Ewan cut short her opinion—he'd heard his father accused of murdering his mother too many times. "But not near as kind or sweet. Remember that, dear Aunt Angela."

Her voice rose to a scream. "Don't you threaten me, boy. I'll ruin you."

"If I were you, I wouldn't threaten. What I said fifteen years ago still holds. Only this time, the odds are evened a bit. I'm not a boy any longer. I'm not leaving this time. I've come to Fairy Cove to stay."

"Blackmailers go to prison."

"Fraud carries a heavy penalty, I hear."

"*I want those papers. I'll buy them.*"

Her voice was higher, and Ewan smiled coldly. Angela's label of "blackmailer" didn't bother Ewan. In exposing him, she'd expose herself, and that wouldn't happen. It was a neat little battle between them, each understanding the base rules. Her panic pleased him; it was little enough revenge for what she had done. He intended to enjoy moments that no court case could give.

"I think of them as insurance. I know the mechanism of Fairy Cove and how you pull strings. Keep out of my way, Angela, and I'll keep out of yours. We have a standoff, and if you don't behave, I'll have to let this town know some unpleasant details about you."

Her breath hissed before the dial tone sounded, and Ewan walked slowly to the window. Just past Main Street to the east and up on a knoll overlooking the cove, the windows of Angela's house shone through the night.

At sixteen, Ewan had moved into the shack behind her house. Because if he remained too near Angela, he wasn't certain of controlling his anger. And he'd stayed in Fairy Cove to protect Hallie as long as he could, to find some way to wrest his little sister from Angela's grasp.

And then he had. In a few short minutes of pilfering through Angela's ornate desk, he had enough to leash his aunt's cruelty. Ewan had used the copier in Fred's tiny home office to ensure the evidence of how she'd managed the insurance money from his parents—investing it in her private funds and using none of it on the Lochlain children. That tiny bundle of papers had rested in his duffel bag for years, but was now with Andrew Larkin's trusted attorney. If anything happened to Ewan, Jack Brown would see that Hallie was protected.

A tough legal fighter from Down Under, Jack loved nothing better than to unwrap fraud and abuse. "You're not really after money, are you, Ewan? This goes deeper than that with you. Auntie used the money from your parents' deaths to build her kingdom, did she? So what's the old girl's weak point?" he'd asked bluntly.

"Control . . . more than money, she needs power. She thrives on her 'Queen Bee' image, her position, her influence, her parties hosted for politician fund-raising," Ewan had answered curtly. "And no, at this point, it isn't about the money she misused."

Jack had flipped a tooth from a shark he'd killed into the air. He caught it in his fist. "Tell your sister to contact me right away—if anything happens to you. I'll be on the next flight. I'll be discreet. I understand the need for a quiet job, because of those you love. But if anything happens to both you and Hallie, I'll take that witch to a courtroom and make enough stink to ruin her."

The boat shop's familiar sounds settled around Ewan. What threat had Angela used to silence young Hallie, to prevent Ewan's sister from telling him of the beatings?

It seemed that his little sister wanted to keep her silence still, and he would give her that; shame wasn't an easy thing to share. Ewan shrugged and turned his mind to the task at hand—surviving in Fairy Cove. He opened his own notebook, the things he remembered while working with his father, the bits and pieces he'd picked up from other handcrafters, and placed it beside his father's. "It's a start, Dad. A fine start."

Cyd lay on her bed, her body shaking as she stared at the ceiling. Though her bedroom was well lit every night, the nightmare still held her. She willed it to end, the terrifying image of a big man reaching for her, leering down at her, the crash of the storm, the yells, and the blood, so much blood on her hands.

Ewan Lochlain had somehow brought the past more vividly alive than it had ever been. Lying in that boat, sleeping off a drunk, Ewan had caused her fears to leap to life— even though it was day. Wearing a mass of long, shaggy, black hair and a beard, Ewan could have been the town's legendary bogeyman.

Cyd tossed off her blankets and walked into the living room, to her small desk, piled high with work. There was no need to turn on the lights, because at night, she never turned them off. As usual, when she couldn't sleep, she began to work, this time planning the renovations to the small house she had just bought and intended to rent. "There is no use stewing about McGruder's tonight. I'll call them in the morning. I'll be feminine and helpless, and they won't be able to say no to an extension. All I need is a little time to make Ewan understand the best thing for everyone."

She glanced at a small gap in the curtain's drape, just enough to let someone from the outside peer into her home. Automatically, Cyd quickly turned to close the shutters and arrange the thick curtain over them. She'd moved twice before, and he'd found her—the towering, shaggy, hollow-eyed Night Man—who looked into her windows.

Cyd closed her eyes against the face that wasn't there.

Safe in the retirement home, Linda Callahan wasn't talking. She wasn't telling Cyd what had happened to that six-year-old child that night, why that little girl couldn't speak for days.

But Cyd knew every time she found one of the carved gnomes or fairies. Whatever had happened that night was unsettled, and someone waited for her. . . .

Her uneven laughter echoed in the empty room. "Maybe I am crazy like Linda says. Maybe nothing happened."

But some man was still wandering at night, peering into windows and vanishing, and no one recognized him. And it wasn't wise to challenge a moneymaking legend, was it? The town loved the legend, because tourists' money flowed freely for the Night Man's souvenirs.

Cyd kept her thoughts to herself, unable to explain her terror, or her shame. Whoever wandered the streets of Fairy Cove at night was the man of her nightmares.


The Other knew the alleys well, where the slivers of streetlights could not reach him. In the night, he had no face or name, moving as he wished.

The legend of Fairy Cove's Night Man had served him well through the years. The town hired several other men to thrill the tourists and make money flow. If they saw his shadow now and then, they only waved, and shouted a greeting. "Hey, Night Man! How's it going?"

This was his life, walking in the night, watching the town's lives, because he had no one to hold him dear.

Rage stirred against his life, against what he had become. He pushed the bitter taste of self-disgust down where it had become the disease that would kill him.

Suddenly, unexpectedly, the devastating pain raked at

him. Intent upon Cyd Callahan, the man had let the pain catch him. He fumbled quickly for the pills inside his pocket; he almost dropped them as his hand shook while raising them to his mouth.

He had only six months to live, and before he gave way to disease, he would kill the woman who had ruined his life.

She'd taken everything from him, and he hated her more each day.

He would make them pay, all of them, the people who had ruined his life. . . .

The man gathered his long ragged coat around him and hunched into the upright collar. A worn slouch hat protected his face as he slid down the alley, past Hallie's back steps and into an empty lot. Then he stepped onto an old forgotten path, nearly covered by brush.

He stopped in the undergrowth behind Cyd's house and noted the lighted windows. The earth was damp with spring, the night air rich with memories.

A woman with red hair shouldn't be alone.

She needed him to take care of her, to be strong for her.

The Other took a red curl, wrapped in pink ribbon from a worn envelope and stroked it lovingly. The strand was that of a child's hair, and he drew it to his face, stroking it along his cheek.

"I've waited so long for you, Molly Claire. You've always been mine. . . ."

# Chapter 5

"Shush, I won't hear of you paying me, Ewan," Sally Donovan said. "If you're going to put this place in order, you'll need good food in you. Here it is, only three days since you came home, and you've done more to resurrect and repair this boat shop than poor old Finlay did in all these years."

She looked around the boat shop, noting the new window, the cleaning he had done, and her four-year-old granddaughter warily inspecting the place. With an approving nod, Mrs. Donovan continued, "Let's see, it was locked for those first couple of years after your parents passed away. Then Angela rented it to Paddy O'Connor, who finally bought it. He rented it at times, too—when he found that he wasn't the boat crafter that your father was. Summer people used to store their small craft and such here during the winter. Paddy had it for less than four years—closed more often than not when he was away on a drunk. He's still around, you know, grumbling about how Finlay played him in that poker game fifteen years ago. Finlay wouldn't go for a rematch, saying he had what he wanted, and I guess he did—keeping it for Tom Lochlain's son."

She lifted the cooking pot from the child's red wagon and placed it on the shop's workbench. "You're almost one of my own. A thank-you is only good manners for a pot of stew or a cake—but I'll take none for a brooch I didn't give you. But it looks like Mrs. Linnea's—the one she placed in her blouse collar, tight against her scrawny neck. Her obituary said she died of natural causes, but I say she died of a cold heart. She preened in church one day, saying that your aunt Angela had given it to her. Angela likes to favor her friends, the ones who have done as she has asked."

" 'Given it to her'? Angela isn't a giving person," Ewan mocked carefully as Mrs. Donovan's granddaughter tugged on his pant leg, silently asking to be picked up. He carefully wrapped the brooch and placed it aside. When Ewan bent and lifted her to his hip, she lay against him with a sleepy sigh. He nuzzled the fresh scent of her hair and swayed gently, reminded of another little girl with bright red hair in tangles and curls.

Molly Claire had been a sweet little thing back then—not the fiery woman whose eyes flashed blue lightning at him . . . and Cyd didn't like her given name, to be reminded of another time when her mother's callers came to stay. . . .

Mrs. Donovan stroked her granddaughter's curls, and said, "I wouldn't say anything about the brooch, Ewan. Simply keep it as a family treasure. There are those about who might think you—well, that you had something to do with Mrs. Linnea's passing. We'd better go now."

Temper flashed in Mrs. Donovan's usually cheerful face, and she spoke quietly, fiercely. "When Angela took you children, Mr. Donovan and I wanted to—well, never mind. We wanted you and Hallie, but with our brood and the mortgage that Angela threatened to raise, we couldn't, and I will regret that until I die. We did offer and try."

After her good-bye kiss, Mrs. Donovan patted his face. "You're like your father, you know, gentle and easy to win a heart. Children sense that right away. I'd keep the brooch, Ewan, and say nothing to raise Angela's evil ways. You know it for your mother's, and you should have it. You got little enough from Angela as it was, and Mrs. Linnea had no heirs. Angela is nervous, you know, sending out her tentacles to find out what she can about you—how much money you have. Be careful, Ewan. She'll run you out if you can. The woman is dangerous. I'd expect a visit from Fred Greer soon. She still sends her husband, poor little man, to do her dirty work. He's retired from the lawyer business, but he's still hopping to your aunt's tune. . . . Keep the mystery of the brooch to yourself and be glad you've gotten something of your dear mother's."

After Mrs. Donovan left, pulling her granddaughter in the red wagon, Ewan slid the brooch into a rusty tool chest. He'd been gone for a few hours that first day, to transfer the ownership to his name, going to the Donovans for supper and later that walk with Hallie to their old home. If Mrs. Donovan hadn't left the brooch, then who had? And why? Angela?

His aunt had proven that she knew how to play games. Perhaps this was only one more. But he wasn't playing; he had no time for anything other than his dream.

Ewan stroked the cord he'd just attached to a control level's plumb. New tools would be expensive, but so was each hour he spent repairing the old, and making new ones. Glue and resin and epoxy would be costly enough. If he was going to create boats from his father's models and notes, he'd need good tools and wood.

But he needed something else, too, a healing time to settle into his new life.

Ewan left the future and concentrated on just that first start, filling the urge to feel wood beneath his hands, to create his first wooden boat, the forerunner to display and figure costs for the kits. But first, he'd take the unfinished skiff apart, working with her until he got the feel of the work.

Sharpening the hand planes his father had used seemed only right. He picked up a box of old wooden screw-and-wedge clamps. Broken now and worn, they would be good enough to use for patterns. He picked through them carefully, placing them on the workbench, then studied the old C-clamps, freshly oiled and waiting. The old adze still needed a handle, and the box of rusty rivets was best tossed away.

Ewan picked up a box of nails, and, as they rattled, his mind turned to the past. His father had been a gentle, loving man . . . one who worked hard to pay his bills and care for his family. Ewan's adult mind recognized the way his father had drawn his mother to him, the soft sighs and kisses as they settled against each other—Tom Lochlain had loved his wife, Ewan's mother. He would never have plotted to kill her for the insurance money—or worse, for the bed of another woman.

Memories of his father in the shop were too painful, and Ewan moved into the apartment just off the shop. The view of Lake Michigan spread endlessly westward beyond the wide windows he'd installed. He'd placed his bed near the windows, where he could watch the moonlight on the waves, or the storms brewing, the clash of thunder, and the fierce strike of lightning. The storms and the wind, the sound of the waves gave him no answers. But the answers were there, and he would find them.

Tom Lochlain's fifteen-foot sailboat had been well kept, light, and strong. The summer wind that day had come suddenly, but hadn't been strong enough to tear the boat apart. Even so, his parents were strong swimmers and their life jackets and perhaps a portion of the boat should have helped them reach either the beach or Three Ravens Island.

Ewan scanned the one-room apartment, now tidy and clean. A small stove stood near a well-used Formica table, though he still lacked a refrigerator. A lamp placed near a sofa with a wooden frame served well enough, and it had taken hours of work to clean the tiny, grimy bathroom.

This was his first real home since his parents'. And from here, he would unravel the rumors surrounding their deaths. . . . Obsessed? Yes, but then a man's family name and his love of his family had to stand the weather.

If Fairy Cove was hiding a secret, Ewan would find it.

Ewan's mind swung back to the mystery of whoever had left the brooch. He couldn't account for his possession of the brooch, though he had the motive to reclaim it. A trail from the dead woman to him would look suspicious.

Perhaps Angela was already planning how she could evict him from Fairy Cove; she knew how to make trouble for the Lochlains. Ewan silently agreed with Mrs. Donovan that revealing his possession of the brooch might not be a good idea just yet.

For the moment, he needed the feel of wood beneath his hand. He needed to find answers, to heal, and to find peace. . . .

*Ewan Lochlain . . . obstinate . . . unreasonable . . . illogical.*

By mid-April, a solid two weeks since Ewan's return, every sight and word of him infuriated Cyd.

Shopkeepers were busy stocking their wares for the coming tourists, and Cyd worked from early morning until dark preparing summer rental homes. Maintaining the small houses herself was just the thing to keep Cyd busy while she planned how to seduce Ewan into selling the boat shop. With a McGruder's extension in her hand, Cyd had taken those two weeks to assess Ewan's actions, looking for a weakness. And damn him, somehow he seemed to have money—money he should have used to help Hallie.

Fairy Cove buzzed with news of Ewan, and none of what she heard suited Cyd. She learned that he had purchased a small, new, apartment-sized stove, electrical supplies, lumber and caulk, insulation and windows. And he was renovating the storeroom for an apartment.

"Rat. You are a rat, Ewan. I had Finlay about to sign, and you turn up," Cyd brooded to herself as she slid beneath a leaking kitchen sink and began to loosen the stubborn old pipes—as stubborn as Ewan.

A visit to Finlay on the morning after Ewan's arrival had only gotten her the news that "Everything is in black and white. Ewan has his father's boat shop. No sense in trying to wrangle it away from him, either, girl."

Finlay's wink hadn't helped Cyd's bad mood. "But I'm sure you'll try, now, won't you? I've got this little bet, you see."

Before she knew it, she'd eaten a sweet roll, laden with calories, from the pastry sack she'd brought Finlay. "And what are my odds?"

The old seaman had puffed on his pipe and tilted his head, laughter crinkling in the lines of his face. "Two to one favoring Ewan. There are still some with faith in your powers of persuasion, though . . . just because they say you've got a witch's fiery blood and could call a man past what's safe, if you ever tried to put a spell upon him, that is."

Cyd didn't believe in spells; rather, she believed in cold, hard cash. "Put me down for five—on me."

"Oh, so little confidence in yourself, dearie?" Finley had crooned, and puffed on his pipe.

"Then make it one hundred. I'll make a lot more than that in commission from the sale to McGruder's."

Cyd tossed her head and decided to put Ewan Lochlain out of her mind; she'd brooded about him long enough. The daffodils were in full bloom all over Fairy Cove. The morning was bright and sunny and fresh, perfect weather to repair the little house. When she'd bought it five years ago, it had been a bargain and had almost paid for itself in rental fees.

In the bare, sunlit living room, she'd set up a small table saw, using the wood scraps for kindling when she needed to light the freestanding woodstove. The gallons of bright new paint would have to wait until a warmer day, when she could open the windows. She'd varnish the new door, though, and change the locks for the incoming renter.

For now, Cyd had everything she needed to work Ewan's stubbornness out of her system. She'd have Ewan agreeing to a sale—there was no way he could turn his back on the profit McGruder's could offer.

Or could he? Ewan was just stubborn enough to dig in—

She didn't want to think about Ewan Lochlain staying in Fairy Cove. Cyd freed the old pipe and decided that she would deal with the rotted wood at the bottom of the cabinet, before installing a new pipe. She stood, turned on the radio, and set her mind to using the crowbar on the wood beneath the sink.

The rental house needed a new refrigerator, and she planned to sell the old one. Once a buyer responded to her ad to sell it in the local paper, the old refrigerator would be gone and the new one would cut energy costs. A new kitchen look—just a new sink and linoleum—would surely draw a higher monthly rate, perhaps from a summer vacationer used to better things at home.

The board broke beneath the crowbar and Cyd knelt to use the hammer's claws on the nails holding the board in place. A nail, just as stubborn as Ewan Lochlain, remained stuck against her efforts. She lay on her stomach, reaching to the back with her hammer.

A creak of a board and a nudge on her leg terrified her. She'd locked the back door, or had she?

The Night Man never walked in broad, bright daylight. Or did he?

Cyd gripped the hammer, braced herself, and eased out of the confinement beneath the sink. On her knees, she heard Ewan's chuckle before she looked up to see him. He held a big, bright bouquet of daffodils. The yellow blooms defined the king-size bulbs she'd planted to offset the little house's quaint cottage look.

She scrambled to her feet and glared at him. "Exactly what are you doing here?"

Ewan grinned and held out the bouquet of daffodils. "Brought you these."

"If you picked them from my property—"

"I did."

Cyd grabbed the bouquet and tossed it into the sink. "I planted those to make this place appeal to vacationing tourists, not for you to pick. Though I love flowers, I don't love them from you. I should have Marvin arrest you for stealing my property."

Ewan's grin widened. "You could try. I gave him some for his wife. Here, Hallie sent her blueberry muffins." He nodded to the sack on the counter. "I've missed you this last week. I was thinking that you might continue bringing Finlay's share to me."

His hands were tucked in his back pockets, the worn navy pea coat open to show his shirt and jeans. Cyd's agile mind ricocheted through the facts: new flannel shirt, jeans, and boots meant that Ewan had extra money to spend, damn him. And that was a barber's haircut he was sporting—the waves neatly trimmed. He just might not be in a tight spot with money, getting that old shop into shape. But then, he should have some money to spend, shouldn't he?

After all, he hadn't helped Hallie at all.

"What are you grinning at?" she asked, when Ewan's gaze traveled slowly down the red bandanna tied around her head, keeping her hair from her face. His slow, intense study took in her paint-stained old sweatshirt and the thermal underwear showing through the holes in her jeans, and workman's boots, no better than his when he had arrived.

"Your boots are new," Cyd stated. "No doubt purchased with Hallie's money."

He frowned briefly, then said pleasantly, "Nag."

"Rat."

He smelled of fresh coffee, soap, shaving lotion, and man, and that dazzling grin and sparkle in his gray eyes would be enough to fascinate some woman—but not Cyd. Ewan Lochlain was wasting his interested, rawly male, sexy look on her.

She jerked her face away from the broad callused hand that came to lie on her cheek, and Ewan's grin widened. "You're all lit up and ready to fight, and I haven't said a word. Makes a man wonder why a woman would get so hot and bothered—just looking at him. I'd rather you placed that hammer on the counter, love. If you don't mind."

Cyd struggled with her temper and slowly placed the hammer on the counter. She clicked off the radio, tugged off her work gloves, and crossed her arms. She leaned her hips against the countertop as she focused on Ewan. "I detest endearments. Why are you here?"

"The newspaper advertisement said to come here this afternoon for the refrigerator and household odds and ends left by renters. But I'm busy this afternoon, shopping for a used truck. I thought I'd try this morning. Are you doing business or not?"

"It's cash only."

"Good enough."

Cyd couldn't move, and it wasn't from fear. Ewan's soft deep voice wound around her with just that touch of his father's beguiling Irish lilt, a gift from his father before him. The past snagged her. Her only safety back then was that of Ewan's and his father's arms, the hugs of Mary, all scented of cookies and love, and Hallie's unwavering comfort.

Ewan's expression darkened, as if he, too, were remembering, and the memories brought him pain. He eased away, and asked quietly, "How much for the refrigerator?"

"Fifty."

He walked to the refrigerator, opened the door, looked inside and peered around the back before he turned to her. "It needs some work. Thirty."

"I could get more, but I just want to get rid of you. It's yours." Cyd forced herself to meet Ewan's searching gaze. She knew what he was seeing—the scared child he'd comforted, the girl ashamed of her mother, the woman still afraid to go out at night. And the girl who gave him her first kiss, offering her body to him all those years ago.

And he was probably wondering just how free she'd been with that body since. But Cyd had seen enough of her mother's active bedroom to know that she needed her self-respect more than a lover, and her defenses ran high.

It wouldn't do to let Ewan Lochlain, or anyone else, know that she was still a virgin—as a known woman-magnet, Ewan would have a good laugh over that.

Cyd wished away the blush that had crept up her cheeks, but it only deepened when Ewan's expression changed to that of a man interested in a woman.

She moved away and walked into the living room. She was shaking, her palms damp with the sweat of fear, reacting now to Ewan's size and strength and masculinity.

The boy who had taken her first kiss was now a man—and something fierce within him could set her off easily. "The rest of it is in here. Odds and ends that renters left and never claimed. It's in my rental agreement, so they're mine and for sale. I cleaned everything—"

When she turned, Ewan was standing too close, staring intently at her, and the heat of his body warmed hers. Startled, Cyd moved away, putting a few feet of new linoleum between them. She frowned when Ewan took one step, then another, blocking her into a corner.

"It's always like that, isn't it, Cyd? You moving away from any man who comes too close? I noticed that when I visited before— Cyd, you still act like a virgin after all these years. And that fear is real. What happened to you?"

Cyd rubbed her damp palms on her hips and crossed her arms on her chest, her trembling fingers digging into her skin. She'd survived and that was enough. Now Ewan's return had stirred something she didn't want touched. "Do you want the refrigerator and anything else? Or will you just get out?"

Ewan's expression hardened, an eyebrow lifting to mock her. "I've got the feeling you're not done pushing that Mc-Gruder deal at me. So if I were you, I wouldn't be cutting off any friendly chats."

"There's a lot of money in that deal, Ewan. Nothing to play games about. You could stand to lose a small fortune— start-up money for some other place, and a little to help Hallie on her mortgage."

"Which you hold. Oh, yes. My sister told me about that, how you've helped her—"

*"Because you didn't."*

Ewan stiffened at that, his eyes narrowing, his jaw setting firmly. "I wouldn't want my sister disturbed by what you think. Hallie has a soft heart. You don't think Fairy Cove is big enough for the two of us, do you? That makes two of you—you and Angela."

"Angela hasn't bothered Hallie in years. You could start her up again. It's just better for everyone if you leave, Ewan."

"Like it or not, love, I've come home to stay."

He reached to twine a finger in the strand of hair escaping Cyd's bandanna, keeping her from moving away. "You're a fine-looking, fiery woman, Cyd Callahan. Not at all the imp that I held years ago, shivering from tales of the Night Man and how he would steal children away. But that fear is inside you still, fear of a bogeyman who doesn't exist, a little something the town uses to put it on the map, to get a few more tourist dollars. . . ."

"I've seen him, Ewan." She heard her own uneven voice, the adamant statement startling her. The bald truth nipped at her once again—that after all these years, she could trust Ewan with her worst fears.

"Have you now? Someone the town has hired to carry on the sham?" Ewan's tone lacked mockery, the same steady tone that she'd known years ago—and trusted.

Damn him. She still trusted him. Some inner sense told her that she could depend on Ewan for safety.

She'd given Ewan too much already, an insight another man might use in business. Uneasy, Cyd shook her head. "I don't want to talk about that anymore."

Raised in Fairy Cove, Ewan knew Cyd and the folklore too well. "To talk of Fairy Cove's Night Man gives him power, they used to say. Do you believe that?"

"Leave it, Ewan," she whispered shakily.

"What does he look like?"

"Damn it, Ewan. I don't want to talk about this."

"Hallie says you still have nightmares, that you won't go out at night. I've been to your office—it has a more-than-adequate surveillance system and locks."

She couldn't have him prowling through her fears. "We've had break-ins, so I installed some—"

"A simple lock is serving Hallie's place, and she's got stock to steal. From what I could see, you've got a computer setup and office furniture that would take a few men and a truck to move . . . and they would be noticed, parked on Main Street. And if you're not afraid to go out at night, why don't you come to dinner at my place?"

Cyd shivered, horrified at walking the streets and alleys of Fairy Cove at night. "Not tonight. I would like to talk with you about the money you can make. I think they'll raise the price, especially after you've fixed up the place. That always raises a buyer's price—"

Ewan moved closer, and braced his hands flat on the wall beside her head. "Tomorrow night, then? That is, unless you have a date? Someone you're seeing?"

He was pushing, and Cyd didn't like it, her temper rising. She lifted her head and met his stare. "No. Don't think for a minute that I'm dating the likes of you, Ewan Lochlain. Or doing anything else with you."

His finger lowered to prowl around the safety glasses draped around her throat. "Oh, I'm wounded. You think I'm out to have you, don't you? And me without a taste of your kiss—except that last going-away one. It was truly fine, Cyd, all hot and wild and sweet as a first kiss should be. It carried me through a lot of lonesome nights."

When Cyd opened her lips to scald him with words, Ewan grinned and tapped her nose with his finger. "Hold that thought. I'll pay for the refrigerator, and I'll be back this afternoon with my truck. We could go to dinner later. Think of it . . . Cyd Callahan, Fairy Cove's top moneymaking entrepeneur, riding around in a beat-up used truck. Of course, it's not quite the fancy new four-wheel-drive model beside this house, with its CALLAHAN REAL ESTATE sign stuck to the door. Truly warms the heart, doesn't it? You, in a beat-up old truck, dressed like that? As if you were a regular laborer and enjoying a carefree date with me?"

She'd struggled for a professional image, and few had seen her without cosmetics, or in her working gear. Ewan was already at work, set to undermine what she had built— distance between her mother's life and her own. "No, thanks. The last time you were in port, you made do well enough—Margo Hanson, wasn't it? They say you went for dinner and stayed for breakfast."

"If that's what they say. Jealous, are you?"

"Not a bit. And I'm not helping you load that refrigerator. I'll be here at three. Come then."

Ewan took his time in answering, then his voice was deep and lilting and intimate. "I always come when a lady asks. Usually. But then, sometimes waiting for the right moment . . . when she is ready, is better."

The underlying double meaning shot straight into Cyd's midsection. She didn't trust the curve of Ewan's lips, nor the grim promise in his eyes.

After he had gone, whistling a tune and walking down the sidewalk toward Main Street, Cyd folded the bills he had placed on the counter and tucked them into her jeans.

In her brooding about Ewan and how he could both make her feel safe on one level—understanding fears that reached from her childhood—but unsafe as a woman, Cyd barely tasted Hallie's muffins. She burned her lip on the hot coffee from the thermos. "You are selling that property to Mc-Gruder's, Ewan Lochlain."

Worst of all his crimes was that Ewan hadn't mocked her when she'd said she'd seen the Night Man. There was only the quiet understanding that he'd given her as a child.

As a woman, Cyd didn't trust Ewan's charm . . . or her feelings about him.

"Good evening, Ewan." Fred Greer nodded to Ewan as they passed on Main Street at five o'clock that afternoon. Fred clutched his briefcase against him, almost as if he feared Ewan would strike him. He adjusted his glasses with a shaking hand. "I heard you were back in town."

"Fred." Ewan's contempt softened at the sight of his uncle. Marriage to Angela was probably punishment enough for not standing up to her—not even to protect children.

A shadow of a man, Fred was well dressed in a charcoal gray fedora and long overcoat. Tall and thin, he hunched against the cold wind. He tugged on his gloves and looked nervously around. "I'm glad Hallie is doing so well at her shop. I would come to see you, but Angela—"

"I know, Fred. She wouldn't be happy. And I'll be seeing Hallie for dinner tonight, so I'll relay your good wishes to her."

When Fred hurried away, Ewan took a deep breath and

scanned the pink horizon and the gray line of clouds above it. The anger he'd once felt for the older man was no longer there . . . only pity. And Ewan had other things on his mind—like Paddy O'Connor's grumblings.

Ewan entered the Blue Moon Restaurant and Bar and found Paddy sitting at a corner table, a mug of beer in front of him. From his sullen looks, Paddy had more than a few beers inside him. Unshaven, the big seaman glowered at Ewan.

"A draft and some fish and chips, when you get time," Ewan told the waitress as she passed.

After a slow look down and then up to Ewan's face, the blonde's smile was sultry and knowing. "Well, hello, sailor. You're who everyone is talking about, aren't you? Hallie Lochlain's brother? You bought the old boat shop from Finlay?"

He appreciated the inviting look, but just then, he wanted to deal with Paddy. "That would be me."

"You've got a bit of a reputation with women. I'd like to see if it's true. My name is Jennifer. Take me out on the lake sometime?"

Ewan settled back to enjoy the play. "Maybe, but I'm probably overrated."

She sent him a flirtatious and knowing look. "Honey, you're a legend."

Just then, Cyd entered the restaurant in a blast of cold wind. Her long coat swirled around her, her face pale amid a storm of wind-tossed red hair. Quivering layers of curls upon curls, still caught by the wind, seemed almost alive.

Ewan's fingers moved as if he could almost feel them within his grasp. He waited for her to see him, to watch her reaction—that hot, fast, wild look that he wanted to—

Across the distance of the cocktail crowd and early diners, her eyes locked with Ewan's. He braced himself against the raw impact of his hunger for her, the need to stake her out and burn away the need that had grown with each visit to Fairy Cove. He ached to hold her as he claimed her lips and tasted that pale soft skin, to feel the beat of her blood beneath his lips.

Primitive? Yes, the need to capture and tame, and perhaps be tamed a bit, too, an equal match to settle the wildness within him.

When he'd collected the refrigerator earlier with Sean, Cyd had been almost as cold as the April day. Now, just to set her off, because that was what Ewan truly enjoyed, he slid his hand to the waitress's hip, smoothing her tight jeans. He'd make no excuses for the life he had led, or the women he had known, at first for comfort and warmth, friendly harbors he'd badly needed and shared.

But none of them had fired him like Cyd. He wondered whom she reached out to for comfort, for arms to hold her safely in the night, another body to keep away the night, another heart pressed against her own.

No one should have the fear that moved inside her, real or not. Despite himself, Ewan wanted to comfort her, and those softer ties caused him to be uneasy.

She wasn't that child any longer; she was a woman who would take what she could—if it put a dollar in her pocket— and walk away without a backward glance.

The smile on Cyd's lips slowly died. Without a word, she turned and walked out of the door.

"So it's like that, is it?" the waitress said, studying Ewan and snuggling closer. "There's more than a few men after Cyd, but she's not buying. They say she's got a cash register for a heart and prefers her bed cold and lonely."

"Well, then, she's not buying, but I've always liked a good game," he said lightly, pulling himself from the need to warm Cyd's cold lips to the one of settling scores with a bully.

Jennifer giggled and patted his chest. "I'll just bet you do. I'll get your brew."

Ewan slid his coat onto a chair at Paddy O'Connor's table and sat slowly. Paddy had aged badly over the years, his gray hair greasy beneath his knitted seaman's cap. A hard life, spent drinking and on the water, had carved deep lines on his face. The cruelty in his eyes hadn't changed. It lingered, a beast lurking within, ready to pounce and hurt. The burly seaman cursed, and Ewan waited until he had finished. "So, now, O'Connor. What's this I'm hearing about you calling Finlay a cheat, and that the Lochlain Boat Shop is rightly yours? Your signature was on the deed."

Paddy swigged his beer and wiped the foam from his lips with the back of his hand. "Finlay caught me when I'd had a few too many."

"That was over fifteen years ago. I talked to the others who were there. You put what you had on the table—what was left of my father's boat shop—and lost it. Let it be, O'Connor."

Paddy slammed his mug to the table. "I earned that property, paid for it, I did. I hear it's up for a pretty penny now with a sale to McGruder's."

Ewan methodically placed a napkin over the spilled beer. Big money usually stirred old grudges. "I'm not selling."

"You'll sell. And I want my share. Cyd Callahan usually gets her way when money is in the mix. She spreads her—"

"Say that, and anything more about Finlay, and you'll deal with me," Ewan warned softly. To the waitress who had just delivered his order, he smiled. "Thank you. I'll pay O'Connor's bill. He's leaving now."

*"No son of a murderer is going to tell me what to do!"*

Experienced with the sound of a brewing fight, Jennifer's indrawn breath hissed as she backed away.

The taunt caused Ewan's blood to run cold; the old pain cut through him—and the rage he didn't trust, once locked inside the boy and ready to break free of the man. Anger curled Ewan's gut and into his fist. "Would you like to discuss this matter in the back alley, Paddy?" he asked coolly.

"As I remember, the last time you dealt with a boy, roughing him up quite a bit. What were the odds then? A thirty-year-old man to a sixteen-year-old boy? Fractured my rib, didn't you? I've been waiting for a return match."

"You were sassing me. I had a right to defend myself. If you don't back off, you'll get a second helping." Paddy glanced at the three men at the bar and nodded.

"Here I am. Anytime," Ewan invited softly. "For you, or your friends."

Paddy started to push back from the table, his hand on the knife at his back, when Sean Donovan entered the restaurant. As though sensing the tension that had drawn the rest of the people to look at the two men, Sean paused, then called to Ewan. "You owe me a beer for helping you with that refrigerator, Ewan."

Ewan understood that Sean was giving fair warning—if there was a brawl, he'd be at his back. "It's always good to have a helping hand. Jennifer, a beer for my friend and some fish and chips for a snack before dinner."

The seaman scowled at Sean and at Ewan and, with a salty curse, hurried out of the restaurant.

Sean sat at the table and reached for Ewan's fish and chips. "He's not happy, and from that look on your face, neither are you. O'Connor is trouble . . . always has been, and if he can make it for you, he will. He works at odd jobs and ships out sometimes, but he always comes back. Word is that drinking and a hard life has gifted him with liver disease, but he's not changing his ways. No one knows what holds him here. He rents a little house from Cyd, up on Brownie Lane."

Ewan forced his tension away and reclaimed his dinner. There would come another time when Paddy and he would tangle. "Your food is coming."

"Hallie says Cyd is in a mood. That usually means you two tangled. She was always like that the times you came home to visit."

Ewan sipped his beer and decided that Cyd would probably have more bad moods, because this time, he wasn't leaving. "Don't you have better things to do than gossip? Like letting Hallie know you're in love with her?"

Sean's wide grin stilled, and he ran his finger around the mug of beer that Jennifer had placed in front of him. "That easy to see, is it? My son is in love with her, too."

Ewan thought of Sean's six-year-old son. Timmy's eyes, jet-black straight hair, and dark complexion didn't come from the Donovans' fair coloring. Just nine months before Timmy was born, Sean's blond wife had been seen with a Hispanic man passing through Fairy Cove. "Do you ever hear from Janie?"

"My ex-wife? No. She was glad to get rid of me and the boy. After he was born, she took my payoff money, signed her name to a release, and ran. Timmy is set to have Hallie for a mother though, pressuring me and trying to sell me to her when he can. She doesn't see me as a husband, Ewan, or as a lover, and that's the bottom line. I can tell you that I don't like that ex-husband of hers. He comes around now and then, just checking on her, I guess."

Ewan frowned slightly. "In the shop? That's the first I've heard of that."

Sean shook his head. "It's not for me to say. She keeps that part of her life to herself. And Cyd has nothing to say about it either. The two of them are very close, closer now than as children—they share something now that they didn't before—I can sense it when they're together. It's there in a look between them . . . O'Connor will cause trouble for you if he can, you know. And Angela is already stirring the rumors about your father. I heard Fred was at the newspaper office, digging in their files for the day your parents didn't come off the lake. She's got him running her errands already, and she won't make life pleasant for you."

"Let her stir. I'm not leaving Fairy Cove."

Sean tossed a fried potato crisp into the air, catching it in his mouth. He munched on it, grinned, then said, "And then there's Cyd. She's set to have the boat shop."

Ewan returned the grin. "Now that's going to be an interesting game."

Sean settled back in his chair and studied Ewan. "She's already visiting all the shops on Main Street, explaining to them how they would have more customers if McGruder's came in, and that they might talk to you about selling."

"Like I said, this could get interesting. You have to appreciate a woman who fights for what she wants."

# Chapter 6

"**I** thought you said you didn't see your ex-husband, Hallie."

In the first week of May, Ewan had had a month to study closely his sister's expression each time her ex-husband's name was mentioned. Her open, happy look slid into a shielded one, and he wanted answers.

A secret ran between Hallie and Cyd; he could feel it at times when the two women shared a look. That uneasiness always prickled when Hallie's marriage or ex-husband was mentioned.

Ewan leaned back against Hallie's kitchen counter and studied her face as she rolled pie dough. The afternoon sun slid through the window to light her face. Easy to read and truthful, Hallie's body had stiffened, her fingers gripping the rolling pin too tightly. She bent to check the casserole in the oven, and the movement shielded her face from Ewan. "Allan comes around."

His sister had never been evasive with him, and Ewan searched for the answers why she should start now. "Why?"

She started working again, in quick, hard movements, and the dough tore. Dipping her fingers in a glass of water nearby, Hallie patted the mixture, closed the hole, and sprinkled flour over it. "I'm almost ready for those apples you're peeling. Better hurry up. You said you were an expert at peeling—all those tons of potatoes you peeled as a kitchen boy."

When Ewan had come to visit Hallie, Allan Thompson was always out of town, a tractor salesman visiting farmers. They'd met just once in passing, and Allan had seemed friendly enough, definitely attentive to Hallie—but even then, there was something about her too-brilliant smile, the nervous way she hurried to make Ewan's visit perfect.

"You never told me what went wrong."

She shrugged and folded the dough once, then again, cutting designs into it. "Get the butter from the refrigerator, will you?"

He handed the small crock of butter to Hallie. She was mixing sugar and cinnamon in a cup and talking too quickly, a sign she wasn't comfortable with the subject. "Timmy was here today. He's so bright. I don't see how any mother could leave such a beautiful child, but Sean is doing a wonderful job as a single father. That old hermit—Peter? He's still out there at one end of the island. We never see him. Norma Johnson—that's the resort housekeeper—in the last year or two, she's lived almost full-time at the resort. She used to go for long drives by herself, and when she came back, she seemed so distracted, so sad. She used to be a nurse, you know."

Ewan noted the slight tremor of Hallie's hands, the way she bent her head to avoid looking at him. His sister didn't want him prying—and probably for a good reason.

"I should have paid more attention. You just seemed so happy, and your letters—"

"I married Allan and I divorced him three years later. Those were my choices. I suppose he drops in now and then to check on me because—because he still cares," Hallie finished firmly. "It's over, Ewan. Six years have passed."

"Sean says Allan comes around, here in the shop. Why?"

"He's—he's only interested in how I'm doing. The whys and hows don't really matter. Now we'll eat while the pie is baking—I had that shipment of blown-glass fairies come in earlier and couldn't start the pie then—then I want you to take a plate to Cyd. When she gets in a snit—and you're the current reason—she forgets to eat, and she can't cook. She ends up eating those awful frozen dinners. Always call Cyd before you drop by at night. I'll call and tell her you're coming over. She's still—she has nightmares. They are horrible."

Hallie turned to Ewan, her expression fierce and unexpected in such a gentle woman. "You and Cyd are bound to tangle, but don't you dare torment her about the Night Man, Ewan. She's done everything she can to cope with her fears, including seeking professional help, and I will not have her frightened any more. She's gone through enough. She was there when I needed her—always."

An image of Cyd's fearful expression that first morning wasn't something Ewan was likely to forget. "I know what it is to be afraid, Hallie. It's no laughing matter."

She reached to kiss his cheek and smiled. "And that is why I placed my first bet on you, Ewan, my very first gamble. I bet that you'd hold the boat shop against Cyd's maneuvering. Don't tell her, of course, she's my best friend. She was just here storming away about you."

"She can't avoid me forever. I've been here a month, and she leaves the minute I come in the door." Ewan glanced at the flower box outside Hallie's kitchen window. The new plants were already promising pansies, and that brought him back to how Cyd had looked with the daffodils in her hand.

Pretty. In her worn clothing and the red bandanna capturing those vibrant curls, she'd looked pretty and sweet and fresh and young.

Ewan shook away the thought. Sweet? Not Cyd. A fascinating witch? Yes, and, despite himself, one he longed to see.

After dinner, Ewan carried a picnic basket filled with Hallie's lasagna and apple pie to Cyd's house. Acting as Hallie's delivery boy had benefits—seeing Cyd again. Beneath bright lights, he knocked the required tattoo on her door and listened to the multiple locks clicking open. Prepared for the delivery, Cyd opened the door; she frowned at him and reached for the basket. At eight o'clock at night, she was dressed in a sweater and jeans, and the light from the room behind her outlined the curves of her body and long, long legs.

The sight of her was enough to take Ewan off course, and he wanted answers from Cyd. Firing straight at her might get him more returns, so he led with a taunt, "So you can't cook and you'd starve if it weren't for the charity of my sister. You've been avoiding me, Cyd. I thought you'd be interested in my progress at renovating the shop."

"I'm not. I told Hallie that I'd already eaten, that I'd pick this up in the morning, but she—"

Ewan looped his fingers around her wrist, just tightly enough to hold her. He liked to hold her, too much, and that discovery brought his own frown. "Not so fast. I want to talk about Hallie."

He didn't like that wary shielding of those blue eyes, as she said, "Ask her whatever you want to know."

Cyd tried to tug away, and Ewan couldn't help smiling, enjoying the emotions on her face—frustrated, angry, and so perfect for the taking. He placed the picnic basket just inside the door and took his time straightening, still holding Cyd's wrist. His need to know his sister's secrets gave way to a desire to kiss the woman who had haunted him through the years.

"I've been wondering about this, how you would taste after all these years," he said quietly, and slid his hands into that warm silky mass of hair, capturing it.

She hadn't moved, her eyes wide upon his face as he lowered his head to brush his lips against hers. He took her breath into him, closing the slight opening. He felt the ripple of fear, absorbed it, ached for the cause of it, and whispered, "There now, Molly Claire Callahan, it's only me."

He'd meant only to kiss her, but instead he placed his cheek against hers. He waited for Cyd to reach into the past, to the safety of the boy who held her on his lap and talked of fairies and whimsy and the brave things he would do in the world. He'd called her Molly Claire then, too, and now the name sat softly, sweetly upon his lips. "Come walk with me, Molly Claire, and I'll show you there is no Night Man on the streets of Fairy Cove. It's only a story, just words that can't harm you. Whoever gave you that fear should have been horsewhipped."

Against him, her body was stiff, her cold slender fingers digging into his wrists.

"It's only a story, Molly Claire, not flesh and blood," he repeated softly against her skin. "And I'm only Ewan, the boy who cut bubble gum from your hair and drank Kool-Aid at little girls' tea parties, now just a man."

Against his cheek, she breathed unevenly, her body relaxing just that bit before Ewan stepped back to study her. At least the fear he'd felt in her wasn't there. Shock turned to fury as Cyd stared back at him. *"Never call me Molly Claire again."*

"You took another name, but the girl is still there, and the fear. . . . I want to know what happened to Hallie's marriage," he said quietly, firmly, understanding her need to separate herself from the child and the safety she'd found with the Lochlains. "And one of you is going to tell me."

For an answer, Cyd stepped back the inches she needed to slam the door in his face.

With a sigh, Ewan sat down on the porch and nodded to the carload of teenage boys who came slowly driving by. They honked, hooted, and called to him. "You won't make it past first base, buddy."

In another moment, the door opened, and, behind him, Cyd said, "Get off my porch."

"Not until I have some answers." He reached into a flower bed near the steps and leisurely picked a stem layered with tiny bell-shaped blooms. "Fairies sit beneath these at night to polish their wings. It's said that the lily of the valley collects moon glow, storing it so that fairies can read and mend their clothes of spiderwebs."

Cyd's brief silence said she remembered his father's stories. Then she said, "I'll call the police. Marvin lives next door. He'll be here in a heartbeat."

Clearly interested in Ewan's progress, the boys drove slowly by again. "Give the guy a break, Callahan."

"Mind your own business, babies," she returned furiously.

"Get much of that?" Ewan asked, and thought he'd do the same at their age. He looked up to enjoy the sight of Cyd simmering, her eyes flashing, her cheeks pink.

"What? Men sitting on my doorstep? You're the only one so far, and that's one too many."

"Unfriendly sort, aren't you?"

Ewan looked at the man walking from the house next door. It would be like Cyd to choose a house with a police chief at the ready. "I believe the police chief is already on his way. Hello, Marvin. I was just waiting for Cyd to put on her sweater and take a walk with me. Come sit with me while she's getting ready."

Behind him, Cyd whispered desperately, "He's carrying two beers. That means he intends to stay a while and talk with you. I can't have you and the police chief sitting on my front porch like some sort of male convention."

Ewan answered quietly, "Then you'll have to hurry up, won't you?"

There was just that pause, then Cyd whispered, "Do something."

"I am. I'm waiting for you. Let's take a stroll around town."

"Damn you."

Ewan slowly turned to look at her again. "If it's to hell, I've already been there. And something tells me that my sister has been, too. And you. But I promise we won't talk about that any more tonight. I give you my word."

He'd given his word to her years ago and wondered if she'd trust him now, or if her fear of the Night Man was even stronger than before. "It's only a story that the shopkeepers keep alive, Cyd. They hire men to do the stalking at night. There's nothing to fear—"

"Good to see you around Fairy Cove. How about a beer?" Marvin Kendrick was a few years older, and a good man, according to Finlay and others.

Marvin was almost to the porch when Cyd sailed out, jamming her arms into her light coat. She nudged Ewan's bottom with her foot. "Come on."

Ewan stood slowly. "Sorry, Marvin. Looks like we'll have to catch up some other time. Cyd wants me now."

Marvin grinned. "Darn. I'll have to drink your beer. Can't have you walking around Fairy Cove with a beer in your hand."

" 'Wants' you," Cyd muttered beneath her breath as they moved onto the walkway. "That will be the day."

With a wave, Marvin moved back into the shadows, and Cyd whispered, "This is nothing short of blackmail, and I won't forget it. You'd just better promise to bring me back here, and to keep your lips to yourself."

When her eyes, expressive in that pale narrow face, darted to the shadows, Ewan ached for the child who had been terrified. But to tease the woman who looked as if she'd run back to the house, he said, "Oh, always, darling-mine."

Cyd walked slowly, glancing fearfully out into the shadows of the street. Her body stiffened as he put his arm around her, yet she didn't refuse the comfort. "If anything happens to me, Hallie won't be happy. And I won't answer your questions about her."

Then Ewan knew that he wouldn't like whatever secrets Hallie protected—because even in her terror, Cyd would not betray her friend.

The Other eased back into the bushes as Ewan Lochlain and Cyd Callahan passed on the sidewalk. In the night, a dog barked nearby, aware that a prowler was near.

He reached into his pocket and tossed the dog a treat, silencing it. Through the years, the dogs in the town's backyards had come to know him, to expect favors in return for silence. He was no better. He'd traded his life, his pride, and his honor for favors and money. . . .

Pain slashed through him, and he quickly swallowed his pills, bracing himself until they took effect. His terminal disease—and hatred—were eating his insides. But before he was finished, he'd punish them all.

She'd taken away his manhood, made him useless to other women, but he'd waited for his time to punish her. . . .

"Molly Claire . . ." he whispered into the fog, and the fragrant night air, loving the taste of her name on his lips, remembering the sweet scent of her childish skin against his lips. She was grown now, looking like her mother.

He remembered Linda Callahan's fair skin and wild red hair and groaned a little, aching for the daughter . . . for the empty years, the need to hold her close that ate at him, and the hatred of the woman who had ruined him.

"Molly Claire, I'll always come back for you. . . . My Molly Claire. . . ."

Alone in her house, Cyd replaced the telephone receiver. She peered inside the picnic basket and selected Hallie's apple pie. Her warning call to Hallie had been unnecessary; her friend knew that Ewan would be searching for answers, for the darkness she'd shared only with Cyd.

The house seemed oddly quiet, the shadows seeming to

quiver as though someone had just passed through it. Cyd could almost feel that someone had been inside, yet the locks had been intact.

She pushed away the prickling of her senses; she wouldn't allow herself to grope for answers in an empty room and fill it with nonsense. No one could have entered her home; it was just as she had left it. . . .

Cyd jabbed the fork into the apple pie and ate, for once not savoring the taste. "For your information, Ewan, as a child, I left Mollie Claire behind and a lot of other things, like my crush on you."

Ewan had seen straight into her terror and made her face it. Walking closely beside her, he'd been the safety she'd had long ago, speaking quietly of the changes in Fairy Cove, the friends who had married, the babies they'd had—

The fog had curled around them, the mist like cold fingers upon her cheek, yet she knew she was safe, because she was with Ewan. He'd moved beside her—big and invincible and fearless, just as he had when she was a child.

He spoke quietly, but his silences told of his brooding, of the boy who had become a man too soon—and who had made Angela back away from the guardianship of Hallie. But for once, Cyd didn't want to ask the whys and hows. With fog softening the images of the buildings, and the waves sounding against the piers, they walked side by side, the years falling away.

Ewan had been perfect, damn him, offering her no basis to be angry . . . except when he had arrived, taunting her and giving her that searching, sweet kiss. Cyd resented the need to slide into Ewan's arms, to open for him, to taste him, to find that wild, hot strength and capture it, just as she wanted to soothe the dark storms that still lurked there.

Worst of all, she trusted him on a level that hadn't changed.

But Ewan stood between her and a great deal of money. If she had to go through him to get it, she would.

* * *

In the morning, Ewan bent to his drawing, carefully measuring the tiny cherrywood model and writing down the measurements for a larger sailing boat, just big enough for two. He'd seen his father take his mother sailing in a boat like that, light enough to skim the waves, and the wind had captured Mary Lochlain's happy laughter, bringing it back to Ewan, the boy—for Tom Lochlain, hardworking family man, who took time to enjoy his wife and their love.

Tom Lochlain wouldn't have wanted the insurance money from Mary's death—he'd rather have had his wife, alive and safe in his arms.

Ewan glanced at the blinking message machine and deleted the one that had been waiting for him last night. It had taken Angela one month to make contact with him again, after circling his purchases and activities.

Now Angela required that he set up an appointment to meet her at her home. Ewan would go to her—but in good time and on his terms.

He pushed away the troubling darkness that somehow never left him. If Fairy Cove was holding any secrets about his parents' deaths—he'd dig them out.

And whatever troubled Hallie, he would discover that, too.

And then there was the hunger for Cyd—to taste those ripe lips again, to burn out the fire that ate at him, to quench the need for her that hadn't died in all those years.

But only when she wasn't clinging to his hand, afraid of the night. He wanted her on different terms—and when he awoke at five o'clock this morning, it was to the hard ache of his body, the sound of his own groan, and the dream of sinking into Cyd's body giving way to the coming dawn.

The bone-deep pain and the way the sheet rising over the erection below his belly said that he was truly lusting after Cyd, a woman who tangled his emotions—took them dancing between protecting the child as he had as a boy and the aching needs of a man. He had no delusions about Cyd—given the chance she would, in a heartbeat, take away his dreams of his father's boat shop.

Money had ruled Cyd for most of her life, and Ewan understood the roots of that driving need; but he would not feed it.

A run at the icy water, a yell and a dive into it had taken away the pain, enough for him to brew coffee and start his day. By working on the skeleton of his first effort, a little flat-bottomed skiff, which could be used as transport to a larger craft, he'd get back into the feel of handcrafting. Only a twelve-footer, it could be rowed, or a small motor could be used. Easy enough to craft and better-looking than aluminum, the small boat was perfect for those who preferred to fish near land in good weather.

He'd learn from his first effort, then gathering confidence and skill, try a second from scratch.

Ewan watched a fishing boat in the harbor, riding the big waves easily. It was an expensive red-and-white twenty-footer, a metal-and-fiberglass monster without the heart put in her by a handcrafter. Dressed in upscale weather gear, the men in the boat were trolling as they headed out for more open water to fish.

Handcrafting and the boat kits business he wanted weren't likely to make a fortune, rather they would fulfill a dream—and reclaim the honor of a family name. Was it only a whim and a dream to build his father's boat shop into what it had been?

Into more than it had been, Ewan corrected. With power tools and equipment, he hoped for a better income on the boat kits. He had enough money to repair the building and roof, and to get a good start—the rest was up to fortune.

But Hallie's money was for her, and it nettled that she'd kept it for him.

The seven o'clock sunlight skimmed through the window

Ewan had recently replaced and painted a bright square on the wooden floor.

And in that square lay the shadow of a cross.

Ewan followed the shaft of sunlight up to the window, where a tiny gold cross hung. Turned slowly by the slight drafts of the building, it was suspended from a nail by a delicate chain.

When the cross lay in Ewan's open hand, he could almost see it at his mother's throat, a gift from her mother, and intended for Hallie. . . .

Angela had said the gold cross was lost long ago . . . yet here it was, gleaming and warm from the sun, worn a bit from wear and love.

Ewan gripped the cross tightly and brought it close to his throat. Whoever had returned it to him knew that it was rightfully that of the Lochlain family.

And the old brooch . . . someone was set on returning his mother's jewelry—but who? And why?

When Cyd's bright hair passed his window, her expression grim and set as if she had war on her mind, Ewan held the cross tightly, feeling the bite of metal and memories. Until he had answers, there was no sense in letting anyone know about the sudden reappearance of his mother's jewelry.

Especially the red-haired woman who had just slammed into the building as if she wanted to start a war. She marched past the skeleton framework of the skiff he'd been working on and braced her hands on her hips.

Ewan's mind danced from the mystery of the jewelry's appearance to the woman in front of him, the way she tilted her head so that her hair spilled over one shoulder, the way her coat opened to show that fine gray merino wool sweater, tightened across her breasts.

"Ah, you're in a mood already this morning," he said, just to start her off and see what was on her mind.

"You know they're talking about us already this morning,

don't you? The bet has just gone up. To match it, I had to wager another hundred."

"Did you bet on me, darling? Or yourself?"

Her sky-blue eyes heated and blazed and from the inches separating them, Ewan almost felt her anger quiver. "Who do you think?" she demanded.

"I didn't think you were a gambling woman . . . since you like money so much."

"Shut up." She glanced at the boat models on his workbench, the drawing pad beside it. "Still playing with boats, Ewan? You can't make a living that way. You'll be living off Hallie unless you sell."

"I'll manage somehow. But it's good to know that you care."

"You're a dreamer, Ewan. Get real. I care about the sale to McGruder's, and you'll run out of money soon enough. Then you'll be sorry you didn't take a better price, and my commission will go down because of your stubbornness. You've already spent a fortune for repairs to this place."

Her long black raincoat had shifted, revealing the gray sweater tucked into a neat waistline, circled by a gold chain. But just past the hem of her skirt and above the high-heeled leather boots was a length of long shapely leg that would run smooth to the touch. . . .

"My father made those boats, and built to scale, I should do well enough. . . . And what are they saying about us, Cyd, that has you so aroused and hot?"

Cyd's slender hand shot out to capture his flannel shirt, fisting it, as she leaned close, and said fiercely, "They're saying that we went for a walk last night, Ewan."

"There's some truth in that, Callahan. We passed a few people on the way. You're out early, making bets and catching gossip, aren't you?"

"Hard to miss when I stopped for a morning paper and coffee at the restaurant. A whole roomful of men—apparently with nothing else to do—sat there grinning at me. Naturally, I had to ask. Naturally, they answered. Between the hoots and jeers, one fact emerged—that exactly at five o'clock this morning, when Courtney Mason was opening up the Blue Moon to start breakfast biscuits, you took a running dive off the pier into the lake. You swam like the devil was after you, then climbed back up the ladder."

Cyd took a breath and delivered the rest quietly, angrily. "They say—and they are wrong—that I'm playing you for the money in this real estate deal. That I'm using sex, and leading you on, and you were so worked up during the night that you had to . . . to cool off. . . . I do not use sex to get real estate deals, Ewan. Ever. And especially not with you."

"I never thought you would, sweetheart. But I've been meaning to talk with you about paying off Hallie's mortgage. Of course, I wouldn't use sex to persuade you. No, I truly wouldn't, not even if you begged me for it." He enjoyed the rosy color rising in Cyd's cheeks, the way her eyes widened until he could see himself in the black irises. "It's almost as sweet as a morning mist before the world wakes to clutter the day, you know."

"What?"

"Wondering what you'll do next." He scratched his chin and eyed her, thoroughly enjoying the sight of her. "You haven't come up with any fancy self-defense moves, have you? Maybe I should be frightened. Dear me, I think I am positively quivering."

A fighter and used to holding her own, Cyd clearly struggled with her temper. "Idiot."

Ewan placed the cross in his chest pocket—it could wait, and so could Angela's explanation of just how it was lost from the family estate. He had Cyd, all stirred and hot within kissing distance. And it would be a shame not to kiss her.

"Oh, well," he admitted softly, "if it's not sex you're wanting from me this morning, we may as well get this over with—since you're in a mood, and I'm damned already."

And then he reached for her face, captured it, felt the fine bones beneath that soft skin, and sealed her lips with his own. He'd intended to taste the fire beneath the fury. But instead, within himself, he found an aching tenderness to soothe and to enjoy at the same time, to share a bit of himself with her—as though he could relax, coming into a good, safe port.

Strange, Ewan thought distantly, as his lips brushed hers and tasted a bit of the corner, and that fine bow of her upper lip, how she gave him something—a gentleness that a man needed to call him home.

Odd, Cyd thought distantly as Ewan's lips brushed one corner of her lips and then the opposite one, how she wasn't afraid, not of the boy or of the man. She tasted a loneliness and an ache, and incredible care not to frighten her, just to hold her with his big, rough hands, framing her face, and the touch of his lips, light upon hers.

She could have moved away. But he'd given her the choice, and she wanted to stay, easing nearer, wanting more.

Ewan's hands slid from her face, but his lips played lightly along hers, brushing and teasing, but never stopping long enough for her to sink into the kiss. He shifted a bit, and Cyd pressed her advantage, slipping closer.

The game had changed, she realized with triumph—Ewan was uncertain and hot and backing away, and the play was all hers. A heady sense filled her: that she was strong and in control in a man's arms, taking what she wanted, demanding his lips open for hers, tasting him in a rich, hot play of tongues, slanting her lips for a closer fit.

The scratch of his morning stubble excited, a contrast to her smooth skin. It was no gentle feeling she had for Ewan Lochlain, rather the need to beat him at his own game.

And she was flying, filled with victory. For once, she'd

gotten the best of him, because his breath was rough on her skin, and the heat from his face warmed her own.

"You're aroused, Lochlain," she whispered against his lips. "In another minute, you'll be embarrassing yourself. It's true then, that dive off the pier this morning was because you were dreaming of me."

Ewan's voice was deep, uneven, perfect. "Just tell me you're not going to have me right now. I'd feel so easy."

Cyd held very still and opened her eyes to meet Ewan's gray ones, filled with laughter.

It took her a full three heartbeats to realize that she had backed him against the workbench. She stood between his open legs, leaning her weight against him, one hand gripping his hair and the other open on his chest—just over his racing heartbeat.

But Ewan's hands were at his hips, gripping the workbench behind him. He hadn't touched her. He'd made her come after him with just the brush of his lips. . . .

The laughter was gone from his eyes, and he held very still, watching her. Then he took her hand, raising it to his lips, kissing the palm. "I'm just Ewan, who used to kiss away your scraped knees, your 'boo-boos.' You caused me a little embarrassment back then, a little girl with a mop of red hair chasing after me," he said very quietly in the lilt that had always soothed her. "And it was only a kiss and freely given. Tell me of your dreams. Tell me why you still fear the night and worse when it storms. There's more to that, than Fairy Cove's bogeyman."

Cyd shoved away and when she did, her thumb caught on a tiny loop of gold chain. Ewan's hand caught on her wrist, his smile disappearing into a frown.

And between them, suspended by a gold necklace, dangled a small, gleaming cross.

# Chapter 7

"What are you doing with that?" Cyd whispered. Her hand trembled, and, on it, the little cross began to dance at the end of the gold chain.

"It was my mother's and grandmother's before her, meant for Hallie one day," Ewan said roughly as he eased the chain from Cyd's thumb.

The cross lay on his scarred palm, and Ewan's fingers curled to stroke it lightly. "Hallie was probably too young to remember this. Years ago, when I wanted to know where it was, some small inexpensive thing to give Hallie from our mother and her mother before her, Angela said it had been lost. And now, magically, here it is."

His fist closed over the cross as if he'd never let it go. Cyd placed her hand at her throat, her pulse racing cold beneath the skin. "That belonged to Patricia Erland. Why do you have it?"

Ewan shrugged and straightened, but Cyd wouldn't let him escape. She put her hand on his arm, felt the muscles bunching there. "Ewan, if you came back for revenge and have anything to do with Patricia Erland's death, do you know what that would do to Hallie? To know that her brother—?"

"Exactly what do you mean?" Ewan gripped the cross in his hand, his arms folded over his chest.

"Ewan, sometime last night, Patricia Erland died. She was an asthmatic, and she'd had an attack. At eighty years old, she wasn't able to reach the telephone for help, or her breathing machine. Her portable tanks were in a closet, and it looked like she tried to reach them, but had knocked over a clutter of her husband's old golf clubs. She couldn't get to the tanks. That necklace belonged to her, Ewan."

"How do you know?"

"I've bargained and traded enough estate jewelry to recognize it. It's worn just enough to say that someone loved it and maybe held it in her hand before Patricia. I liked that. And I liked the idea of rescuing it from her. It's not expensive, but it's a sweet piece that I wanted for myself. In fact, I'd go so far as to tell you that I had my eye on it, when and if that old woman died and it came to auction. I make it my business to keep an eye on Angela's old crones."

Ewan stepped toward an old wooden box, which he placed on the workbench. "Come here, Cyd."

He carefully lifted the lid, taking out a small square of cloth, and eased back the corners to reveal a brooch. "This was my mother's, too. My father gave it to her. I found it, the second morning I was here. The cross was hanging up at that window; both were placed so I would find them."

Side by side on the cloth, the old jewelry caught Cyd's breath. "Mrs. Linnea died last October. Marvin said that she was missing a piece of jewelry. As her executrix, Angela had asked him for it. And she asked for the cross this morning, too. It couldn't be found."

Leaning close to Ewan, Cyd barely realized that he had his arm around her, drawing her closer, protectively, just as he had on their stroll in last night's fog.

"I was in Sydney, Australia, six months ago," he said thoughtfully. "Had a bit of a layover from pneumonia, and there are medical records to prove it. Flu had taken our whole ship, and we worked a bad storm just before arriving, worsening our condition. Andrew, my employer, was very sick, and required intensive care until we could put his schooner out to sea again."

Ewan's gray eyes had darkened, and the tenderness with which he spoke was undeniable as he continued, "There are plenty of witnesses who know I stayed with Andrew, caring for him with a full-time nurse, while we sailed his last voyage. I can prove where I was at any given time, because I helped finish his affairs, including getting his schooner back to Maine for a fancy sailing school. . . . And I didn't have anyone do the job for me. I expect Angela would be asking about the jewelry. She doesn't like things to escape her keeping, or rather, she likes to know where her possessions are."

Cyd looked up at his profile, the hard edges and his set jaw reflecting his distaste of the past. "Like Hallie."

"Yes, she would consider Hallie to be hers, and she would be able to keep tabs on Hallie." Ewan turned slowly to face her, and brushed a tendril away from her cheek. "Which brings me back to my sister. I'm going to find out what she's hiding."

Cyd's instincts to protect her friend lifted instantly. "She's not a girl any longer, Ewan. She has a right to privacy, even from you."

"And that brings me back to the mortgage you hold over her. What will it take to buy you off?"

Cyd moved away from him; she thought of how Hallie had come back to Fairy Cove that night, bruised and terrified. She had just filed divorce papers and had taken a beating for it. When Mr. Allan Thompson had arrived at Cyd's door, demanding his wife, he was in for a surprise. Cyd's revolver aimed below his waist had a lot to do with making him see things her way. If Allan had pressed charges against her, Cyd would expose him for what he was, and that wouldn't serve him well in the tractor-selling business.

She couldn't keep Allan from visiting Hallie—because Hallie forbade that intervention. But Cyd let Allan know that if he made any wrong move, she'd run him down and make him pay—painfully. It wasn't a threat, rather a promise, and Allan knew it.

"Hallie needs to make her own way, Ewan. It's important to her as a woman. But you could have helped her, and instead you had to have this—" She waved her hand at the old boat shop. "*This.*"

Ewan's head went back as though he had been slapped. "I'd watch that, if I were you, Cyd. My sister's issues, and what I want to do, are separate."

"Don't you dare make trouble for Hallie, Ewan. Everything in Fairy Cove has settled down, and you're set to stir it up again. Did you have anything to do with either of those women dying?"

"No, and you have my word on that."

"Your father used to speak just like that, as if he'd die first, before breaking his promise. For that reason, and because of Hallie, I believe you."

"Speaking of my sister, I hear you have my father's armchair?"

"Because he made me feel safe, and it makes me think of him."

Ewan shoved his hands in his pockets, studying her in that quiet way. "A child should feel safe, and so should a woman. But you weren't safe as a child, were you, Cyd? Did you ever ask your mother about why you might have those nightmares?"

"I tried. My mother isn't the talking sort. She doesn't want to remember what she was. She's not well, and maybe it's best for her to forget."

Cyd reached back into the night, when the terror came, a shaggy man with his hands outstretched, reaching for her as she lay in her child's bed. He smelled of whiskey, his eyes burning at her, and suddenly the storm was inside her tiny bedroom, fierce and ugly, and then her mother was sobbing. . . . Now that man prowled the night, and peered into her window—he wasn't a legend or folklore, he was real, waiting for her—

And the tiny carved fairies and gnomes he still left on her doorstep proved that he hadn't forgotten her.

Cyd shook away the nightmares and drew herself back to the present, leaving Ewan's question unanswered. While Hallie deserved her secrets, so did Cyd.

Because she had to sit, to absorb the fact that Ewan possessed the jewelry of Angela's friends, who had spread the malicious rumors about Tom Lochlain, Cyd eased onto an old chair. She placed her high-heeled boots on a stack of lumber. "Then, Ewan, old buddy, someone is out to make trouble for you. It wouldn't do for you to show off jewelry that had been stolen from dead women. Angela would pounce on that fact in a minute. You're not exactly on her list of favorite people. Anything she could do to remove you from the scene, she'd do. You're a reminder she doesn't like having around."

"Let her pounce." Ewan tilted his head and studied Cyd. "Enjoying yourself, are you, Ms. Callahan? To picture me as a murder suspect? Maybe you placed that jewelry here."

From the way his mouth curved and the laughter touched his eyes, Ewan was enjoying testing her. His supposition was meant only to get a rise out of Cyd—they knew each other well enough for the banter, and it was safe play—his kisses weren't.

"But then, Mr. Lochlain, how would I know that was your mother's jewelry? It would break Hallie's heart to have you accused of thievery—or worse. And I wouldn't do that to her, not even for a hefty percentage of a sale. I'd say you'd defend yourself when needed, but there's just something old-fashioned and gallant about you—like that stroll around town last night—that says you wouldn't hurt women, or the elderly. And from the looks of you, rather what you don't have, you're not a thief either. Or you'd have come a little further along in life. You'd have new tools, instead of making your own and repairing what was left lying around here."

"So kind of you not to suspect me of foul play. As for our walk last night, my dear, I was only staking a claim. Just letting everyone know that I intend to have you."

"Dream on."

If Ewan's smirk could be packaged, Cyd could sell it at outrageous prices. It packed enough punch to weaken her legs when she stood. "See you around, chum. And you can leave a message on my machine anytime you want to negotiate the big fat price you'd get for selling this dump."

His voice wrapped around Cyd as she walked toward the door, holding her. "There's no need to let Hallie know about the jewelry, Cyd. If someone is out to plant evidence, naming me as a thief or worse, I'd rather keep that fact quiet— for now."

Cyd hurried out of the boat shop, shaken by Ewan's kiss and the fact that his mother's jewelry had suddenly appeared, taken from the homes of the dead women. Someone was out to make trouble for Ewan, for one reason or another.

And Ewan wasn't letting secrets lie, either Hallie's or Cyd's.

But then, *she* didn't know the secret her mind held, and tossed back to her in nightmares, the images unclear and shifting in the storm—but the chilling fear remained.

She didn't know why the Night Man came to peer in her window and why he left her the gifts—unless it was to remind her that one day he would finish what he started. . . .

Cyd shuddered and lifted her face to the cool bright May-morning sunlight. She'd had enough practice, putting her terror into a drawer during the day—but she always pulled it out at night, especially if a storm was brewing. . . .

But the day had other flavors, and the memory of Ewan's kiss remained, the taste delicate and warm and tormenting, just light enough to hold her in place, to make her come after him. The sound behind her caused her to look over her shoulder, and there was Ewan, standing in front of the boat shop that he was set to defend. As he watched her across the distance of the harbor's waves, his arms were crossed, his legs braced apart. The kiss he blew her did what it was meant to do—torment her.

She saw Sean on another pier, filling his motorboat with gas, getting ready to go to Three Ravens Island for the day. His big grin and wave said he knew about Ewan's dive into the lake.

Because Cyd was Cyd and the town had always talked about her, she walked to where Sean stood grinning. "Kiss me, Sean, and make it good. I'd like to give the town something else to talk about."

With a quick grin, Sean looped her into his arms and gave her a kiss that took away her breath. He held her inches above the wooden pier and grinned. "How'd I compare?"

Sean had wrapped a friendly arm around her often enough, and fear hadn't leaped into her. He'd kissed her. But the friendly kiss didn't raise her hunger for more as Ewan's had. "You compare quite nicely. Thanks. I'll do the same for you sometime. Have you kissed Hallie yet? Like a woman you want?"

His expression stilled. "She doesn't see me that way."

"Take my advice. Make her come after you. It's not something a woman can forget."

"How long do you think that will take? It's been a lifetime already. And by the way, my friend Ewan over there is scowling at me. You'll protect me from him, won't you?"

With a laugh, Cyd eased away. Then because Ewan was watching, she stood on tiptoe to kiss Sean. "You're always good for me, Sean Donovan."

"My pleasure," he answered with a grin. "Now, if you could just help me a bit with Hallie, I'd appreciate it. Just a kind word now and again."

On her way to Hallie's for one of her delicious blueberry scones, Cyd turned to meet Ewan's dark stare with her own. She ignored the wind whipping her hair around her head, the strands clinging to her cheek. Ewan might be a bit wiser on handling a woman, on knowing how to make her ache, but the hard evidence he had pressed at her stomach had told her that he'd ached, too.

She'd have to work on that game—tormenting Ewan and taking her revenge.

She could hold her own with Ewan Lochlain, anytime, anywhere.

And someone was out to frame him for thievery—or worse.

And damn, because he was her best friend's brother, she'd have to protect him.

Angela had given his mother's jewelry to her friends, had she? Ewan thought angrily. How was his aunt going to explain that fact if she accused him of thievery? That she'd sold the jewelry to pay for Hallie and his upkeep? The pieces were inexpensive, their value measured in sentiment, rather than dollars.

Or perhaps, as Sally Donovan had said, the jewelry was cheap payment for her cronies' dirty work, the vicious rumors they spread? For making Angela look as if she had a heart of gold, taking the orphaned children?

Anger had almost cost Ewan hours of work. He'd been refashioning the center molds, the skeleton upon which he would build his first skiff. It would be hours until he answered Angela's recorded demand that he appear at her home, and he intended to take his time, cooling his mood. Errors in the creation of the skiff and notes taken wrongly would be costly. His success depended on correct notations, transferring his father's model boats into reality, then into designer kits for the do-it-yourself wooden boatbuilders. Once that project was successful, he intended to hold classes in the shop for those who wanted to make their own boats.

It was a long, expensive road from creating his first skiff and maybe his second or more, to marketing the packaged kits. Ewan propped the center molds to one side and glanced at Hallie's shop. After Cyd had kissed Sean, she had walked into Hallie's Fairy Bin, and she hadn't come out—unless she'd used the back door of the apartment.

When the telephone rang, he automatically reached for it. "Lochlain."

"I've got a chum here who wants a good boatbuilder—a sweet little dory for his daughter-in-law, who likes to fish, taking her peace away from my son's wild horde of children. D'you suppose you'd be interested?" Finlay asked between puffs of his pipe.

"I'm closed for general business, Finlay, but open for friends. Tell your friend to drop by for a chat and use the buzzer by the door. I'll keep his request in mind for when I'm better settled."

Finlay puffed his pipe. "We were just wondering—not that we have to know, you understand—but wondering just the same, if you've any idea that Cyd could wrangle a Mc-Gruder deal out of you. Seems like she just left the shop in a snit and kissed Sean to make you smolder a bit."

Ewan smiled slightly. He'd done more than smolder, and Fairy Cove was on the alert for changes. "How am I doing in the bets?"

Finlay puffed a bit more. "You're ahead. But Cyd has her ways. She's won more than she's lost. She's a fighter, boy, but I'll give you a bit of an edge, since you asked and all— she's not been in love, that the boys and me know of. It's only money that puts a sparkle in her eyes, not a man. Since you're a handsome lad yourself, mind you, we're wondering if she might be of the other sort, in which case the game is in your favor."

Ewan tasted Cyd's hungry, seeking kiss still on his lips. The heat burning low in his body denied that she was "of the other sort." In their eighties, the "boys" probably knew the details of Cyd's affairs, the whos and whys. "She hasn't been interested with anyone?"

Finlay's chuckle irritated. "So you're curious—already warmed up and ready, eh? This should be interesting if Cyd decides to use her wiles on you. She's had a bit of a rough start, with her mother and all. She's had a few boyfriends, but when you pried the lid off the matter, you could see she was after business, not love. So the boys and me prefer that you be a gentleman with Cyd, as you always were a bit of a scamp with women."

After the call ended, Ewan's hand slid over a smooth oak plank leaning against the wall. He was still aching for Cyd, wanting to feel all those sleek warm curves pressed against him.

Ewan stared out of the window toward Main Street and the water beyond. Sean had passed the boat shop's pier, motoring out to Three Ravens Island. Seagulls hovered in the blue sky above him, using the wind's drafts to stay aloft. Sean's grin and wave said that he knew a game was brewing between Ewan and Cyd and that he knew he was only a pawn to be played between them.

Paddy O'Connor leaned against the side of the Tobacco Shop. He smoked his pipe, one foot braced back against the wall. With a grudge against Ewan, Paddy was definitely a candidate for planting the jewelry. Always up for easy money and mischief, Paddy was making it known around town that the sale to McGruder's was actually meant for him.

Sooner or later, Ewan and Paddy would meet, and this time, Ewan wasn't a boy outmatched by a bully.

Paddy shoved free of the shop's brick wall and moved down the street, hunched against the wind.

Ewan watched him round a corner and decided that Hallie's invitation to have scones and coffee would be a nice break—before he responded to Angela's message. And if Cyd was still in the shop, that would be a bonus. He had an admitted hunger to see her—and an unsettling tenderness at the thought of it.

As Ewan walked along the pier and crossed Main Street to enter Hallie's shop, he smiled a bit, amused at how he ached to see Cyd.

The bell over Hallie's shop door tinkled a welcome, and, after entering, Ewan closed the door slowly behind him.

The stillness in the air warned him—so did the way Cyd stood protectively next to Hallie, behind the counter. Both women's faces were pale and tense.

But there was a difference—Cyd's vivid blue eyes didn't flicker from the man to Ewan. Her expression said she didn't like the big man on the other side of the counter—Allan Thompson, Hallie's ex-husband.

The sudden way Cyd moved close to Hallie spoke of protection; it wasn't difficult to imagine the women's hands linked tightly below the counter.

Hallie's expression was just as tense, but with a touch of something Ewan didn't like—fear. Her uneven voice came across the cluttered shop. "Hi, Ewan."

He reached to silence the bell, wanting no interference in the prickling danger he sensed. Hallie's smile at Ewan was forced and tight, and the quickly shielded surprise and fear in her eyes almost tore his heart away. His sister didn't fear him—but perhaps she feared his arrival at that moment. Why?

"Hi. Cyd . . . Allan. . . ." Whatever he'd interrupted wasn't pleasant, Ewan decided as he studied Hallie's ex-husband. Allan's smile was too bright. Cyd's rage and Hallie's fear was palpable.

With a wide smile, Allan stuck out his hand. "I heard you'd come back. Going to stay around a while this time?"

"I'm staying. Are *you* around much?" Ewan ignored the offer of a handshake. He didn't like what he was thinking—that Hallie was afraid of Allan. Or that she was afraid that Ewan would discover something she'd rather hide, and he wouldn't be happy. Hallie had that same wary look when she feared trouble was afoot, and she was the cause.

Allan's easy, confident attitude was just as Ewan remembered. With a wink at Hallie, Allan explained, "I like to keep an eye on Hallie, just to make certain she's okay. Who knows, she might decide to come back to me one day."

"It's been six years, Allan. That isn't likely," Hallie stated unevenly. "We're just friends now, Ewan."

Ewan didn't miss the tense set of his sister's body. Or that Cyd's lips had just silently formed the word "bastard."

"Allan was just leaving," Hallie said unevenly, the sound uneven and husky as she glanced nervously at Ewan.

"But, Sugar—" Allan began.

"Get out," Cyd ordered coldly. "There's no reason for you to hang around."

"Cyd, I want to handle my own . . ." Hallie's tone admonished, and Ewan didn't like the undercurrents in the tiny shop at all. Cyd was in full protective mode, her blue eyes blazing at Hallie's ex-husband.

"It might be a good idea for you to leave, Allan," Ewan said quietly.

Allan's eyes glittered with rage, but the smile remained. "You'll be gone soon enough, Lochlain. You're not the staying sort. Hallie needs a man—"

"Who will do what?" Ewan invited softly, more certain now in his suspicions that Hallie had been abused.

The flush on Allan's face and the way his eyes glittered weren't friendly. Ewan's own dark mood was fast rising; if his suspicions were right, Hallie had been a battered woman, and she'd come to Cyd for protection—because she was ashamed and because she didn't want to involve people whose families might suffer.

Angela wouldn't have been on Hallie's list of protectors. And her brother hadn't paid enough attention to her welfare; Ewan had missed what he was seeing now—but then, he'd been too busy putting money in his dream to hold the boat shop to notice much else. "Oh, I'm staying. But you aren't, Allan."

"Now, look, Ewan. Hallie will come around, but not if you and Cyd interfere—"

"It's been six years, and if you haven't made progress since then, it's her choice, and there's the door. Use it."

Allan's easygoing mask slid into one of bitterness. "You haven't heard the last of this, Ewan. Angela said she was going to send you on your way soon enough."

Again that was that uneasy ripple amid the fairies in the shop—or was it his sister's fear? Of what? "Now that is interesting news. You know Angela?"

Ewan didn't like the way Hallie looked at Cyd, the silent message flowing between them—one that warned a secret was better than giving him the truth. Then Hallie admitted quietly, "Angela introduced us."

One fact leaped to two ugly ones, and Ewan didn't like the sum total: Angela had intentionally plotted to match Hallie with Allan—an older, experienced man to a young, innocent girl. Hallie hadn't a chance. . . .

"You'd better get out of here now," Ewan ordered Allan.

When Allan blustered out of the shop, toppling a display of handmade birch baskets, Ewan turned to the two women. "All right, let's have it. He beat you, didn't he? And Cyd, stay out of this."

Cyd's anger swerved from the man bristling past the front window to Ewan. She rounded the counter and pushed both hands against his chest. "I will not. Don't you dare talk to Hallie that way. Don't you dare bully her. Back off."

"She's . . . my . . . sister. I should have known." The full impact of what Hallie must have gone through had blindsided Ewan. Rage knotted his gut, burning him with the need to follow Allan and give him a taste of what Hallie had known.

"She didn't want you to know, you idiot," Cyd shot back, and gave him another light shove. "She didn't want anyone to know. Got that? And no one is going to know."

Ewan leaned down to meet Cyd's flashing blue eyes. "This is between Hallie and me. She should have told me. I could have—"

"Men!" Cyd snarled. "Leave her alone. If you want someone to fight with, try me."

"Oh, I'll do that, all right. You could have gotten in touch with me."

Cyd's hands went to her waist, her eyes narrowed up at him. "I didn't know at the time, you idiot—"

"Stop calling me an idiot—"

"Well, you are."

Ewan glared at Cyd, and she returned the favor. He barely noticed Hallie moving between them. She stood with a hand on each one's face, a gentle caress. "If you two want to fight, please don't do it in here," she said quietly. "Allan stops by now and then. It's nothing to start a war over. I loved him once, but now it's over. I do think he is concerned about me, and I like to think that I can handle my own affairs."

Cyd threw up her hands. "I don't get it. He's a beast, and he's after you. He wants a piece of what you've built. He's Angela's pet watchdog. Don't tell me you'd actually go back to that—that bastard. I don't know how you can even stand to be in the same room with him."

"It's important to me that I face the past and understand it. I can manage him. But I can't bear to see my best friend and my brother arguing. You're breaking my heart, the two of you. I love you both."

Ewan and Cyd stared at her, unable to speak, and Hallie began to smile. "You should see the two of you now, each speechless and with a totally blank expression. I bet it's the first time for either one of you."

When a tourist, easily spotted with a Fairy Cove logo on his new ball cap and a camera draped around his neck, came into the store, Hallie said quietly, "Now behave, the both of you. While I'm waiting on this man, I want you both to go to the back and get a blueberry scone and a cup of coffee or tea for Cyd. Don't either one of you go after Allan. I want you to sit down and make up."

"Not with her."

"Not with him." Cyd noted the direction in which Ewan looked—the one Allan had taken. Ewan's body was tense, almost vibrating with anger. There was no mistaking the hard set of his jaw, that narrowed look—he intended to give Allan a taste of his fists.

Across the distance of the shop, Hallie's expression silently begged Cyd—Stop him. Don't let my brother get in trouble and ruin his chances here. Keep him away from Allan, just until he cools down . . . "Cyd, would you mind please?" she asked quietly as three more people entered the shop.

When Hallie looked at Cyd that way, there was nothing she could do. "You're coming with me, Ewan," she said.

His silence spoke of revenge, the need to go after Hallie's ex-husband hadn't dimmed. He was still focused on the door, a hard muscle contracting in his jaw. There was no mistaking the set of Ewan's body—as if he wanted to take Allan apart.

"Huh?" he grunted, but Cyd knew his mind wasn't on the question.

Cyd spoke in hushed tones. She had to get Ewan's attention and fast—or he'd follow Allan. From the expression on

Ewan's face, the consequences right now looked like murder. "Come on. I've just been delegated to babysit you. Hallie is too sweet, and she loves you and I don't. But right now, you're needing someone to keep you out of trouble. You're no good to anyone if you're put in jail for assault, and Angela can get Allan to testify to anything. Think of Hallie."

Now Ewan turned to her, his smile a mere showing of his teeth. "You? You're going to babysit me? You, who kept this from me when I could have helped?"

No doubt drawn by the growl in his tone, the tourists turned to look at Ewan, and Hallie's expression had turned to panic. When Ewan took a step toward the door, Cyd caught his arm—beneath her fingers and his coat, his arm was ridged with muscle. "You're staying with me."

Ewan looked down at her hand, then at Hallie. He didn't like the fear and worry in his sister's expression; she'd had enough of both. With a grim nod, he followed Cyd out of the shop.

Surprised that Ewan had controlled the temper she'd read in his taut body, the locking of his fists, Cyd noted how he searched the streets—no doubt looking for Allan. "Don't you dare," she said.

Hallie was depending on Cyd. . . . She had to hold Ewan until his rage cooled. But how?

For Hallie, Cyd would do anything— She laced her fingers with his and waited for the solid lock as he automatically tightened the hold. If Ewan wanted to go after Allan, he'd have to drag her, and she would go limp, her body deadweight. "I'll tell you everything, but at my house. Look, you've got two pieces of jewelry that you can't explain. They belonged to dead women—the women who started rumors for Angela. Think of Hallie, Ewan. What it would do to her if you were charged with assault, or worse. Even though you were in Australia when Bertha died, Angela could start suspicions that you had something to do with her death.

"My sister wouldn't believe that. Not for a moment."

"True. But if you take Allan to task now, Hallie won't like it."

Cyd prayed that Allan would not appear, not drive by, because she wasn't certain if she could hold Ewan, his angry savage storms almost thundering across the clear, calm day. There was just one place that she could be certain Ewan wouldn't see Allan. "Can you cook?"

His head reared back and he stared blankly down at her. "Hell, yes, enough to get by. What's that got to do with anything?"

"I can't. We're going to my house, and you're going to cook me something." If she could just keep him away from Allan . . . Cyd watched Ewan's expression, the indecision, warring between rage and control, and prayed good sense would win. "I've never failed to do what Hallie asks. And she's the reason you're coming with me."

Cyd tossed her briefcase and coat onto an armchair she'd upholstered herself, a pretty little thing with curved cherrywood arms and legs, a real thrift shop find. Ewan stood in the center of the small, comfortable room, and the violence in him caused the air to quiver.

She pushed her hair away from her face and blew back a persistent curl. It flew around her now, reminding her that she had very little control over her life these days.

But she'd had enough of violence and ugly moods, and she wasn't having any of it in her home. Cyd nodded to the other big chair, sitting in a shaft of sunlight, and waited for Ewan to follow her look.

Next to the chair was a reading lamp and a square walnut table to hold her books and magazines. In front of the chair was a chunky stuffed ottoman, which she'd covered in the same floral pattern as her drapes and accent pillows. "That's your father's chair. He was a good, kind, thoughtful man. Sit in it and think, Ewan. When you've cooled down a bit, we'll talk. You are not going to worry Hallie anymore. She needs to stand on her own, not have you play big-boss brother. It's important to her."

Ewan took up too much space, his dark masculinity emphasized by the room's delicate jade and mauve shades. His worn workman's boots looked as if they would leave permanent marks on her thick carpeting.

Cyd yanked on Ewan's jacket, none too gently, an indication that she would take it from him. He allowed her to strip it from him. Cyd pushed him and he turned frowning down at her. "Lay off. I've been maneuvered enough for one day."

"Stop being so surly. You'll have to adjust to life here in Fairy Cove, and that means you can't go threatening everyone who ever caused problems for you—like Paddy O'Connor. Or Hallie's ex-husband."

"He hurt her." Ewan's dark tone said he was brooding revenge.

"Hallie is handling the past. But not if you go in swinging and ruining the life she's built. Don't you dare, Ewan Lochlain. It's very important to her that she handle her own problems. Now sit down until you cool off." Cyd placed his jacket over the back of a used sofa that had only needed a bit of foam and thread, and it was as good as new.

Ewan studied the big armchair, a soft beige weave covering it. "That's Dad's chair. It's different than I remember."

"So is Hallie. You can't take her hard-won independence away from her, Ewan. She's fighting for it every day. She doesn't want to be victimized anymore. Not by Angela, or by Allan. . . ."

Ewan eased into the big chair, his hands spreading on the rounded arms. "You look like him," Cyd stated quietly. "Exactly like your father."

"So they tell me. But there's a big difference between us: he saw more good in people than I do, and I'm afraid I'm not as forgiving as he was. But if any part of Dad is in me, I'm grateful. He was a good man."

He looked at the chair and spoke softly, "I remember my mother sitting on Dad's lap, in this chair. They loved each other."

"I remember." The memories tangled softly between them, and Ewan's dark storms seemed to ease. Cyd had gotten him here, now what was she going to do with him?

Ewan's dark head lay back against the chair, his eyes closing. "I should have checked on Hallie. I should have been more alert to how she acted. It was all there, and I didn't see it. Maybe I saw what I wanted, that she was happy enough."

Cyd sat on the arm of the sofa and decided against leaving him alone. She eased off her high-heeled boots and wiggled her nylon-clad toes against the lush carpeting.

"I did check on her, Ewan. And I knew something was wrong. Hallie wouldn't answer questions, and she hid what happened. Until that night she came to my door—and there was no hiding the damage he'd done. He came after her—here, and it was the only time I'd ever pointed a gun at a man. I'd have shot, too, and he'd never have had a woman again. Drunk as he was, he understood, and I wasn't having him come near Hallie. And she didn't want Angela to know, either. Or anyone else. *You won't tell anyone, Ewan.*"

"Sean? Does he know?"

"No. He would have gone after Allan, too, and there would have been trouble for Hallie. She doesn't want that, and you're going to have to get used to the idea that she needs to stand on her own feet. Don't take that away from her. She's worked too hard to stand on her own."

Ewan's big hands spread on the arms of the chair, gripping it. "How does a woman who barely weighs 115 pounds manage to stand on her feet when a man, taller than her and outweighing her by sixty or so, is hitting her?"

When the violence stirred in him again, Ewan looked as if he would walk through her locked doors to get to Allan. Cyd hurried to him, sat on the footstool, and bent to untie one of his boots. "That's something I don't want to think about. And neither does Hallie. Now you can sit there and brood, or you can cook me something to eat."

She levered off his boot and began on the other one. When freed, she knotted the laces together and tugged them tight. She gave him a look that said she'd finished his chances for escape.

That was the first time Ewan's mouth softened. "Exactly what are you doing?"

He was mocking her. "I've tied the laces, so you can't leave when your temper moves you. This carpet is expensive, and I don't want it ruined, and you're not going anywhere without them."

His eyes darkened, and he reached to skim his hand over her hair. "You've got the wind in your hair, the fresh scent of the sea."

His violence had been replaced by something else she didn't trust. Cyd pushed the strands away from her face and, with his knotted boots in her hand, eased back onto the sofa, her legs dangling over the end. "I'm exhausted. Dealing with you does that to me. Now either sit there in that chair and calm down, or get in the kitchen and cook me something. Hallie makes me buy eggs from old Sarah Jones, whose chickens are her only income. Do something with them."

His chair was near where she lay, and Cyd felt Ewan's sock-covered toe rub her insole as he said, "I saw you punch in the codes to reverse the locks. You're not just keeping me captive until I agree to that McGruder's deal, are you?" he asked in that lilting, deep tone.

Cyd groaned and shifted her feet away from his foot. She dropped his boots on the floor beside the sofa and covered her eyes with her hand. "That's another matter. But you should consider it. Even if you do have a fat bank account. Oh, don't try to tell me how hard times are. I have ways of checking what goes on in this town. Your deposit could choke a horse, and you didn't help Hallie when she needed it. You should have sent her some money, Ewan."

"And ruin your interest rates on her mortgage? Wouldn't think of it. According to my sources, your love life isn't exactly active. Why not?"

His hand circled her ankle, stroking the nylon covering it, and Cyd instantly tried to jerk it away. Ewan's light grip held briefly, then released. The light creaking of the chair said he'd left it. She looked up to see him standing above her, his expression closed and dark. Cyd knew a man's dark moods, had seen them often enough, starting from her childhood. "My mother told me that all it took to ruin a woman's life was one wrong man. You're definitely a wrong man for me. It will never happen, Ewan."

"Care to take odds?" he asked slowly, his gaze traveling down the length of her body. And though his stance was casual, she remembered how dangerous he could be with just a kiss—making her come after him for more.

Cyd jackknifed into sitting position, then stood. Directly in front of her, Ewan blocked her passage, and he did not move back. With her Franklin stove on one side, Ewan in the middle, and the big chair on the other, Cyd had no easy escape.

"You can kiss me, if you want," he offered a little unevenly in that deep lilting tone.

At the boat shop, she'd had a disturbing taste of him, and now Cyd didn't trust her reactions. With as much dignity as she could manage, she stepped onto the sofa, placed a hand on the back, and stepped down to the other side—and free passage.

She looked across the couch to Ewan and wished she hadn't—his pleased smile was enough to stop any woman's heart. "Don't get any big ideas. I'm doing this for Hallie," she said unevenly.

"It's a dangerous thing, bringing a man into your little fortress, dear heart. Why there are even shutters on the inside of the house. I could stay in here for days, and no one would know that I'm your prisoner. I'll wager I'm the first man here. Am I?"

His question had a deeper meaning, and one Cyd preferred not to answer.

Ewan spoke quietly, sincerely. "This is the house you always wanted, isn't it, Molly Claire? A real home, polished and clean and comfortable? Maybe it's time you thought about that other house, the one you won't go in, the one outside of town that you bought when you could. The old Callahan house is empty and going to ruin. Maybe there are more locks than you have here that should be opened."

She stared at Ewan, unable to answer, unable to tell a lie. Because Ewan knew the truth of what drove her, the whys and the hows.

He knew that Cyd still desperately wanted to know her father's name—the green-eyed man who had made her mother feel like a lady, whose private waltzes made her love him enough to forget caution and give him a child.

Then, with a nod, Ewan moved into her kitchen—a homey, efficient one, well stocked with glass canisters and a fat fairy godmother cookie jar. She heard the pots and pans rattle slightly. The refrigerator door opened and closed, water ran from the faucet, and the sounds all seemed to echo in Cyd's taut, trembling body.

Ewan was right: She had him, and now what was she going to do with him?

# Chapter 8

"Just how long do you think you can keep me prisoner?" Ewan asked as he washed the dishes and placed them in the rack.

"You're staying with me until you calm down and promise not to go for Allan—or Angela. She'd love that, you know, you causing trouble—putting yourself in her sights."

"So now you're my protector, are you?"

"Hallie is too soft. She loves you. Since I know you for what you are, I'm better for the job. You had that money. You should have helped her. But you put yourself first, didn't you? As always."

Seated at the chrome-and-Formica table, she helped herself to another slice of bacon. The woman had a healthy appetite, and just watching her devour food was enough to make Ewan debate her other needs. The house bore her arousing scent—fresh like sea air, sweet as mountain flowers, with the bite of cloves.

And despite her low opinion of him, it had been too long since Ewan had had sex, he thought darkly, as Cyd delicately licked her fingers. She glanced at him, and Ewan didn't bother to hide his bold stare.

"You're hot for me," he said, just to get her simmering. "There's going to be talk about how you had your way with me, trapped here for hours. I think that when I leave, I'll stagger and fall as if I've exhausted myself satisfying you."

"You haven't changed at all. You're still maddening."

The flush that rose from her throat fascinated him. He wondered if it covered the rest of her body—but the kitchen was too close, and he purposely shifted the subject before he embarrassed himself. "I'm going to talk with Angela. It's inevitable."

"If she learns you have that jewelry, she'll point the finger of suspicion right at you. Marvin will have no choice but to question you, and that will upset Hallie."

He nodded, agreeing to the truth of Angela's powers. "You'll have to let me go sometime, sweetheart."

"If you think I'm enjoying this, you're dead wrong. I've got a business to run, you know, and I don't usually take this long for lunch." Fed, Cyd stood and stretched her arms high in a feline movement and yawned. The gray sweater tightened across her breasts, sending a hot jolt to Ewan's midsection as she continued, "And while we're here, let me get the portfolio of McGruder's proposed layout. You'll see that it is just perfect for the setting at the boat shop. People go for that rough wharf dining experience—"

She stopped and stared at Ewan, who didn't shield his desire. Her hand raised to smooth her hair and knocked a hanging plant. She steadied it, sniffed, and turned stiffly, leaving him alone.

Despite his hard, aching body, Ewan smiled—Cyd was definitely aware of him . . . and on the run. The telephone rang, and in the other room, Cyd's husky voice answered.

Taking his time, Ewan walked to her and slid his arms around her from behind. She stiffened slightly, cradled the telephone on her shoulder, placed her hands on his, and tried to pry them free. Failing that, she tried to move away, and placed a kick that missed. He grinned as he nuzzled her ear, felt her quiver, and settled in to taste her.

"Yes, he's here, Hallie. Nothing is going on. We're just sitting here talking. . . . Here, talk to him—"

Cyd turned slightly to him, and as she did, their lips brushed, tasted, and brushed again. "It's Hallie," she whispered unevenly to him.

"Mmm." Taking the telephone and cradling it on his shoulder, Ewan eased down onto the old chair with Cyd on his lap. Thoroughly enjoying himself for the first time in ages, Ewan held her still, watching those flat-out hot emotions burn him. She was mad, of course, furious and fascinating.

Held down by one arm over her stomach, his hand spanning her hip, and her hands caught by his, Cyd lay still and glared at him. "He's being as obnoxious as ever, Hallie," she said loudly. "I thought boys stopped this stuff at a certain age—old age."

"Be nice, Ewan," Hallie said with laughter in her voice. "Drop by the shop later, will you? Or for dinner?"

He grinned as Cyd blew a rippling strand of hair from her face. "I might. Cyd is trying to keep me busy. I've fed her lunch, but there are other things she wants me to do."

When Hallie said good-bye, Ewan released the telephone from the cradle of his throat and shoulder. "You're not going to hit me, are you, darling?"

"You haven't changed in years. You're still the same, showing off—"

"Not the same," he said quietly, releasing her and locking his hands behind his head. She was too lovely and steaming, sprawled across his lap, her sweater pulled from her waistband in the tussle, her hips soft and curved above his erection. Only a bit of cloth separated him from sliding into her warmth, a bit of cloth that kept him from tasting those soft breasts.

But this was Cyd, who deserved better than a quick satisfaction on a sunny afternoon. "If you wanted to distract me from knocking Allan around a bit, you've done that—temporarily," he said tightly.

She sat up, but didn't move from him. "You're going straight to Angela, aren't you?"

"Damn straight. She deliberately set Hallie up with Allan. I'll get to him later."

If he could just lift his eyes from Cyd's hardened nipples thrusting against her sweater, he might be able to move.

Cyd crossed her arms in front of her chest, shielding her body from his stare. "I'm not moving. You're not going to make trouble for Hallie."

He ached in places that needed smooth, tight, soft, moist relief, but Ewan wouldn't unlock his hands, he wouldn't touch her. "If we keep sitting like this, something sure as hell is going to happen."

With a delicate sniff, Cyd straightened and eased off his lap. He admired the way she pulled herself together, smoothing her hair and clothes with shaking, slender hands that he could almost feel against his skin. And because he could take no more without crushing that wild-flowing froth of red hair in his fist, and capturing her lips, Ewan reached for his boots and unknotted the laces with a flick of his finger. "You've got a thing or two to learn about knots. We could work on that, if you're interested."

With his boots on his feet, the laces retied, he stood. "I've got people to see."

"Angela."

"That would be herself. But first the newspaper office. I want to review those articles again—on what happened the day my parents didn't come off the lake. I might have missed something earlier." Ewan reached for her sweater, which had come partly untucked. He gently slid it back into place, removing himself from the temptation of lace and silky skin. He bent to kiss her briefly, and while Cyd stood there, her eyes wide upon him, he tugged on his coat.

"I'm coming with you, Ewan. Hallie would never forgive me if you—"

"What I have to say to Angela, I'll do alone. I'm not in the mood for a tagalong."

With that, he walked to the door and punched in the code she'd used earlier, not an easy one to forget—his sister's birthday.

Cyd had stayed.

And he had not.

And Hallie had married a man who abused her.


"You're back to make trouble, Ewan Lochlain. Don't think you start it in Fairy Cove. I've had you investigated. I know that you worked for a millionaire, taking care of him and his needs, as he sailed that silly boat. No doubt you scammed a dying man. You came back with money in your pocket— that's a sizable deposit in the bank." Angela's shrill voice cut through the suffocating air of her study.

Filled with shelves of books, a marble fireplace, and Queen Anne furniture, the study provided the elegance Angela required in her home. On a delicate cherrywood table was an ornate china tea set, a china cup and saucer on her desk. Swags and lengths of wine-colored drapes covered the tall windows, the sheers softening the cold day outside. Angela's face bore the same bone structure as Ewan's mother and sister, but the lines were cut deep by bitterness and greed. Beneath the layers of powder and paint, lay a simmering hatred that had taken years to understand.

Everything in the two-story house and its manicured grounds, including an English garden in the back, had been designed to showcase Angela's wealth. Ewan wondered distantly if the hedge between the sculpted shrubs and the roses and the beds of herbs still hid the shack where he had lived.

As a teenager, he'd had a cheap woodstove for warmth— if he stood close to it, he roasted on one side and froze on the other. Food came more often from the Donovans' table than the cook at the Greers' back door. But he'd do it again—for Hallie. He searched Angela's face and wondered what Fred had ever found to love.

"I see you've still got your hooks into everything that happens at Fairy Cove," Ewan said easily, though his emotions were simmering. Memories tumbled over him, biting and snagging and infuriating.

"I make it my business to care for the community—yes. When riffraff appears, we generally see that they leave."

"But Paddy O'Connor bought the boat shop from you at a cheap price. So you're running with the likes of him now, are you? Why so cheap, Angela? After a mug or two, Paddy was quite free with information. Enough people heard him."

Angela stiffened and snapped at him. "It was going to ruin. No one else wanted it. It should have been burned. I see you're just as insolent as you always were, forgetting my kindness to you and Hallie."

"Kindness, was it?" The house brought back suffocating images of Hallie, trying desperately to please. And he'd done his best, but Angela's cruelty came out immediately, and he'd rebelled. At twelve, he'd taken her belt away from her. At fourteen, he'd held her bony wrist, keeping her hand from slapping his face. That was when, venomous and hissing, Angela had told him how she hated him—because he looked like his father, and called his mother a "slut." At sixteen, he could have run away, and didn't—because of Hallie.

He'd gotten Angela to promise that she wouldn't hurt Hallie again—but she had, blackmailing the sweet girl by threats of "putting your brother away in prison where he belongs."

Ewan had been extracareful not to break the law, because Hallie needed him nearby.

And all the while, Ewan had watched for something to hold over Angela—until he got it.

Before Angela closed a connecting door to her parlor, Ewan noted the airless room where he'd discovered Hallie cowering after a blow. The memory was still painful— She'd been a fourteen-year-old girl, working too hard to tend her aunt's wishes. And she'd committed the dire crime of breaking a single china cup. At eighteen and with his sister hurting, Ewan had faced Angela. She'd gone pale when he told her about the incriminating copies that he had tucked away. Angela had nervously agreed to signing over Hallie's guardianship to the Donovans. Before Ewan left Fairy Cove, his sister was living safely with the Donovan family.

Because of a single china cup, Hallie had been hurt. . . . Ewan forced away the ugly memory and glanced around the room, looking for a picture of his mother. He found none. But then, Angela wouldn't want to be reminded of her twin, would she? Mary Lochlain had a gentle heart—and she had captured the man Angela had wanted. "No pictures of your dear family, Angela? Your twin?"

"None are necessary. I remember quite well."

Fred peered into the study and nodded. "Ewan, I'm so glad to see you."

"Fred," Angela rapped out. "You have something to do, don't you? You were going to research that property on Elfindale Street, weren't you?"

His uncle stiffened and nodded. "Yes, yes, of course. Good-bye, Ewan."

Another man might have ignored her sharp prod, but years of marriage to Angela would change anyone, Ewan decided. He pushed away that brief spark of sympathy for Fred, the man who had allowed Angela's abuse.

When Fred silently closed the doors, Angela closed the one to the parlor. Ewan understood: The gloves would be off, the threats on the table. Without invitation, he walked to the tea set and poured a cup, cradling the delicate china in his hand as he sat down. The chair was big, supple leather, and masculine—probably chosen for the businessmen Angela corralled into her schemes.

He studied the cup, so translucent he could see the shadow of his finger through it. "Let's just do this, shall we, Angela?"

"I require respect. Hallie still calls me Aunt Angela."

"I don't."

"Let's get to it then," Angela stated briskly. "I want you out of Fairy Cove. I'll buy out whatever investment you have in the boat shop and make it worth your while. With an extra amount, I'll expect the return of the documents you stole from me. And you're lucky that I don't report you for blackmailing. How much?"

Ewan sipped the tea and wondered how his mother could have come from the same womb. Silence hung in the room, and he let it fester and build. Angela knew that in exposing Ewan, she would reveal her own nasty little secrets. He didn't want her money now; he only wanted her to know that in their little game, he wasn't powerless to fight her.

He took his time in answering—in his own way. "I've always wondered what happened to my mother's jewelry. Not much of it, was there? And Hallie's dolls, the ones she loved so much . . . her little tea set . . . the little music box in which my mother kept her trinkets and gave to Hallie. Hallie should have those things, Angela. Do you know where they are?"

Beneath her carefully applied paint and powder, Angela's face paled, her body stiffened. "Absolutely not. Things were sold, to pay for your keep. Your parents owed bills, and there wasn't much left to you. You know that."

"Oh, yes, I do. Payments must be made. My mother had a locket, not an expensive piece, but one that opened several times—it held your parents' pictures, my father and Hallie and me. And there was a ring, black onyx with silver filigree, a sweet little thing, a courting gift from my father. You wouldn't know where any of those would be, would you, Angela?"

He noted the trembling of her hand as she covered the other one and the finger that bore jewelry Ewan remembered very well. He'd noted the silver filigree and onyx ring earlier, and it had taken a firm hold on his patience to wait for the right moment to claim it. "I'll take it now, my mother's ring. It belongs to Hallie," he said quietly as he stood.

"I don't know what you mean. I have no idea where those pieces are."

"Oh, I think you do." Then Ewan held the cup away from him, the delicate little bone china cup with the flowers and the gold. He opened his fingers and let it drop, shattering and breaking on the silver tea service. "I'll take that ring now."

"It's mine," she yelled shrilly. "You can't have it. You broke my china cup!"

"And what are you going to do about it? Try to use the belt on me like you did on Hallie?" He held out his open palm and indicated the ring with a glance. "Now."

Trembling, Angela jerked the ring from her finger and threw it at him. "It is *my* ring, but if you wrongly think that it might be Mary's, then it's yours. I have no idea what happened to that other jewelry. You and Hallie cost a fortune to raise, there were expenses to be paid."

Ewan's fist tightened on the tiny ring. "But then, you had all that nice fat insurance money to handle, didn't you? The money Fred invested? Oh, yes. The figures I found in your desk and that I copied revealed direct transfers from insurance deposits into your accounts, then into investments. It was a very neat money trail, Angela. I kept it with me for a long time, did a bit of research on my own, and now it's in the keeping of an attorney I trust. If anything happens to me, or to Hallie, that information goes right to the authorities, with my personal notes of your motives, of course—

jealousy, greed, little things like that. Think of it, Angela. You would be shunned. After all, who would want to come running at your invitations—if certain matters were brought to light?"

Because he feared what else he might do, Ewan walked from the room.

Angela's shriek followed him. "Ewan Lochlain, I want the copies of what you took."

"Sorry," he said, but he wasn't. Then with his hand on the knob of the front door, Ewan stopped.

He turned to look at Angela. He wanted no doubt between them, about what he knew and understood, the evil that ran deep in his aunt's heart. "There are things that I know now. How you looked at me when I began to develop . . . it is even more uncomfortable now—now that I am a man and realize what went through your mind. Because I look like my father, the man you really wanted? The man who scorned you for my mother's love?"

With a hiss, Angela stiffened back against the paneled wall, her hand upon her cold breast. "That isn't true."

Speaking very quietly, Ewan served her another truth. "Allan Thompson is your doing, a way to control what you couldn't have. You knew exactly what he was, and you set him up with Hallie. Did he report to you how he beat her? How she cried?"

"Allan is good for Hallie. She needs a stern hand. If Cyd hadn't interfered—that daughter of a prostitute—Hallie would still be married."

"I'm grateful to Cyd. Hallie only needed love. Something you can't fathom. Be very careful not to upset the delicate balance between us, Angela, because I am not feeling friendly. But the Lochlains have had their share of gossip, thanks to you. I'd rather keep Hallie safe from more. Unless I'm pushed, I'd rather not peel back the lid on our family secrets," he warned, and walked out into May's clean, fresh air.

On the porch, he looked down at Fairy Cove, the town and the harbor, and saw the perfect view of the boat shop. How often had Angela stood in the same place and lusted after Tom Lochlain, her hatred for Mary growing?

From where he stood, Ewan located the boat shop. Why hadn't Angela destroyed it? She certainly had the man to do it; Paddy O'Connor had done enough for Angela in the past. It would have been so easy to pay Paddy to "accidentally" drop a match on inflammable cleaning rags.

But Ewan knew—the boat shop was a trophy in Angela's twisted mind, something to hold in her claw and savor. . . .

And it was only this morning that Ewan had learned Angela had set Allan Thompson on Hallie. That thought set Ewan to walking quickly toward Fairy Cove.

Locked in his thunderous thoughts, the memories clashing with his fury, Ewan tried to ignore the woman who swung into step at his side.

But Cyd lengthened her stride to match his. "You're in a fine mood."

"Get lost, Red." He had an appointment with his sister's ex-husband, one to even the score.

"I thought you might be difficult."

Cyd's fingers clasped his hand and cold metal circled his wrist. When Ewan stopped, she ran into him, stepping back a little, though her hand lifted with his, joined by steel links. He bared his teeth, mocking her. "Handcuffs? Is that the best you've got?"

"I promised to babysit you, and I'm doing it." She pushed her face up to his, the wind catching the curls. A soft fragrant drift of Cyd's hair hit Ewan's jaw, clinging to the late-afternoon stubble there. "If you're headed full steam for Hallie—don't. She's building her pride, and I won't have you tearing it away with what she should have done. She's doing the best she can, and I—"

With his free hand, Ewan fisted the blaze of burnished red

hair, tethering it back from Cyd's face. Bright sunlight
danced across her lashes, her eyes slitted clear blue and icy
as, unafraid, she stared back at him. "Don't think I'm backing down from you, Lochlain. I promised Hallie that I'd
keep you out of trouble, and I will."

What simmered in Ewan, dark and brooding within Angela's house, burst into clear bright anger. He moved his
handcuffed hand behind him, so that Cyd stood close and
taut and just as angry as he, her arm circling him. "What
gives you the right to step into my business, Ms. Callahan?
What make you think that you can order me not to speak
with my own sister?"

"You idiot. Men don't understand. Do you think she wants
to relive all that with you? To rake it like an old cow pile and
make it fresh and stinking again? Today was enough. You
looked as if you could murder Allan on the spot. But it isn't
Hallie that you're after now, to drill the gory details from
her. It's to make Allan pay. Hallie doesn't want you to start
life here in Fairy Cove with an assault and battery charge.
You're coming with me, Ewan . . . until you cool down."

"You're renting a house to Paddy O'Connor. Where is it
on Brownie Lane?"

Cyd frowned slightly. "Why?"

"I've just put two and two together, and Paddy's name
keeps coming up. I've spent time in the newspaper archives,
refreshing what I remembered. Two years after my parents
died, Angela sold the boat shop to Paddy for a pittance—
he's given enough people the details. Finlay kept the exact
figures. I want to know if they are connected and if Paddy is
planting the dead women's jewelry on me."

Cyd's eyes widened, clear and blue. "That's a stretch,
Ewan."

"If Angela knew I was coming back, so did her boy,
Allan. They could have worked together—Angela letting
it be known that the brooch and the cross were missing.

Allan could have planted them in the boat shop."

His body had taken his mind to other things, just that quick, just by the curve of Cyd against him. He looked at her hand, open and braced on his chest, then at the softness of her lips. "You did not need to handcuff me to hold me close, darling-mine," he whispered. "Though the experience is interesting. Shall we go somewhere, and you can have your way with me?"

Her head jerked back, and her anger seared him. Holding her hair, Ewan drew her back, his lips brushing her parted ones. "There's always this, isn't there?" he asked. "The fire between us . . . the need to challenge and bring to heel. Do you ever wonder what would happen if we freed it, the need to burn each out and walk away?"

"Not with you, Ewan Lochlain. I've got better ways to spend my time. You've got enough beds waiting for you here in Fairy Cove, no less the world. I'm not going to be one of your backups when you have nothing better to do."

"What makes you think I'd be that 'one wrong man'?"

"Volume," she answered simply. "You've always been ready to supply the demands of any nearby and willing woman."

"Not for a long time, Cyd," he answered seriously. "I was looking for something years ago, a bit of warmth that I couldn't find anywhere but in sex. I've changed."

Ewan thought of Irene Larkin, Andrew's daughter, and the first woman in a long time. When Andrew was dying, Ewan recognized the need for comfort when Irene came to him. And he gave her what she needed, nothing more. For her part, Irene gave him a woman's softness, and that was enough.

Ewan had Cyd shaking, on the run, and his senses told him to pursue. Beneath the stroke of his thumb, her skin was smooth and warm and enticing. "What are you going to do with me, now that you have me? Use these handcuffs much, do you?"

When Cyd fumbled in her pocket and withdrew a key, Ewan bumped her hand gently. The key flew into the air, and he caught it with his fist. "Angela is watching from the window. She thinks we're lovers, darling-mine."

Her head turned to find Angela in the window, and Cyd lifted a hand. The gesture wasn't sweet, and Ewan chuckled as he placed his arm around her and guided her toward the lake. "Naughty, Cyd. I'm shocked. Truly I am."

"That snooty old bag. I am taking her down if it is the last thing I do."

"Then here's a tip. She's after some property on Elfindale Street."

Cyd blinked, and Ewan enjoyed watching her vivid expression, a young shark ready to snatch away dinner from an older one. "Give me that key. I've got things to do. That Elfindale property is a fine old house, perfect for a bed-and-breakfast. *My* bed-and-breakfast. I've been circling it for years. Hallie could provide the scones and I could find maids, and—give me that key!"

"That will have to wait. Come on. I need to talk to Hallie. There are things she should know. She should have you by her when she hears them."

Cyd frowned, searching his face. "Be careful, Ewan."

"She'll need you. Will you come?" he asked gently, and already knew the response.

"Of course."

Ewan locked his hand around Cyd's, then slowly refitted his palm to hers, lacing their fingers. She had a good strong feel to her, beneath the curves and that flashing temper. He'd have to be careful of her, because she brewed tender feelings in him that he'd sealed away long ago—

"He muscled me all the way here. I would have come without all the macho bull," Cyd protested as she pushed her elbow against Ewan's midsection. On his way to Hallie's,

Ewan had let nothing stop him. When Cyd had balked at crossing the street, he had merely wrapped his free arm around her waist. Then he lifted her feet from the sidewalk and carried her all the way to Hallie's back door.

She'd called for help, but Sean had doubled over with laughter; Marvin pretended that something out on the harbor needed his attention. Finlay, smoking his pipe and sitting on a sidewalk bench with his elderly friends, chuckled and asked if Ewan needed help.

Inside Hallie's small kitchen, Ewan had tugged Cyd upon his lap. His free arm held her still easily. "She's not in a good mood," he informed Hallie, who was smothering laughter.

"You're an idiot," Cyd stated darkly, and moved to another chair.

Ewan unlocked the handcuffs and passed them to her. But his hand replaced the metal, his thumb caressing her inner wrist as he studied the faint marks on her skin. He drew her wrist to his lips, smoothing them over the marks. "You might want to save these for more private times between us. Though I can be quite obedient without them."

"You— Hallie, Ewan went to see Angela, and he's taking his evil mood out on me." Cyd stood, removed her coat, and hung it on the hook by the back door. She took the cup of tea Hallie offered and leaned back against the counter, a safe distance from the man she wanted to— She looked at the pot of pasta Hallie had been rinsing in the kitchen sink, then her eyes narrowed at Ewan.

"I wouldn't, if I were you." Obviously still struggling with his need to find Allan, Ewan stood. He leaned back against the wall, his arms crossed. "There are things to say, and none of them sweet," he said finally. "Your best friend should be here. Cyd would have come anyway. But the tussle took away a little of my steam from seeing Angela."

"Be careful, Ewan," Cyd warned for the second time.

"You're in a nasty mood today, and I won't have you hurting Hallie."

Hallie frowned and looked from Cyd to her brother. "If I find that the both of you are protecting poor little victimized me," she said very quietly, "you'll neither one have another muffin or pie or scone from my oven. Say what you have to say, Ewan."

He slid his hand into his pocket and pulled out a tiny ring. Gleaming filigree and shining onyx looked delicate upon the wide span and calluses. "This was Dad's courting gift to Mother."

Hallie's eyes widened. "No, you're wrong. I've seen Angela wearing it—"

Ewan moved to place the ring on Hallie's finger, a perfect fit. His expression softened, and he ran a gentle hand over her head. "It was Mother's. She put it away when you were five or so, saving it for you."

When she sank to a chair, Cyd eased into one nearby, placing her arm around Hallie's shoulders. "Tell her the rest, Ewan. She needs to know."

With a nod, Ewan seemed to brace himself before speaking. "Someone placed Mother's brooch in the boat shop, where I would find it when I arrived. And just today, the tiny cross that was also meant for you by way of our mother's mother. The brooch had been in Mrs. Linnea's possession and the cross came by way of Patricia Erland. Mother's jewelry was Angela's payment to her cronies, I suppose—the witches who spread rumors about Dad. With Mother's brooch and cross in my keeping, it could look as if I somehow helped those old women die."

"No!" Stunned, Hallie was on her feet and went to hold him tight. "Nothing is going to happen to you, ever again. We won't say anything about the jewelry, and no one will know—"

"Except whoever delivered it. It was placed deliberately,

where it couldn't be overlooked, Hallie." Across her head, Ewan met Cyd's eyes and he spoke gently. "You should have told me, Hallie . . . about your marriage . . . what happened to you. I would have—"

"You were doing so well, working for Andrew and being so kind to him. I should have been able to handle myself better."

"Against a bully who outweighed and outmuscled you?" Cyd couldn't resist muttering. She saw Sean's wind-tossed blond hair cross the window in the alley and was on her feet, jerking open the door. "Get in here."

A scowl had replaced Sean's usual easy grin. He shut the door behind him with a quiet violence that shimmered in the room.

"A gathering of the clan, is it?" he said, and reached for a cabinet to take down a whiskey bottle. He poured an amount into a cup and glanced askance at Ewan, who nodded. Sean handed another cup to Ewan, then downed his drink quickly. "Hallie uses it for colds, but it's a hot temper I'm brewing now."

His eyes had never left Hallie, and the Irish accent passed down to him by his ancestors emerged in a dark tone. "I've just lost my good nature, and I really regret that. Truly, I do. I was just putting gas in my truck when Allan Thompson pulled up on the opposite side of the tanks. Mad, he was. He started spewing unkind words about the Lochlain family— especially Hallie. I had to remind him of his manners and send him on his way, but I've got a picture of what happened in your marriage. You could have come to me."

"You what?" Hallie rounded on him, her finger jabbing his chest. "You hurt Allan?"

Sean's defense of his actions was sturdy. "He swung first. I had to defend myself. Did you know about this, Ewan?"

"I just found out this morning. He's Angela's doing. Hallie was easy game—"

Hallie's hands went to her waist, and the anger leaping to her eyes burned a straight line to both men. "I resent that. It makes me sound like I don't have a mind, that I need big strong men to protect me. Are you set to make me relive that nightmare? Do you both think you can fight my battles for me?"

"Did you go for the jaw, Sean?" Ewan asked curiously as he poured Sean another drink. "I figure Allan's is glass."

"Nah, for the midsection first. He's soft."

"And a bully," Ewan added darkly. "He hurt Hallie."

"He said she liked it," Sean returned, and drank the whiskey quickly.

"I haven't finished with him," Ewan brooded.

"Stop!" Hallie raised her hands. "This is my business. I will handle it," she stated unevenly. The men were talking about Allan's punishment, and she would have none of it.

"He's a worm, a regular slug. I'd like to have a go at him myself, but Hallie made me promise." Cyd's label for Allan snapped across the tiny kitchen.

Hallie took the cup from Sean's and Ewan's hands and pointed to the back door. "Out. Get out of my home, all of you. And you, Ewan. If you lay a hand to Allan, you'll deal with me."

Ewan's eyebrows went up, almost comically, the little sister he'd always protected telling him to shove off. "If he comes back, I'll want to know."

"If Allan comes back and gives one hint of a threat, I will deal with him. The both of you are not taking that away from me. And I want to know what Angela said, what passed between you. But right now, I'm so angry that I don't trust myself. Allan is a businessman, not a rowdy. He was outmatched by Sean, a great big hulking brainless good-looking Viking—"

Cyd let out a long, knowing whistle, and both men looked at her. "You should have told us," they accused in unison.

"I promised," she said. "You wouldn't have me break a promise to Hallie, would you?"

"Yes. In that case, yes, I would," Sean stated firmly.

"Do you suppose I could have a splash of that whiskey?" Hallie asked wearily, rising to pour her tea into the sink.

"You really think I'm good-looking?" Sean asked carefully, stepping closer to press her. "A Viking? You like the Viking look, do you? You like me? A romantic 'like'? My sister says that a Viking is a romantic image for women, isn't it?"

Hallie blinked up at him and in the small kitchen, backed against her brother. "Did I say that?"

"You did." Sean's blue eyes held Hallie's stunned gray ones, as he said, "I'm sorry, Cyd. But from this moment on, my heart is taken."

Cyd couldn't help smiling. One good thing had come of the day, a slip of Hallie's tongue would have Sean dancing around her, changing the course of their friendship, deepening it. "Well, ta-ta. I've put in my time babysitting Ewan and keeping the world safe, so I'm off to count my money."

She wouldn't let them see her fear, as late-afternoon shadows crawled into the alley. Night would soon be coming.

"Out. Get out, you two muscle-for-brains overgrown boys," Hallie was saying. "The both of you walk Cyd home and see that she's safely inside."

"Can I come back? I'd like to talk more about how good-looking I am. I come from a long line of Vikings, all quite handsome, they tell me," Sean stated cheerfully.

"*Out!* And Ewan, I want to know everything. I mean everything. I will not have you leaving me out of this, either. You're my brother. I'll stand by you, no matter what."

Ewan caught her close, his voice uneven against her hair. "You give more than you get, Fairy-Girl. You'll tell me if that ex-husband comes around, won't you?"

She pulled away and looked straight at him. "Leave him

to me, Ewan. It's a matter that I have to close. Until today, he wasn't a problem. Cyd set him off earlier, then you came, and suddenly, Allan . . . he changed."

"Like he really is beneath that bullshit charm." As Cyd passed Hallie, the women's eyes locked in silent understanding; Hallie had struggled for her independence, and nothing, not even Ewan's love, was taking that from her. With a quick hug, Hallie told Cyd she loved her.

"My hero," Cyd whispered, filled with pride for her friend. Through the years, Cyd had needed to know that she was loved by someone, and Hallie had given it freely, endlessly.

Hallie reached for a thermal lunch bag and draped the long strap over Cyd's shoulder. "I love you, but get out. And by the way, my brother made no living off me, so don't even think that for a minute. He won't touch the money I saved for him, the money he sent me every month, no matter how he skimped on himself. It's still there in the bank."

"But I thought that—"

Hallie leaned close to whisper against Cyd's cheek. "I had to do it by myself. You understand better than anyone. Don't blame my brother, Cyd. He's fighting far more of a burden than I. He feels guilty because he left me, when it was all he could do. He was only a boy, and Angela wouldn't have let him earn a living here—worse, she might have done him injury. And now, more guilt has been added to the pile, because of what he learned today—about Allan. Men are a different breed, you know. They're fierce and prideful. But they need the gentler sort, too. You give Ewan that, even when you're fighting. You take him away from the darkness, that awful brooding."

Cyd didn't want to think that she gave Ewan anything; they'd battled for years, and he'd taken her first kiss ruthlessly, leaving no man to compare. "I have no softness in me. You know that. They say I have a cash register for a heart."

Hallie patted Cyd's cheek. "Tell that to someone who doesn't know you. I think you are filled by softness and heart and love. Oh, I do. I truly do. That's why you set up a mortgage plan that I could meet, and I desperately needed that."

"Profit. That's my only motive." But Cyd's blue eyes spoke of her love for Hallie.

"Sure. Now get out."

# Chapter 9

Because she worried about Cyd, Hallie went outside and watched her brother and Sean leave, with Cyd walking between them. Her hair caught the wind, flying out behind her, a vibrant banner of curls against her long dark coat. Tall and brooding, the men walked on either side of her.

They were a sight, Hallie decided with a smile, the best of her life—Cyd, Ewan, and Sean. Two noble, brooding warriors with a strong, good-hearted fighting witch between them—unstoppable, sweet, dear, lovable. People strolling on the sidewalk and around the piers stood and looked at the powerful, stormy trio.

Suddenly Cyd placed an arm on each man's broad shoulder, and their arms crossed her back, hands at her waist. With a whoop, Sean and Ewan lifted her off the ground, and Cyd's laughter came floating back on the cool breeze.

The little boy who had come to stand beside Hallie giggled. "My dad is so funny. He plays with my uncles like that, and sometimes they pick up Grandma and toss her real easy between them. She likes it, I think, though she scolds them. Dad says he and Ewan were friends since they were little boys, and Cyd played with them, too."

The memories of young Sean and Ewan disdaining the company of a little sister and her friend caused Hallie to smile. She stroked Timmy's glossy black hair, and he leaned against her. "They used to do that same thing, years ago. Cyd loved it then, and she still does. She's missed them all being together—but don't tell her I said so, okay? She likes to think she's all grown-up and above such things. But she loves them both—like friends. Like you and Sophia Sanchez." But Cyd's feelings for Ewan ran deeper than those of a friend, Hallie thought.

She glanced at Sally Donovan and nodded, acknowledging the familiar transfer of the little boy while she shopped. "So your grandmother is shopping next door and you're to stay with me for a few minutes, is that right?"

"Grandma likes you. That's weird, swinging Cyd between them. But it looks like fun. He should act that way with you, then maybe you'd marry him. Or I will—when I get big."

Hallie bent to kiss the boy's cheek. "But then, Timmy, I could already be married by the time you got old enough to ask me. How about some cookies? Did you play with Sophia in school today?"

"Yuck. She's a girl. I play with boys."

Hallie ruffled his hair. "That will change. Look at your dad and Ewan playing with Cyd."

In the peace of her small living room later, Hallie curled up on the sofa and tugged a favorite yellow afghan over her. She sipped chamomile tea, trying to steady herself. The silver-and-onyx ring had been her mother's, and Angela had kept it from her. . . .

Someone was out to frame Ewan; they had placed the dead women's jewelry in the boat shop. Who was it? "Don't think you're keeping me out of harm's way, big brother. I will not have anything happen to you," Hallie promised quietly.

But Cyd had already happened to Ewan. Edgy, sharp-

witted, and feminine, she would be just the challenge Ewan
would lock on to. His hand had captured Cyd's on the table,
strong and dark against her finer bones and light skin, and
the looks that passed between them clashed and heated.
Their reckoning had always been there in Ewan's visits
home, in the way Cyd eased away from him, her tart defensive answers to simple exchanges.

Hallie smiled softly and sipped her tea. In the quiet,
peaceful room she'd created, she said aloud, "If ever there
was a woman to capture Ewan's heart, to reach inside him, it
would be Cyd. And it would work the same for him. But I'm
certain that neither sees it that way."

Big and bold, the picture of a tall blond Viking, Sean
Donovan leaped into Hallie's mind—as if he was ever far
from her thoughts. In her temper, her tongue had moved beyond her mind's keeping, and she'd given away a secret
she'd hidden for years. A patient man, he'd corner Hallie one
day, and she'd have to be ready to protect her heart. She'd
given it away freely once, and no man was taking away the
strength she'd carved for herself.

" 'Good-looking,' " she repeated, regretting that she'd released her private thoughts.

The small silver filigree ring gleamed in the soft evening
lamplight. Angela had it all this time, had she? Mary
Lochlain's jewelry had been parceled out to Angela's
friends, and now someone was out to make Ewan pay.

But who?

Paddy O'Connor for certain, who bore a grudge against
Finlay and Ewan.

Angela—Hallie preferred not to think that her aunt would
sink so low.

And Allan. In his fury, he had already sworn that no man
would have Hallie, except himself. In her marriage, Hallie
had feared that threat, but until today Allan had seemed
pleasant enough. And she'd wanted to handle her own af-

fairs, backing away from no one. If he felt Ewan was protecting her, Allan might—

Hallie shuddered and held her ring hand close to her heart, protecting it with the other hand. She fought the memories crashing back upon her, tender loving young years and then—then Angela's cold resentment. "You look like your mother, the slut. . . . Stupid clumsy girl. . . ."

Sean Donovan had been like a brother.

Hallie couldn't ruin both their lives by thinking she could be as any other woman, free to love and be loved.

Ewan Lochlain, the image of Tom, was set to defy her, was he? Then he had a lesson to learn. . . .

Angela stood by the study window overlooking Fairy Cove and brooded over the threat Ewan posed. After all these years, he still enjoyed holding those papers over her head and threatening to destroy everything she'd built. "Blackmailer."

She automatically straightened a fold of the drapery and discovered a tiny doll on the carpeting. The housekeeper sometimes brought her youngest child to play as she worked—when she thought her employer wouldn't be home. Angela left the proof where it lay, because children weren't allowed in her house. But Angela knew everything that went on in Greer House, and in Fairy Cove.

Two of her closest friends had died recently, and the jewelry Angela had given them wasn't to be found. They were cheap pieces, unfitting Angela's status and wardrobe. But Mary had loved them, wanting them for Hallie and Ewan.

Angela kicked the doll lying on the floor. Her mother had always loved Mary more, giving her the cross that Angela had desperately wanted. But Angela had always wanted everything that Mary had cherished—even a man.

Where was that jewelry? If Ewan had spotted her ring— Tom's courting ring—then he'd remember the other pieces.

He had asked specifically about his mother's jewelry. Angela sniffed haughtily and rubbed her ringless finger with her thumb.

Everything Mary had was cheap and worn. And yet her twin had been happy.

But Mary had had Tom Lochlain, hadn't she?

Angela's eyes narrowed on the moonlit silhouette of the boat shop down on the pier. Ewan had demanded Tom's courting ring right off her finger!

She fought the edge of panic and fear. The boy didn't have his father's loving heart. If tested, Ewan's cruel streak could match her own. They would play his game, opponents holding threats over each other—she, with the ability to tug Hallie's tender emotions, and Ewan lording his precious papers over Angela.

She'd find those papers and the jewelry. She'd leave the young pup nothing. How dare he make such statements in her own home?

Evidently money was in Ewan's pocket, and he wasn't fearful of her power. She'd have to remind him. . . .

Mary and Tom had finally gotten what they deserved, and once she had the blackmailer's papers in her possession, Ewan might find the same end.

If he didn't tear her life apart first. . . . She didn't trust Ewan Lochlain. His temper was too fierce, and one wrong push could take him running to the authorities—or to kill her.

Would he actually kill her? Did his hatred run that deep?

Hers would, and Ewan was of the same blood. . . .

Angela's hand lay protectively on her throat. She refused to be afraid of a troublemaker. She would simply cultivate Hallie's trust and use it to get those papers. . . .

"Fred!" she called shrilly into the intercom.

From his office, Fred's mild voice returned, "Yes, dear?"

"Deduct 25 percent from Maria's next check. She knows that only her two oldest daughters are allowed in my house, and only to clean. She knows she shouldn't bring that youngest one, and yet here in my office is a doll, proof that the child was here."

Angela wouldn't be afraid of Ewan Lochlain. She ruled Fairy Cove, and it was only a matter of time before Ewan fully understood that. . . . Perhaps even tonight.

Ewan stepped back into the shadows of Main Street's alley. The heavy footsteps and the low voices of the three men following him told him that they weren't used to stealthy work.

The leaves on the street's tree rustled like secrets tossed by the slight damp wind. On the lake, moonlight caught the froth sliding on the sand and danced a trail across the lake's endless black swells to Ewan.

He mentally wove the facts into a blurred tapestry of intrigue. Someone had planted stolen jewelry to throw suspicion upon him. But who?

He'd stirred hatred in someone—most likely his aunt.

And maybe his blood, akin to hers, wanted a dark revenge. If evil prowled the night, perhaps it rested within him as well, because he was in a mood to use his fists—a "devil's mood," his father had called it, when his own ire was tested.

Ewan glanced at the owl's journey across the moon. Somehow, the jewelry, Angela, and Paddy were all connected with the Lochlain family's past. But how? Did the women die of natural causes—or had someone helped them along, and the beloved jewelry of Mary Lochlain had become sick trophies?

Whatever the reason, they could point suspicion to Ewan.

Angela was definitely a candidate, her hatred of Mary still vivid after years. But even she wouldn't steal from her supporters.

The footsteps sounded closer, big men huffing to walk fast. A man's gruff whisper slid through the night, "Bastard. He's slipped away. Maybe he's gone back to that red-haired witch's place, leaving Donovan out of it."

"He's got a sister. Pretty—"

A cold, deadly fury slid over Ewan. His hands closed into fists.

After delivering Cyd to her home, and turning to walk toward the lake and the boat shop, Ewan and Sean had noted the trio. The men stayed a distance behind, obviously following them and staying to the shadows.

After an argument, Ewan had sent a reluctant Sean home to his son; Ewan preferred to keep his friends away from the trouble brewing—and harm.

With a brawl or two behind him, Ewan's senses prickled warningly. If Angela was behind this, then the game had gotten even more dangerous . . . and he preferred to know the faces of his hunters.

When the three men passed the alley, Ewan stepped from the shadows. "If you're looking for me, I'm right here."

With two of his friends, Paddy O'Connor's small soulless eyes and heavy jowls caught the streetlight. "Lochlain!"

Ewan smiled and ducked the first heavy fist. "You've gotten slow in your old age, Paddy."

To the other two men, Ewan spoke very quietly, "Touch my sister, and you won't touch another woman."

They were on him then, but Ewan had learned a few tricks from a friend who was a black belt master. He moved quickly, using just enough force in a blow to one man's throat to cause him to gasp and double. A quick chop brought the second to his knees, then only Paddy stood crouched and ready to fight.

"Shall we?" Ewan invited coolly.

"None of that fancy stuff," Paddy said, lifting his ham-sized fists.

"Playing by the rules now, are you?" But Ewan obliged, weaving and putting just enough force into his fists to make Paddy stagger backward. He grunted as his back hit the streetlight's metal post.

Enraged, the heavier man growled and rushed at Ewan, landing a glancing blow on his cheek. Ewan went for Paddy's soft midsection, hammering quickly until the seaman doubled and backed against the storefront. His friends hurried into the night, and Ewan glanced at the police car that came to a stop.

"Later, Lochlain," Paddy gasped.

"You've got that right. I'll want to know what ties you to Angela."

Beside them now, Marvin held his flashlight high, catching Ewan's and Paddy's faces. "Problems?"

"Just a little chat between friends," Ewan answered, straightening Paddy by pulling up his coat's lapels. "Isn't that right, Paddy?"

"Uh." Paddy's grunt served as agreement.

Marvin's expression said he doubted the friendly chat. "You can go, Paddy."

He watched Paddy move into the night, then said, "Ewan, that's a nasty scrape you've got on your cheek. It needs attention. I'm on my way home. My wife could patch you up—or of course, there's Cyd," he added with a wide grin. "Women love to baby heroes. And I've got this little bet to tend, you see. A wound like that might throw the odds toward you."

"Cyd?" The novel idea that Cyd would tend him was too fascinating to pass, and, moments later, Ewan rang her doorbell.

The porch light pinned him instantly. Ewan heard the rustle behind the door, noted the shadow in the peephole, and decided to add a groan loud enough for Cyd to hear.

"Louder," Marvin coached from the bushes.

Ewan braced a hand against the doorframe for effect and groaned again.

The door swung open, and she stood, dressed in black satin pajamas that offset her pale face.

He could have clasped that face between his hands and

taken that wide saucy mouth with the hunger that sprang instantly hard and low in his groin. But to his unsteady noble credit, Ewan managed, "If Hallie sees this, I'm in for it. Can you fix me up?"

Of course he knew how to tend himself, to minimize bruising; but fascinated with Cyd's stunned face, Ewan settled in to enjoy his helpless male role.

"I should let you die," Cyd stated bluntly, but not too gently tugged him into her house. "Don't bleed on anything. Don't move. I'll get a towel—no wait, come with me into the kitchen. This carpet is—"

"Ahhh . . ." Ewan faked pain, testing Marvin's theory that women loved to hover over the wounded. He leaned slightly against Cyd as she helped him into a kitchen chair.

She eased his coat away. "I'll say this for you, Lochlain, you know how to stir things up. You've only been here just over a month. What happened?"

"My friend Paddy and I had a discussion. Don't tell Hallie. She's got enough on her plate."

"And don't you dare add to it by jumping Allan."

"It's just possible that he put that jewelry in the boat shop. I will have to ask him about that sometime."

"You do, and he's certain to turn you in—or tell Angela, and she'll see you in prison. Keep quiet about it, Ewan." Cyd leaned over him, inspecting the cut closely as she dabbed a wet towel around the area. "Andrew Larkin's money won't do you any good there. Oh, yes. I've been too busy to research deeply, but a few hours spent online was most informative. I hadn't realized just how wealthy Larkin was, enough to commission an 1812 schooner and bankroll sailing around the world. As a millionaire's right-hand man in his last years, you were certain to come away with a nice piece of the pie."

Ewan jerked his head away from her hand and stared up at her. "That wasn't why I stayed with him."

She replaced her hand to his head, firmly tilting it down the better to tend the wound. "No, I didn't think for a moment that it was. I'm glad he had you."

"Andrew had a daughter. Irene was with him, too." Why the devil did he think he had to bare his life to Cyd?

She dabbed hard just once. "Pretty?"

Upscale and pleasant, Irene had loved her father. She'd left her busy life to sail his last dream and care for him. One day, she would run Andrew's empire, but in those awful last painful months of his life, Irene was only a woman who needed a friend—and gentle sexual comfort without strings, easy for them both. "Not too ugly."

Ewan had an excellent view of Cyd's breasts, his senses catching her feminine scent. He closed his eyes and wallowed in the soft light touches, the feel of her fingers on his skin. The game had turned on him, his need to be near Cyd growing.

Was he so far gone on Cyd already? Needing this tender sense of home from her as he had no other woman?

With a tired sigh that he felt down to his bones, Ewan laid his face against her breasts. He rested against Cyd with a sense that she gave him comfort, even with her dark tempers and her scolding. She felt like home, and he hadn't been home in a very long time. . . .

She stiffened, but didn't move away. Beneath the satin, her heartbeat kicked up, and her breath ran ragged in her throat.

"Damn you, Lochlain," she muttered, even as her fingers moved in his hair to draw his head closer. As she would a child, Cyd rocked him gently against her. "This is no good. I'd rather have your tormenting than this."

"I'm tired, Cyd," he admitted quietly, his arms slipping around her. Her senses leaped into warning mode even as her heart softened. Ewan's fatigue came from years of fighting and worrying, of a young boy doing his best for his sister . . . of a man who wouldn't admit the fear of failure circling him.

The snare was soft and tempting, to play the woman's part, easing a troubled man—a world warrior—simply by holding him.

But her relationship with Ewan wasn't simple, and Cyd feared her tenderness for him. When she eased away slightly, Ewan's smile was weary and accepting as he stood.

With a sigh, he ran his hand over her hair, letting a curl twine around his finger. He gently tugged it. "I used to clean the rubble from this. I'm sorry that life wasn't kinder to you," he whispered in that deep, lilting, almost musical tone she remembered from childhood.

In this mood, Ewan was more frightening to Cyd than in his dark brooding. "I'm making it just fine, Ewan. I don't need your sympathy. I just scooped up that Elfindale property for a sweet, sweet price. Angela will burn over that one, and poor Fred will catch it for not moving faster. I just haven't decided to make my move on her yet."

"Always defensive. . . ."

His fingers eased her hair back from her face. The desire of a man leaped into his expression, and heat danced between them, shimmered intimately in the shadows. "Still. And yet, it's not always sympathy that I'm feeling for you."

"I know—" She frowned as Ewan tensed and stared at the window.

"Something moved outside. A man's shadow just showed through the curtains. If Paddy and his friends are prowling around here, I won't be so gentle to them this time," he stated quietly, and brushed past her.

Cyd reached out instantly, catching Ewan's arm. She didn't conceal her terror. "Don't go. It could be . . . him."

" 'Him'? You're being stalked, Cyd?"

Embarrassment gave way to stark, flashing fear. "The Night Man. I see his shadow sometimes. I see his face, his eyes."

"Cyd." Ewan's tone was a gentle reprimand that Fairy Cove's legendary bogeyman wasn't a reality.

Cyd hurled herself at him, circling his body with her arms. "Ewan, please don't go."

He folded her close to him. "You're shaking, Cyd. That was a man's shadow. If there's someone out there, I want to know who he is. While they might have failed with me, they may have come after you."

Terror that she'd held for years rushed into words as she huddled against Ewan. "He leaves things on the doorstep, in the morning—fairies and gnomes. I have a whole box of them. He's been leaving them since I was eighteen. I haven't told anyone, not even Hallie. I don't want her to worry. Please don't go outside, Ewan. When I lived at your old house, I thought I would be safe there. But he found me. He found me when I moved here. Sometimes . . . sometimes I feel him in my office, or in a rental . . . or sometimes it feels as if he's been here—right here in my home."

"I doubt it. You've got plenty of locks, Cyd." Ewan held her closer and smoothed her back. She could feel him thinking—

"I tried psychiatrists. I've tried tranquilizers, but I'm not doing more of that after seeing my mother's addiction. He's a reality, Ewan. Don't go outside. Please."

"Angela could have sent Paddy or Allan—"

"This man is tall and lean. His eyes are—they are empty and haunted. He wants something from me—he wants to hurt me."

Though unspoken, Ewan's thoughts leaped to her, and Cyd shoved back from him. "You think I'm crazy."

"I think you're upset. Any woman would be with a stalker circling her."

She locked her arms around herself, her fingers digging into the satin. "I can manage. You can go. Look all you want. You won't find him. No one has, not in years, and other people have seen him, too."

"Come here, Cyd. Let me hold you."

She was shaking, terrified, and couldn't let Ewan see how badly she needed him. "I'm just fine. You can leave now."

Instead, he moved toward her and scooped her up in his arms. "Shh."

Ewan moved into her living room and sat with her on his lap. In his father's big chair, he eased her head down to lie on his shoulder, next to the steady beat of his heart. "Fairies and gnomes, is it? Well, let me tell you what I know of them. . . ."

"Ewan, this is serious. Those were meant as threats. I don't want people to think I've lost my mind like my mother. You've got to promise not to tell anyone."

"I won't." Ewan's hand smoothed her hair, and his voice was low and steady. " 'Twas a dark day with a storm brewing when the Fairy Queen called her court to the giant mush-room canopy. With tiny wings quivering upon their shoulders and with clothing as fine as the finest of all spiderwebs, the fairies perched upon the blades of grass and the tiny toadstools. 'A spell has come upon us, you see, and one of us is really the Troll of Kilkearny.' "

"That may have worked when I was a child, Ewan, but I've grown a bit. It won't work."

"Won't it? Give it a try, Cyd."

"Sure. Go ahead. Embarrass us both."

Cyd relaxed slightly, comfortable with the boy within the man as he continued, "Well, all the fluttering of wings and whispers of the fairies caused the gnome who lived within the tree root to surface with his warty nose and his peaked ears. Birdlike, he searched the fairies, all shimmering in the dim light, and one with a tiny flower serving as a cup for a fresh raindrop. But Mr. Gnome had a kind heart, and was truly a prince under an evil witch's spell. 'A troll, you say? I can sniff a troll as I would an earthworm or a nit burrowing under a kitten's fur. Let me sniff about to find him—' "

Ewan's nose burrowed close to Cyd's throat, and he sniffed loudly. The play took Cyd back to another time, and she couldn't help giggling, just as she had as a little girl.

Then suddenly, she was leaning back, looking up at Ewan, and the magic turned into a steady hum. Or was that the rapid beat of her heart?

Her hand lay upon his face, bones unforgiving beneath the rough evening stubble. Ewan's gray eyes had darkened, and he turned slightly, kissing her palm. "Don't be afraid, Cyd. There's been too much of it in the past."

"You were afraid of failing Hallie, weren't you?"

"More than I can say. She believes in me."

"You didn't fail, Ewan. You won't fail. Angela won't label you as she did your father."

"*Mislabeled*, you mean," he said broodingly.

Then quick to change his mood, Ewan studied her. His teeth nipped her hand and laughter lit his eyes. "You've given up the idea of selling the boat shop to McGruder's then?"

"No. You can build boats anywhere. The place makes no difference."

"But it does . . . to me. Are you going to let me kiss you?"

Cyd should have moved away; instead, her fingers had locked into his hair, urging his face to hers. For once, she let a man inside her emotions, the hunger and the fire, breathing his breath, letting her softness flow beneath his roaming hands.

She slid her hand along his throat, tested the strong, fast beat there, before moving lower. Inside his collar, she found skin, almost burning with a sensual hunger that matched her own.

Smooth and hard and rippling with checked power, his broad shoulder tensed beneath her prowling fingers.

Ewan's hand lay open and strong upon her hip, fingers digging in as if he meant to keep her—until when? Until he was done with her, then he'd move on?

She should know better, a woman who knew only that her
father had green eyes and that he loved to waltz. . . .

Cyd tossed away thought when Ewan's fingers moved up
slowly to unbutton her pajama top. His finger traced a slow
straight line down her body, from her breasts to her waist,
hooking inside the elastic waistband of her pajama bottoms
and tugging lightly.

Then Ewan's hand returned to her hip. He eased away and
lay with his head back, eyes closed, his breath ragged in the
silence. Beneath her, his hips moved restlessly, and layers of
cloth did not conceal hard, jutting desire.

Ewan was giving her time to escape, to choose, and Cyd
could no more move than she could stop touching him.

His hand opened to smooth her breasts, to heat and cup
them gently. "It's been a long time for me, Cyd. Are you
shaking because you're afraid of me—or is it the fever I see
in your eyes?"

"I haven't decided to have you yet, Lochlain. And my
choices are always on my terms," she managed breathlessly.

"That's my girl. Always wrangling." He smiled slightly,
the light catching his black eyelashes, sending shadows
down his cheek. He'd been the most beautiful boy she'd ever
seen—and now, mature and rugged, even more desirable.

Then suddenly, his body tensed and he tugged her against
him, pushing aside the cloth until skin burned skin. Again,
he held her hair, holding her face close to his, and the storm
clashed once again between them, hot and furious. "Be careful, sweetheart."

"Just like a man," she returned, even as her heart raced at
that primitive beckoning. "Brawling one minute and wanting sex the next."

"It's true, I am a man. And I know when I've got a willing
woman in my arms."

"In your dreams."

"Maybe." His eyes narrowed downward, to where her

pale skin lay against his body, to where her breasts lay pink and round and rose-tipped against his hard muscle and tanned skin. "I like the look of this, you and me," he stated roughly.

She'd known that men could be aroused by the look of male and female pressed together. But she hadn't known that she was just as susceptible to that man's hungry look, her heart pounding, her body waiting, trembling down low and aching—

Cyd slid her fingers through Ewan's hair as he slowly lowered to taste her body, to nuzzle and suckle, and take away her breath. Or was it her soul?

As she floated and hungered, Ewan turned her body to straddle his, his hand cupping her bottom, fingers seeking a deeper, intimate warmth, even as his lips prowled her throat, his breath hot and uneven against her skin.

With layers of clothing between them, her body matched the rhythm of his, rise and fall, thrust against thrust, and within that storm, she knew her power—and Ewan's over her.

"Enough," she whispered against his lips, and bit his bottom lip.

He breathed deeply, and one long stroke of his fingers noted that she was moist and soft and aching for him. "Afraid?" he drawled huskily.

"That I can't handle you? No."

"Mmm. Interesting. You're burning for me, Cyd. I could have you."

"You wish. I've enjoyed this, only because I had nothing better to do."

"Ah. A way to pass the time. A useful tool, so to speak."

She shrugged and eased away, standing and turning to button her top. When she turned back again, it was to Ewan, towering over her. He tugged her into his arms and fused her open lips with his own, burning her. It was no gentle taking, but it was a match to her own shaken emotions. He took everything until her fingers dug into his shoulders and her tongue met his own.

Cyd wanted to brand him then, so that Ewan Lochlain would want no other woman.

She dug her nails into Ewan's hard shoulders, reminding him that she was no easy catch, that she could hold her own with him.

Then suddenly she was pushed away, shaking and unsatisfied. Ewan's cold smile and flashing thunderous eyes said that he'd call his own time. His eyes ripped down her body as though he knew already the heat within it, as though he could feel her burn for him. "I'd know your scent anywhere, Cyd. You're aroused, and it's enough to make me forget a few rules between us. But I don't think that either one of us would appreciate a quick relief or its repercussions. I'm going to check outside. If you see a shadow, it's mine. Do you have a flashlight? I want to see if your stalker left any footprints in the flower beds."

"In the toolbox, by the door." In another few heartbeats while she weighed her fear against attacking Ewan, he closed the door softly behind him, the automatic locks set.

Cyd watched his shadow move outside her window, the slash of the flashlight against the night. Then Ewan rapped on her door. "Cyd. I'm going now. Call Hallie to tell her I'm coming. I want to check on her, and I'll call you later."

She opened her lips and closed them again. An invitation to Ewan now could be taken wrong, and she wasn't ready to sacrifice herself for safety's sake.

Or so Cyd tried to make herself believe.

# Chapter 10

After a visit to Hallie's, Ewan held the sack of food she'd sent in one hand and with the other, the boat shop's broken padlock. The marks on the wood said a crowbar had been used for entry and not too skillfully, either. "You owe me a lock, Paddy," Ewan said quietly. "We're going to have a little chat about your window peeking. I'll let Marvin know *after* you and I have had our private meeting."

Ewan entered the dark boat shop, flipped on the light and scanned the big room. Everything was in its place. Ewan slid the interior iron bolt closed on the big door and listened to the familiar sound of waves hitting the wooden pier, the creaking of the wood's resistance, the flap of plastic on an upper window he'd not yet replaced.

A quick search of his apartment revealed it to be just as neat. He placed Hallie's food into the refrigerator and walked back out into the boat shop.

On the floor in front of the workbench lay a few screwdrivers and a bevel board with his father's initials, T.L., cut into the wood. A screw clamp and a wedge clamp lay a few feet away. The angle of the tools was careless, as though they had been tossed aside.

On the workbench, copper rivets had been placed in a neat row as if they had been meticulously studied.

Ewan had left the broadax on the workbench, stripped of its old wood handle. The metal head still gleamed with a heavy coat of oil, in preparation to work with the rusty spots on it. There was something about the whetstone his father had used for sharpening. . . . It bore the oil from the ax's head and had been replaced to the workbench, not at Ewan's right-handed angle, but at a leftward one.

Next to the whetstone, the wooden toolbox had been rifled, an old sheath knife placed back at a left-hander's angle. It also bore a streak of oil from the whetstone. . . .

Ewan carefully nudged aside the other tools and found the jewelry gone.

He leaned back against the workbench to think. Paddy had swung with a meaty right fist; his left didn't carry the weight.

Someone had been very busy that night. Could Allan be looking for ways to cause trouble?

Was Allan prowling around Cyd's house, trying to frighten her? He'd have the motive—because Cyd had protected Hallie. . . .

Ewan shoved past guilt that came when he thought of Hallie's abuse. He slid a compact two-way unit from his coat pocket. On impulse, he telephoned his sister and waited, hoping she was safe in her upstairs bedroom. She picked up and sleepily murmured, "Hello?"

"This isn't Sean," he teased, making light when his fears ran deep.

"Don't forget to warm the meat loaf. I won't have you eating it cold," Hallie returned sleepily.

He listened to the sound of her bedclothes rustling, the flop of her body upon the mattress and the puff of a pillow being adjusted. Tomorrow, like it or not, his little sister was getting new doors and locks. Ewan spoke carefully to avoid frightening her. "I left a two-way hand radio by your bed. Pick it up and call me now. Just punch the button—"

"Allan wouldn't—"

"Do it."

With a sigh, Hallie flipped on the unit and the loud squelch shot from Ewan's unit. "Turn the green button to the left, Hallie, and talk to me."

Her metallic voice sounded impatient. "You're worried that whoever is leaving the jewelry might be watching me, too. I'm quite safe, really. But with Mother's jewelry turning up, something is afoot. Did you call Marvin?"

"No. If Angela is playing games, I'd rather keep it in the family. And I'm not too fond of explaining something that was stolen from me, that logically shouldn't have been in my possession. . . . Keep that unit with you, Hallie."

Ewan remembered Hallie's firm bid for independence, and added, "Please. For me? To make me feel better?"

She sighed again. "I guess I could do that. Did Cyd get one, too?"

"She will. The jewelry is gone. Someone broke in tonight. I'll be over tomorrow and put on new doors and locks. Meanwhile, tuck that hand unit in your pocket."

"Oh, Ewan. I'm so sorry. Because you remembered it, that jewelry was probably more important to you than to me. I'm sorry it's gone."

"I'll find it and whoever is playing pack rat. See you tomorrow."

"Ewan, I want to know exactly what you did to get Angela to transfer her guardianship of me to the Donovans. I have a right to know."

"I'd rather keep that to myself. It's a darkness that would go with a woman who would beat a defenseless girl."

"I'm not a girl any longer." The declaration was there again, a woman demanding her own rights, not the protection of an older brother.

"I'm not ready to explain parts of what happened, Hallie. I haven't worked them out myself. I only know that Dad had no part in planning Mother's murder . . . I know they loved each other," he stated quietly and hoped she'd understand.

It wasn't like Hallie to push and pry, and, trusting Ewan, she accepted his wish. "Come for breakfast. I love having you home, sitting there drooling as if you've never had a decent meal."

"If Sean starts courting you seriously, three will be one too many at breakfast—"

"That's not going to happen. See you in the morning."

A motorboat sounded distantly in the night, and Ewan hurried to unbolt the door. But when he threw it open, he heard only the rhythmic sound of waves hitting the pier.

Because he had to know about the woman whose scent still clung to him, whose safety came second only to Hallie's, Ewan dialed another number.

Cyd's tone said she was wide-awake and edgy. He pictured her prowling her house like a caged tiger. He pictured her lying soft and curved within his arms. Once more, he heard the deep yearning purrs, tasted the silkiness of her skin. . . .

"Want me to come over?" he asked casually, trying to soften his need to hold her safe and in truth, to lock his body deep in her hot, sleek one.

"Get lost." After a slight pause, she added sharply, "Unless you called to start negotiations for a sale. Are you ready to sell the boat shop?"

Ewan smiled tightly. Cyd, in business mode, was already calculating her profit. "I think Paddy and his gang prowled around your house tonight. I'll talk to Marvin tomorrow— and definitely Paddy. Good night, darling-mine."

He studied the tiny sliver of carefully placed wood near his boot. The sliver remained wedged in the exact place he'd put it, between the old boards. His model boats and notebooks of plans and notes had been untouched.

Someone had placed the jewelry in his keeping, then they'd taken it away.

Someone was playing games that Ewan intended to uncover.

Cyd awoke to her own scream and images of a big man bending over her, hands reaching out to her, his breath foul with liquor—"I'll be back for you, my pretty," he'd said, his eyes glittering with lust. . . .

She sprang out of her tangled covers, running for the window's slice of daylight. Cyd tore open the curtains and the shutters to the bright morning. She placed her open hands upon the cold glass, absorbing the safety of sunlight and day.

With Ewan's return, her nightmares had become more vivid—ever since she'd found him sleeping in that boat, his beard black and his hair shaggy around his head.

But last night, the nightmares had mixed with images of Ewan moving over her, in her, his body slick and hard and demanding against hers.

Her lips remembered the tempting nip of his, her breasts ached for the cup of his hand, the stroke of his thumb across her nipple, peaking it. . . .

Cyd showered hurriedly, trying to erase his touch, and meanwhile her ache had turned to fury.

Who did Ewan think he was, to call an end to their fever?

Oh, she wasn't done with him yet, not on this war. . . .

She hurried to her kitchen, brewing coffee quickly with shaking hands. Ewan simply terrified her—for what he knew about her, for the gentleness and understanding that mixed with a man's primitive hunger.

Ewan terrified her because of her own need to clash and defeat him, a woman taking what she wanted.

He terrified her on another level that she didn't understand, something that colored her nightmares. . . .

Cyd dressed quickly in a warm black sweater, black jeans,

and walking boots. If Hallie could meet her fears, so could Cyd. . . .

"I am a grown businesswoman, and I can handle Ewan," she stated shakily. Then she checked her office messages, made a few return business calls, and braced herself for the day. She called Hallie to reassure her. "I won't be over this morning. I have a lot to do today."

"Ewan came back here last night. I gather you two fought. Don't hurt him too much, will you, Cyd?" Hallie teased, unaware that Ewan had been in a brawl.

The quiver that passed through Cyd's body said it still simmered with Ewan's touch, the need to have him. "I can't promise anything where he's concerned. He's on the make, Hallie. And I won't be used. I know the male animal, whether he's your brother or not."

"True." Humor circled Hallie's tone.

Cyd smiled and couldn't resist teasing her friend. "So have you seen Sean? The guy you called 'good-looking'? Your Viking?"

Hallie's silence said that she was aware of Sean's desire for her. "Okay, then. Have a good day. I've got customers. Call when you can," Hallie stated briskly, and the line went dead.

Cyd's smile widened as she slid into her black leather jacket and shouldered into her backpack. "About time."

She reset the alarms and hurried into the garage, revved her pickup and backed onto the street. With determination and a firm to-do list, Cyd shot into the morning.

Because before night came, she intended to understand her fears better.

And to rid herself of a new hunger—Ewan.

The double doors to the boat shop were closed to the warm early May day. Odd, Cyd thought. Usually, they were wide open and the sound of Ewan's hammer and saw could be heard.

She tested the single entry door, found it slightly ajar, ignored the buzzer, and pushed the door open. If it was privacy Ewan wanted, that was too bad. Cyd was only there as a favor to Hallie, bringing Ewan a basket of food.

At the workbench, Ewan was bent over a notebook, a pencil in hand.

At three o'clock in the afternoon, shafts of sunlight cut through the high windows. Dust particles circled inside the sunlight. They seemed almost as trapped within it as Cyd felt after a grueling day of fighting her past.

She didn't feel thirty-one; in her ongoing battle for the truth, she was at least a hundred and one.

Whatever was trapped inside her mind, terrifying her with nightmares, was also hiding within her mother. And earlier today Linda Callahan wasn't talking when Cyd asked about the cause of her nightmares. When pressed too close, Linda had hummed a waltz that seemed trapped in her mind; she'd ignored Cyd's questioning about the identity of her father.

Was it someone she saw every day? Did she pass him on the street every day?

It could have been . . . It could have been any man with money to pay for her mother's services. . . .

The riddle of her father's identity went round and round as Cyd held the food basket that Hallie had sent for Ewan. Cyd leaned back into the shadows, watching him.

Light caught the hard angles of his profile. Big and angular, power in his broad shoulders, legs stretched long from his perch on the stool down to the worn, sturdy boots on the floor. Raw and male and tough, Ewan was no sweetheart beneath his lilting deep voice and his teasing play. He was a taker, the same as she, set on his course.

She'd be making a bargain with the devil if she took him to her bed.

Yet a part of her wanted to come into his arms for comfort. Part of Cyd wanted to hold Ewan, to give him ease as she had last night when he'd simply leaned against her. She'd felt the weight of his struggle, the pain, and the unique comfort that she could give a man simply by holding him. . . .

But another part of Cyd wanted to take. . . .

"Just one wrong man will ruin a woman's life," her mother had said, and Ewan was definitely that wrong man.

Cyd mentally crossed Ewan off her day's to-do list. He was too unpredictable now—and for that matter, so was she. She was too tired to play his games or to fight him.

"I know you're there. You might as well come over here, Cyd," Ewan said suddenly, without looking up.

Cyd moved across the room briskly, and Ewan continued making notes. She hadn't thought of him as a businessman, with pads and pencils and a calculator resting beside a high-priced laptop. He ran a finger down the list of numbers in his worn notebook and punched numbers into the laptop. It sprang into life, pie graphs divided into different colors.

"New laptop?"

"No, but it needed some work and programs, and Andrew's techs sent it here. I told them to wait a bit until I'd settled in. I'm settled."

Another quick jab of his fingers and three-dimensional lines in the shape of a small boat filled the screen. Beside it, a list of numbers cross-referenced the alphabet labels. "A skiff?" she asked, leaning closer.

"Flat-bottom . . . my father's design, but I've tweaked it a little at the hull, and added my own signature to it. How long has it been since you've been out to Three Ravens Island?"

She scanned the scrap of paper with doodles on it and saw the makings of a Lochlain logo. For a heartbeat, she almost felt sorry for Ewan's dream of using his father's boat shop, because it was bound to be hers. "Three Ravens Island? Long enough, I guess. Maybe on a picnic at the end of last summer when Hallie wouldn't visit Sean without me. Why?"

"I was wondering about Peter Hedwig, that old hermit. He's a highly educated business dropout. He used to run a small motorboat from Three Ravens Island to Fairy Cove for supplies and an occasional load of financial magazines and newspapers."

"He's still there, living at one end of the island. In return for the seeds and necessities Sean and Norma provide for him, Peter supplies them with fresh vegetables and fruits for the guests, and Norma cans the rest. Sean gives Peter the same privacy as his grandfather Donovan did. Peter didn't stay long at last summer's picnic, but did take the leftovers. I think Norma has taken a fancy to him—or at least they had several very private conversations that day."

Ewan's silence said he was once more absorbed in numbers as the laptop's boat shifted into another view. He'd surprised Cyd, working with electronics and numbers and notes, and she struggled to recover from a Ewan she didn't know. Intriguing? Yes. Dangerous? Yes.

"Hallie sent food," she said finally, depositing the basket on the workbench. She was bone tired and yet fascinated by Ewan enough to watch him at work. "Are you hungry?"

"Mmm."

He noted another figure, and flipped the pages of his notebook, making another note.

Cyd opened the basket and looked inside. She selected a small bag of pumpkin and raisin cookies and tucked them in her backpack. Ready to fall onto the closest flat surface at her house, she straightened the backpack's shoulder strap, and said, "I'm leaving. Don't bother to say thank you."

"Mmm." Ewan flipped back the pages to another note and jotted a figure. He reached for a calculator, punched in numbers, then wrote in his notebook.

"You can't actually be planning to make something of this place, Ewan. Let me sell it for you. At some point, Larkin's money is going to run out, and you'll have nothing—not even this."

"Mmm."

She leaned closer, instantly focused on the chance that Ewan had changed his mind. She placed her backpack on the counter, and said, "Is that a yes? Yes, you'll let me start negotiations with McGruder's?"

He slapped the notebook closed and reached for her with one arm, drawing her between his legs. He searched her face and eased away the silky tendrils from her cheek. "Hallie said you've had a bad day."

Ewan's thumb gently stroked her cheek. "You've been crying. Want to tell me about it?"

She didn't deny it; Ewan had known her for too long. Cyd never let anyone see her cry. Hallie had shed enough tears of her own, and Cyd didn't want her more disturbed. Then she'd learned long ago that predators took that as a sign of weakness.

Cyd stiffened back from him, though she could have circled those broad shoulders with her arms, and rested her head upon them. "No more than usual. I visited my mother. She won't talk about what happened to me as a child. She won't give me the name of my father. All that I know of him is that he has green eyes and they waltzed and he treated her like a lady. She loved him. He gave her something she never had—and me, of course. She hums that waltz over and over again. It's like that song is holding the last thread of her sanity."

Ewan's thumbs massaged her temples, easing the headache there. It would be so easy to lean against him, to feel his safety. But she wouldn't; then Ewan was taking the choice from her. He drew her gently against him, rocking her with his body, his fingers massaging her scalp. "You're tired, Cyd. No sleep last night?"

She fought resting against Ewan completely. In her emotions, the boy and the man tangled together, and she found it difficult to separate them. Concern might come from the boy of long ago; taunting could come from a man who wanted her to ache for him. Ewan could be reminding her that sex brewed between them, unwanted and unfed, but still simmering.

Cyd did not intend to release the tension she felt with Ewan until she was ready and had decided her course. But a visit with Linda had skewed Cyd's priority of burning sex with Ewan out of her system. "I hear you talked with Paddy today and informed Marvin to watch out for him stalking me. You and Sean installed new doors and alarms at Hallie's. You've had quite a day yourself."

His thumb rubbed tiny, gentle calming circles on her temple and his other hand slowly massaged her nape. "You've got some tension cords there. Relax. . . . Do you think those two women, Mrs. Linnea and Patricia Erland, died of natural causes?"

His question surprised her. Cyd drew back to study Ewan's face. "Yes, I do. Don't you?"

"I don't know. They had the years and long-term illnesses, heart and asthma. Both of those can kill, especially if enough stress is induced. Hallie probably told you that the jewelry has been stolen. I regret the loss. I wanted her to have it." He studied Cyd's hands, resting within his. Her fingers seemed so fragile in contrast to his. "Hypnotism sometimes brings out hidden memories. Have you thought of trying it?"

"Maybe I don't want to know, Ewan. Maybe it's better left alone," she answered unevenly. Linda wasn't always coherent, the effects of past and present drugs added to a prostitute's share of torments. "And you're wrong about Paddy stalking me, looking in my window. He's not the man. It's all too easy to reason, but it isn't the truth. There *is* a Night Man, Ewan, and not just one for the tourist trade, either. I have those gnomes and fairies to prove it."

Was the man her father? Had he kept track of her through the years?

Was he a married man who couldn't reveal himself?

Did he love her?

Then—why couldn't he love her?

Ewan nodded slowly and brought her hand up to his lips. His breath warmed her palm. "This place was settled by the Irish and the Scots. Fairy tales are a part of the town, bred into us. It could be anyone who understands that lore, using it."

Cyd's free hand gripped his shirt. "You believe me then. That the Night Man is real?"

"Maybe not as a legend, but as a blood-and-bone man. The carvings could be courting gifts. That was common enough in the old days, they say. My father courted my mother by bringing her little pretty stones from the lake, a pretty piece of driftwood, a bouquet of flowers. What are they like, the gnomes and the fairies? Have you shown them to Hallie? Maybe they were bought in her shop—"

"I was eighteen when they first started arriving after his visits. I didn't want to tell anyone then. I still don't. My mother's mental illness, her dependency on drugs to remain calm, taught me that much. I didn't want people looking at me like that, and I'd had enough of pity looks. And Hallie didn't have the shop then. They couldn't have come from there."

Ewan's kiss brushed her temple. "When I left, you were a pretty thing at sixteen, very sexy."

She didn't trust his sensual tone and moved slightly away. Ewan could take control of a situation too quickly, whereas Cyd preferred the upper hand—and the choices. Standing this close, feeling both feminine and hungry for him, underlined the danger of a woman giving herself to a man.

She'd walked in to finish the last item on her frustrating day's to-do list—to finish her hunger for Ewan, to burn it out of her. An hour should do it, she'd thought as she'd carried the basket inside, or maybe less, if she was fast enough.

Then she'd be free of him. She'd return to her own keeping, safe within herself without that nudging ache that one look at Ewan could bring.

She'd know how he touched and took, and there would be no more mystery to Ewan Lochlain. He'd be like any other man . . . or would he?

Ewan folded his arms and looked down at her. "What's that getup? The black leather jacket, all black down to those boots? Not that it isn't a great look, but unusual for a top-notch, business wheeler-dealer."

"I had a lot to do today. I tried to slay a few ghosts. It didn't work."

His amused expression stilled, and bitter lines deepened around his mouth. "Slaying ghosts, or the past, isn't easy work."

"You're needing more here than the work, aren't you? You're needing to heal. But Angela will drive you out any way she can."

"No. Not until she has what she wants from me. I have enough leverage that she'll keep her claws from Hallie in case I can't make a living here."

"What do you have on her?"

He smiled coldly. "Now that would be telling, wouldn't it? What's the point of a secret if too many people know? Still, it's leverage that keeps Angela in check. It's a bargain, we have—my dear aunt and I. I like having that bit of power over her, even though I know she'll play her games. Maybe I'm as perverted as she is, enjoying the game between us. Who will win, I wonder?"

"There's more to it than that. I can understand punishing her, making her wait to see what you're going to do. But whatever you're holding disturbs you so much that you don't want to expose it—perhaps because you don't want Hallie hurt. . . . And just maybe, you have feelings for Angela, too—she's your mother's twin. It can't be easy to face her and not think of your mother."

"She's nothing like my mother."

"Sometimes the mind and heart don't agree, Ewan."

Cyd turned toward the workbench, eyeing the notebook he'd just closed. It never hurt to know figures when negotiating a business deal. "Paddy dropped a month's check in my office door slot with a note that he was 'taking a vacation.' If his check bounces once more—he's out of my rental house. I suppose you're the reason he paid early."

"We had a chat after lunch, in the privacy of the alley behind the Blue Moon . . . just to clear up any misconceptions." Ewan's arms framed her body, his hands braced on the workbench, his hard length pressed close against her.

Then with ease that sent shock through her senses, his lips bent to press against the side of her throat at the same time he slid the shoulder strap of the backpack from her. "Have dinner with me. I'll cook breakfast for you in the morning."

Cyd's defenses leaped into action, and she ducked under his arm. She snared her backpack and changed the last to-do item on her day's list—that of burning Ewan out of her mind and body. "Let me know when you're ready to talk numbers on the sale of this place."

His next question caught her midstride on her way to the door. "You never go to your old house, do you?"

Ewan's softly spoken words wrapped around her, imprisoning her. "No."

"I'll come with you, if you want. Right now. There's at least a good three or four hours of sunlight left."

"No." She couldn't move, her body cold, her mind leaping into terror—and she didn't understand why. She fought images of the grove behind the old house, where her mother's customers used to hide their cars.

"I'll help you tear it down and clean the lot as if it never existed."

Ewan was pushing, delving too deeply into images she didn't want to remember, into a darkness she'd rather bury forever. . . . She pivoted to him and fought tears that leaped from her terror of the past. "I can manage quite nicely without you, Lochlain. The only things we have between us are Hallie and a damn good business deal."

With a tilt of his head and a narrowing of those pewter-colored eyes, Ewan tied his arrogance into a verbal bow. "Is it now?"

Cyd stepped out into the early morning and inhaled the mid-May fragrances of earth and flowers. Almost seductively, the fog curled around her house and lawn, layering out onto the sidewalk. Daylight topped the shadows and the misty layers, the air cold and moist against her skin.

After almost two weeks of restless nights with Ewan's sensual challenge grating at her, Cyd had dressed quickly in jeans and a warm sweater and tied her hair in a ponytail.

Ewan's challenge—if she had visited the house that held too many bad memories—had nudged her for the last night.

She chose not to drive, to have people notice her truck, to know that she was prodding her past. For the most part, the residents of Fairy Cove were still grumping about getting up, or leaving for work. She might just be out for a walk, searching for new rental property, hunting for potentials. If they saw her, they'd yawn and pour another cup of coffee. They were used to Cyd prowling the town, ready to scoop up cheap property herself, or to massage a deal for her percentage.

Determined to meet any challenge Ewan could place before her—and needing to face her own fears, Cyd walked briskly to the end of Delaney Street and turned onto a side street. The homes weren't as well kept in this part of town, and more than one backyard had trash the city wouldn't al-

low in the front. Just past those homes and out of the city
limits was the old shack where she had lived—a place where
a prostitute could ply her trade, and behind it, a grove of
trees where "respectable" men could hide their cars.

Was the man with the emerald green eyes respectable, the
man who was Cyd's father? Or was he just another predator
who caused Linda to love him and give him a child?

Few even knew any structure existed within the overgrown yard. A high board fence sprayed with graffiti and
overgrown with trees and vines sheltered the house from the
country road. Behind the house, the grove of trees loomed
only as an indistinguishable shape in the mist.

Brush tore at Cyd's clothing and skin, just as fear pricked
her emotions. Leaves, holding the fog's dampness, brushed
against her legs. Something scurried away and rustled the
underbrush. Birds, waiting for full light and disturbed by
Cyd's passing, flew into the sky, and the rapid beat of their
wings echoed that of her heart.

Above her, sunlight was just touching the tops of the trees,
and she moved in the shadows below—just like the memories that would not come clearly to her.

What had happened to her twenty-five years ago? How
could a six-year-old girl remain frightened inside a woman's
mind? What lay trapped inside her, screaming to come out
with every nightmare?

Vines crawled over the windowless two-room shack, the
roof and porch sagging.

Who brought the carved gnomes and fairies to her
doorstep now? Who wanted to torture her?

Angela? That was possible, a snarling old dog protecting
her territory against a younger, up-and-coming.

An old customer of Linda's?

Her father? A man she'd never known? Who was he? Why
did Linda keep his name from Cyd?

Cyd rubbed her face with her trembling hands and braced

herself against the fears screaming at her, telling her to step back outside the physical barriers—and seal away her childhood.

Damp with fog and aged with mold, the house silently echoed with male grunts and primitive sounds and scents, with drunken laughter and the drowsy silence that drugs had brought.

Cyd closed her lids against the burning tears. When she forced them open, the shadow of a big man moved through the mist toward her. She opened her lips to scream—because the Night Man was real, coming for her in the dim light and shadows. . . .

# Chapter 11

"It's only me, Cyd," Ewan said softly, slowly. In the shadowy dim light, he instantly recognized Cyd's terror and stopped moving toward her. "Cyd, it's Ewan Lochlain."

Was that the sound of dew dripping from the leaves? Or was that the sound of Cyd's heart beating as fast as a bird's, trapped within a snare and almost loud enough for him to hear?

In the mist and shadows, Cyd stood frozen. Her hand covered her mouth, her eyes huge and rounded in her too-pale face. The brambles had tugged away tendrils from her ponytail, and the dim light settled upon her hair in a soft eerie glow.

Ewan wanted to go to her, to hold her.

Instead, her fear bound him still, giving her time to recognize him.

"I thought you might come here. It's like you to pick up a challenge, and I knew when I asked you about this place, that you'd be circling it. Hallie called last night. She said that you wanted to walk this morning—not something usual for you—and I guessed you'd picked your time to come here. I thought maybe you'd need someone with you." He spoke of having an early breakfast at Hallie's, of everyday things like Mrs. Mason's butter melting into the blueberry scones, of his sister's idea to produce and sell her favorite fudge recipe at the Fairy Bin.

Cyd's expression was the same as when she'd discovered him sleeping in the boat, the same silent scream of terror.

She trembled, and focused on Ewan, did not notice the man behind him. Ewan raised a hand to signal Marvin to remain still.

"It's only me, Cyd," Ewan repeated softly, and took a step closer for her to see him better, to recognize him.

"Ewan?" Her voice was only a breathless thread, barely sounding above the steady drip of water from the leaves.

"Yes," he repeated, moving closer. "It's only me, Cyd. Like you, I decided to take an early-morning walk."

She looked up at him, blinked several times as if clearing away another image, then her hand came cold and trembling to trace his face. Ewan placed his over hers, pressing it against him, giving her his warmth. He ached for what she would go through later, when she learned of the body, buried long ago in the shack's backyard.

"Ewan." Her voice was uneven, but she'd recognized him.

"And Marvin. We're here together. Cyd, I found something—it's not pleasant—and called Marvin. His car is on the other side of the grove. He's put in a call for the medical examiner. Since it's your property, you're going to be questioned, and probably Linda, too."

"My mother? Why? No one has lived here for years. What do you mean, 'a medical examiner?' What did you find?"

"I was just looking around the property, trying to figure out what would be the best place to start—in case you decided you did want to clear it. I circled the house and took a walk through that overgrown grove behind the house. I lifted an old fender and—"

"What did you find? Why is Marvin here? Why call the police? Why call the medical examiner?"

Ewan held his breath and looked at Marvin, who had come to stand beside him. Then he looked back at Cyd, who was gripping his hand tightly. "A skeleton, Cyd. It's been there a good long time."

By early afternoon, the medical examiner's informal report stated that the skeleton was that of a tall man. John Doe had likely been killed and buried twenty-five years earlier. Erosion had caused a tree to topple, and when the roots were exposed, so was the skeleton. Nature had allowed the body to be exposed from what probably had been a three-foot-deep gravesite. An obvious deep crack in the back of the skull would have come from a blow and had probably been enough to kill the man. The facial bones had been destroyed, or carried away by animals and, though missing teeth, the man had had no identifying dental work.

Twenty-five years ago, Cyd would have only been six. The connection was too strong, the nightmares and the timing of the man's death, but Cyd couldn't remember the details. She couldn't provide the details of a child's memory, rather the nightmares that aligned with this man's violent death—the blood that would have been everywhere—the blood she remembered on her own small hands. . . . *Who was he?*

Stunned, Cyd could do little more than answer necessary questions in Marvin's office. One investigator interviewed her and took notes. At times, Ewan spoke quietly at her side, and his hand was wrapped warm and safe around her cold one. The medical examiner's van was parked by the grove. A team of men working the crime scene were tramping all over the area, picking at anything, taking pictures and videotaping.

Cyd had answered the primary investigator's questions. Yes, she'd purchased the property when she was just twenty.

The investigator pushed her for answers—Why buy a worthless piece of property outside the city limits? The house was in a bad state then, overgrown by brush, but somehow it held a part of her life that belonged to no one else.

Did she know anyone who might have been killed?

Did she know why . . . ? Why? . . .

Cyd couldn't explain the most obvious question—Why hadn't she done anything with the property when she was in the business of real estate and remodeling to resell or rent houses?

How could she explain what she didn't understand—that somehow the house had to stand, untouched, until she could deal with her own past?

At six o'clock that evening Cyd, Ewan, Marvin, and an investigator were in Linda Callahan's room.

Because Cyd was her mother's guardian and, if she admitted the truth, because she really did love Linda, Cyd sat near her at the interview. The retirement residence was expensive and conservatively managed, and provided the best health care for patients either too elderly to care for themselves or who could be gently managed, such as Linda.

A nurse hovered nearby, concerned that her patient would be overly distressed by the investigator's questions. "Linda," Marvin asked gently, "do you have any idea who the man might be?"

Though the questions were handled delicately, Linda's slight grasp on reality suddenly dimmed. As if frozen in another time, she closed her thin lips and stared out of the window, her expression blank. She began humming a waltz, so softly it could barely be heard.

Cyd sensed that Ewan was comparing her mother's face to hers. Physically, they were similar, but there the resemblance stopped. Emotionally, they were night and day—because Cyd was never letting a man use her. Long ago, she had promised to be her own person, to have the money to live as she wished.

Linda Callahan had been readily available to men, and whatever she might have been as a woman—she was now a pale, thin, empty shell, staring sightlessly out to the manicured lawn. She hummed that endless waltz as if she clung to it, as if it kept her thin line of sanity anchored and safe.

"She does that—sealing me away—when she doesn't want to remember. When something really bothers her. I pushed her really hard two weeks ago, probably too hard, because I wanted—I wanted my father's identity. She started that song then, too," Cyd stated softly and took her mother's cold hand. The bony fingers wrapped tightly around Cyd's. Linda's eyes darted to Cyd, and for a heartbeat fear mixed with what Cyd tried to imagine as a mother's love. She adjusted the warm blue shawl around Linda's lap and legs.

Then suddenly, as quickly as Linda's mind leaped from reality into other times in her life, she turned to Ewan. "You!" she hissed, her bony hands curling into fists. Her eyes were bright blue and vivid with violence that shook her thin body. "You! How I hate you."

The nurse moved forward, a prepared needle ready for use. "She does that sometimes. Usually it's a man. We don't know why. She's never hurt anyone. If she did, she'd have to be placed somewhere else."

Then just as quickly, Linda's expression cleared, and she stared, eyes devoid of all expression, at Cyd.

"Who are you?" Linda asked her daughter.

They'd finally found the body.

The Other sweated as he fought the pain, waiting for the pills he had just taken to slide into his system. How much time did he have left? Enough to make her suffer? Enough to kill her?

After twenty-five years, Linda Callahan's feeble mind

could not recall the truths of what had really happened. But he knew everything.

Or perhaps Linda knew, and knew what could happen to her daughter if she went to the police.

Sweet Molly Claire. . . . Yes, Linda would protect the girl with the red hair like hers.

Sweet Molly Claire, who had always been his and soon she would know to whom she belonged. . . .

An unexpected jab of pain in his belly almost doubled him. In the alley, he gripped a window ledge until his hand ached, and his forehead was wet with sweat. He waited for the pain to pass, concentrating on how he would kill again. How he would enjoy the fear in her eyes—

The early mid-May evening was damp and heavy, the waves sounding on the beach as he leaned against the alley's bricks. He watched the city's patrol car glide by on Main Street. Upset and gossiping about the skeleton, Fairy Cove's residents were staying in tonight. Marvin Kendrick was at his office, dealing with investigators.

He leaned against the alley wall, beneath Hallie's kitchen window, and strained to hear voices within the apartment. Hallie and Cyd were talking quietly, the words indistinct and blending with the sound of a television program.

His pain lessening, the man moved silently, sliding through the shadows. He moved from Hallie's alley, to a lot covered with weeds, then an overgrown path that led to Cyd's backyard.

The man hurried to Cyd's back porch, to the door with all the electronic locks and dead bolts. He rapidly punched in the access code for the locks and slid his key into the dead bolt.

Excitement raced through him. Cyd never left her home overnight—only on rare occasions did she stay at Hallie's apartment—and when she did, he prized his brief time in her home, prowling through her life.

Once inside, he moved through the familiar shadows, inspecting how Cyd lived, her sewing machine, her desk, then her bedroom.

The room was very feminine. With a tight smile, the Other noted the absence of masculine influence. Cyd was too smart to get tangled with any man—it would take a special man for her to leave her safe moorings.

"Good girl," he said, and walked into the kitchen, noting the fat fairy godmother cookie jar. He lifted the lid and peered inside, taking one of Hallie's cookies. Strolling back to the tiny living room, he settled into the big wide chair Cyd had reupholstered.

He ate the cookie leisurely and imagined himself living here, with sweet Molly Claire.

Curiosity pushing him, the Other stood to open the drawer that held the tiny perfect carvings. He selected an ugly gnome, studying it. "She used to love dolls. Does she touch you? Hold you?"

How odd, he thought, that Cyd didn't display her excellent collection of fairies and gnomes, but kept them private. They seemed to wait for their moment—

As he had always waited. . . .

But then he knew about privacy and the dark secrets that ran through Fairy Cove's streets. At night, secrets slid through the house's open windows and to his listening ears. He held them like treasures, waiting, always waiting to use them.

And then because time ran short and Cyd could return soon, the man replaced the gnome, reset the locks, and eased into the night.

He needed to rest, to save his strength to kill again and soon, finishing his very private revenge . . . before he died.

"I've got to go home," Cyd stated unevenly as she stood up from Hallie's dinner table. She glanced outside, clearly uneasy. "It's night already. It seems like a hundred years since

this morning. They'll have more questions in the morning—
I didn't know there were so many questions. . . ."

Hallie looked at Ewan, who nodded and rose to his feet.
"Let's stop by my place first, Cyd."

"Why?"

He ached for Cyd, for the confusion and pain she couldn't
explain. "To pick up my shaving kit and a few necessaries.
I've got to secure the boat shop against prowlers. There are
things I have to put away—that pretty little laptop. I'm staying the night with you."

Cyd's slender hand rose to rub her forehead and she
gripped the back of a chair for support. "I can't deal with
you now, Lochlain. Pick another day."

Hallie rose to hold Cyd close. "You'll stay here, with me,
then. I'd like that . . . for the company."

There were no secrets between the friends, and Cyd held
Hallie close. "I have nightmares, Hallie. They'll be worse
tonight—I can tell. I feel them coming sometimes after visiting Linda. I can't do that to you. I won't."

"My brother, then. It's one or the other of us. You're stuck
with a Lochlain tonight."

"Damn. I know that tone. You're set to have your way."
Then with typical brass, Cyd flashed Ewan a nettled look.
"If you're going to be around, you'd better stay out of my
way."

In the boat shop, Cyd stood with her arms crossed, staring
out into the night as Ewan moved around the tools at the
workbench. She turned to find him crouching in front of it,
his hand on a floorboard. "Loose," he explained briefly. "I'll
have to fix that."

Cyd turned back to the lake's rolling swells. She felt safe
with Ewan, and the thought that she needed him close tonight nettled. "There's a boat motoring out to Three Ravens
Island."

He stood and came near her, angling his head close to hers

to see the tiny white trail across the black water. "I've noticed that once or twice since I've been here. Lovers, maybe? Sean returning after checking on his son? Peter, the old hermit?"

"Peter does make the trip sometimes still. He's a poor old thing, his clothing in tatters. Sean has a couple of honeymooners now and then, but it's too early in the season, and they'd be tucked in bed by now. It's probably only a fisherman who stayed too late at the Blue Moon and needs to hurry home to his wife. . . ."

Cyd rubbed her cold hands together. "People are looking at me and whispering. I can't take any more today, Ewan. I can't. Twenty-five years ago, I would have been six, and that is when something happened to me. I remember my mother giving me drugs that made me sleep. I didn't want them, but she said it would calm me."

She shook her head to dislodge her mother's whisper, the look of fear and tenderness that sometimes filled Linda's blue eyes. "That skeleton could be why I have nightmares. Maybe the man in them is the dead man. Maybe it's his blood I see on my hands—from the wound. They say that there would have been a lot of blood."

Desperately tired, her mind tried to find reason in the day's findings. "He's not my father. I know he's not. I know that my father is still alive. I feel it. At times, I feel other things—like I'm being watched. I . . . try not to give in to my senses prickling, those little chills. I don't want to—become like my mother."

She rubbed her hands briskly, but the chill remained. "I don't know who my father is, and I don't know the man who looks in my windows, who leaves those fairies—"

After years of desperation, hope leaped within her. She hurried to kindle it. "Maybe you're right—that someone interested in me is giving me the gnomes as a courting gift—yes, that would be right, maybe a married man who strayed. That happens sometimes. I can deal with that. Then the

Night Man, the one that I know, not the tourist legend, is really a man, a window peeper who's really harmless and not dangerous at all—"

She gripped Ewan's hand and asked huskily, "Could it be that he's my father?"

"Cyd . . ." Ewan couldn't help her, but he understood her lifelong insecurities about her unknown father.

She turned suddenly and burrowed into Ewan's shoulder, gripping him tightly. Against that strong shoulder, the warmth of his throat, she freed her tears. After hours of moving through the investigation in a state of disbelief, almost numb to her own emotions—or perhaps what the little girl inside her knew was too terrifying to release, she simply rested against Ewan. "I don't think I can go anywhere. I can't move another step. I want you to hold me tonight, Ewan . . . and hold me tight when the nightmares come . . . stay with me."

The safety of her locks and shutters gave way to the need to have Ewan near, to feel his warmth and safety, to hear his voice. She trusted him on one level, that of understanding her fears and not mocking her. He was still the Ewan who held her as a child, who gave her more comfort than anyone, except Tom Lochlain. She leaned back, shaking in his arms and tried a brave smile. "I'm not asking for sex, Ewan. Just the safety that you give me. In my house, alone, I'll—I don't know what I'll do, and I'm not taking pills to sleep. If you laugh, I'll quite simply—"

He frowned slightly, and placed his hand along her cheek. "Did you think I'd laugh, when you need me? I know what comfort can be, Cyd. I can give you what you need tonight."

"Just don't talk any more about—it," she whispered, and once more held him tight. "Damn."

"You really should stop cursing, Cyd," he whispered, and she clung to the humor in his tone, anything but the horrible day that had just passed.

But Ewan stood strong and warm and safe against her. His

arms held her tightly, and for a time, she gave herself to the rocking of his body, the humming of the old familiar Irish and Scots songs against her cheek, effectively locking everything else away. . . .

In her study above Fairy Cove, Angela replaced the telephone in its cradle. Her informant would receive a reward. The birdlike store clerk would do anything to gain favor and a better position—and her rented room above a shop on Main Street was perfect for spying.

Angela looked into the night, and the window threw her reflection back at her. For a heartbeat, as always, she thought she saw her identical twin Mary, and a shiver ran through her before she focused back on the hatred that always drove her. "So the witch has taken my nephew to her bed, has she? But then, what could anyone expect from Linda Callahan's daughter?"

Perhaps Cyd could be tied to a murder, or had witnessed a murder and Linda Callahan—the possibilities of what she could do to the women stormed into Angela's mind. Gossip sometimes could be used to twist the truth—just that bit, for Angela's revenge. There were secrets brewing in her town, and she needed to know what they were. "I wonder who took the brooch I gave Bertha and the cross I gave to Patricia? With Ewan recognizing his mother's jewelry, it won't do to hand him more ammunition."

Ewan was toying with her, making her squirm; Angela understood that well enough. Later, when he was finished with his play, and if he could, he'd tear apart everything she'd built.

Angela sensed that Ewan didn't want reimbursement of the funds she had misused, and she wouldn't lower herself by asking that direct question. This wasn't about money and legalities— His need ran deeper, to twisting the screws of his revenge.

"Takes one to know one," Angela whispered. Panic raced through her. She couldn't bear to lose her influential position in Fairy Cove, in her different charities and clubs. She couldn't bear for the state and national political candidates who had been helped by her fund-raisers toss her away—but they would, because gossip and implications of fraud could stain their careers. What if no one came to her tea or holiday parties and balls? And the guests of honor—they'd turn her down, preserving their own reputations. . . .

She'd worked too hard to elevate herself. The slightest whisper of gossip could cause her to be blackballed from the elegant societies she'd fought to join—

Angela felt the elegant, powerful world she'd built slipping away from her. *She'd be no one again.*

She almost feared Ewan. Almost. With a predator's sense of danger, Angela knew that she needed answers. She called shrilly, "Fred? Fred, come in here."

"Yes, Angela dear?" Fred came into the room, his glasses catching the dim light.

What a weak man Fred was, Angela thought, hating him even as she needed his expert services. "Fred, what do you know about the medical examiner's van recovering a body from the old Callahan place?"

"It's a skeleton, Angela. No one knows who the man—"

"I've already heard that it was a man, Fred. I always know what's going on in Fairy Cove. I know that the investigating team is asking questions about a man missing twenty-five years ago and asking people to come forward. They're questioning people now. Cyd has already been questioned, and her mother. Is there anything more?"

"People are upset. The whole town is talking about the discovery and wondering who the man could have been. The investigating team is headquartered at Marvin's office and still working tonight. They have rooms at the motel, but no one knows how long they are staying. That's all at this point."

"You'll keep on this, of course." She attempted a winning

smile that sometimes gave Fred just that remembrance of Mary, her twin. He always worked better when reminded of Mary's timid soul—but if he could be duped, it wasn't Angela's problem. "Any word of where the brooch and cross might be, Fred, dear?"

"No one has seen them, dear."

"I have to have them. You know, of course, that Cyd and Ewan are an item. They're in bed together now."

She waited, hungered for the shock on Fred's face, to surprise him out of his complacent, dull shell.

Instead, he said, "I thought that might happen. There are bets on it in town. Is there anything else you needed, my dear? I've still got accounts to go over."

"No, but any news you have, Fred, you'll pass on to me, won't you?"

Alone again, Angela started to twist the little ring that reminded her of Tom Lochlain and how he should have been hers.

Her barren finger reminded her of Ewan and how she had to remove him from Fairy Cove.

Angela's eyes narrowed as she noted that the lights had gone out in the boat shop. Fury burned her as it had years ago, and she hissed, "He's sleeping with her. Tom is sleeping with her and not me."

She'd used Tom's name, and not Ewan's, the thoughts and the words twisting, echoing in the shadows. Angela blinked, surprised that the years had leaped away in her mind, to when she was young and craved Tom Lochlain more than she craved status. Other than the ring that she had kept, Mary's pitiful jewelry had gone to three women—Bertha Linnea, Patricia Erland, and Thelma Brit.

Where were the brooch and the cross? Careful inquiries had brought Angela nothing. As the executrix for the wills of Bertha and Patricia, she kept a detailed list of their belong-ings, and the jewelry hadn't been included in the inventories.

Angela had to have the missing jewelry. She wanted to recover anything that might point a suspicious finger at her. Ewan was no fool; he already had incriminating evidence that she had misused her authority as executrix of his parents' pitiful estate.

On impulse, Angela called Thelma Brit, who suffered from sleep apnea. The whir of the machine that kept Thelma breathing when her natural processes failed, sounded briefly on the line before Thelma answered. "Yes?"

Angela paced her questions carefully, until she asked the one that mattered, "Dear, would you please return the locket that I gave you years ago? Fred has just reminded me that it was a gift from him when we were first married, and he's distressed that I'd given it away. I should have remembered, but we do forget, you know. I'll be happy to replace it with a new one, a better one."

"No. I've promised it to my son. Danny says it's unique, not like today's stuff."

After the call ended on a frosty note, Angela whispered, "Oh, you'll give it back. One way or another, you empty-headed twit."

She turned back to view the boat shop. The building and pier leading to it should have been burned years ago. But it was a cheap payoff for Paddy, and she'd needed his services now and then. Since Finlay couldn't make it thrive, the shop had posed no danger. But Ewan, settling in to stay, was a different matter.

The young pup dared to challenge her, did he?

Did she fear him, that one day he would come after her, that thunderous fury in his hard face?

The uneasy answer slid across her lips—"Yes. . . ."

Angela mentally prowled around the identity of the skeleton. Paddy might know—perhaps he had played a part in it.

Paddy, who needed to be more careful with the notes she'd given him, little directives that were too physical for Fred to accomplish.

Paddy's drinking and brawls had taken their toll, and at times he grimaced with pain. "It's nothing, only a bad meal. It will go away," he'd said. But she'd seen his stark pain too often—he'd chosen drink over life, but all she needed of him was just a little more—

Angela could feel someone waiting to hurt her. Hatred seemed to be palpable, prodding her senses, chilling her skin. . . .

Not sweet forgiving Hallie . . . not Ewan, because he'd never hurt a woman, even in revenge. . . . It had to be Cyd!

In the past months, Cyd Callahan had let her hatred boldly throb out of her, and it had grated at Angela's senses. The young witch was coming after her. . . . With her hand on her throat, Angela backed into the shadows, fighting panic.

Angela shivered and pushed back her fear. The body had made her uneasy, a reminder of how she'd turned Linda Callahan to drugs and desperation. The past had stirred secrets in Fairy Cove, and she knew that someone, something wanted revenge. Ewan? Definitely. Cyd, positively.

Angela had to contact Paddy. He could deal with Cyd, and maybe his match was overdue to burn down the boat shop. "Strike and strike first, I always say. If Ewan wants to play games, then we shall. And that witch may be younger, but she's met her match in me. We've circled each other long enough."

"This is childish. I could go home. I *should* go home," Cyd whispered sleepily in the shadows of Ewan's bed.

"Do you want to?" Ewan lay stretched on the opposite side of the bed from Cyd. The sweatshirt and pants she'd borrowed only made her seem more feminine. And her scent, a touch of flowers and spice, had stirred him into a tight sensual knot.

Moonlight skimmed across the water. It slid through the bare window facing the lake and danced a mottled design across the ceiling of his one-room apartment.

Ewan had placed his hands behind his head to keep them from Cyd. "I thought we settled that. You shouldn't be alone. Today was too hard on you, and you're not taking something to sleep—you need to sleep, Cyd. You were riding on an edge earlier, though now you've relaxed. Hallie would have my scalp if I took you home and left you, and it's too late to wake her. She got up even earlier than me to work on her new fudge recipe. . . . I didn't realize Linda was in such a state. . . . I asked you if you want to go home now. I'll go with you."

"No. I don't want to move. My mother has been that way for years . . . the result of drugs mostly and alcohol. But there are times when she just closes people away and hums that same waltz, like today. She's not likely to recall the names of her customers—or the name of the man you found, even if they do somehow identity him. I'm never going to forget those bones, strewn by animals," she whispered. "I don't want to go to sleep. That's when I remember her starting to drink heavily—when I was six. Maybe that's linked to the dead man. She's not talking, and I can't remember. . . . You're still wearing your jeans."

"I'm modest," he lied. Intimate talk with Cyd's warm, long curved body on his bed had spiked his need of her. But Ewan had promised himself to be noble, giving comfort; she'd been through so much.

Cyd's drowsy tone, her scent, and the sight of her tousled hair, free upon his pillow, silky soft curls that he could almost feel against his skin—

"Sure. Tell another one." Cyd turned to her side and raised up on one elbow to look at him. "You're upset, too. Why?"

The need to make love to Cyd hummed in him, that was why.

"It's not every day I find a skeleton and then terrify a woman when I walk toward her." That image had nudged his mind throughout the long, hard day.

He could almost hear Cyd's brain working, churning the events of the day and struggling for her priorities, for her survival.

Cyd's switch to business prodding was a safe mode for her and predictable. "You know you should sell to Mc-Gruder's. You're just being difficult."

Ewan smiled briefly. It was in Cyd's nature to push for what she wanted.

"I'm just waiting for you to settle down to sleep, then I'm moving—"

Cyd suddenly sat up. "Let's take that skiff you're working on out now. The lake is calm enough, isn't it?"

"It is. But the boat isn't near ready, and neither am I."

"You used to take me out on the lake."

He snorted at the memory of an older boy, stuck with a younger sister and an unwanted tagalong girl. Yet he had taken them when he could, because they both had needed him.

He caught Cyd's feminine scent as she moved, and his senses stirred. Cyd was in his bed.

There had been other beds and other women. But none of them had been *his* bed, and the taking of this woman would go deeper than the physical jolt. His life was already tangled enough—

He just might crave her after one taste. . . . "Let's go. I'll walk you home, if that's what you want."

Cyd lay back down again, her hair flowing across the white pillow. "I think you're right. I need to work off what happened today. Thanks to my mother's preferences, I'm careful how I work off tension. I have an exercise set under my bed. One of those foldaway things."

Ewan didn't want to think of Cyd's bed, that feminine ruffles-and-pillow affair he'd noted through an open doorway. He sat up, his bare back to her. Cyd could be as unpredictable as the wind—and he didn't trust himself.

Behind him, the bed creaked and shifted as if Cyd had stood.

"Ready to go now, Cyd?" he asked, his body throbbing, his mind filled with the image of Cyd straining, working out—"You could use a bit of tension release. It will help you sleep. I don't have any exercise equipment here."

Her breasts, warm and soft and tipped with buds, etched against his back. "I'm staying. I'll work off my tension here."

He stiffened and placed his hands over the soft ones prowling his chest. "No."

Her teeth nipped the side of his throat, and the hard flesh of his body tightened instantly. "No?"

"Just what do you think you're doing?" he asked roughly, as her fingers slid across his belly and down to unsnap his jeans.

"I had a goal the other day—when I visited Linda, trying to get her to name my father," Cyd whispered as she nipped his shoulder. "I thought I'd finish everything that bothered me in one day, the day you said I'd been crying. But after visiting her, I couldn't finish my plans. . . . You've been on my uncompleted to-do list for almost two weeks. I usually take care of matters right away."

"Change your to-do list. I'm not taking advantage of you. Not tonight."

Her hand smoothed the evidence of his need, held tight within the confines of his jeans. "Give in, Lochlain. You're hard as a rock and shaking. I know what I'm doing. Stop trying to be noble."

Only Cyd could reach into his light grasp on nobility and honor and tear them into shreds. That nettled—that she could circle his control and sense his weakness. "So you'd rather have all the bad stuff over in one day, would you?

Stop playing games, Cyd. I could be that one wrong man, remember? And just maybe I'm not easy."

"Maybe you are. I don't have a stitch of clothes on, Ewan.
I'm naked. Think about that." Her breasts nudged his back,
and Ewan, despite his intentions, rubbed back against her.

He'd thought he was past shocking. Yet Cyd had zeroed in
on a streak of protective gallantry that he thought he'd lost
long ago. "Damn, Cyd. Women don't just come after men
like that. There are rules."

"I'm playing. Are you?"

Ewan could refuse.

People had sex all the time, Cyd told herself, arguing with
her defenses that no man had penetrated. It was merely a
way to pass the time until morning and another grueling day.
Merely a way to take the edge off tension . . . exercise, if she
thought of having sex with Ewan that way.

She had a minor problem, since she'd never had sex before, but then she'd always been a fast learner.

When Cyd was a teenager, she'd asked her mother how she
managed to take man after man to her bed—and feel nothing.
Linda had spared her daughter nothing. "How do I do it? It's
mechanical. There's no feeling. You do what they need, but
keep yourself apart. There's no emotion in it. You keep yourself safe inside your heart. Then they're done and gone."

Cyd knew the mechanics of sex. She wasn't letting Ewan
into that safe center of her. Her hunter's instincts rose, a
challenge before her, and maybe something more. Ewan's
resistance only fired Cyd's need to challenge him and to win,
to have her way.

Ewan Lochlain had been ruthless when he'd taken her
first kiss, branding her. Now she intended to leave him with
a memory he wouldn't soon forget.

Cyd lined up the facts: She had never seduced a man, but
the past day had been unusual and terrifying. It called for

drastic action—for the reality of fire and emotion that she knew simmered within Ewan.

She needed to pit herself against something, and, at the moment, it was Ewan. She'd tasted his hunger, had seen it in his eyes, had felt it in his body, that ripple of raw heat and power that said he was a man, needing a woman.

If he refused—

Then Ewan turned and caught her hair with his fist—not painfully, but in a way that told her that she had him.

She had him. She'd set the snare, and he was hers. She needed to claim Ewan Lochlain tonight, to make him hers—because everything else in her life was surreal and unknown and shaking.

She'd wanted him since forever, and now she would have him, burn him from her dreams. . . .

Ewan was bending over her now, a sexually experienced man who knew how to handle a woman's body. Above her, his face was honed and savage, his eyes like silver, flowing down her body. His free hand skimmed over her, heating as it passed.

"You want me," she whispered unevenly. The physical mechanics were there, that hard prod against her thigh. Mechanics, Cyd thought, not emotional bond. . . . She wasn't letting Ewan into the safe center of her heart and soul—she'd keep that for herself. . . .

"Yes." The answer came as a raw, reluctant growl.

"Then?"

"Then this—"

She met his lips with her own, tasted the fire between them, flowed beneath him as he stripped away his clothing.

Held tight against Ewan, Cyd sighed, because this was what she wanted, to be claimed and to claim, to burn away everything else. His raw breath stirred her own, his mouth moving upon her flesh—surprising her with the flick of his tongue.

She dug in to hold him, because he wasn't getting away. Ewan was hers for now, one true thing in her life that she trusted on a level she trusted nothing else. In a storm of hunger, he matched her perfectly—no easy gentleman, but one who knew what he wanted, what she wanted.

Ewan came bold and hot and full to where she waited and softened and ached. His fingers stroked her, slid inside to take her higher, and then he began to fill her.

Arched above her, muscled arms shaking as he braced himself away, Ewan stopped. She caught her breath at the gentle bump within her and he eased back slightly. He scowled down at her, his shoulders bunched and tense, his thighs quivering inside the cradle of hers. His voice, when it came, sounded strangled and raw. "Cyd . . . you're a virgin."

She locked her legs tighter around him, sank her nails into his muscled, taut buttocks. "You're not going anywhere, Lochlain. Not now. I've got you."

"This is no game, Cyd. Once it's gone— You picked a fine time to— Cyd, you should tell a man things like that," he rasped unevenly.

"Are you going to lecture me on what good girls do or don't now? You did that years ago. What's the matter, Ewan? Haven't you had a virgin before?" She was desperate for him, hurting a bit, but she was also frustrated and losing her temper.

"No. Of course not," he stated bluntly, indignantly.

Cyd couldn't help smiling. Ewan, uncertain and locked in desire was just too perfect for the taking. "I suppose I'll have to go easy with you then."

"You wouldn't know how."

"I learn fast."

When Ewan hesitated, Cyd sensed him withdrawing, struggling against his desire. Ignoring the slight pain within her, Cyd raised her hips suddenly and brought Ewan home.

His desperate sound, the way his body shook told her he

was still fighting, and Cyd played to win. Her body trembled, and she accepted that first times usually caused a woman's body to react like that.

She hadn't expected the excitement, the startling waves of emotion hitting her. . . .

"Is this the best you've got?" she whispered unevenly, shielding her uncertainty and the slight pain.

She wasn't prepared for the tender smile, for the way Ewan stroked the damp hair from her face, for the way he lowered his lips to kiss her gently. Then with slow magic, he completed the lock, resting upon her lightly.

Cyd lay quietly, rocked by emotions. There was more than a physical tangle of bodies and limbs. Ewan was sharing a part of him that had to do with caring, controlling his body, being very careful to wait for her. He wasn't using her, rushing on with his own needs; rather, he moved slowly. Cyd floated amid those light, teasing kisses, the gentling stroke and caress of his open hands. She gave her body to those safe open hands, her lips and mouth to his, and let herself flow—

The first time the riveting jolt came, Cyd wasn't expecting it, nor constrictions of her body, the pulsing of Ewan's body becoming hers. Hers. She'd come so far to meet Ewan here, like this, through years of sparring with him and with herself, and now—

When the gentle storm slowed, Ewan lay still upon her, braced away slightly, his hands stroking her, his heart slowing as she held him.

Cyd felt as if she'd relaxed for the first time in her life. Was that tenderness she felt, flowing warmly, gently through her mind? Whatever the emotion, it gave her peace—and a unique sense that she'd given Ewan more than sexual pleasure. That he'd come needing her for more than her body— And as a woman, she had comforted that unspoken need.

She smiled against his hair and slid off into sleep with the thought that she'd captured Ewan for this time, when she needed to be close and safe.

She sank into the first peace in a very long time—Ewan resting against her, as if he'd found his harbor after years of hard storms. . . .

Cyd turned on her side with a sigh and let herself slide softly into oblivion.

But not before she felt Ewan spoon against her back and gather her closer. His big rough hand stroked her hip and her thigh and rose to cup her breast. It skimmed downward slowly, his fingers spreading upon her thigh.

Cyd smiled softly. She could handle Ewan Lochlain.

When his fingers dug in slightly, she frowned, uneasy with the possessive gesture, the claiming. "Asleep, are you, darling-mine?" he whispered huskily against her ear, then nibbled a bit on the lobe.

With a faked sigh, Cyd pretended to sleep.

But that wasn't going to be with Ewan's hands and lips prowling on her skin.

"Yes, I'm asleep," she whispered desperately, as Ewan turned her to her back and began kissing her.

"Later . . ." This time, Ewan was even more gentle, their lovemaking almost dreamy and soft and sweet.

He held her close later, soothed her with his hands, and hummed a forgotten lullaby.

"I could kill you. I didn't want it that way, not so—so tender," she whispered unevenly as her tears slid down her cheek. He'd taken a part of her, not just her body. Cyd had felt as if she were a flower, opening her petals, slowly, beautifully to the sun. Emotions, she thought, damned silly emotions that she'd promised she wouldn't have, separating her body from her safe place— Ewan had reached into her most private heart, a place so scarred it would never be touched.

He nuzzled her hair and kissed her forehead. "Shh. Go to sleep. You've definitely put in a very full day."

"You won't blow this out of proportion, will you?" she heard herself ask drowsily, still fighting to keep sexual pleasure from that inner safety she'd fought a lifetime to protect. "I wanted you. I took you, and that's about the sum total. . . ."

Ewan's arms around her tightened. His fingers stopped caressing her shoulder. His leg, rough against her thigh, flexed just that bit. "Wouldn't think of it. Go to sleep."

The pain had eased slightly, enough for the Other to slide into his lonely, narrow bed for a few hours' rest—something he rarely gave himself now, driven by revenge before he died.

He raised the soft curl of Molly Claire's hair to his face, stroking it against his skin.

No one would believe that Ewan Lochlain had simply found the brooch and the cross in his shop. If he had reported the dead women's jewelry, rumors would be flying of how Ewan was out for revenge, and he was too smart to let that happen.

With the discovery of the body, Fairy Cove was unsteady, humming with gossip, searching for reasons and testing the past.

But the man was too clever to get caught and only had a few months to complete his revenge, to complete the circle. . . .

She'd destroyed his life, and she would pay. She'd taken what he loved dearly and his manhood.

He enjoyed punishing her, watching her fear what she didn't understand.

She would understand soon enough, because she would die, and soon. He couldn't leave her alive as he went to his grave.

He settled into sleep with a slight smile. He still had time to play with her fear—before the disease couldn't be controlled by the pills in his pocket, before his pain demanded his own death. . . .

# Chapter 12

Ewan stared down at the mussed bed, the tiny bloodstain that marked his taking of Cyd's virginity. With dawn lightening the sky, he'd left her sleeping soundly. But while he'd showered, Cyd had left.

He scrubbed his hands over his face and tried to align the earthshaking facts.

He was now in the unsteady position of a man who had taken a woman's virginity. Ewan had thought—no, he'd known—that Cyd had had lovers. She had that knowing look, the slant of her eyes, the sensual way she moved. . . .

But then, she'd been shown by a mother who'd known an army of men.

And it was likely that Cyd had promised she wouldn't become like Linda, that she'd keep her body and her heart for herself. *I thought I'd finish everything that bothered me in one day. You're on my uncompleted to-do list.*

"On her to-do list, was I? Just a little something to ease her tension, like whatever equipment she keeps beneath her bed?"

Ewan's gut squeezed as he remembered the barrier that he had met inside her. He heard the echo of her slight cry. He felt again the shock of her body, and the warm slick tight depths of her. . . .

She hadn't known how to move against him; he'd had to gently tutor her, no easy task to move slowly when his need for her ran so high.

When he would have withdrawn, she initiated the thrust that took him fully into her. . . .

Cyd Callahan was a virgin and he'd taken her twice—the second time to give her a woman's due, the sweet tenderness of caresses and kisses—and she'd cried. . . .

Ewan cursed beneath his breath. He wasn't prepared for the emotions disturbing him, the waves of tenderness mixed with frustration and guilt. Cyd was his first virgin, and the primitive sense to claim her again seemed to roar through him.

He'd never wanted to possess a woman, to put his mark on her so deeply that she'd never forget—

Last night, he'd felt that primitive urge, to mark this one woman as his own.

Ewan shoved his fingers through his hair and shook his head. But when he closed his eyes, he saw Cyd in his bed—sleeping deeply, curled like a child, dark circles beneath her eyes, her face too pale amid that froth of red curls. . . .

"On her to-do list," he repeated darkly, his temper brewing.

This was his bed. Not some rented room, or a beach, or the woman's bed . . . but his bed, in his first home. That should amount to some obligation, some tie Cyd couldn't dismiss easily as she went on with her life, and probably sex, without him.

Ewan placed his hands on his hips and stared out to the lake beyond the windows and cursed. "It's a black day for you, boyo," he murmured aloud. "You're feeling like a virgin yourself, and you're shaky on what to do about it."

Damn it, she'd cried, the tears dampening his chest. Not a sniff or a sob, just the warm plop of teardrops hitting his skin. It was true then, what his father had said long ago—

that the silent weeping of a woman could make a strong, fit man feel helpless and weak and ineffective.

Ewan dressed quickly. Cyd was no sweetheart, and she'd gotten to him. If he let her, she'd unman him.

She'd left him feeling as if he'd dropped the protocol ball for virgin taking. Where was his morning-after? She'd left him nothing. He'd wanted to—do the gentler things a woman should have after her first time.

Ewan had to find her. Cyd wasn't leaving him to feel guilty and helpless . . . and deserted, and vulnerable. He wasn't the guilty party. Cyd had started, initiated lovemaking with him, and pushed him when he could have stopped . . . withdrawn—

What if she needed him now? What if she was trying to untangle yesterday's discovery by herself?

What right did she have to leave his bed before they settled what had bloomed, sweet and tender and hot, between them?

"My brother seems in a bad mood for some reason," Hallie stated as she straightened a garden fairy who'd come to rest too close to the edge of a glass shelf.

Cyd pretended not to notice the male who had just stepped into the shop and stopped the tinkling of the bell with his upraised hand.

She'd faked sleeping as Ewan left the bed, then hurried to her home. She hadn't answered the telephone, letting the answering machine record Ewan's voice, "I'm coming over. You'd better be there."

In a heartbeat, she was dressed and hurrying to the post office, walking quickly up and around the faster route Ewan was certain to take. Cyd didn't want to face Ewan, not the morning after he'd made the discovery that she wasn't a worldly woman. Not the morning after she'd discovered that there was more to sexual pleasure than the body's needs.

The wash of tender emotions as their bodies met had shocked her—the give-and-take, the gentling she'd given and received after—she hadn't wanted that, not that. . . .

She hadn't known what to do, how to face Ewan with all that churning inside her, the newness of emotions she hadn't wanted. . . .

But now, there he stood, unmovable, his legs braced as if for a fight, a big flower bouquet in one hand and a scowl on his face. "You're a hard one to catch, darling-mine."

To Hallie, he nodded and began to make his way to Cyd, his eyes locked upon her. "Cyd had a bit of a bad day yesterday—that unexpected skeleton, you know. A bad session with Linda followed to top it off, then she showed her lack of sensitivity—to me—and she has some explaining to do. You might not want to be here for the bloody war."

Hallie's eyes widened, looking from Ewan to Cyd and back again. "I'll be right back. I've forgotten something in the kitchen."

"I'll go with you—" Cyd began, already in motion and fearful of this determined Ewan.

Ewan wrapped an arm around her and tugged her close. "Stay, dear heart. My sister can manage on her own."

While Cyd swallowed that last bite of blueberry scone, Hallie left the room. Ewan held her tight against him, and that quiver of last night's sensuality leaped into a full blast of heat. He leaned to lick a crumb from her lips, and, with his hand on her hip, his desire pushed solidly against her, he smiled.

It was a wolfish, angry show of teeth. Then the words came fierce and low, lifting the hair on Cyd's nape. "So you had me—in my bed—and ran away before I could make breakfast and serve it to you. You pitched the morning-after protocol in the trash. That's unfair, and not a bit romantic, don't you think? Not to give a man the fighting chance to even up before you leave?"

He stepped back abruptly, leaving her to grip the counter. "I've got a little present for you."

Ewan thrust the bouquet at her, and the full red roses quivered between them. "Here. You like surprises, don't you? Well, I don't."

Cyd tried to glare at him. But her rising blush wasn't good for a keep-your-distance effect. Ewan stiffened and frowned at Hallie, who had just come back into the shop. "This is private."

Hallie looked as if she'd burst into laughter at any minute. "Ewan, I have customers coming in the front door now. You'll have to take this someplace else."

He turned to Cyd and demanded, "Your place or mine?"

"It's a business day, Ewan. I've got to go down to the police station and see if—"

"By yourself, I suppose. So then, when you need me, I suppose you'll come calling. I'm expected to be available, of course."

"Jerk."

"Witch."

Hallie giggled and gave them each a little shove. "Get out of my shop. I'll talk with you later."

Outside the Fairy Bin, Ewan took Cyd's arm. "If you're going to the police station, I'm going with you. But first we're having breakfast."

"No, thanks. I've already had a scone." Cyd glanced at Ewan's hard expression and dropped her argument on the sidewalk. "You're upset. Why?"

He turned to glare at her and demand, "Now just why would I be? Could it be that you left before we had time to sort this out? Like why you were still a virgin? Like why you didn't tell me? *Like why you chose me?* Why am I the lucky—rather unlucky guy? That's quite a burden to put on a man, but then you're just evil enough to make me feel guilty."

Cyd couldn't stop blushing.

And she couldn't stop the tears from brimming in her eyes as she looked up at Ewan. Ewan was angry, and she'd hurt him somehow, injured some male pride she didn't understand. Sex was sex, wasn't it? Men usually had what they wanted, then they left—the only thing that was different was that this morning, she had left. What difference should that make?

Yet here Ewan stood, glowering at her.

She had his bouquet in her hand, and the world was unsteady.

"I don't like this," she managed unsteadily.

"What? The morning after? Dealing with life? What's the matter? Did I get too close to whatever you're set to protect? What did you expect?" he drilled.

She eyed Mr. and Mrs. Louis, who passed near on the sidewalk, and whispered, "Do we have to do this now?"

"What's the matter? Aren't you prepared to handle me out of bed? Oh, wait. If I'm only the equipment you use to relieve stress, maybe I should be beneath the bed."

"You're being ridiculous."

The wind caught Ewan's hair, taking it back from his dark scowl, the hard set of his lips and jaw.

"You're very emotional, Ewan . . . and unreasonable. Men and women share beds and nights all the time. Life goes on."

She didn't trust the angry flare of his nostrils or the narrowing of those steel gray eyes. "We're not dealing with an average situation here, Cyd. You've tossed me a hard one. I'd thought you'd crossed that line a long time ago, most do. But it was your first time—and mine, too, if you want the truth of it. How do you feel?" he asked in a low voice that seemed to shake all around her.

She ached in places she hadn't known existed. She didn't know what to do with Ewan, all puffed up and volatile. She didn't know why her hands gripped the roses as if she'd never let them go.

She didn't know how to stop blushing. "What do you mean that it was your first time?"

"Exactly that. The women weren't virgins. You were my first. That's a hard thing to do to a man, Cyd, even for you."

She'd thought him experienced and unshakable, and yet— "Can we do this some other time?"

"No. Are you okay? Should you see a doctor?" Ewan was too close, looming over her, sheltering her from the wind. His hands framed her face, making her look up at him. He searched her face and she could find nowhere to hide. "I used protection."

She remembered that moment when he'd pulled away just that bit. She tried a shaky smile to shield her unsteady emotions. "Always at the ready, I imagine. Probably cartons of it ready for duty."

"Don't push it, Cyd. Why me? *Why did you choose me to be the first?*"

"You're under no obligation, you know. I have no expectations, if that's what's worrying you. You're not committed."

His eyes narrowed dangerously again and Cyd felt his anger bristle around her, so strongly that she backed a step away. Ewan caught her arm and stated grimly, "We're having coffee, if nothing else."

He didn't talk during the breakfast at the Blue Moon, rather he leaned back in his chair. Ewan stared at Cyd as if he were dissecting her and what he would do with her. "I suppose your view of lovemaking would be skewed," he said finally, decisively.

"Stop." Her hand trembled as she replaced the coffee mug on the table and the liquid sloshed onto the surface.

Ewan looked meaningfully at her as he blotted away the coffee. "For now."

She couldn't stop blushing or fidgeting, her hands trembling as she held the bouquet. There was a difference about

Ewan that she didn't trust or understand: the way he moved close to her, his hand riding her waist. With Ewan at her side, their bodies brushing, Cyd felt softer and delicately feminine—and that terrified her. She'd always been so complete, so strong and independent by herself.

Cyd was still dealing with those new emotions when they walked into the police station, Ewan at her side.

He stayed close during the next round of questioning, taking her cold hand in his. Ewan was silent and grim as he walked Cyd to her office, still moving close and protective, his hand on her waist. Inside, he walked around the sleek, ultramodern office, his hands in his back pockets.

He turned to her finally as she fiddled with her messages, trying to avoid looking at him. "I need to know that you are okay," he said huskily.

Of course she was just peachy. A body had been discovered on her property. The suspected murder would have dated back twenty-five years ago to when she was six years old and had been traumatized so badly that she required sedation. Linda had glossed it all over through the years, and now her damaged mind couldn't release the secrets it held. Why? What had happened?

Could the dead man be Cyd's father?

Could her father be the Night Man?

Was it only a drifter's bones that now lay on the medical examiner's slab?

And then there was Ewan, the sensuality between them that threatened to heat even now . . . and how she longed to move into his arms. But she wouldn't. She knew better than to get herself entangled in a love affair with any man. She'd seen firsthand what men could do when the dark, ugly beast in them arose. It wouldn't do to let Ewan heat her blood. Not at all. "I'm fine. Please leave."

"One other thing—call me if you get scared again. Or if you need me to be with you during the interviews. And when the investigation is done and the property released, I stand by my offer to help you clear that place."

With a curt nod, Ewan walked out of Cyd's office. Only when he was gone did Cyd gather up the bouquet that she'd tossed carelessly on her desk and hold it close, nuzzling the fragrant petals.

Blushes and tears weren't for her, she decided, and briskly placed the roses in water. She had a good deal on her desktop: McGruder's offer to buy the boat shop. To keep herself from brooding about the investigation—and Ewan's unexpected emotional revelations, and her own shattering ones, that tender emotions could bond with sexual encounters—Cyd picked up the telephone. She knew how to handle business, anyway, if not Ewan and her unstable senses. Keeping in contact with McGruder's was a definite must. Determined now to place herself in a mode she understood—that of making money, Cyd picked up a pen.

Another thought caused her to drop it. She'd dreamed about Ewan for years, and now she was finished. She could place her unsettled feelings for him aside.

Her free hand skimmed across the roses, and she replaced the telephone in the cradle. Ewan would have paid a pretty price because they weren't in season.

Because she couldn't resist, Cyd bent to nuzzle the soft blooms again, to smell the fragrance.

She was finished with Ewan Lochlain. She had crossed him off her to-do list. *The End.*

Cyd trembled, and that slight intimate ache reminded her of their bodies locked, Ewan's hard face above her, honed and fierce, his muscles quivering within her grasp. Yet despite his primitive expression as if nothing could distract him, Ewan had handled her gently.

He was upset and angry just now, and concerned for her.

Cyd placed her hand against her cheek and discovered another blush.

That wouldn't do at all. She could handle one night with Ewan Lochlain and get on with her life as usual.

Suddenly her senses shifted and her office seemed too still—as if someone had been here. . . . The hair on the back of her neck lifted, goose bumps rose on her skin, though the room was warm. The sensations chilled her, like heartbeats of someone else pushing at her own— There were times, when she walked on the street that she had those same feelings, like she was being watched. . . .

Of course people watched her, Cyd reasoned. She dressed well, cared for her body, and—

Cyd wrapped her arms around herself, trying to shake free of the chilling wary sense that someone prowled through her life. . . . She was just emotional, that was all. Ewan, in a storm, would cause anyone to be upset.

Cyd pushed away her uneasiness, and yet the sense that someone had been in her office came crawling back. . . . Who could it be? Or was she her mother's child, her mind slipping?

"Cyd Callahan comes from trash, Ewan. She probably knows more about that body found on her place than she's admitting. As little as I thought of your father, I don't think it is wise for you or Hallie to associate with Cyd. You were with her—all night—just two days ago. Cyd only left yesterday morning, running like the devil was after her. Don't deny it."

Angela's bald statements echoed in the airy boat shop. Her perfume bit into the scent of fresh wood and caulk.

Ewan didn't like the image of Cyd fleeing his bed, but he wasn't giving that information to Angela.

He leaned back against his workbench and crossed his arms. A queen of the realm, addressing the lower minions, Angela was prowling in his shop. Her overt purpose was to underline her power in Fairy Cove.

But somehow Cyd had wrested free the little shop and Hallie's Fairy Bin from the rest of Angela's Main Street property. Hallie had explained briefly that it was a loophole that Cyd had found, allowing an immediate purchase for cash at the end of the lessees' contract. The current lessees had wanted no more part of Fairy Cove, or Angela, and didn't object to Cyd's buyout plan.

Angela's harsh voice echoed in the silence of the boat shop and any reminder that his mother's sweet soul wasn't shared by Angela.

Still. His mother had had a gentle heart, and she would have protected her twin.

Just as Hallie would do, should Angela need her.

Then perhaps, just perhaps, he didn't want any part of his mother's life dirtied by gossip. Somewhere deep within him, Ewan would protect Angela, too—up to a point. But if she crossed that line . . .

Angela's glance around the shop was disdainful. "Everyone still remembers Linda Callahan. She plied her trade outside of town. No one would allow her to live inside the city limits. Cyd isn't any better. She's only bedding you to get this place. She's got a big money deal brewing. I have my sources, you know. Apparently your affair with Cyd—what that Molly Claire girl calls herself now—hasn't worked out, because she's only been here once. You haven't been seen with her. But then, it wouldn't be wise during an investigation of a body to rake up all the facts about your father, would it?"

Ewan's gut tightened. "The facts? The gossip you and your cronies created, you mean? After the insurance money was safely in your pocket?"

Honed for the charge, Angela pivoted to him. "There is a prison penalty for blackmailers. It's only because of my twin sister that I don't turn you in."

"Family love and all that. We both know the cards we're

holding on each other, Angela. Don't threaten me again. And I hear you're visiting Hallie, and she's your leverage over me. But she knows that I have something that protected her before I left Fairy Cove, the reason you so readily turned her guardianship over to the Donovans. We all know what we know. You can drop the honey, Angela. Now why did you really come here?"

His aunt hesitated only a moment, then stated, "I want you to take McGruder's offer. It will be good for the town. A chain like that can advertise and perhaps triple the tourism traffic that we have now."

Angela studied the window's view of the harbor. Instinct caused him to toss her the next question: "Cyd doesn't know that you're behind the McGruder's offer, does she?"

Angela glared at him, her lips in a tight red line, a verification that she'd been at work.

"I see," Ewan said slowly, watching his aunt's expression. How could two sisters who shared the same womb be so different? He tried his suspicions aloud to test Angela's reaction. "You're probably a shareholder. And you want to put an upstart in her place—a prostitute's daughter challenging you in your own territory."

Angela's face paled, her eyes small beads of hatred. "She's getting too uppity. I don't like it. Take the offer. It serves everyone, even that red-haired tart."

Ewan went cold with anger. "You probably knew that McGruder's was looking for a place along the lake. Somehow you managed to funnel that information to Cyd and sent her in to do your dirty work, to soften Finlay. A boost in tourism would mean a hike in income, and you could profit, right? Cyd's percentage would be chicken feed to what you would gain in the long run, and you'd let her know that when the time was ripe."

"Don't you defend Cyd Callahan. You're only one of many men sniffing after her."

"I was only testing the waters, Angela, but I see my guess is right. You are behind the McGruder's deal. . . . The investigation is ongoing, but no man has come up missing during that period of time. Cyd is not a suspect, neither is her mother. . . . It won't do to start rumors about Cyd. She knows how to play your games and win. She may come after you, Angela, and somehow I think you understand that."

"Sell and I'll see that you have stock in the McGruder's chain."

"Angela, I intended to keep this muck within our family, such as it is. . . . I don't want Hallie facing more gossip because of my mother's love for you, and the pity my father felt for you—"

Her eyes widened. "Tom pitied me?"

Cut for cut, Ewan thought, blood against blood and just as fierce and ruthless. For a moment, he almost pitied his aunt and resented the softness. "He wished you well, and you really repaid both their kindnesses, didn't you? If you ever, ever have anyone break into my shop and steal what is mine—what is my family's, again—I will release all information I have about just how you got such a financial grasp on this town. That ring Hallie is now wearing was just the start. And don't try to get it from her. She's stronger now, no thanks to your boy Allan's abuse. I want my mother's locket and anything else of a sentimental nature that you've given or hidden away."

Angela looked stunned, her lips opened almost comically, like a fish landed on sand and gasping for water. "What do you mean?"

"I mean that someone broke in here, the Lochlain Boat Shop, and took what was mine. I didn't report the theft. I know that they were left to throw suspicion on me. I just want them back. And if Allan Thompson is still reporting back to you, give him the message that if I see him in Fairy Cove, the results won't be pleasant."

Fear seemed to come alive in Angela's expression, her face pale. "What was stolen?"

"Something that was mine."

"I need to know what it was, Ewan. Tell me." Angela's voice was soft and uneven, and a long-ago memory of Ewan's mother shifted in the shadows.

Angela straightened, and her hand went to her throat, a protective gesture. "Did you take anything that belonged to my friends? If you did, I won't say anything. I just want to know."

"You should know exactly what I am talking about, Angela. You're out to make trouble for me. Missing jewelry in my possession and me with a motive to have it would—"

Angela's clawlike, blue-veined hand gripped the unfinished skiff as she seemed to brace herself. After a moment, she said, "You're taunting me, Ewan, playing a cat-and-mouse game. I'd advise against that. Until you have proof, don't accuse me of having anything to do with breaking into this . . . this dump."

"Sell that McGruder's stock now. Get your claws out of my father's life."

"How dare you!" Angela hissed.

"And stay away from Hallie. I know you've been prowling around her shop. If you don't, I'm going to take the gloves off, Angela."

"It's a store. I have a right to be there, just like any other customer. She likes me."

"I don't. And it's me you have to deal with."

When Angela hurried from the shop, Ewan frowned. His aunt's surprised expression was too real, wiping away her arrogant confidence. Fear had paled her face and shaken her body.

Someone had planted the dead women's jewelry on him, and just maybe it hadn't been Angela's doing.

And someone *else* had stolen the cross and the brooch.

But who?

* * *

Angela hurried into her home, locking the door behind her. The elegance she'd desperately needed wrapped around her. But as fear crawled inside her, her social trappings meant nothing.

The house smelled of polish and window cleaner, the carpet in her study bore the marks of a daily vacuuming. Maria Sanchez and her two older daughters had left, their work done. The cook had the day off, and Fred was likely to be at the bank, depositing late rental checks.

A terrifying silence fell upon Angela. She'd made enemies, of course. That was expected in business.

Dealing with Hallie was one thing; Ewan was another. He held a blackmailer's fist of goods tucked away in an attorney's vault and he wasn't bluffing. Or was he?

*She could lose everything!*

Angela forced herself to breathe . . . and think. Ewan was still tied to his family honor. And he was on the hunt to salvage his father's reputation.

But the brooch and the cross were missing. The locket was safe, for now, and Angela had to get it back.

The locket . . . the brooch . . . and the cross. Ewan was searching for the locket, and "what is my family's" could mean the brooch and the cross. *They were left to throw suspicion on me*, he'd said, and the dead women's jewelry found in his possession would do that.

Ewan could be lying. He could be torturing her. Where were the brooch and cross?

Her fingers shook as she unlocked the desk in her study. She took a small handmade key meant to fit into a very special lock. The other key was large and old and fit a camelback trunk. Angela hurried up the stairway to the second-floor landing, turned into an alcove, and stopped in front of the tiny door of the attic. With shaking hands, she unlocked the door and hurried up the narrow stairway.

She reached up high to a hidden ledge and removed another key. Using it, she opened another door and stepped inside the attic. Angela stopped to study the musty shadows, then walked to pull a sheet from the locked trunk.

Angela used the old key to unlock it. Filled with Tom's and Mary's sentimental treasures, it also held Hallie's and Ewan's childhood toys. She quickly surveyed the untouched contents. The envelope with the tiny pictures of Mary's family was there, emptied from the locket Angela had given Thelma Brit. Hallie's tea set and dolls, family albums that Mary had lovingly created and the rest remained safe.

Angela touched the stack of letters that Tom had sent Mary, all neatly tied with a faded blue ribbon. They were really meant for Angela, not Mary. They were really *hers*, just as Tom was.

Everything was just as Angela had left it.

She closed the trunk, securing the things she had to hoard, keeping them from everyone else.

When she turned the key again, a tinkling melody played eerily, muffled inside the trunk. The jewelry box, with a tiny ballerina circling to the music, had been Hallie's favorite.

She was right to keep anything she wanted, Angela told herself. Ewan and Hallie didn't deserve anything. They were ungrateful for the care she'd given them.

Poised to leave, Angela listened until the sound died.

The shadows seemed to shift, and her flesh turned cold. Ewan's return to Fairy Cove had unsettled the past, and danger stirred around Angela.

She hurried downstairs, forcing herself to breathe quietly as she called Thelma Brit. Thelma was yawning when she answered. "I didn't sleep well again last night. My sleep apnea, you know. I was afraid to do more than doze. The machine that is supposed to keep my breathing regular as I sleep must have malfunctioned. Danny, my son, says that he'll adjust the machine when he can get to it. I've never been technical. . . . For some reason, there have been endless calls from salespeople lately, disturbing my daytime naps. I'm too tired to fight with you over that locket, Angela. . . . No, you may not have it. Anyway, the clasp is broken."

"I'll come pick it up and have it repaired, dear," Angela offered carefully. At seventy-eight, Thelma had become peculiar and suspicious. If she knew that Angela wanted it, Thelma wouldn't release it easily. She hoarded everything, and her home was a jumble; it would be impossible to find a tiny piece of jewelry.

Angela had to get that locket.

"I'm taking a nap, Angela. I just told you that I'm having trouble with the machine and not sleeping well. The other day I fell asleep while driving. The locket was a gift. You gave it to me, and you're not getting it back."

"Thelma, I will have that locket," Angela said fiercely. She hung up and tried to stop shaking from anger.

Or was it fear?

Bertha Linnea and Patricia Erland had died recently. Bertha's delicate heart and Patricia's extreme asthma, added to their age, were enough reason for them to die— But what if someone had pushed those fine edges, stressing the women, causing their deaths? Had someone killed them and taken the jewelry?

Could she be next?

She'd started many rumors about Ewan already. But was it possible that in reality, he was a killer?

# Chapter 13

If ever he wanted to lay his hands on a woman, it was Cyd.

Ewan had given Cyd one week since they'd made love, and that was long enough. She'd been avoiding him, and he'd given her a bit of space to deal with the trauma the skeleton had dragged from the past—and to realize that she couldn't just have a private to-do list with him on it.

He'd track down that red-haired witch and settle—what?

His need to see Cyd did not sit easily upon him, a man with one plan on his mind, to succeed and clear his father's memory. He lifted his face to May's morning sunshine and told himself that a woman was a woman, no more than that. Yet that thin membrane he'd penetrated haunted him. So did the hunger he didn't want . . . that feeling of coming to home port after a very long, hard voyage. . . .

Ewan hefted the boards from the back of his pickup up to his shoulder. It would take a few trips to carry the lumber from the parking lot near the pier to the boat shop, but with each load, Ewan brought his dream closer. The pine and oak lumber was good, the best cuts from a private mill and seasoned well. The scent of wood mixed with the fragrance of midmorning coffee and breakfasts served at the Blue Moon Restaurant.

The fresh taste of new beginnings lingered in the sunlight, the seagulls keening and circling out on the water. The waves caused the wooden pier to creak beneath Ewan's boots, a familiar sound of home—

At eighty-five, Clancy Tremayne wore his waders and stood in the shallow waves. Up on the sandy beach, his bait bucket sat beside Clancy's folding chair. Like a silver thread, his line sailed out into the water.

Finlay was making his way down the steps from Main Street to the beach, where, no doubt, he would advise Clancy on his casting technique.

An elderly man and woman strolled along the sand, and a long-legged girl, wearing earphones, a sweatshirt, and cut-off shorts jogged past them.

Ewan carried the boards to the front of his shop and deposited them against the building. He studied the hoist above him, the one that he would use to lower his personal skiff into the water. The cable was new, the pulley oiled and repaired, the beams sturdy. The wooden ladder that would take him from the pier down into the boat would need replacement.

He'd need to test his first skiff right there. He'd sit on a box and row, before placing the seat and the oarlocks. With proper placement, the boat would be level and the transom would ride clear of the water, no matter what the load.

Working night and day had kept him busy, but his mind always turned to Cyd and her terrified expression when she saw him walking toward her that morning—

Ewan watched the girl run down the beach, her jogging shoes tossing up puffs of sand, a black Labrador at her side.

She had nice long smooth legs that any man would admire—or want to touch.

And that brought Ewan's mind back to Cyd's legs, how they had run smooth and strong beneath his hand, how her thighs had quivered, how the shock of his body breaching hers had caused them to stiffen. . . .

He'd taken her maidenhead—an old-fashioned term, perhaps, but the significance of why Cyd had chosen Ewan for that purpose haunted him. He felt like a boy, uncertain and proud. The idea of showing off his first complete skiff, the way she handled in water, to Cyd caught him. He longed to see her hair catch the sun and the wind on the lake, her face lift to it in pleasure. . . .

Had she thought of him at all?

Could a woman give herself to a man for the first time and not think of him every night as Ewan ached for Cyd?

But then, Ewan reminded himself, Cyd had not had an easy young life. Linda's profession had probably left little room for illusions—or tenderness between a man and a woman.

Ewan had called her at night, finding in Cyd's voice the fear she controlled by day. More than once, he'd started to walk to her house. But Hallie had said that Cyd was very shaken by the discovery of the body. And clearly, Cyd did not want Ewan near her as she fought her nightmares.

Too bad his sympathy was at low tide and his need at high, Ewan thought as he saw her striding along the street, the sunlight catching the rich red tumble of her hair.

A boatbuilder of experience would call a fine handcrafted vessel "eye sweet," and the label well suited Cyd. The wind pushed her sweater against her breasts, her slacks following the curve of her hip and the length of her legs. She swung her briefcase as if it were a part of her.

And she had placed Ewan on her "to-do" list, doing him well and good.

The thought burned and nettled, and Cyd had set him aside easily enough, cutting him away from the fears that stalked her nights.

Cyd would ignore what had happened between them, would she?

A creature of habit, Cyd was heading for her blueberry scone at Hallie's.

A man of need, Ewan had his own "to-do" list.

Cyd forced herself to swallow the last bite of her morning scone. The big man who had just entered the Fairy Bin and had reached up to silence the door's tinkling bell didn't look friendly.

Her body leaped into warning-alert, because she knew his body well, had felt him move upon her, with her, in her.

Ewan's long-sleeved gray T-shirt fit his muscular shoulders and chest tightly. The knife sheath attached to his belt revealed a large, worn handle.

His smile did not reach his gray eyes. His voice, smooth and lilting and deep, seemed to purr dangerously over the shop's happy clutter. The sound wasn't a welcome, rather a warning. "Hello, Cyd."

"Ewan. I was just leaving." Cyd turned to Hallie, whose tightly pressed lips and sparkling eyes said she was struggling against a grin. "I'll call you later."

Because Cyd would have had to pass Ewan if she left by the front door, she said, "I'll just use the back door, if you don't mind. I know the code. I'll wash my teacup on the way out."

She turned and hurried into Hallie's kitchen at the back of the shop. One look at Ewan, and she knew he was after her.

And she knew why.

The sight of Ewan dried her mouth and made her legs go weak. She could still feel him inside her, filling her. She could feel his hands and mouth on her, the weight of his body, the scent of him, the way his breathing came rough and hard and his heart pounded—the way he gave himself to her. . . .

And Ewan knew how she felt, because his body had tensed, almost as if it recognized hers, the pulse deep inside her. . . . His eyes had narrowed just now as she fought her blush. There was no doubt that Ewan knew her senses leaped at the sight of him.

She'd given him something no other man had claimed.

And a bit more, an inner softness she had sworn to protect. She wouldn't live the life her mother had— All it takes is one wrong man. . . .

With shaking fingers, Cyd washed Hallie's plain white cup and turned it upside down on the draining rack. With one week of answering questions and trying to pull answers out of the shadows, and nights of nightmares mixed with erotic sensations that Ewan's lovemaking had caused, Cyd's nerves were stretched taut.

She quickly punched in the series of numbers into Hallie's back door alarm lock, exited, and pulled the door tightly shut behind her.

When she turned, Ewan was at the bottom of the wooden steps.

"You look like hell," he stated pleasantly. "What's the matter? Too much on your 'to-do' list?"

"This isn't going to be pleasant, is it?" she said casually, as she took the two steps down to face Ewan Lochlain. He'd been her first love. He'd taken her first kiss, and he'd taken more—more than she wanted to give again.

He bristled with anger, and smelled of wood and man and heat so rich and wild, she could almost feel him within her again.

Ewan reached for a curl near her face and wound it around his finger, studying the shades against his skin. While his touch was light, his words were savage. "No, damn it, you red-haired witch. You're in my blood, and I'm in yours, and you know it."

"I don't have my mother's weaknesses, Ewan. I'm not her."

"You would have seen too much, too young. It's left your view of life skewed, and you're afraid. I'm not. I'm damned angry."

When Cyd attempted to push past him, Ewan wouldn't move out of her way. She should have known Ewan wouldn't allow that. In the shadows of the alley, he caught her face, turning it up to him. "You're blushing again, Cyd. That must be embarrassing for a woman who likes to be in control."

"You've made your point. Back off."

His hands eased their grip, his thumb stroking her hot cheeks. "I like you like this . . . hot . . . frustrated . . . wary."

"It happened."

"*We* happened. You're too pale, and there are dark circles beneath your eyes. You haven't been eating well, or sleeping. I think we should remedy that, don't you?"

"I'm not going to bed with you, Ewan."

His smile wasn't nice. "Did I ask you? Women should be courted, shouldn't they? Or do businesswomen just take what they want now? I was thinking we should have a nice civilized lunch and decide the rules of this game."

"The only thing we have between us is the sale of the boat shop. The investigation doesn't leave a lot of time to rehash—"

"Oh, we've got a game between us, sweetheart, and it's running fast. You can't take this back . . . it really happened. A man should be prepared when he goes to bed with a virgin. That really wasn't fair, Cyd." Ewan's cheek rested against her own, and he whispered, "There's plenty of time for you and me to chat. What else is on your list today?"

He studied her and frowned. "And why are you trembling? We've argued toe-to-toe before, and you can hold your own with me. Something else is going on inside you. What's wrong?"

The soft concern in his expression and voice caused her emotions to shift from keeping herself free of any "game" with Ewan to that of needing his strength. Cyd wanted to move into Ewan's arms, to let him hold her safe. Instead, she gripped his arm and gave him the bald, desperate truth that churned inside her. "I hate this . . . this weakness. I can't sleep at all. Everything is all tangled up. It's you. It's him. It's the body and the nightmares."

Ewan stood still, his body warm against hers. Then his indrawn breath hissed by her cheek, and he suddenly stood free, his hands in his pockets as he studied her. "You're on edge, Cyd, and scared. Whatever happened to you as a child has been raked up again. Let me help."

"I just want it all to be over . . . for the investigators to leave. When they do, everything will be just the same."

He could have teased her. He didn't. Instead, Ewan nodded, his expression guarded and hard. He wouldn't like her putting lovemaking with him into a brew that included her nightmares and her mother's very busy bed. That injured dark male pride showed in his voice. "Just let me know the next time I'm on your to-do list."

"Tonight." Cyd's need surprised her, the words flowing out into the day. She couldn't spend the night pacing and alone again. She knew Ewan was bruised and brooding, but still, she needed his safety. "Tonight," she repeated firmly.

His black eyebrows jammed together in a fierce scowl. "What?"

"It would be nice to see you tonight. Dinner, maybe?"

Ewan studied her face, his expression wary. "So proper. But then, you still think you have a chance to get me to sell, don't you?"

She'd needed him and had stepped out of her pride, and that had cost. Cyd managed a businesslike tone, because she wasn't going to beg. "Look. It was just an offer for dinner. Take it or leave it."

"Oh, I'll take it. My place or yours?"

"I . . ." Confused, Cyd wasn't prepared for Ewan to leap so quickly.

"Mine," he said firmly. "I've got a fond memory of you

there. In my bed. A man's bed, in his first real home is very special, don't you think? And what happens there?"

"I never thought that would upset you—"

"Well, do think about that, darling-mine. I'll see you to-night." Then, with a light kiss on her cheek, Ewan strolled away from her and onto Main Street.

Cyd didn't trust herself to walk. Instead, she sank to sit on the steps and stared at the worn bricks on the other side of the alley.

The back door opened and Sean Donovan walked past Cyd and down the steps. He stopped whistling long enough to say, "Beautiful morning, isn't it?"

"No," she answered bluntly.

Sean didn't seem to hear Cyd's reply as he walked from her out toward Main Street. His whistling echoed against the brick walls.

"Your brother," she said fiercely when Hallie came out-side to hand Cyd a cup of tea. Hallie sat and sipped from her own cup.

"I've got troubles of my own. Sean Donovan," she stated simply, and stared at the bricks. "He kissed me. Not a broth-erly kiss at all. Simply dragged me into the kitchen, lifted me up to sit on the counter, and put his hands on my face. He kissed me. Sean Donovan kissed me just now."

Cyd studied Hallie's flushed face and smiled. When Hal-lie was near, Sean's eyes didn't leave her. "Did you like it?"

Hallie glared at her. "Did you? Sean has kissed you often enough. I saw that."

"Sean wanted to make you jealous, and you know it. And he kisses quite well. He wouldn't take something you didn't want to give. You kissed him back, didn't you?"

Hallie's frown deepened. "Stop smirking."

They both turned to stare at the bricks, to contemplate men, and to sip their tea. Then Cyd said, "I will not be like my mother. But I'll take one bit of her advice . . . she said that all it takes is one wrong man."

"You're not your mother. And I've had a wrong one. I don't think I want another, right or wrong."

"Sean would never hurt you." Cyd turned to Hallie. "Do you think Allan could have anything to do with the jewelry planted at the boat shop? Or with it being stolen?"

"Allan is capable of anything, when things don't go his way," Hallie stated darkly.

"If he comes near you, Sean and Ewan won't be happy. I wouldn't like to see the both of them out for revenge. Could Paddy have anything to do with the jewelry, or some of his men? He'd have a grudge against Ewan. And then there's Angela."

"She's been around more lately. She's family, a part of my mother and of me, Cyd."

When Cyd lifted that one well-shaped eyebrow, questioning Angela's motives, Hallie said, "I know. She wants Ewan to leave. She's made that clear. But my brother is here to stay. He's determined to rebuild our father's name. Ewan won't be budged."

Cyd stood and stretched. "He might just sell, if the money was high enough."

Hallie smiled and shook her head. "He won't. This isn't a matter of money."

"Well, I've got to go and take care of mine," Cyd said, and kissed Hallie's cheek. If she was going to meet Ewan tonight, she might as well come prepared with a higher offer from McGruder's.

She resented baring her unsteady emotions to Ewan earlier, but they'd leaped out of her before she could stop them. She trusted him, damn it, and why did he have to let her know that she'd been the first woman in his bed, in his first home—and that it went deeply with him?

That she'd been a virgin had set him off, and Ewan had come after her with fire in his eyes, a big bouquet of roses, and that air of male possession.

It was only sex, Cyd told herself. Yet the need for sex wasn't the reason she'd bared her fears to him earlier; it was because on some deep level she trusted Ewan.

Not once had he said anything about her losing her sanity. He'd known her fear that she might become like her mother, he'd seen her stark vulnerability and hadn't taken advantage. "Let me help," he'd said, and she'd known instinctively that he meant it.

On the other hand, he was still brooding about her "to-do list" remark.

Cyd inhaled the May air, the freshness of the flowers blooming in the sidewalk boxes. It appeared she still had a thing or two to learn about Ewan, and herself, when dealing with him.

She'd see him tonight, and that thought set her mind and body humming. With no small effort, Cyd tried to focus on outlining her plan to McGruder's for more offer money.

At noon, Cyd's hand shook as she replaced her office telephone to its cradle. "Someone in Fairy Cove was a major stockholder in McGruder's and just sold all their shares this morning? And now, McGruder's wonders whether the site will be right for their place? After I've put all my work into that deal? Who could have had enough stock to—?"

The answer that came back was Angela Greer.

"You can't blame me," Angela told Cyd an hour later, "if you lost the commission on that boat shop. Blame Ewan Lochlain, not me."

"Oh, he'll sell. But not when you'll make a profit. That profit will go to me, Angela. Every day, you'll look down from this room and think about how much money you lost by selling your stock. And by that time, I'll own those shops on Main Street. Or I'll see that the people renting them can make arrangements to buy, if they want."

"I don't know what you're talking about."

"I have my sources, the same as you. It only took one phone call to learn that you were a major shareholder in Mc-Gruder's and that you sold your stock."

"You called a man, no doubt. Someone whom you've slept with?" Angela prodded too sweetly. "It should be easy for you, a prostitute's daughter, to get what you want from men. And you don't even know your father's name."

"I know that he danced with her, in private, and treated her like a lady. I don't remember him, but I do know she loved him. . . . My mother was capable of great compassion and love, Angela. Have you ever truly loved anyone?"

In the shadows of Angela's elegant study, Cyd's blue eyes flashed, and her mouth moved hot and furious. "Tom was a loving man, too, and it was no wonder he chose the sweet and gentle twin. They had love between them, you bitter old biddy. Tom Lochlain would have never harmed Mary, much less tried to kill her. You planned the whole McGruder's deal, didn't you? You were planning to set me up all the time, have me do your dirty work? Think of it this way, you old bag—it cost both of us. You could have raised the rent on every shop along Main Street—except mine and Hallie's."

Cyd pushed Angela down into a chair, leaning over her. When Angela reached to slap her face, Cyd clasped her wrist. The girl was strong and fierce, and for a moment, Angela feared her.

"I bet that burns your butt, doesn't it? How I was able to find that loophole and take them away from you," Cyd stated and sat back on Angela's well-ordered, expensive desk. She shoved a stack of papers onto the floor. "Hallie is wearing her mother's ring. It's been on your finger for years. Now I wonder where the rest of her mother's jewelry and the personal mementoes that are not in Lochlain possession could be."

The blood in Angela's body suddenly went cold. Cyd knew something about the missing brooch and cross. "I don't know what you mean."

"Of course you do. You're a spiteful old bag. You want to cast suspicion on Ewan, but that idea didn't work, did it? I see that you do know what I'm talking about. You just went white."

Cyd deliberately pushed away a stack of envelopes, ignoring them as they fell to the floor. She watched Angela reach for the telephone. "I wouldn't do that. Paddy is gone. I'm his landlady. I know you call him in now and again for dirty work, when a little muscle is needed. He's afraid of me, you know. We settled that hash long ago."

"I don't know what you mean," Angela repeated unevenly.

"There are things I know—like how Paddy came to bully my mother and since he is linked to you, I suppose that was your dirty work. I know you set him on a shopkeeper who stood up to you and intimidated his family. Oh, yes, Angela. I know he does your dirty work for you. But you can believe I know how to play and start rumors, too. Oh, yes, I remember Hallie's and Ewan's bruises. And you threatened Hallie that if she told Ewan, you'd see that he was put away for incest—she asked me what that word meant, innocent that she was—that she still is in some ways. And then you set Allan on her, didn't you?"

"Allan Thompson was the best thing that could have happened to Hallie. She would still be married to him if you hadn't interfered."

"Well, I did. And with Ewan home, Allan was lucky to get off with his life." Cyd had stood back and crossed her arms and studied Angela. "You hate me. You always have. But I'm not Hallie."

"I don't know what you mean. You can't come in here and threaten me," Angela managed finally.

"That property on Elfindale? That was just a start. I am going to take Fairy Cove away from you and leave you with nothing, Angela. And the only way you can possibly stop me—because I am younger and stronger and better than you are—is to go to my mother and apologize for making her life miserable, for making certain that she couldn't find honest employment when she tried."

"Apologize? To Linda Callahan? Never! Not ever while I draw breath. Your mother was a prostitute."

Cyd seemed to shimmer and tighten as though she was about to burst. Her eyes burned blue and bright to lock with Angela's. Then she said quietly, "I know what my mother was. My mother had more heart and compassion and love than you will ever know. In effect, she was more woman than you could ever hope to be. I feel sorry for you, Angela. I really do. But that won't stop me from ruining you."

With her head high, Cyd walked out of the study.

Alone with the slam of the house's big door echoing in the house, Angela's hands shook as she tried to pour a cup of tea.

The expensive design of the cup and saucer mocked her. Ewan had deliberately broken a china cup to make his point. While Ewan's anger had been cool and controlled, Cyd's was all flash and fire.

"Apologize to Linda Callahan? Never," Angela repeated to the empty room. "I'll see Cyd dead first. She's gone too far. How dare that bastard child of a prostitute attack and threaten me!"

Cyd Callahan was sharing Ewan's bed. What if they united, sharing the information he stole from Angela? That young witch would possess everything that was Angela's—respect, power, influence. Cyd would eventually take over Angela's investments, her property, her money. And Ewan would be the instrument by which Cyd, the daughter of a drug-addicted prostitute, would control Fairy Cove.

"That evil little tramp . . . how dare she?" Angela stalked the length of her study, furious with Cyd. "How dare she actually come to my own home and accuse me of knowing anything about the body at Linda Callahan's house. How dare she accuse me of ruining lives and child abuse—child abuse. I merely reprimanded those two when they needed it. Tom and Mary had let them run wild. Those children came here with no manners, no manners at all. Cyd—Molly Claire—is no better than her mother was, whoring after men."

Angela paced her study, punched an intercom button, and yelled, "Fred, you should have never let that Callahan girl into the house."

But Fred wasn't in his office. He had left immediately after letting Cyd into the house. Fred would pay for that. He would be hiding at the bank, trying to escape Angela's anger for losing the house on Elfindale . . . to Cyd Callahan, of all people.

Angela hurried into her private bathroom and locked the door. She quickly took a mild tranquilizer and repaired her makeup. "That girl. She has always been trouble. And I have ways of dealing with problems. If she thinks she can challenge me for Fairy Cove, or for anything I have, she is going to pay a big price. She needs to be removed once and for all. I'm certain Paddy and Allan will be most anxious to help with that matter."

Restored and confident, Angela returned to her study. The gardner and his helper moved outside the window. The sounds in the kitchen said Edna Whitehouse was busy at work. . . . And the hand-carved German grandfather clock wasn't ticking— "That Cyd-girl probably touched it," Angela hissed.

Yet Cyd had never come close to the clock; it had been ticking just minutes before she had arrived.

Angela listened to Greer House and to the racing beat of her heart.

Like a great hungry beast, the silence roared and terrified her.

Angela pushed the intercom button for the kitchen. "Edna, turn off the stove and leave quickly. Now . . . don't argue. Now."

Once alone, Angela hurried to the attic, where she could be alone with Tom, to hoard him to herself. Tom, the man she'd always loved, who should have been hers. . . .

Ewan turned to the woman who had just slammed into his shop. He closed his notebook, turned off his laptop, and gave Cyd his full attention. She was dressed in a black sweater, slacks, and high heels, and a temper. She thumped the roses she held against her thigh.

"You're early. It's only four o'clock."

"I'm not coming to dinner." Her blue eyes held his as she walked the length of the boat shop to stand in front of him. Along her face and down her nape tiny spirals of silky hair quivered.

She slapped the rose bouquet against his chest, and Ewan ignored it.

He reached for the tight prim knot of hair on top of her head and found the pins, tossing them away. His open hands caught the rich tumble and closed possessively in the curls. Ewan held her still when she would have stepped back, ignoring the swat of her free hand and the bash of the roses against his head. "You brought me flowers? How romantic."

"They're just to keep the score even."

A rose petal tumbled down his forehead to his nose, and he blew it away. "Oh, there's no equaling the score between us. I know that I'm the first, and I know that you trust me on some level or it wouldn't have gotten that far. Now what's this about?"

"Angela was behind the whole McGruder's deal. I just got it out of her. She set me up, made me work my butt off, then she sells her stock. McGruder's has found another place up the coastline, the sale is set, and I'm missing a nice big fat commission. Now the only reason that she would back off for a deal that would fatten her pockets is if someone—you, most likely—made her. You're the only one who did not want this deal to go through, Ewan. You muscled Angela somehow and made the deal fall through."

"You can survive without that commission."

"Stop playing with my hair."

"But I still remember it, spread across my pillow. It's not a sight a man can forget."

"Try. You can build your boat shop somewhere else. This deal falling through cost me three hundred on top of what I lost in commission. I'll have to pay Finlay—unless you finally see reason and I can find another buyer."

"I'm sorry about the three hundred. But think of it this way, you helped Finlay get a few necessities for his apartment."

The roses bashed his head again. "You won money on that bet, didn't you?"

"I knew I wasn't selling, dear heart. I couldn't pass a sure bet." Against him, Cyd's curves and heat had done their work, and Ewan's body was hard and hungry. "So, are you going to kiss me or not?"

Cyd shook free of him and turned away, but not before he caught her blush. She turned to toy with his tools, running her hand up and down the smoothly worn handle of the hammer. The gesture mimed another that brought blood pounding through his body. Ewan fought the tension in his body, then gave in to it.

He moved behind Cyd, framed her with his arms, and gripped the workbench. He bent to taste her throat, nibbling on the silky skin there and testing the warm flush that had just risen in her cheeks. At least he wasn't alone in his desire. His body clenched as her fingers stopped to rhythmically grip the handle.

Ewan removed the hammer from her hand. Cyd's fingers

stroking that hammer had almost undone him. "I've missed you," he whispered rawly.

He couldn't ignore that heady female fragrance, combined with the roses', or the slight quiver that passed through Cyd's body. Ewan kissed the other side of her throat and nuzzled his way to her ear.

Cyd stood away from him. Her thigh bumped a sawhorse, and, unbalanced, she shot out a hand to steady herself.

At least that was some concession that he had an effect on her, Ewan decided. He took a step toward her, and Cyd backed away. "Nervous of me, are you?"

"Not a bit."

"Shy then. Was it bad with Angela?"

"I've never been shy in my life. The meeting with Angela was full-scale war. She hates you, Ewan. And me. And definitely my mother. Of course, she brought up that old history, threw the body buried at the old house at me, and added the necessary low blow—that I don't know who my father is. In return, I had a few things to say about how she treated Hallie and you. It wasn't pleasant. She should not have called my mother—or me—*that* B word. And while my mouth was running full speed, I told Angela that I did not think it was possible for your father to plot your mother's death. Tom Lochlain was a loving man, and I am going to make that old biddy apologize to my mother."

"That should be interesting. Good for a few more bets, if anyone knew . . ."

"What are you holding over her, Ewan? I know she's put a squeeze on you, pressuring the shopkeepers. But then I did that, too. They agree with me, you know, that a restaurant with a view of the lake and plenty of atmosphere would raise Fairy Cove's tourist trade. . . . Angela has half the town council in her pocket. Why hasn't she gotten the town council to pass restrictions that would run you off this pier?"

"We respect each other, Angela and I. Call it a standoff, if you will. But for Hallie's gentle loving heart, I might be—well, I might not be kind."

"That's what I thought. You're protecting Hallie from Angela. Somehow you've held her off for years. . . . And you're afraid that somehow you might fail or have to leave, or worse, and you want to ensure that Hallie will be left alone."

Cyd was too perceptive, and Ewan ignored her curious look. He asked the question that had been bothering him. "Did you ever tell Angela or anyone other than Hallie about your fear of the Night Man? Is it possible that she would have someone stalk you?"

"No one but you and Hallie knew. And Tom and your mother. Do you think Angela might hire someone to stalk me? For this long? Since I was eighteen? You know, sometimes I come into my house. It's been locked all day, and yet somehow, I feel someone has been inside. I have that same sense in my office. It's not possible. Both places are well secured."

Ewan didn't want to add to Cyd's fears—how easy it was to disarm locks and alarm systems purchased at discount cities and installed by do-it-yourselfers. "I wouldn't put anything past her. She put Allan onto Hallie. And the town hires men to play the part. Tourism has to be supported, you know."

He hated to see the shadows come back into her eyes, and the fear, and sought to distract her. "Why are you here early, Cyd? To tell me what you think of me?"

"Yes. I think you are a rat. And arrogant. And—"

Ewan moved closer, and turned her face to the light. Cyd lowered her lids, but he knew her expression well enough. "There's something else, isn't there?"

Cyd placed her forehead against his chest. Her hands slid to his waist as if she needed him for mooring. "I'm afraid for Hallie. And Angela—Angela seems afraid, too. The identity of the skeleton isn't known yet, and I'm afraid to ask for a DNA test, if that's possible. I don't even know that— What if he's my father? What if he isn't? I don't know what to do. Maybe I don't want to know, and I'm afraid for my mother. You're a catalyst, Ewan. You've only been here less than two months, and something is happening in all of our lives—"

Ewan pressed her caressing hand flat against his stomach. "You're playing with my belt buckle, dear heart. Before I misunderstand and chart my course, I'd like to know what that means."

Cyd looked at him and said, "I'm very tense, Ewan. It's been a really, really bad day. It's been a bad week."

"Am I on your to-do list, then? Exercise equipment, so to speak?"

"I suppose that still nettles, but the truth is—yes."

He brushed her lips with his, tasted the full rich promise of them, then moved his hands down to her breasts. "You're the first woman to bring me flowers. I'm feeling delicate and vulnerable. You could probably have your way with me."

Caressed gently, her nipples peaked instantly. Cyd's rising color and uneven breath wasn't because she feared him, or that she'd had a fight with Angela. She'd come to him for comfort—after telling him off, of course. But there was more beneath Cyd's need. She was afraid of the tender moments passing between them, and if she wanted to label it "lust," he would oblige.

Ewan bent to nibble on her ear and smiled as a telltale quiver shot through her body. "You know I'm a sensitive sort. I can't have you thinking I'm easy."

He read the uncertainty in her eyes, warring with her fear of losing herself, and he ached for the damage done long ago.

Then Cyd's fingers caught his hair. "You should sell this place, and you know it. You're just being stubborn. Just lock the door. This won't take long."

"Won't it?" Ewan asked, even as he made his own plans, and settled in to feast upon her.

*  *  *

In the shadows of an alley, a man lifted his face to the new moon.

Power filled the Other now, not pain, and soon he would have his due. He'd waited too long, the hours ticking by at a snail's pace. At times, waiting had seemed as endless as the lake's great waves, but soon . . . soon. . . .

The investigators could do no more at this point, moving on to a fresh murder site, the newshounds at their heels. Cyd wasn't in her house, locked tight against the night. Ewan Lochlain's short presence in Fairy Cove had unsettled the past's murky currents. Everyone knew that he'd tear the town apart, searching for the secret of his parents' death.

And the man in the alley knew everything . . . because he was a part of Fairy Cove's dark side. . . .

He knew that Cyd Callahan feared the Night Man and why. That she had taken Ewan Lochlain as a lover wouldn't stop her need for money or ease her pain, or unlock her memory of that stormy, terrifying night.

The man watched a mouse scurry down the alley. He could give Cyd Callahan what she wanted, what she needed, but it was too soon.

How he'd loved that fiery red hair. How he'd loved the scent of it, the silky feel of it against his skin. . . . Had she known that he had loved her forever?

All the pieces were there, and he would slowly, slowly draw them together in a noose. He would enjoy fitting it to the woman who had ruined his life. To watch terror fill her eyes.

*She'd* dared to threaten him.

He wallowed in the bitter taste of revenge. *She'd* caused him to lose his pride, and for that she would pay.

He wanted to hurt her. To terrify her. To let her know that she couldn't escape him, couldn't avoid the fate he had planned for her.

It was only a matter of time before all his careful planning came together, and she would pay the final price for ruining his life. . . .

He closed his eyes and inhaled the night, the scents of spring and fresh beginnings, the sound of the wooden piers creaking against the force of the water, the slight breeze hissing through the treetops.

A burst of drunken laughter, a woman's high-pitched giggle sailed down the street. The man eased deeper into the alley. He knew them all, watched them all.

By night, he walked the streets and haunted the alleys. He'd stand for hours outside Hallie's apartment window, waiting for her to turn off the lights, listening to the sounds of her settling— Sweet, innocent, unsuspecting Hallie, the perfect victim, struggling against her life. . . .

Pain sent its prying fingers into his body and he had to hurry, to finish his work, his revenge. . . .

# Chapter 14

Cyd awoke to the sound of waves crashing in the night. Fear instantly chilled her, past nightmares clawing at her as she tried to surface completely to reality and her surroundings. With her heart pounding wildly, she looked to see if her windows were still locked, the shutters closed—

But she wasn't in her home. She picked at details, one by one . . . on a big bed . . . waves . . . wood creaking . . . a new moon beyond the huge uncurtained glass windows . . . a big shadowy apartment, the walls no more than weathered planks. . . .

Then she remembered the past frantic hours of lovemaking as if their hunger had waited too long. . . .

Ewan had held her, soothed her gently when they had rested. As she'd pitted herself against him again, he'd laughed outright, a rich, carefree, delighted sound.

The playfulness of a boy had given way to the gentle hunger of a man.

Cyd smiled in the shadows and stretched, her body filled with a luxurious, soothing peace. She hadn't known couples could play and tease and laugh while making love. They'd teased each other, and once rolled off the bed onto the floor.

Wrapped in each other and a sheet, their laughter had stilled, and that lovemaking had been very gentle and seeking and slow. With the rhythm of the waves below her, and Ewan's body above, blending with hers, Cyd had forgotten the darkness haunting her life.

She'd thought only of the man making love with her, how reverently Ewan touched her, how his hands skimmed over her breasts, her sides and waist, how his thumbs smoothed the bones of her hips. While his lips had slid gently over hers, his breath uneven and warm on her skin, Cyd had stroked his face and somehow knew instinctively that she eased him, gave him something he hadn't found before. Ewan had laid his face against her throat and relaxed against her, even as they made love. A slow, easy sweep of his open hand along her thigh, to the back of her knee, drawing it higher, began another journey upward.

The little seeking kisses Ewan had given her were like presents, and Cyd had opened herself to him, gave him something she hadn't known existed.

Later, she'd lain curved to the window view of the lake, and Ewan had spooned his body around hers, scooping her a bit closer. They'd watched the night and listened to the water and between them, silence was enough. He'd taken her hand and brought it to his lips, and she'd turned slightly to meet his kiss.

His gentleness was more frightening than his fierce need, the moments when their bodies seemed to fight each other, slick with sweat . . . when she held Ewan with all her strength and he withdrew; then he lifted her hips higher, allowing a deeper fit.

Cyd stretched again on the bed—Ewan's bed. His scent, blended with the poignant sexual one. He'd given her pleasure and his gentleness changed the dark memories she'd had as a child. . . .

The thin silver crescent of a new moon suited Cyd, a new beginning that she traced with a fingertip.

Was this how her mother had felt with that "one wrong man"? As though she could float forever in their special moments together? Was that "wrong man" Cyd's father? Who was the man found at the old Callahan house?

Alone in Ewan's bed, Cyd listened to the rhythmic sound coming from the shop. A dim light shone from the apartment's opened door. Rising slowly, Cyd slid into Ewan's discarded T-shirt and followed the trail of light leading to the work area.

A work light had been drawn low from the ceiling, circling the man bent over the upside-down framework of the skiff. Wearing only boxers and worn loafers, Ewan planed a long curved section of wood, fitting it over the loose boards on the bottom of the boat. His notebook lay open on the board bottom of the boat, and Ewan measured the keel at different places, noting each separately with a slash of his pen.

The muscles of his back moved rhythmically, gleaming, as Cyd leaned against the apartment door, admiring his body. The strength of muscle and bone was there, but also a lover's touch as his fingers skimmed the wood—roughly scarred and callused, exciting hands that had driven her to the heights and soothed her later.

Bent to his work, Ewan's hair curled a little at his nape and softened his harsh features.

In profile, the slant of his cheekbone gleamed, shadowed by his long lashes and heavy black brows. She could almost feel that strong jaw, feel its hardness beneath the stroke of her fingers. She could almost feel his mouth upon her, demanding, soothing, giving, taking. . . .

Cyd smiled slightly, admiring Ewan, locked in his work.

Still caught by his notes, Ewan glanced at her, then back at his work. "Wear shoes if you come in here."

She slid into his work boots at the apartment door, and they clumped as she came to stand beside him. "I've forgotten a few things," he said thoughtfully. "It's coming back. It's damn slow work—good work. But this first time—"

"You're afraid."

"Yes. I thought I had what I needed, knew what I needed, but a handcrafter like my father usually has a few tricks of his own. There are a few of his boats still around—dinghies and skiffs, maybe a dory that's still good—and I've made offers on them. I'll study them. I might miss something in measuring the model to a larger scale."

He glanced at the small boat that Cyd had lifted to study. "It's a model for the skiff. I thought it would be a good start. She's light and tight with a double-planked bottom. Good for a fisherman and around the waterfront. She'll tow well, and make a good tender for a larger craft. She's a twelve-footer. I've got a fourteen-footer in mind."

Ewan lifted the keel, braced it on the bottom of the boat, and shaved off another curl of wood.

Cyd turned the tiny wooden boat in her hands, a tiny, perfectly detailed skiff. "You took this with you when you left Fairy Cove. I thought it was a toy."

"It was a dark day when I left Fairy Cove. I wanted to take you and Hallie with me."

"You were only a boy, Ewan. You did what you could."

"Hallie," he said quietly in a tone laden with guilt. "She paid a big price. I've yet to have that talk with Allan."

He turned the keel and fitted it over the loose boards at the bottom of the boat. "That 'toy' is my father's work. Thanks to Sean, who helped keep them dry, I have different models in safekeeping and a good set of Dad's notes. With careful measuring, it's a good model for the real thing. It's going to be a long hard year, Cyd. Maybe two before I start shipping kits. I've already had to restart several times. I've miscalculated. If the kits are made up with my mistakes, it will be hard to recover from a bad start. Word travels fast."

The disgust in his tone couldn't be ignored.

"You'll do it, Ewan," Cyd said softly. He'd come from a boy to a man, back to make his dream come true.

"That I will, love." He smiled briefly, ran his hand over her hair, and leaned to kiss her nose. "Now put your arms around me and hold me for a minute while I finish this."

But Cyd was already leaping into Ewan's idea of marketing boat kits and the money to be made. She walked around the skeleton of the skiff, studying the lines. "I could do this."

Ewan straightened and clearly amused, lifted an eyebrow. "Oh, could you now?"

"It's only wood and a few tools, add in some glue." Cyd was in earnest now, plans to make money scurrying through her brain. "I can run a saw. I've lived near this waterfront my whole life. How hard could it be? After I'm done renovating Elfindale House for a bed-and-breakfast, I just might—"

Ewan closed his notebook. "You're turning me on . . . walking around like that, wearing my boots and T-shirt. Do you know, love, what it does to a man to see a woman wearing his clothes and looking all soft and rumpled and warm from his bed? His bed where he first discovered just how sweet and innocent she is, despite all her huff and brass? Where she's cuddled against him in her sleep and done other delicious things before she was truly awake?"

Cyd looked across the width of the skiff to Ewan and found his tender, playful expression. She felt a blush heat her cheeks, her heart pounding, as Ewan walked slowly toward her.

He smoothed her cheek and studied her face. What was he seeking? What did he want?

"You're not afraid now, are you, love?" he asked softly.

"No. Not of you. There's something else that moves in me . . . from another time . . . from another man. But I'm not afraid of you."

"That's good. Because when you looked at me that morning at your old house, and your eyes filled with terror—it isn't a sight I want to see again, you afraid of me." Ewan reached to pull the chain on the light, and the shop was sud-

denly dark and silent—and they were together, enclosed in a
perfect place, the world at bay. . . .

When Ewan lifted Cyd into his arms, his boots fell from
her feet. Because she was exactly where she wanted to be
then, Cyd wrapped her arms around him and snuggled close
as he carried her to bed.

"You're not going to fail, Ewan," she whispered against
his throat.

"No, I'm not."

"But think of somewhere else to put your shop, will you?
The location is supreme and I can still find a buyer for you."

"My brain is too busy thinking of what I'm going to do to
you, love. Or what you are going to do to me."

Cyd nibbled on his ear. "Me first."

Cyd awoke to bright daylight and to Ewan, fully dressed and
sitting up beside her in bed. Clean-shaven and showered, he
didn't look up from his notebook. "You're not going anywhere until we've had a decent breakfast. We didn't get to
eat last night."

Cyd flattened to the bed, shoved the hair from her face,
and blinked against the bright sunlight. She rose on her el-
bows, searched for a bedside clock, and found none. "I have
an appointment with the man I've hired to clear the Elfindale
House's backyard and plant an English garden. I'm truly
hoping there aren't any bodies there. Angela has had the
only herb tea garden and sculptured maze in Fairy Cove.
Mine is going to be ten times better. What time is it?"

Ewan turned a page in his notebook and placed his hand
over her forehead, pushing her head back to the pillow.
"Early. Lie still. But you're not going anywhere without
breakfast . . . here, with me. Running out won't do, not this
morning. Now take your shower, and I'll make breakfast."

"But—"

When Ewan leaned over her, his expression was grim, his

voice deep and fierce. "There are rules to this game, love. I'm not going to sneak into my woman's bed. You'll have to deal with that, love. If it's an affair we're having, then I'll have no other woman, and expect you to do the same."

"You know I'm not—I'm not like *her*."

"Oh, I truly do, since I'm your first." He caught the hand Cyd swung at him and kissed her wrist. "We're in a storm, love, and we're to ride it out, one way or another."

"I set my own rules," she whispered desperately, and feared that she had given Ewan too much.

"Change them. Breakfast will be ready when you're done with your shower."


Ewan admired the woman who stepped fully dressed and perfect from the tiny bathroom—almost perfect, except for the fire in her blue eyes, the wild toss of her damp red hair, and her full, well-kissed lips.

Not an easy woman, he thought, but one crafted for heavy storms and easy sailing with plenty of fighting heart—enough to stand up for what she wanted. And from the feel of her in his arms, Cyd just might want him—enough not to walk away easily.

He'd have to play a dainty game with her, because he was no sweetheart either, not when he had set his goals. And because locked deep inside Cyd was a terror she didn't understand, and he couldn't bear to hurt her. . . .

Cyd faltered for only a heartbeat upon seeing Hallie and Sean, seated around the tiny wooden table, having breakfast. The roses she'd given Ewan were battered and limp now, forgotten during the night. But still they were precious to him, and he'd placed them in a glass jar on the table. Hallie had added an aspirin to perk them up slightly.

Cyd glanced at the bed, which was neatly made now, then away from Ewan as she straightened and pasted a smile on her face. "Oh, good morning, everyone."

Glorious, Ewan decided as he rose to pull out her chair. Most of all, he admired the way she threw herself into a tussle.

This morning, that tussle was with herself. Cyd wouldn't give herself over lightly to an easy relationship; she'd seen too much when she was too young and gotten a dim view of what men wanted—and how they could hurt.

But there would be no denying that they'd had each other, branded each other during the night.

Cyd ignored him, of course. And so, of course, he had to brush a kiss along her warm cheek and nip her ear, enjoying the slight quiver that shot through that long, fine, luscious, silky-smooth, strong body.

Ewan sat beside her and heaped bacon and eggs and fried potatoes onto her plate. "Hallie brought muffins and butter. And Sean."

"I did not bring Sean." Hallie poured coffee from a battered pot into Cyd's cup. "He brought himself."

"I was lonesome," Sean said quietly.

Hallie leaned back to stare at him. "The Donovans just have at least ten people at their house every morning for breakfast. The place is busy as a beehive, and there is a horde of children running everywhere. How could you possibly be lonesome?"

"For you," he answered simply, his eyes sparkling as he teased, "You wear the scent of baking like perfume. Vanilla is . . . erotic."

Hallie blinked at him and turned to Ewan. "You encourage him. You two are no better than when you were boys, out to cause trouble, tormenting anyone in your path."

Sean grinned widely as he said, "Ewan promised to help me today with my passenger boat. I was to come early and help him pack caulk and tools. If you're in a mood later, we could go out to Three Ravens Island. I'm taking out supplies that Norma has ordered. In another week, we'll be stuffed with dreamy-eyed honeymooners, wrapped so close in each other that they probably won't care what they eat. You can take some of those fabulous muffins for Peter."

"How is Peter? Still guarding his privacy?" Ewan asked as he noted that his sister let Sean hold her hand beneath the table.

Sean scooted nearer Hallie's chair and placed his arm around the back, toying with her hair. She pretended not to notice, but Ewan noted with satisfaction a slight softening of his sister's spine, the way she tilted her head to Sean's touch.

"Peter knows you want to talk with him about your parents," Sean continued. "But he's not offering to come to you. He was close to your father and has little to say on that matter."

Ewan buttered another bran muffin and spooned strawberry jam over it. He ate a half and put the other on Cyd's plate. She had already worked her way through the potatoes, eggs, and bacon he'd served her.

He appreciated Cyd's healthy appetite, because he knew how much energy she had expended during the night. Ewan couldn't resist—he ran his finger around her ear, fascinated by the shape of it, and the heat that suddenly leaped to Cyd's averted face. "Peter comes to Fairy Cove sometimes, doesn't he? By boat?"

Sean shook his head. "Not often. He talks with Norma more than to me, and she gets his supplies. I guess he misses a woman's touch. He comes to the resort and they talk. He's asked for privacy on his land and I never go to the piece of land my grandfather designated to be Peter's alone while he lives."

Ewan sat back to watch Cyd devour her food and reach for more. When she licked a buttered crumb from her lips, his body tightened and as though she sensed his need, Cyd glanced at him and delighted him with another blush.

And he had to kiss her. "You're lovely in the morning, darling-mine," he whispered against her cheek. "You wouldn't be embarrassed, would you? Now that our affair is sealed and stamped and the truth is out?"

She straightened and narrowed her eyes at him. "Not a bit. But you're far too sure of yourself."

"Then that blush says you're shy of me. You like me. You like me," he singsonged, richly enjoying himself in his own home—so to speak—with his woman, his sister, and a dear friend. His family, a new one, that he had needed badly through the years, was all together this morning.

"You're so full of it."

Without missing a beat, Cyd turned to Hallie, who was obviously at the point of giggling aloud, and created a distraction. "What do you think of this apartment? It could use a little color, couldn't it?"

"What's wrong with it?" Sean asked, frowning, as he scanned the spartan appearance of Ewan's apartment.

"Not a thing. It's got what I need," Ewan stated with a careless shrug, though he was uneasy now. Cyd had that lit-up look as if she had a brand-new project in mind.

"No color at all," Hallie stated thoughtfully as she studied the apartment. "Seems very—male."

"That's because a man lives here," Ewan said, set to defend his territory. He didn't like the women's shared look. Then Cyd rose to take a measuring tape from her briefcase, and Hallie stood to take one end of the tape.

The women stretched the tape across the huge bare windows overlooking Lake Michigan, and Ewan didn't trust Cyd's "Mmm." Or how she quickly made notes and studied the room, as if ideas were leaping into her head. "It's all about atmosphere. In the shop, a few blue glass balls and coarse fishnet draped around the ceiling and walls would give more of a look. Maybe hang an old wooden fishing boat at serving height. With an iced shrimp buffet inside it—and in here, maybe an office, or a private dining room. But if you're living here, sleeping here, it should definitely be more eye-appealing."

She turned to the sound of the buzzer at the shop's door, and Ewan gave her a warning frown. "Don't even think about it. I like it how it is. No frilly woman stuff."

"This place is perfect to draw another buyer. One with deeper pockets." Cyd's look at Hallie was meaningful. "Your dear brother quashed my deal with McGruder's. Angela had frameworked the whole deal, to her benefit. We hashed that out yesterday. And I'm not happy with Ewan's part, either. They've got something between them, Angela and Ewan, and if it's what I think it is, it's a last-man-standing game. I've planned for years to have that game with Angela."

Hallie shook her head. "It's always been that way between them. I wish—"

"We're not going to be a happy family," Ewan stated, and wished for Hallie's sake that he'd softened his words.

Cyd held his eyes. "I want to make this clear. What's between Angela and me is just that. I want to take her out myself, and I don't want anyone fighting my battles for me. I've come this far on my own, and if you think I'm going to let you take over—"

Ewan could tell she was just winding up and gave a time-out signal with his hands. "Yes, dear," he said in an unlikely meek tone.

He smiled at Cyd's gasp, and Hallie's giggle followed him out of the apartment.

When Ewan opened the shop's door, Finlay came in, grinning. "Sean and Hallie are here, or so says the gossip. Not much is missed when you sit on Main Street's spit-and-whittle bench overlooking this place. And it's likely that Cyd never left last night, so she should be here, too. When night came, we just moved to a good window at the Blue Moon Cafe. Am I to believe that there would be tender hearts here who would want to feed a poor old man?"

He leaned close to whisper, "Angela's got her back up.

She's already had Fred place calls to the shop owners that their rent might be raised. She's called the entire town council separately, of course, pushing for Elfindale Street to be rezoned for commercial shops—body and mechanic shops, signs and cabinets, and that sort of thing. That bed-and-breakfast that Cyd just bought will be smack-dab in the middle of machinery and noise and delivery trucks. This because of the fur that flew yesterday and that, no doubt Cyd whispered in your ear. . . ."

Finlay placed his gnarled hand on Ewan's shoulder. "Better watch your back. Angela can get mean, and Cyd is set to fight. That old witch has already planted gossip that Cyd knows more than she's saying about the body."

Ewan nodded; he'd expected that move, and despite Cyd's orders, he wasn't staying in the background if she needed protection. "Do you know where Paddy is?"

"Not a word about Paddy. But someone saw the Night Man again last night. Paddy used to have that job a while ago—prowling around town and haunting the waterfront, scaring the tourists. . . . Get out of my way, boy. I'm headed for the smell of good food and lovely women."

Finlay hurried toward the apartment, but the expensive black car prowling down Main Street caught Ewan's attention.

"Keep on your side of the fence, dear Auntie," he warned silently, and closed the door against her prying. The game between them had just kicked up in pace. Cyd would want to handle the Elfindale squeeze by herself, but if Angela's goons laid a hand on Cyd—

"I'm sorry, Angela. There's no word of the locket yet. I'll keep asking," Fred said quietly.

Angela stood by her window overlooking Fairy Cove's streets. In the last week of May, Thelma Brit had just been killed in a one-car accident—smashing her car into an electric pole.

And the locket Angela wanted badly wasn't in her possession. Thelma's son, Danny, understood the hefty price Angela would pay to get it back, and he was now scouring his mother's cluttered house. A pack rat by nature, Thelma had her usual hiding places, and her son knew all of them—because he'd been privately selling away her things.

Elderly and suffering from severe sleep apnea and sleep deprivation, Thelma's death had not been questioned. She had simply gone to sleep while driving.

And the locket Angela had given Thelma was lost.

Three of her friends had died recently, and Ewan Lochlain just *had* to be responsible . . . or in some way connected to their deaths.

Now he'd teamed with that young witch, Cyd, and the two of them were set to unseat Angela, to destroy her.

And Marvin, the chief of police in Fairy Cove, wasn't pressing an investigation. He wouldn't be intimidated either. "I'm sorry about your friends' deaths. But Angela, they had severe health problems and some years on them. If the medical examiner doesn't question their deaths, I'm not going to either," Marvin had said.

He was only a young pup and still had to learn his lessons, Angela decided briskly.

"Where is Paddy?" she asked Fred as casually as she could manage. Fear tightened her throat and shook her hands.

"I have no idea, dear." Fred looked up from his paperwork. "You know that young family you want evicted will draw community sympathy. Her husband's lingering illness has hurt their finances, and with three little ones—"

"I'm not in the sympathy business, Fred. Partial payments won't serve. We can raise the rent for that property, and instead of maintaining year-round, we can get decent summer people in there."

"Yes, dear."

On her return to her office, Angela passed Maria Sanchez as she was polishing the curved cherrywood banister that led upstairs. Because she was frustrated and fearful of her power slipping away, Angela needed to rule someone, and Maria was convenient. Since Maria's work was flawless, Angela chose to recall a previous offense. "You understand that you must never allow young children here. They are destructive. Your older daughters may come, as long as their work is good. The next time I find a child's toy here, your paycheck will be lowered double the amount."

"Sorry, ma'am. I know. You told me before when you found the doll. But as I said, I could find no one to keep Sophia and I—"

"No excuses. I'm just reminding you of what can happen if you don't follow my rules." Feeling a little more in control of her domain now, Angela walked briskly to the kitchen and spoke to her cook. "Edna, I am having the city council members over for tea this afternoon. Please prepare a light buffet lunch in addition to a lemon pound cake. I want the men to feel especially comfortable and they like to eat—cold cuts perhaps, something for a good sturdy sandwich. Prepare the dining room, will you? I don't want that mess in my study."

"But ma'am, there is little time to shop—"

"Goodness, Edna. It's only nine o'clock in the morning. You have plenty of time until three o'clock. You can call the grocer for delivery of what you need. No excuses now."

In her study, Angela looked down at the Lochlain boat shop. "Where is Paddy?" she repeated to herself. "He should be needing money by now. And Cyd does need a reprimand. I will not tolerate her sass. Linda is where she belongs, and I'll see that Cyd follows her mother's path. Unstable, the both of them."

She started to turn the tiny ring on her finger, Tom's courting gift, and frowned at its loss. Angela's mind started turning on ways to work Hallie's soft heart. If Hallie were to return the ring—as a gift of family ties—Ewan couldn't protest.

But where was the locket that Ewan had sought? Where were the brooch and the cross? Was Paddy playing games, not answering her cell phone page? Did he have anything to do with her friend's deaths? Would he come after her next?

Angela could feel her power slipping; she sensed the danger prowling near her. She fought her panic with the promise that she would destroy Cyd—and cause Ewan to fail, to lose his pride and send him off again.

She placed her hand on her fast-beating heart. Ewan looked so much like Tom . . . that he took her breath away. . . .

Where was that locket?

"It's only the first week of June. Elfindale House will be ready for a few guests by July. Reduced rates, of course, because fine-tuning will have to wait until the season slows. By next year, the Elfindale Bed-and-Breakfast's rates will be both reasonable and profitable. My English garden is going to be wonderful, stuffed with herbs and flowers and a wonderful maze. The fountain will take some doing, but the garden will be bigger and better than Angela's. I might invite the Garden Club here for teas. It could become a ladies' teatime regular. It was a good investment—"

Cyd stopped talking and watched Ewan run a skilled hand over the Elfindale house's banister. This morning, he'd insisted on walking her home. It was only six o'clock and Fairy Cove was quiet and Cyd couldn't wait to start her day. With Ewan's hand linked with hers, it seemed only right to bring him to her newest and proudest acquisition.

In her mind, Cyd saw the empty two-story house filled with vintage furnishings. She had the perfect long and well-used wood family table stored in her garage, amid a collection of knickknacks and quilts that would give the bed-and-breakfast a homey look.

"Rooms. We'll have to knock out a room or two, and the bathroom will have to do for now. It's rough now, but the house is sturdy. I can just see white wicker furniture and ferns for the front porch, a few flowerpots here and there . . . The banister is cherrywood—it can be revarnished for now, but the stairs have to be good and sturdy. . . . The contractor is already updating the wiring, and the roof will hold until next year. . . ."

Cyd smiled as she remembered how Ewan had looked when she'd entered the shop the evening before—damp from a shower, his jeans's top snap undone, brooding about a miscalculation in his notes. The shop's double doors had been open, letting the cool early-summer air into the shop.

He glanced at the pull-along cart she'd eased inside the door. "Blinds for the apartment," she'd explained because she knew that scowl—Ewan was too deep in his calculations to be distracted. "Is anyone else here?"

"No. And the curve of this damned thing is all wrong. I didn't allow enough for the depth. The hull has to be broader by an inch. . . ."

Cyd had eased the pull-along cart into the shop and closed the double doors, placing the board that barred them into place. She had locked the single door and walked into the apartment, pulling the cart behind her. She had closed the door quietly, leaving Ewan to his calculations.

Because she was wearing her good slacks, she'd slid them off and stood on a chair to lift the first sea grass blind over the window. Then the next of the three blinds. A quick hammer-and-nail job would do to temporarily hold them in place.

She'd taken off her silk blouse to protect it, and with the blinds unrolled, she'd stood up on the chair to make a firmer job of it.

Intent upon getting the job done quickly, before Ewan could object, Cyd hadn't heard him enter the apartment.

When two gentle hands cupped and smoothed her bottom, Cyd's mind had stopped.

It had started working again when Ewan's hands came around to cradle her breasts and one took the hammer from her. His heat and his hunger circled her, his mouth roaming open against her ribs, then lower to cruise her hips, his fingers sliding up beneath the elastic of her briefs, stroking and taking her breath away.

He had turned her slowly and lowered her against him. Ewan's darkened gaze slowly roamed over her hair, her face, her shoulders, and down to where her bra cupped her breasts. His hand on her back had opened, easing her closer to him, her pale skin and lace pressed close to his tanned hard chest. "I like this," he whispered rawly. "You against me."

Ewan had picked Cyd up in his arms and carried her to his bed, easing down upon her. He'd come to her with a long sweet kiss, so tender it terrified her.

Now, with a black T-shirt and worn jeans and workman's boots, Ewan studied the Elfindale house with the eye of an experienced handcrafter. "She'll do," he said finally.

"I want you to see the kitchen. I've got a lovely old family-style table that will be wonderful for serving." Cyd led the way into the kitchen and suddenly stopped, a chill raising the hair on her nape.

From behind, Ewan's hand rested on her shoulder. "What's wrong, Cyd?"

"I feel something. It's like someone is watching me. I've always felt it—" Her panic rose, fear of the Night Man choking her. But it was morning, and the house was empty.

A branch scraped a window, and Cyd shivered, then braced herself. "Sometimes I feel like this in my house. Like someone has been there, and that isn't possible. My house is always locked, the alarms set. There are times when I'm fixing up the rentals, or remodeling, and I feel—my skin seems to prickle as if someone has been in the room. I feel like that now—that someone has been here, waiting for me, always waiting for me."

Ewan turned her slowly to him, holding her face in his hands, looking deep into her eyes. "There's no one here but you and me, Cyd."

"There was someone here. Someone who wants me. I know it. I can feel him."

"Cyd, if you had estimates done, repairmen here, and people looking at this place to buy—"

She shook her head. Her body was cold, despite Ewan's arms around her. Against his throat, she said, "No. It's different. I can feel him waiting . . . for me."

Cyd held Ewan tighter. "I was excited to bring you here, to show you my new toy. But I felt it outside, that someone was watching us. You think I'm—"

"No, I don't. I think that Angela has probably set one of her flunkies—Paddy, maybe—to following us. And that your senses are telling you the truth."

Cyd rested against Ewan, then she eased back. "There are things I knew and have forgotten. The body at the old house wasn't the only thing there. I've just remembered something else. Whatever I could find of your parents' light day sailer that washed ashore, I hoarded there. I don't know why. I just know that I wanted to keep Tom Lochlain safe somehow, and your mother, and it was the best that I could do. I simply forgot. I'm sorry I didn't tell you sooner."

"Maybe you needed to forget. Let's go," Ewan said grimly.

# Chapter 15

"The investigators knew this cellar was here. I told them. They went down there, rooted around a bit, and saw nothing of interest. I was so overwhelmed by the body that—I haven't remembered this in all these years."

With Ewan at her side, Cyd glanced at the broken windows of her old house, their ragged edges of shattered glass glinting in the afternoon light. She rubbed her arms, her flesh and her soul both chilled. Somehow she was trapped back in time, a terrified six-year-old once more.

"We'd gone away somewhere, a little house, I remember. A man came now and then and brought groceries, a few toys. Linda said nothing had happened, but I knew. . . ."

What had happened?

What had not happened? Her mother had been beaten badly several times, the drug use increasing. . . .

Ewan's hand, strong and safe, locked with hers. Despite the sunlight filtering into the damp, secretive shadows, Cyd felt the nightmares crawling inside her . . . waiting.

"Thank you, Cyd. I know what this must have cost you, coming back here."

"She wanted you to know. I'd forgotten that. No one paid

much attention to a little girl and her poor mother hauling what looked like scavenged firewood back to the house. My mother even asked for the pieces, begged for them when necessary. I don't want to think of how she paid— The investigators removed the brush covering. They searched it thoroughly. Linda— Mother helped me put them down there. I remember how she worked, sweating and desperate, to help me cover that cellar door."

Ewan bent to lay aside rotted boards. "It looks like two or more layers of wood here."

"Linda thought that we should put doors over the cellar one, to protect it, she said. She even painted the doors with weather-resistant paint, and tucked plastic sheets over the layers. Ewan, she told me that one day you would want these . . . that something you would want to know lay in the pieces. She said you'd know. To have something of your father, I suppose."

Crouched and carefully lifting the boards the investigators had carelessly thrown across the cellar opening, Ewan looked up at her. His expression was so fierce and determined that— "What's wrong, Cyd?"

She swallowed that jolt of fear, because she didn't understand why at times Ewan could terrify her. He was her lover. He'd never hurt her. . . . "Nothing," she said finally.

"I think that Linda knew something about my parents' deaths that day. Did she ever say anything?"

"She said that all it took was one wrong man to ruin a woman's life. . . . Only that your parents loved each other very much, and that Tom Lochlain was the best man she'd ever known. She wished that my father had had his honor and pride. She made me promise not to tell anyone about the pieces in the cellar. It was our secret."

Ewan stood and bent to kiss her briefly. "You're cold and shaking. If you want to leave now, I'll understand."

"I should have told you sooner."

But Ewan was already moving down into the old cellar, flashlight in hand.

In the underbrush, a rabbit stared at Cyd. Birds flew from the old grove as though startled, as though someone had frightened them.

Cyd fought panic; she wouldn't allow her fears to drive her from the old cellar. Ewan would be trapped—she took another breath and steadied herself. There was no one in the old grove of trees, the birds settling upon the limbs. A gust of wind had disturbed them, that was all, she told herself. Yet the feeling that she was being watched lingered, raising the hair on her nape. "Ewan?"

He appeared in the dark hole and brushed cobwebs from his hair. "I don't know how you and your mother managed. There's a lot of wood down here. Some of it is rotted now. I'll get Sean to help. We'll haul it to the shop."

Ewan came up the concrete steps beside her, took one close look, and said, "No more for you today."

Cyd couldn't move as Ewan covered the cellar opening. Then, somehow, she was sitting beside him in his pickup, and his arm had drawn her close.

"Okay?" Ewan asked as she looked back at the old house.

"I never thought about how hard Linda worked until today. How she fought for the pieces that washed ashore. Without drugs and alcohol, she was determined. I remember her shaking and sweating and struggling against her addictions."

Ewan was silent for a moment, then he said slowly, "I want to buy this place from you, Cyd."

"What?"

"You were terrified just now. I don't like that. Either let me buy it and deal with clearing it, or let me help you change it."

Cyd shook her head. "There's something about it that holds me. I don't know what. It's got to stay here, just like this, until I know why it holds me."

A man who had his share of fighting the past and one who understood Cyd's very personal battles, Ewan nodded. "When you can, show me what you remember of those pieces, where they were. . . . Some of them had been hacked. This is just the evidence I've been looking for, Cyd. Someone deliberately used an ax on that wood. That mahogany and oak and cedar didn't break as easily as the spruce and pine. The chopping marks are still there."

"I'll take you there now, if you want. I remember where we found the pieces. Linda told anyone who asked that we wanted it for the stove. Maybe she—"

Ewan studied Cyd's hand, measured her fingers against his own. "She is a small woman. She wasn't likely to be handling a woodman's heavy ax. The question is, who knew that my parents had started taking regular outings. Every Tuesday or Wednesday afternoon, depending on the weather, they had 'their date.' "

He started the pickup. "It would take a man's strength to use that ax."

"Paddy?"

"I checked. Twenty-one years ago, when my parents died, he was in Chicago. Someone else did that damage."

"Ewan, I think someone has been watching us—here."

He scanned the house and the brush. "Where?"

"From the grove, where the men used to hide their cars."

Ewan turned off the motor and slid from the pickup. "Come on."

Minutes later, after picking their way through the brush, Ewan crouched to examine the grove's freshly bent grass and broken twigs. "You're right. Someone has been here. The question is who?"

Paddy threw his duffel bag onto the small neat cot. He scanned the shack hidden behind Greer House. He noted the broom and bucket, the plastic jugs of water on the floor, the radio, television, and the earphones that he had been ordered to use. The carton of cigarettes was there, his favorite brand and some Cuban cigars. Paddy swept a hand to the table, and claimed a bottle. "Ah, yes. The whiskey, Angela. Only the best from your cabinet."

The familiar envelope had been taped beneath the old table, stuffed with cash, a down payment for the job he would do. No notes this time, the old girl had said, only cellular phone contact, coded messages left in his text mailbox.

"Cyd. Accident," was the order that Paddy would relish completing.

He drank thirstily, then crouched to open the electric ice chest on the floor. Stuffed with cheese and ham and cake, it was enough until— "Until you bring me more, Mrs. Greer."

The whiskey had burned a path to his stomach—lighting the pain there—enough to make him gasp and double. With a shudder, Paddy straightened, furious with age and doctor's orders. He'd always done as he wanted, and no doctor was telling him what to do. No sissy diets for Paddy O'Connor; he'd drink what he wanted and eat what he wanted.

He lit a cigar, puffed it, and released a series of familiar coughs. When they ended, he settled down to enjoy the luxury Angela could provide. This would be his last job for her. Then he'd find the note written twenty-one years ago and blackmail *her* with it.

Paddy relished the idea of the fancy Mrs. La-De-Da Angela Greer, lugging his needs to him like a servant. He settled down to enjoy himself, keeping out of sight as Angela had ordered. When Cyd was killed, it would be best no one knew he was in the area.

At four o'clock, Cyd walked beside Ewan on the beach north of Fairy Cove's harbor. Acres of sand stretched along the shoreline, tufts of tall grass bending in the wind. "That's it,

Ewan. All I can remember. Mother worked so hard collecting the pieces, but there was little left."

Ewan noted the waves, the way the wind topped them with whitecaps. He mentally drew a map of where the pieces of his parents' sailing boat had been found and gauged the distance out to Three Ravens Island. A good man with a light, fast sailing boat, Tom Lochlain could have managed the minor squall that had come up that clear day. He could have made it to shore, either on the mainland or at the island.

The charred pieces of the boat logically should have washed toward Fairy Cove, with the body of his mother. . . .

Cyd studied him. "Ewan?"

"I know in my gut that it was no accident. No life jackets washed ashore. Only pieces of the boat here, and my mother's body near Fairy Cove. I'm drying the wood now, carefully, and maybe I'll never have proof. I want to talk with Peter."

"Peter isn't always chatty. You'll get more by going through Norma."

Ewan glanced at Cyd, the wind scooping her hair up and sailing it around her face, bright tendrils catching the afternoon sun, striping them across her pale skin. The day had been harsh to Cyd: the memory of her mother working desperately to save the pieces, preserving them as best she could, and more—the terrified child coaxed back into reality by her mother's care.

To distract Cyd, to pull her from the darkness that seemed wrapped around her now, Ewan wrapped a finger in a silky strand and studied the fiery glints amid the dark. "Have you set siege to Angela yet?"

The Cyd he knew came back to life, temper flying. "Ask the council to her teas, will she? She'll have to play a better game than that."

Ewan enjoyed the lift of her head, the fire in her blue eyes. He couldn't resist brushing a kiss on those lovely, smirking lips. "You've got her set in a trap, do you?"

"I did a little research and guess what? Elfindale Street has an over one-hundred-year-old tree on it called a 'Peace Tree.' At the turn of the last century, politicians gathered to plant it in the name of peace. Articles have been written about it. The historical society is set to defend it. That historical society has council members or ones married to historical society members. They network with state and national societies. Protests have already started flooding city hall. A senator grew up on that street, and a few other well-placed state and national dignitaries are related to families who once owned those houses."

She met Ewan's second kiss and arched against him, her arms around his shoulders. "I made a few calls. The local historical society, of which Angela is a member, is now circulating a petition to renovate that street, and my bed-and-breakfast is going to sit right smack in the middle of it. My renovation plans have already been cleared, but I intend to keep the integrity of the house. . . . Angela will back down, because of the pressure. Gee whiz, she's been foiled again. After she lost out on my office and Hallie's shop, she had Fred running offers to me every day."

"That should keep you busy for a while and off the sale of my property."

"I've been thinking about that. The boat shop is perfect for a restaurant. I could—"

"No."

"If you would only listen to reason—"

Ewan traced her eyebrows, sleek and high and arched. He ran a fingertip across the long fringes of her lashes, darkened by mascara. "I like you better without this, when you're all drowsy and soft and sweet against me."

"I always put on full makeup when preparing for war—or a business deal."

He enjoyed the richness of color, the contrast of fair skin and blue eyes, the warmth of her cheeks. Heat leaped between them, fierce and hungry as a summer storm. Cyd's hands gripped his jacket, and her eyes darkened, filling with him. She studied his lips, his face, and seemed to go inside herself.

Ewan understood. Cyd was remembering their lovemaking. He could almost feel himself inside her, the textures and scent of a woman he desired more than any other. His hands sought her hips, drawing her close against his body, already hard and jutting.

The wind rose and whispered through the trees, bringing the fragrances of earth and grass, and seagulls screamed out on the lake. Yet Ewan and Cyd stood, wrapped in their own burgeoning storm, a mix of sensuality and tenderness.

He opened the top buttons of her blouse and hooked his finger in her lacy bra, tugging it.

Against her throat, Ewan breathed her scent, caught the wildness of it, the fast beat of her heart. He gave himself to feeling, just feeling her soft and sweet and breathless against him. "I like how your breath catches, as if you don't know whether to release it or not. Then, finally, you have to. It's like that when you make love. You hold until the last minute, then there's that delicious minute when you come hot and fast and shatter. All those little purrs and ohs, and ragged breath."

"You're already aroused. You'd better be careful. You'll talk yourself into embarrassment."

Her hands smoothed his chest, ran up and down his sides, and latched on to his belt, tugging him closer. Her tongue was agile in his mouth, sucking his. She drew back and gave him a delicious smirk. "Think about that for the rest of the day."

Cyd looked down to where his hands were busy, unzipping her slacks. "No bed, Ewan. Just acres of gritty sand. Not a blanket in sight. You're too big for the front seat of the pickup, though I heard you were pretty agile in one when you were a teen. Dear me, I guess you'll have to wait."

"Will I?" Ewan enjoyed Cyd's tease, because even now, her breasts were hard-tipped and etched his bare stomach, his shirt and jacket pushed aside. "If I have to wait, there's no need for you to suffer."

Cyd lifted an eyebrow. "I think you've got that reversed. I'm just fine."

"You will be."

He released her bra, eased it aside to take her nipple into his mouth, to roll it on his tongue, just as his finger slid inside her moist heat to stroke another button . . . and Cyd tensed, her body beginning to pulse, her head thrown back. When he cupped her, she braced herself and gripped his arms. "Stop playing, Ewan."

But he'd drawn back to look at the reddish curls moist and soft in his hand. "It was something I had to see . . . I've been wondering. There was no time before—"

Cyd's arms locked tightly around his shoulders, her hips moving in the rhythm to his hand. Her breath uneven, her hair flying around her head, stroking his face like red silky whips, her mouth parted and sweet, her eyes half-closed.

She began to quiver and tighten, then he couldn't wait . . .

Ewan back-walked her slowly to his pickup. He cupped her breasts, playing with her nipples, tugging the peaks, caressing her breasts. He looked at them in his hand, and his look of hunger dried Cyd's throat.

"You're perfect," he whispered, the wind catching his hair until she had to smooth it away from his face. She caught the heat from his flesh, felt his pounding need within her own rushing blood. His eyes were slits between his black lashes, his look consuming her.

The urge to cover herself gave way to a surprising boldness, and she pressed against his chest, loving the texture of burning skin and the chafe of hair against her own sensitized flesh. She ran her hand down his jeans, found that hard, bulky shaft beneath the cloth, and stroked him.

Play, she thought, confident in herself now. Playing with Ewan, but on a different level, trusting him and herself. She wanted to devour him, and fought the tremors in her body, the intimate clenching that ached for him— "I'd have you now, but we have a problem—"

"Do we? We could make do, you and me," he had asked rawly as he nibbled on her ear.

Ewan Lochlain was a six-foot-three adventure, just waiting to be experienced. She leaned forward to lick his nipple and felt the jolt hit his body, the taut lock of his muscled thighs against her own. Cyd had as much power over him, as he did— at the moment—over her. "I've always loved making do."

"That's my girl."

"I'm not your girl."

He grinned, but there was still that dangerous edgy look, the color riding high on his cheekbones, and she knew she'd follow him anywhere. . . . She felt young and riding the edge of life, filled with her own power and a joy she couldn't explain.

While she was still laughing up at Ewan, he turned her slightly and eased her slightly over the truck's fender. He arranged her jacket to cover her body against the metal, then against her back, gently pressed her still.

"Ewan?"

"Coming, love." His body pressed against hers, his lips open on her throat. He eased her briefs and slacks lower, then his body pressed against hers. The blunt nudge of his sex against her own moist femininity startled her at first, then Ewan's deft fingers found that intimate place, stroking her as he slid slowly upward.

"Okay?" he asked roughly, while her body accepted the fullness of his.

"I . . . don't . . . know," she managed, as sensations poured over her, and her hand found the hood ornament, gripping it. She stood on tiptoe, pushing back against his slow thrust.

She fought flying out of herself, holding him tightly within, holding the hood ornament in her left and the thin blade of a windshield wiper in her right. She had no time to think, just to feel him inside her, stroking, filling, withdrawing. . . .

He withdrew slightly and nudged gently back into her. His body still covered hers from the back, his lips against hers. She turned slightly, meeting his kiss, his tongue. "I think I'm going to—"

When he stroked more quickly, she heard the crack of metal as her own cry flew into the clear blue sky.

Then Ewan was pressed heavily against her back, breath dragging slowly, heavily along her hot cheek. His hands came to fold over hers, and his smile curved along her cheek. "You broke my hood ornament and my windshield wiper, love."

Her hands still tightly gripped the shocking evidence. "You're proud of yourself, aren't you? Making me—"

He kissed her cheek and chuckled. "Oh, I made you all right."

When she couldn't think of a reply, Ewan kissed her cheek again and eased away. He patted her bottom and gave it a kiss, and still Cyd couldn't move. She was still holding the hood ornament and the windshield wiper when he turned her and pulled up her briefs and slacks.

Ewan's look was tender and knowing as he buttoned her blouse. "You're shocked, aren't you? Does it help to know that I am, too?"

"I don't think I can move. My legs—" She blinked and stared at him. "You're shocked?"

Ewan bent to kiss her and draw her against him. He rocked her gently. "It hasn't meant anything before. . . . You're scaring me, Cyd. You're still holding that ornament and the windshield wiper. Do you intend to use them on me?"

"No, no, of course not. I'll have them repaired. I . . ." She stared up at him helplessly, feeling the warmth of their love-making and warmed by something else.

*All it takes is one wrong man. . . .* Her mother's words

circled her, flew into the leaves above her head and out into the dark swells of the lake.

She held the metal tightly on her lap as Ewan drove back to Fairy Cove. He looked grim, and she sensed him moving into working with the puzzles of the wood, the wave action, and his parents' deaths.

Her fingers ached from gripping the metal. She couldn't give herself so easily . . . could she?

*All it takes is one wrong man. . . .*

"I want to go home," she stated suddenly, desperate for the stillness of her home without a brooding male to clutter her thoughts.

He turned and lifted an eyebrow. His hand stroked her thigh. "I thought we'd have dinner. I'll cook, or we can eat out. Or order in."

"I want to be alone."

In Fairy Cove, Ewan pulled alongside Main Street. He turned off the motor and stared at her. "I don't. I didn't give you much back there. Not what you deserve."

She glanced at the gray sky, where it met the black lake. In a few hours, night would come, and her fears. "I want to be home before dark."

"What just happened now, Cyd?"

She watched Angela's car slow, the older woman peering at her. Angela's sneer damned Cyd for her mother's fate, a woman with her color high, her hair mussed, a man bent intimately close to her. "Please take me home."

"Will you invite me in?" Ewan asked as he toyed with her hair.

"No. It's been a long, busy day."

She eased across the width of the seat and looked away from Ewan's cold expression. *All it takes is one wrong man. . . .* Had her mother felt so wonderful and sweet and flying on air?

Ewan started the engine and guided the truck out into the

street. "You're not your mother, Cyd. You're strong enough to handle bad weather. I shouldn't have taken you like that."

"Sex is sex. Need for a need."

Ewan was silent until they pulled into her driveway on Delaney Street. He turned to stare at her, his eyes silver in the shadows of the cab. His deep raw voice cut at her after she slammed the door. "You can keep your trophies—the hood ornament and the wiper. Pleasant dreams."

He reversed too quickly for her to return them, and Cyd hurried into her house and safety—from Ewan and from the Night Man.

Inside her locks and shutters, Cyd stood very still, her body chilled.

Somehow the Night Man had been inside her home; she felt him there still, in the shadows, waiting—always waiting for her. . . .

The Other smiled slightly as he stayed in the shadows on the opposite side of the street from the Blue Moon. At almost closing time, Ewan was easily seen, sitting alone at a corner table.

Clearly, Ewan was brooding, ignoring the waitress who came to rub his back. She positioned herself beside him, bending to reveal her well-filled cleavage, and Ewan didn't turn from staring at the table.

Jealousy rose and spiked in the man. The image of his father, Ewan drew women's attention the same way—without trying. They held a power that the man wanted more than anything, to make women desire him.

He'd stood in the grove, watching Ewan and Cyd at the old house, wishing that a woman would lean against him like that, trust him. There, Ewan had touched Cyd like a lover, comforting her. At the beach, he'd held her close after their lovemaking—if that's what it could be called.

Watching them, the man had given that privacy. But he

hungered for the intimacy and the tenderness later, the softness of that red silky hair against his face.

Yet Cyd had not let Ewan into her lovely little feminine
home.

The man fought his rising pain and smiled bitterly. He had
so little time remaining to finish his work, to kill again. . . .

# Chapter 16

After Sean had helped deliver the old boards to the boat shop, Ewan studied them for only a short time. But his mind was on Cyd and how she had hurried away from him, from what they had. With a frustrated groan, Ewan decided to brood alone over food and beer at the Blue Moon.

Hours later, Ewan had stayed away from his apartment and the lingering scent of Cyd in his bed long enough. At one in the morning, the Blue Moon was empty, and the bartender wanted to close. Ewan could not avoid returning to the boat shop; he was in for a long, very hard night, aching for Cyd.

The visit to the old Callahan house had started Cyd's mind flipping through the unpleasant past.

*All it takes is one wrong man to ruin a woman's life. . . .*

But then Ewan was guilty, wasn't he? Of using Cyd, taking her the quickest way for them both without much foreplay or a leisurely comfort later? Of reminding Cyd of her mother's profession?

Ewan breathed deeply, inhaling the sweet air of home. He understood Cyd's background. He understood that it was difficult for her to realize that tender emotions could run with sex.

He understood that he needed her, the sweet essence that was Cyd—Ewan smiled slightly, thinking of Cyd's many facets—biting, exciting, challenging and perfect.

Standing on the pier in front of the boat shop, Ewan automatically searched for the dimmed lights of the Fairy Bin on Main Street. Earlier, he'd seen Sean and Hallie walking together, probably from the Donovans'. Body language said that Sean was in pursuit, leaning closer, protectively toward Hallie . . . and she wasn't moving away. Rather, she was looking up at Sean.

Hallie had let Sean and Ewan know several times that she could handle Allan and Angela. Their protective interference would not be allowed, or excused. But if Angela ever raised her hand again to Hallie—Ewan did not want to think of what his cold anger might do.

Allan was another matter—Ewan knew exactly how to respond to a bully who had abused Hallie.

And of his own guilt? How could he erase leaving his fourteen-year-old sister behind to face all that?

Ewan reached into his pocket and retrieved his keys with his left hand, sorted through them, and with his left, reached for his new padlock. His fingers tangled in thread and Ewan bent to inspect the padlock. A gold chain had been wrapped around the padlock, and from it dangled his mother's locket.

His fingers shook as he carefully unwound the chain and lifted the locket, a fragile thing in his hands.

And Angela had been hunting it, according to Marvin. She said she wanted a memento of Thelma Brit, some small thing they both loved. Thelma Brit's son was tearing her house apart, searching for it—Angela had offered a tidy sum. But a thing that small and with Thelma's tendencies for hiding, the locket might never be found.

Yet it gleamed in the palm of Ewan's hand, and its appearance there could place him under suspicion. If anyone connected the other two pieces of his mother's jewelry with

Ewan, then the locket—he would definitely be a candidate for what? Did someone murder those three helpless women?

Ewan scanned Main Street, and his gaze slid up to Greer House where Angela probably stood, spying on him. Waiting to see if he'd go back to Hallie's, waiting to see if he'd walk to the police station.

If she wanted him to be suspect in theft, or murder, he wasn't playing. Inside his apartment, Ewan carefully opened the locket to find it empty.

According to Marvin, Thelma Brit's lack of sleep had caused her accident—asleep when she drove straight into an electric pole at sixty miles an hour.

She had a machine to help her sleep safely. But according to Hallie, Thelma had looked exhausted and distracted while visiting the shop. Sleep deprivation could be the reason, or someone could have deliberately, methodically distracted Thelma. Her son, Danny? A gambler who sold her things when he could?

Ewan clutched the locket in his fist. By asking for the lost locket, Angela had created a perfect frame for murder—and Ewan would be suspected. . . .

Angela. His dear aunt might have found a way to remove him from Fairy Cove.

Ewan began to work on the pieces of his parents' small sailing boat, no more than a mast and a sail, carefully using a magnifying glass to pick at the rot and inspect the hacking marks. The pieces were too small for a natural accident—someone had deliberately chopped them into shorter lengths. . . .

He took one piece and placed a blackened tip on paper. The resulting black line was that of charcoal. But then the beach was used for parties and any wood at hand was used. . . .

The telephone's shrill cut through the silence. Cyd's uneven whisper caught Ewan, chilling him. "Ewan?"

"What's wrong, Cyd?"

"He was here, about an hour ago. I saw his shadow outside my window."

Ewan gripped the telephone receiver until his hand ached. Cyd hadn't called him at first. Instead she'd waited—and feared. "Why didn't you call me sooner? Do you want me to come over?"

"No . . . no . . . I . . . I'm sorry I called. I need to handle this. I can manage . . ."

He ached for the child and for the woman, needing to hold her. He decided not to tell her about the locket; he didn't need to add more to her fears tonight. "Cyd, that business about a Night Man is just legend, and something that serves the shop-keepers to promote souvenirs. I'll come over and we'll talk."

"It's sex you're after, Ewan Lochlain." *All it takes is one wrong man. . . .*

The bald, true statement raked him. "That's an option. I'm greedy, you see. For you, as much as you are for me. It won't do to deny it."

Then because he was lonely and cut and a bit perverse and Cyd was Cyd and the night was long, and he wanted to give her something more to think about than the Night Man, Ewan added, "I haven't tasted you all over yet, love. That hunger is in my mind, what lies between those silky legs of yours. I know for certain how you'd look, riding me, all wild and bloomed with heat, squeezing—"

He listened to her silence, her ragged breathing, and added, "Right there, on the peak of what's burning you, you're beautiful—eyes closed, going into yourself. . . ."

"You looked!"

"At everything."

The line clicked off, and Ewan poured a whiskey neat, a good Irish blend, and with a shot glass in hand, settled down to wait. Cyd was most enjoyable when she was angry, and he'd bet on that hot temper of hers. Fully dressed, Ewan kicked off his shoes and settled on his bed, drawing her pillow to his face. He could smell flowers and cinnamon and al-most feel her hair sliding silkily across his skin— With a smile, he reached for the bedside telephone. "Yes, love?"

The silence at the other end was telling. Cyd wasn't letting him get ahead in the sleepless night business. If she needed company, but was unwilling to have him in the flesh, he'd give her comfort over the telephone. She might rile and rage at him, but it would take her mind off the Night Man legend.

Ewan smiled and settled in for tormenting her. "You miss me, don't you, darling-mine?"

"I'm lying here naked," Cyd stated slowly, huskily, after a heartbeat. "Naked and warm and dewy."

That one sentence jolted Ewan; he almost choked on the drink he had just sipped. His hand shook as he replaced the shot glass to the table.

"I'm running my hands over my body now, and oh yes . . . oh yes, I'm so ready and wet and—ohhhh!"

"Cyd." Ewan's admonishment sounded low and raw, his erection pushing heavily at his jeans.

With a sultry laugh, Cyd added, "Pleasant dreams, chum," and the line clicked dead.

Ewan downed the whiskey in one gulp. Then he had to smile, because Cyd could hold her own, and he enjoyed the battle—and the tenderness between them. On an impulse, he rang her.

She breathed quietly, then answered sweetly, "Yes, Ewan?"

"But then, love, isn't it rather lonely afterward? When you like to cuddle and sigh and hold on to something other than your pillow?"

Her laugh was low and wicked and knowing. "You, Ewan?"

"Me, specifically, love."

"But how could I do that to all the other women who need you, specifically?"

"They'll have to suffer on without me. I'm taken."

After a disbelieving silence, Cyd's "Good night" was firm.

"Good night. Call anytime. I'll deliver."

"I just bet you will."

"I mean it, Cyd. If you get scared again, call me. If it's Paddy, he's on my list to see, and so is Allan. If not, whoever it is should be caught. If you don't want to call Marvin, I'll come right over."

At three in the morning, Ewan had not slept. He lay on his bed, staring out into the black waves, his mind too restless to sleep. He'd gone over the national weather maps, the topography maps, and methodically pieced together the day his parents died. Ewan's mind churned with dates and bits of information, and the locket, the missing brooch and cross, tormented him.

And was Cyd snug and sleeping, dreaming of him, wanting him?

The solid bump of metal against a wooden pier said a boat rode the swells near the shop. A motor started, revved, and purred out into the lake.

Ewan dressed quickly. If he couldn't sleep, he'd follow whoever roamed the distance between Fairy Cove and Three Ravens Island. He grabbed a key for Sean's extra motorboat and ran from the shop. Running from boat to boat docked at the stalls, Ewan found the one he wanted, a small, tight runabout.

Whoever was headed toward Three Ravens Island was an expert with small craft. Though Ewan could no longer see or hear the boat, the direction was enough.

It led to the northern end of the island, where Peter the hermit lived.

Ewan pulled closer to the sandy beach, cut the motor, and let the waves carry him to a ramshackle dock. A hand on the warm motor told him it had been used recently.

The man standing on shore yelled, "Get out of here. This is private property. You can't have your wild parties here."

"It's Ewan Lochlain, Peter."

A shotgun's warning blast sounded over the waves. After a silence, the hermit called. "I don't care who you are. Leave me alone."

"I want to talk with you about my parents' accident—"

Another warning blast closed any conversation and Ewan turned his boat, heading back to Fairy Cove.

After hours of frustration and prowling along the beach, Ewan sat at Hallie's breakfast table.

When Cyd arrived, carrying her briefcase and a paper sack, and wearing a spiffy yellow sweater-and-pants outfit and a too-brilliant smile, Ewan studied her. "You look like you didn't sleep well last night."

He expected Cyd's quick, tart reply. "You either?"

Hallie nudged Cyd into a chair and served her coffee and a freshly baked orange scone. "Ewan has good news for you, Cyd. Tell her."

Cyd plopped the sack in front of Ewan. "Car parts. Yours."

Ewan ignored the sack with the hood and wiper blades; he was too busy dealing with his hardened, aching body. Cyd's blue eyes held his as she ran her finger across the scone's orange glaze, then sucked the tip.

"Here, let me do that for you," he offered, and took her finger to his mouth, licking it slowly.

"You said something about good news?" Her voice was uneven, breathless and perfect.

Ewan held her hand in his, bringing it over his heart. "Peter the hermit is the Night Man—"

"No, he can't be."

"He might fit the description. He motored from Fairy Cove to Three Ravens Island early this morning. I followed him. He's an unfriendly sort. I'm going back today, if you want to come. He might be more receptive in daylight. He knows I want to talk with him. You could be my good luck piece—he's rumored to like you."

"You should go and see him, Cyd," Hallie soothed. "You'll feel better."

"No." Cyd shook her head and bright sunlight caught sparks on her hair. "I don't believe it. Peter would have no reason to—"

Hallie stroked Cyd's hair. "I think you should see him for yourself."

"I'm not going. No. I have business to take care of now."

When Cyd left quickly, Hallie said, "She's afraid, Ewan. For other people, it might be simple, but Cyd fears something she may not want to know. Her nightmares are terrifying. Give her time."

"I knew I shouldn't have come."

Cyd paced her room at Three Ravens Resort, her arms around her body. She turned to look at Ewan, who was leaning against a wall, studying her. "This is crazy. Or maybe I am. But Peter Hedwig isn't the Night Man. There is no Night Man. I'm just imagining that I feel someone watching me. I've *always* imagined it. I want to go home."

As thunder crashed outside the windows, so close it seemed on top of the resort, rattling the windows, Cyd knew that a return boat trip to Fairy Cove was too dangerous, and the decision to stay overnight was wise. Rain slashed at the glass, presenting a watery view of her own frightened expression. If she could only stay awake, the nightmares wouldn't come. . . .

Ewan stared out the windows, and from his brooding expression, Cyd knew he was thinking of the light, fast, summer squall that had taken his parents' lives. He took her hand, warm and strong around her own cold one. "Peter is downstairs, in the kitchen. He's getting the supplies that Sean and Norma brought over today. I'm going down to talk with him. Coming?"

"I . . . don't want to be alone here. You're staying with me tonight, Ewan. And don't torment me."

With a grim nod, Ewan bent to kiss her cheek. "I'm afraid that for tonight, I'm your tagalong. That reverses things a bit, doesn't it?"

Cyd wasn't in a mood to be teased, reminded of how, as a little girl, she had followed him everywhere—because he gave her a sense of safety. He still did, even as he terrified her in other ways.

She shivered, her senses prickling warningly as the wind howled outside the resort. "I hate storms."

"I know. Let's go downstairs."

When Ewan and Cyd entered the kitchen, the tall, thin man seated at the table opposite Sean turned to them.

Cyd recognized Peter Hedwig instantly. Despite his shabby appearance, Peter Hedwig still gave the impression of the intellectual professor that he had been. Roughly dressed, obviously wet from the rain, he sat easily with a teacup in hand, one knee casually over the other. Workman's boots without laces lay open to reveal black socks with holes. His battered umbrella, more spikes than cloth, sat opened on the floor by the back door.

Fragrant with Norma's stew and baked bread, the kitchen continued the woodsy exterior look of the resort with its wooden shingles, log walls, porches, and railings. The kitchen served as a dining room, the tables covered with red-and-white-checked oilcloth. The walls were well-varnished, gleaming logs. The gingham curtains on the windows added a homey effect, with small pots of herbs catching the light. A large washer and dryer stood at another corner, near a table stacked with folded laundry.

"The storm will pass soon," Sean said quietly, as thunder cracked outside the resort. "It's a good sturdy place, Cyd. And the honeymooners upstairs aren't noticing the storm. I've sent word back to Hallie. She knows we're all safe. Meanwhile, eat a bit and relax."

Sean pushed away his plate and sat staring at the storm.

From his wistful expression, Ewan knew Sean was thinking of Hallie. The men shared a look over Cyd's head, and suddenly Sean stood and walked from the room.

"He's brooding a bit, wishing for that sister of yours, Ewan Lochlain," Norma Johnson said quietly. "He'll be trying to call his son now, and Hallie. His ache is plain to see. He's wanting a family, and I don't blame him. Life is long and cold without—without a partner to care for as one ages."

Familiar in her kitchen at one end of the dining room, Norma Johnson was in her sixties, running a little to the plump and comfortable side. An apron with pockets covered her faded blouse and jeans. She studied Ewan closely, her kind face thoughtful. "You do look like Tom. I hope you eat like him, too."

With the ease of a woman used to visiting and working and making others comfortable, Norma placed a basket of freshly baked rolls on the table. "Butter beneath that lid and jelly in the jar . . . honey in the pot, if you like. Help yourselves and mind, no cutting off fingers with that bread knife."

She passed the man seated and staring at them. "This one here isn't much for talking. You remember Peter Hedwig, our own resident professor and gardener. His summer vegetables are wonderful. He grows enough for me to can and to serve the guests. He has a regular little apple orchard, and grapes, beautiful grapes, enough for a little homemade wine. That jam comes from his berry picking. Peter, Sean brought some more seeds. I put the packages in your basket."

"My father always spoke well of you, Peter. And I remember how you and he talked, years ago," Ewan said. "I've been wanting to get better acquainted."

From beneath a mass of gray hair and thick, wild eyebrows, Peter's bright, intelligent eyes studied Ewan. "You would be Tom Lochlain's son."

"Yes. I was here early this morning." Ewan placed his arm around Cyd, easing her into a chair. He sat to place his arm around her while Norma poured tea and placed bowls of stew in front of them.

Peter's stare shifted to Cyd. "You've got Linda Callahan's look. You would be Molly Claire. Little Molly Claire. Such a little ragtag, funny little urchin you were, but you made it. I hear them talk of you, proud of you, they are. They call you 'The Challenger.' One day, you'll put Angela Greer in her place. It was a person like her who turned me against human elements, preferring my own company. It was quite the scandal, of course, and I won't talk about it. You shouldn't think badly of Linda. She did the best she could. I understand that she still does."

With teapot in hand, Norma stared at Peter. "That's the most I've ever heard you say."

"I can converse when needed. She's a good girl, Molly Claire is. She's taking care of her mother when another might have turned away. But as a rule, I just don't like people, preferring my own company—and those who feed me, of course."

"Sean brought you some newspapers and books," Norma stated meaningfully.

"And of course, I like Sean, who brings me newspapers and books," Peter amended.

Peter turned to Ewan. "You look like your father. Tougher, maybe. More scarred by life, but you've got Tom in you—a good man. He did not turn from me in the most difficult period of my life. He always listened and understood. They came hounding him, ready to prove my guilt, and Tom sent them packing—Angela and her cronies, determined to have me out of Fairy Cove. When Tom spoke, people listened. They adored Mary, as did I. The witches couldn't stand that. My debt to him is so enormous, I could never repay it. However, you are not Tom, and I owe you nothing. I know nothing of what happened the day your parents died, and I don't want to be your friend. Leave me be."

With that, Peter stood. Norma helped him into a worn, long, all-weather coat. She adjusted a heavy-looking backpack onto Peter's shoulders, and the hermit lifted the picnic hamper from the table.

"I could help you carry that," Ewan offered as he stood.

Peter's reaction was instant and fierce. "I said, 'leave me be.' Never come to my end of the island again."

"If it's not going to be pleasant discussion between us, then here it is: I studied the winds that day, and the waves would have carried the remains of a boat, or my parents if they were wearing life jackets, to your end of the island. I have some of those remains, no more than rotted chopped pieces of wood, but I know my father's work, the way he notched and fitted. Someone set fire to them, probably built a beach fire. My mother's body washed ashore near Fairy Cove. Those pieces came in more south, as if someone had—"

Cyd reached for his hand. From Ewan's set expression he was determined to push Peter. "Ewan, don't."

He scowled down at her. "He knows something."

Peter stared at Ewan. "I know that you are not to speak with me again. Thank you for the clean laundry and food, Norma. You and Sean are both treasures. Remember me to your mother, Molly Claire. Good evening, everyone."

With that, Peter picked up his umbrella and strolled out into the storm.

As the storm gathered in intensity, the thunder came crashing down, and streaks of lightning cut across the night. Ewan watched Cyd lie in the bed beside him. Even with the curtains drawn, the room lit each time lightning came close, and Cyd's torment would not be calmed by soft words and soothing caresses.

At times she seemed to doze, and just as Ewan slipped into sleep, her terrified, childish cry would split the night.

Norma had come, softly knocking at the door. When Ewan had pulled on his jeans and opened it, the housekeeper said, "Poor child."

She touched his cheek lightly. "You're a good boy, like your father. You're caring for her tonight, aren't you? And worrying a bit for what is stalking her mind tonight?"

Ewan turned toward the woman tossing on the bed. "I want to help her, and I can't. She's exhausted, and still—"

Norma's hand was over her heart. "I know how you feel, loving someone, unable to help."

"Peter? I thought I saw his shadow earlier, there by the woods. I can see how someone could take him for the legend, for the Night Man."

But Cyd had studied Peter closely and firmly declared him not to be the man in her nightmares.

For a moment, Norma hesitated, then whispered, "I've loved only one man in my lifetime, but his heart is tied to another. You're like him in so many ways. I see it in how you care for her—always there, always with a soft word and a gentle touch when she needs it. It's not a lover she needs tonight, but the friend that you have always been. She's terrified, isn't she? More than the usual? Poor girl."

Sean came next, knocking softly. He handed Ewan a bottle, a glass, and a deck of cards. "Peter's homemade wine. He calls it, 'Comfort.' I heard Cyd down in my office. It's this old place with its vents and cracks. I put the honeymooners in rooms that have been treated for sound—I haven't reworked this room yet. I never knew a woman could cry out from her heart like that. Long night for you as well, right? Maybe this will take the edge off. Give her a drop as well, if she wakes."

Ewan settled down to the sound of rolling thunder, spears of lightning and Cyd's whimpers and cries, her nightmares pursuing her. The storm rose again, and suddenly she sat up with a scream that tore his heart.

He hurried to her, bending to soothe her, to bring her back. Suddenly, Cyd lifted her hands as if to protect herself. Her eyes were wide, locked on him, her body trembling as she tried to scoot away, and instead tangled in the blankets.

"Don't you touch me!" The childish cry terrified Ewan, and when he reached for her again, she cried, "Mama! Mama!"

"Cyd! Wake up!"

"Don't you touch me! Mama said it's bad to touch me like that. I don't like you! Stay away from me!"

Each time Ewan reached for her, she cried out again, "Mama! Where are you? Mama!"

"It's Ewan, love. Just Ewan. Remember me? Ewan and Hallie." He could think of nothing else, but to sing softly to her.

His heart pounded as she stared at him, her terror still for the moment, waiting . . .

Then Cyd whispered, "Ewan?"

"Ewan," he stated firmly. "Can I hold you?"

"Ewan," she cried, lifting her arms to him. "Hold me. Please hold me."

He sat carefully on the bed, folding Cyd into his arms, resting his chin above her head and rocking her. "Cyd, you were having a nightmare."

"You think I don't know that?" she demanded unevenly.

Ewan smiled slightly. Crisp and tart, she'd come back to him, and that meant she was more herself. "Tell me about what you just dreamed. Maybe that will help. It's something from when you were a child. You called out for—"

"Mama. I always want my mother to save me. And in my dreams, she does."

"It was a man, wasn't it? Someone who—"

"Who wanted me," Cyd finished, huddling closer. "Oh, Ewan, it's awful. Two men are fighting. My mother is crying and protecting me. The storm is outside, then suddenly everything is still—too still. My mother said I must never talk about that night, that it didn't happen, but it did. Some of the man's blood was on my clothes, I couldn't get it off. He was lying facedown in blood, so much blood and . . . my mother was holding an iron coated with it."

Her fingers clutched at him, and her terror leaped in her eyes as she looked up at him. "Ewan, that man—the dead man—told me that if I didn't do what he wanted, the Night Man would get me. That someday he'd come for me. I remember his voice, the way he acted out the part of the Night Man, frightening me with that old legend. He said there were prices to be paid, if I wanted to live—if I wanted my mother to live. He said the Night Man would wait for me, no matter how long it took, and he'd come for me. I know it's just a story, and the town fosters it for the tourists' enjoyment, but I can still hear him telling me what the Night Man did to little girls who didn't obey and be quiet about— I was so scared of doing something wrong, of the Night Man—"

Cyd hurried for breath, then said, "But I never let him touch me. Ever. And that's why they fought, my mother and the other man. Because of me. Because of me, someone died, Ewan. I don't know who the other man was, but he helped my mother bury that awful man— The man, the skeleton, at the house . . . There were two men fighting, and one died, the bad one, the one that—"

The rising panic in her voice warned him; Cyd needed a distraction and quickly. Ewan held her closer and eased into bed beside her. Her body shook against his and her hands were too cold. "Shh, Cyd. Listen to the rain now, Cyd. Gentle rain, no storms now. Just rain that the flowers need to grow."

She was quiet, holding him tightly. Ewan sensed her straining to distance herself from her memories, blended with the nightmares. "And Norma's town garden, behind her daughter's house. It needs rain. She grows beautiful roses."

"And Hallie catches the rain in a bucket to water her house plants. I bet that bucket is on her back porch right now."

They talked of the people in Fairy Cove, the gardens, Finlay's favorite pipe tobacco, and Hallie's Fairy Bin, how she had changed her life.

As the storm faded and the house settled, their sharing moments were punctuated by a brush of lips, a tender shared kiss. "This is nice, Ewan. Do you do this with all your girlfriends?" Cyd asked as she finger-walked down to his navel and circled it with a fingertip.

He trapped her hand and brought it to his lips. "I wouldn't call them girlfriends, exactly. Talking about life in Fairy Cove wasn't on the agenda."

Cyd's fingers brushed his lips. "But I know your secrets. Why you're driven, and why you're afraid. You're not going to fail in developing a Lochlain boat shop, and I can see the idea of boat kits working."

He chuckled at that. "Enough to try it yourself?"

"It wouldn't be difficult. And you know that I'm right about selling the boat shop and making a profit off it to start a better location. Location, location, location, Ewan."

"What's this I've found?" he asked to distract her, and to please himself with the soft flow of her breast in his hand.

The soft intake of her breath and the sigh that released it was encouraging. But Cyd returned huskily, "I'm not going to give up. You'll see things my way."

Ewan buried his face in her hair, inhaling the sweet, exotic fragrance. "Did I tell you that someone left my mother's locket at the shop? I think Peter knows something about my parents. I'm going there, tomorrow, welcome or not."

"He's such a sweet man. I thought Thelma Brit had that locket. Angela has been scouting for it, offering a reward."

Ewan tensed as Cyd released the snap on his jeans. "It's

the same game as the brooch and the cross. But I have the locket, thanks to a new and better padlock. It's Angela's games, no doubt. If all three of those pieces came directly from the houses of the dead women to me, I'd be a prime suspect if their deaths were murder. Or at the least, I could be accused of stealing. Peter knew I wanted to talk with him, and he's avoided me. That shotgun blast didn't sound friendly. He's a crusty old—"

"Shh. Peter likes me. You heard him in the kitchen. I'll soften him with my wiles and get him to talk with you. But don't push him, he's too much like you—stubborn and uncooperative."

Ewan couldn't move, staked to the bed by Cyd's agile tongue circling his nipples. "'Uncooperative' because I'm not selling my shop?"

"No, because you're wearing too many clothes."

"Is this better?" Ewan asked after he slipped off his jeans and shorts and tossed them aside, returning to lie beside Cyd. He placed his hands behind his head and waited. "I suppose I can sacrifice myself. If you need me to help you sleep for the rest of the night, the least I can do is to oblige."

"Definitely." Her hands were busy already, finding him, and Ewan sucked in his breath.

He tossed a pillow on top of the vent that might take any sounds to Sean's office, then called, "Sean, if you're there . . . leave."

Ewan turned his attention back to Cyd. The tension in her body had eased slightly, and her bare thigh crossed his. Her hand stroked his chest, toying with the hair there, then skimmed downward. . . .

"Um, Cyd? I'm doing the comforting here."

"It's not comfort I need now. Try cooperating a little. You know you need me."

"Ah. That. The reason my hood ornament and the windshield wiper are missing from my pickup. I've got fond memories of that vandalism."

Then Cyd was moving over him, taking him.

Ewan gave himself to making love with her, forgetting everything else, but how she moved, how she sighed, how she tasted, how her heart beat against his. . . .

# Chapter 17

"Why me? Why did I have to offer to charm Peter into talking with you? This isn't a trail, it's nothing but brush and—" Cyd gasped as a small branch, laden with raindrops swung back at her. She blocked it with her arm and stepped around it. With Ewan in the lead on the overgrown trail to Peter's, Cyd grumbled, "You did that deliberately to stop me from talking."

"You haven't stopped griping since breakfast," Ewan corrected, his mind on the hermit, what he knew of the Lochlain's death. He tugged Cyd's hand, increasing his pace as he broke through the dense brush. The trail was overgrown, but obviously used. "Now, come on. Sean thinks we're still in our room, and so does Norma. They know you had nightmares last night and are letting you sleep in."

"Well, I'm not, am I? No thanks to you. There's still fog on the island. It's only eight o'clock. Someone cost me a great deal of sleeping in this morning. . . . This isn't a real path, Ewan. It's overgrown and—stop that. Stop letting those branches hit me."

"They're only tiny branches, and at least for a minute, you stop yammering."

Cyd stopped walking, and, when Ewan turned, she glared at him. "Orders, Ewan? 'Yammering,' is it? You can charm Peter by yourself. Because of the storm, I couldn't wash my clothes last night, and I'm still wearing the same thing as yesterday. I made myself a promise that I would wear clean clothes every day, and now here I am, with you, being battered by wet branches, my jeans soggy, my hair a frizzy mess. You know what rain and damp weather does to my hair and—and stop smiling. You look like you just had the whole jar of candy, or caught the biggest fish, or just—"

If he'd had time, Ewan would have told her how gorgeous she was, all lit up with temper and with her cheeks flushed and her lips slightly swollen from his kisses. Better timing wasn't on his mind when he stated, "You look like a rain forest goddess, a whole bouquet dancing with color, shimmering with raindrops . . . Perfect. My goddess, by the way. You're moving in with me, or I'm moving in with you. It's time. I want you in my bed, or me in your bed, to wake up every morning and enjoy all those little stretching movements and yawns, and sighs and—"

"You are so full of it, Lochlain. A goddess—"

Cyd stopped and, caught by a new thought, narrowed her eyes at him. Her finger jabbed his chest. "You watched me again last night. Every time I— You take up too much of the bed, Ewan."

He studied her hair and picked a collection of tiny rubble from the damp reddish spirals. He pulled one straight and let it spring back into a coil, just as resilient as Cyd. "Because I'm after you, love, needing to cuddle. Could we do this some other time?"

"Cuddle. That isn't what you did last night. My muscles ache—"

"From wrestling me into submission." He kissed her nose. "Let's go. Use your wiles. Charm Peter . . . I really need to talk with him, Cyd."

She snorted and eyed Ewan's grin. "Okay. But you owe me."

"Of course. You're my girl, aren't you?"

He adored her brusqueness, meant to conceal her gentler emotions, when she said primly, "It's a little late for that. We're both past thirty, you know. And neither one of us is sweet. I just want to get back to my closet and my hair-taming gel. Let's go."

"Age doesn't matter. It's the good feeling you give me and maybe I give back to you." Then, with a grim nod, Ewan turned to the path again, leaving Cyd to follow. Leaving her to mull her rain-goddess position, and that of being Ewan Lochlain's girl.

They pushed through the brush and came into a small clearing that opened onto a view of the sandy beach and the lake. Fog hovered above the water, concealing Fairy Cove. A small wooden cabin sat in the middle of the clearing, surrounded by several large gardens. Solar panels gleamed on the cabin's shingled roof, and what looked like a water collection pipe system ran from the gutters down into a reservoir.

A small shed sat a distance from the cabin, overgrown with vines, and wooden shingles green with moss. A hoe and a shovel were propped near the shed's open door. It swung wider as Peter stepped out. He stood still for a moment, then walked toward them. "The only reason I'm not getting my shotgun is because of Molly Claire. Would you share a spot of morning tea with me? Hallie sent some lovely orange-flavored scones. The pot is under the towel, there at the picnic table. Pour, will you, Molly Claire? It's so nice to have a woman's hands, graceful and capable, pouring tea."

The hermit came to stand beside them, studying Ewan carefully. "Come. It's time, I think, for the son of Tom Lochlain, stubborn as he is and set to destroy my peace, to ask his questions. I've been expecting you. The tea service, cups and saucers, are on the table. I do enjoy my morning tea. We try to keep on schedule here, my good friend and I."

Cyd's look up at Ewan warned him not to push too soon, to let the hermit take his time.

Seated at the table, Cyd poured three china cups of tea.

Peter looked up at the sky, and said softly, "Pour another cup, will you dear?"

Then he looked past Cyd and Ewan and called, "Oh, Tom. There's someone here to see you. Come on now, time for morning tea."

When Cyd and Ewan turned to the tall stooped man approaching them, Peter cautioned quietly, "His condition is worsening. Schedules are so important . . . to keep his routine. Do not upset him. You'll see. It's time, I think, for you to meet my friend."

" 'Tom?' " Ewan repeated, as the man came nearer . . . and his features reflected his own. The stride wasn't his father's, strong and sure. This man's gait was uneven, as if he wasn't certain about his bearings.

Ewan's every muscle strained, his heart pumping wildly as he recognized his father. Peter spoke quietly. "Tom isn't having a good morning. The storm last night upset him. He can sense them coming, and that is when—when I have to watch him closely. It is then that he steals away onto the lake and to Fairy Cove. He's quite skilled at taking our boat across the lake. When he returns, he is terribly distressed for days, perhaps weeks. Sometimes I think he does it because he wants to die, to be with Mary. I found him washed ashore, unconscious, after that horrible storm."

Cyd's fingers bit into Ewan's forearm. "It's him," she whispered desperately. "He's the man who looked into my windows. It's the Night Man. . . ."

But Ewan couldn't move, watching the man—his father—come across the clearing.

"No, my dear. It's not the legendary Night Man who the shopkeepers use to boost their sales of absolute trash—cups, hats, and such. It's merely Tom Lochlain, dealing with his guilt and what is left of his life. Let him lead you. Ewan, be careful. I know you are shocked now, but Tom must be treated gently. Norma and I have kept him safe against the cruel world for twenty-one years."

Peter's gaze shifted toward the beach, as if remembering—"At first, Tom could not bear the guilt of your mother's death. Or of seeing his children's eyes . . . his motherless children. I have never seen a man grieve so deeply. He wanted to kill himself, blaming himself. He wouldn't go back to Fairy Cove, couldn't bear life without his Mary. He only wanted this place. I feared what he would do, if left on his own, grieving. . . . After the first flurry of the accident, I began hearing rumors—absolute lies about Tom, and I knew their origin—Angela. She had to destroy what she couldn't have—love. And I knew what Angela was capable of, how she would see him put on trial for murder. I couldn't bear that to happen, not to someone so dear to me."

Tom Lochlain's hair was long and gray, his eyes haunted, but they warmed when he came to stand close to Cyd. "Molly Claire. Here, I've got a present for you."

From his pocket, he slowly took a small carved fairy and placed it in her hand. "How is your mother?"

Cyd's eyes were shimmering with tears, and Ewan watched her struggle for control. But then he wasn't certain of himself—his father was alive. Alive for all these years. . . .

Awash with emotions, Ewan fought against his rising anger. "Life could have been so different," he heard himself say, the raw tone drawn from his heart.

Cyd's elbow nudged his stomach, a silent warning to watch his words. "My mother is well. It's lovely here," she said. "Thank you for the fairies. I adore them."

Tom smiled and nodded, "And the gnomes. I thought you would like them, too. I have a little boy and girl, you know. But I can't go back to them. They'll have good care. They're better off without me. I caused my wife's death. My little girl will grow up to look just like Mary. How I loved watching all of you play, my Hallie, Ewan, my son, and you, Molly Claire."

Ewan stood to his feet, fighting his rage, and Tom stared at him. "You remind me of someone."

"I should, damn you."

Peter was instantly on his feet, clearly alarmed. "It's all right, Tom. He's only a visitor—"

"*'Only a visitor!' I'm your son—Ewan!*"

Instantly, Cyd stood in front of Ewan, her fingers biting a warning into his wrist as she talked softly to Tom. "I kept all of the fairies and gnomes. I still play with Hallie."

"My little girl, Hallie."

"Yes, your little girl. She's grown a bit, as children do," Cyd added gently.

Tom's gaze shifted to Ewan. "You look like someone I once knew. . . . My boy isn't this man. Oh, my boy is a devil of a lad, he is, always tormenting the girls. But he's got a good sturdy heart beneath the devilment, a good lad—I have to go hoe my beans now. Ah, there's Norma. . . . Norma, it's going to be a fine crop this year."

Norma came walking quickly from the woods. "I'd love to have my tea now, Tom, if you don't mind. Go ahead. I'll come see the garden later."

When Tom ambled toward the garden, Ewan's fist hit the table with enough power to make the tea service dance. He looked at Norma, then back at Peter, and his curse burned the damp, morning air. "You could have done something for him, for us. Does Sean know, too? How many know?"

"Not Sean. He has enough dealing with his life and this place," Norma said quietly as she watched Tom gently hoe a row of newly sprouted green beans. "Tom likes rows, everything in its place. Hoeing the garden rows gives him comfort. He was in a terrible state. We couldn't bear to turn him over to—to anyone who might not understand."

Ewan shook off Cyd's restraining hand. "Do you have any idea what Hallie and I went through? With Dad—with him, we could have managed."

"No, you couldn't have," Norma said quietly. "He said he couldn't bear to look at his children, knowing that he'd killed their mother. And Hallie looks so much like Mary. I think he would have harmed himself."

Cyd placed her hand on Norma's arm. "You love him, don't you?"

While Norma looked at the man in the garden, Peter answered softly, "Enough to tend him when he needed medical attention, transporting him far away from Fairy Cove for treatment. As a former nurse, she knew the protocol for transmitting and handling patients, and put herself in a great deal of danger by duplicating and forging records. Doctors and dentists seldom question nurses with mentally troubled patients. When needed, Tom became Peter Hedwig. Sean's grandfather, who owned Three Ravens Resort, knew and kept the secret to protect Tom."

"I want to talk with him. Now. He had no right—" Ewan turned to Peter, furious with them.

"Tom Lochlain never intended to do anything but take Mary sailing. A wind came up suddenly, and Tom said—when he gradually came back to himself—that he should have been able to sail to Fairy Cove, or to the island. He went over and over it. The strange thing is, he said that he and Mary felt so sleepy after they ate, barely able to rouse."

Peter's hand shook when he sat and quickly sipped his tea. His eyes narrowed as he seemed to focus inward, remembering what Tom had said. "The boat wasn't responding, then there was a roar of wind, and suddenly it tore apart. He'd made certain Mary was wearing her life jacket, but he wasn't. Tom fought to save Mary, but he couldn't. He didn't remember how he got here. He only remembers fighting to save her. Her life jacket wasn't—something was wrong with it."

The hermit slowly, precisely folded his cloth napkin as if he were putting thoughts in line. "The odd thing is that they must have been a distance out on the lake, not in the area between Fairy Cove's harbor and Three Ravens Island, which is where he usually sailed with Mary. I . . . after seeing Tom's horrible state, how he didn't want to live, I knew he couldn't bear to see Mary as she was. I took the liberty of taking her to Fairy Cove, where she could be found for a proper burial."

Ewan was on his feet, his hands braced on the table as he stared furiously at Peter. "*You did what?*"

"Ewan . . ." Cyd cautioned softly.

"I did the best I could for dear Tom—and your mother." Peter looked at Tom, who was slowly, methodically hoeing the garden. "At least he makes sense of the rows, if not his loss. He was able to control consequences. I never want to see a man grieve like that again. Once he knew that Mary's body had washed ashore, he did nothing but stare at the lake, wanting to be with her. For the most part, now, that is behind him."

Norma placed her hand on Peter's shoulder and looked at Ewan. "You're upset and—"

Every particle of Ewan felt raw and exposed. "And I've got a right to be, haven't I? You kept him from his family. We needed him."

"Perhaps we just did the best we could for Tom. Perhaps it was wrong to burn the pieces of the boat and the life jackets that washed ashore, but they were ugly reminders to him."

Peter's thoughtful frown deepened. "Strange thing about those life jackets. The canvas was empty of the buoyant filler. I found the filler down the shoreline . . . and the jackets' straps had come off somehow. . . . I should have set the fire back from the beach, but it seemed safer—a storm took the pieces away."

He shook his head as if shifting back to the present. "Tom is safe here. We're caring for him. Norma and I are getting quite good at researching on Sean's computer, when he isn't around. And we keep updated on the latest medical changes for his condition. Between us, we've become quite expert, the professor and the nurse. He has medication, but he's progressively getting worse. I beg you—let him have what he can, tending his garden and carving his fairies and gnomes for Cyd. He still believes Hallie is getting good care, and that Cyd needs the reminders of love more. Please don't take that away from him—it would mean the end of the man."

"Why did Tom come to see me?" Cyd asked quietly, her hand tight in Ewan's.

Despite his own trauma, Ewan understood that Cyd needed answers, too. He put his arm around her and drew her close, his eyes never leaving the man in the garden—his father.

"Because Tom wanted in some simple way to ease what you had seen, to remember that not all men were evil. The memory caught somehow in his brain, a little girl getting the worst of life. He wanted better for you, and he gave you what he had. He doesn't know why now, but it gives him pleasure to carve whimsy for you. He was just coming home, walking from a friend's on a stormy night, when he heard Linda Callahan scream inside her house. The man who was trying to—you were only six. She'd just taken a terrible blow when Tom arrived, and the man—"

*"Was that man my father?"*

"No, my dear. Years ago Tom said he knew the identity of your father, but now that information remains locked inside him. He said only that your father was a man desperate for love. But the other man, the man who died, was a brute. He fed off helpless women. He and Tom had a terrible battle right in front of you, and then—then Tom fell and hit his head. The man continued beating him, and Tom couldn't fight—Linda hit the man with an iron, killing him. She'd already—her life had been difficult already—and Tom buried the man to keep her, and you, safe. Angela hated Linda, and made her life even more difficult. But for some reason, Linda wanted to stay in Fairy Cove. She fought to stay. I think she loved your father dearly."

"You are saying," Cyd stated shakily, "that she loved him, and he was only looking for—"

"Someone to love. You'd better go now, before Sean comes looking. Please," Norma said quietly.

"You think I'm going to leave now? He's my father. Damn all of you," Ewan erupted, fighting against his past, stunned by the discovery that his father was alive.

Peter shook his head. "You can come back. But I agree with Norma. It's time to go."

"We'll be back tomorrow. I want to talk with him," Ewan stated furiously. "I'm not done with all of you."

"Have a caution with words, young man. Tom's memory moves back and forth. He went into the boat shop one night, broke a lock, and he was terribly distressed for days. He couldn't remember the tools and what they did, but he knew that he had used them. They fit his hand, but not his mind. He showed me a brooch and a cross and asked me to keep them. He didn't know why, but they were important to him."

"He took those from my shop. They were my mother's." Ewan remembered the odd placement of the tools on his workbench, and those dropped on the floor. His heart clenched painfully, because he remembered his father's sure hands on the tools, making wood into boats. "The tools were laid at a left-hander's angle, not mine. I use my right hand."

On the way back to the resort, Cyd grabbed the back of Ewan's jeans, holding on until he stopped. "Don't you dare say anything to Sean. You're upset, Ewan—"

He turned on her, furious with life, his father, and himself. Emotions hit him like a bitter ocean's thirty-foot waves—

cresting, swamping, and hitting again. "I've got a right to be, don't I?"

"Think of what's best for Tom. And for Hallie."

"If she knows he's alive, she'll come here. She looks exactly like my mother. It's sure to set him off. Damn it, Cyd. I feel so—"

Cyd hurled herself against him, her arms around his waist. "Ewan, hold me. Hold tight. You're trembling. You look as if you've—"

He held Cyd close and buried his face in her hair. "What? Seen a dead man? My long-dead father? It's all a big joke, isn't it?"

"You are not going to work through this in a few minutes. Peter said we can come back, and we will, tomorrow."

Ewan felt so helpless, the past twisting with reality, his throat tight with emotion. He gathered her closer, ashamed of the tears burning his eyes. "Cyd . . ."

She stroked his hair and kissed his cheek. "I know, Ewan."

Hallie studied the little music box, the tiny ballerina pivoting slowly to the music. Obviously worn and loved, the music box played "Twinkle, Twinkle, Little Star," and was probably collected at a yard sale or a church bazaar. "I had one just like this once," she said, and bent to give Timmy a kiss on his cheek. "Thank you. I adore it."

The little boy beamed. "Grandma put the new pink satin in it."

"I love this so much, I want to put it where everyone can see it. I'll put it in my front window during the workday, where everyone can see her dance. Then at night, I'll take her to my apartment, so she can rest."

Hallie glanced at the window, hoping to see Sean's boat in its stall. In the early afternoon, it remained empty, though he had called. Sean had informed her that Ewan and Cyd had had a restless night and needed their sleep this morning. They would return with the honeymooners from the resort.

"There, the ballerina should have friends, don't you think, Timmy?" Hallie placed the music box in the window amid the fairies. While she stood admiring it, her arm around Timmy, Angela swept by.

In another minute, she was back, peering down at the music box. Hallie recognized Angela's fierce, furious expression and braced herself as her aunt swept into the shop.

"Exactly where did you get that?" Angela demanded, pointing at the little music box.

"It was a gift from an admirer." Hallie eased Timmy to one side, her hand on his shoulder to keep him safe.

"I gave it to her," Timmy stated proudly.

Angela's fury focused on the boy. "You! How did you get it? You stole it, didn't you? Somehow, you managed to steal it."

"Angela—" Hallie warned softly, fighting the memories of that shrill tone, the fear it brought. A glance at Timmy's pale face, his huge rounded eyes told her that the boy was experiencing that same emotion.

"It's bad to steal, Mrs. Greer. Everyone knows what happens to people who steal."

"But you did, didn't you?" she demanded harshly.

Timmy held Hallie's hand, and Hallie found herself shaking, wrapped in the past and Angela's abuse. "Leave him alone, Angela."

"It was a present from Sophia," Timmy said. "I told her boys didn't like ballerinas, but I knew someone who would. She said that was okay."

"Sophia Sanchez. Then she stole it. It's mine, and I want it back."

Hallie spoke very softly, controlling her tone for Timmy's sake. "Timmy, it's time to go home now. You've done nothing wrong. I love your present. But I want to speak to Mrs. Greer. Okay?"

When the little boy hurried out the door, Angela reached for the music box in the window.

Hallie found her hand extended and gripping Angela's wrist before she knew she had acted. With her other hand, Hallie retrieved the music box. "If you want it badly, there must be a reason. Don't you ever, ever talk that way to Timmy, or any other child. Don't you ever come to my shop again. Don't you ever—"

"How dare you!"

"What are you going to do, slap me? Do it, Angela. Try. I can defend myself now. This time you'd have an adult to deal with. I don't know what Ewan has on you, but it was enough to make you back off. Now I'm telling you the same, back off. If I hear that you have dismissed Maria Sanchez as your housekeeper, or that her family has suffered in any way, I will tell everyone how you treated me. It wasn't pleasant."

Angela drew herself up in her power-threatening mode. "They won't believe you. You're just trash. You come from trash. You *are* trash."

Hallie shivered and realized it was from her just-discovered temper. "I have heard that for the last time. Leave my store."

"I'll run you out of Fairy Cove. I'll—"

"Just try."

Who was this person, this Hallie who defended a little boy, a cleaning woman and her family, herself, and her property? Where did this new Hallie come from? When Hallie settled down for a cup of tea a few minutes later, she was still shaking from reaction to her memories of Angela's abuse—and from reaction to her newly discovered anger limits. She'd also just discovered that she could handle a terrible situation. She needed no one to protect her. Layers of self-disgust seemed to peel and fall away. . . . She wasn't a victim anymore. She could fight for herself. . . .

She wound the music box and let the music calm her, the tiny ballerina circling on her pedestal. Hallie frowned and somewhere in her mind, the music blended with another music box. It was blue and dented— Hallie picked up the music box, and on the bottom was scratched, "Hallie."

For the next hour, between a few customers, Hallie replayed the music and tried to deal with the past and the discovery of the music box. Her mother's brooch and cross had already been found and stolen. Ewan could be accused of murder because the women who had owned the jewelry were now dead. The music box had been in Angela's possession. . . .

The facts went round and round, and Hallie needed to see her brother and Cyd—and maybe she needed Sean's strong arms, too. Yet the stall for Sean's Three Ravens Resort boat remained empty, except for the lake's black waves. He'd be bringing the honeymooners back today, and Ewan and Cyd—

Hallie was not in the mood for Allan Thompson, who entered the store smiling at her.

"If Angela sent you, you can tell her that I'm not done with her. You obviously know that both Sean and Ewan aren't nearby, or you wouldn't be here. And that says Angela has been keeping track."

How could she have seemed so helpless, needing someone to protect her? How could she have let this man abuse her? Why hadn't she left at the first slap? Why?. . . .

Anger filled her, so fierce that it knotted her fists, and for the very first time in her life, Hallie wanted to hit someone—just once—and that someone was Allan.

Unaware of this new Hallie, Allan smiled winningly. "Now, honey. Angela may have introduced us, but I knew the minute I saw you that you were for me—"

The anger Hallie had just discovered rose and crested again. "Right for you to do what? How does it feel to be a big strong man, hurting someone so defenseless?"

"I've changed. If you come back to me, we can work things out."

"How much money did Angela pay you to try that one?"

Hallie demanded, furious that she had once been fooled so easily.

That was the past, she reminded herself, and settled in for the last confrontation she would ever have with Allan.

His expression darkened into the savage mask she remembered. But with her temper to defend her, Hallie said fiercely, "You'd like to hit me now, wouldn't you?"

"You need it—"

Hallie grabbed the broom next to her, turned the handle toward Allan, and jabbed threateningly below his belt line. "Don't knock over anything on your way out, or I'll send Marvin after you with a destruction of property charge. Marvin has his own way of dealing with men who abuse women."

She jabbed again. Stunned, Allan started backing away, his hands lowered to protect himself.

"Oh, yes," Hallie said, surprised at her own fury. "I have a need to hurt you there. So you had better leave."

When Allan hurried out of the shop, looking quite flustered, Hallie heard herself laughing. She felt young and free and—and strong. A new Hallie had come to her, filling her with joy. She knew who she was—a woman with heart and power and love. But also a woman who could protect herself—and others, if need be.

Hallie had to tell someone. To share with someone she loved . . . Sean. He'd been so careful with her, fearing that he would hurt her, barely drawing her close, always watching his strength and his hunger.

She hurried back to her apartment, closing the bathroom door behind her. Unbuttoning her blouse quickly, Hallie studied her breasts, lifting them in her hands. Sean's hands were much bigger than hers and—and he was much bigger all over. She closed her eyes and in her mind, saw him without his shirt, working on the docks. Hunger stirred within her, the need to smooth that strong back, to feel it move under her hands—

She could feel herself getting ready for this new Hallie. A new Hallie. A new woman. A new life . . .

Hallie tugged away the band of her ponytail, played with her hair and a sultry vamp expression in the mirror. Today was a perfect time to start a new life, casting off all her fears of sex and men—and Sean's love.

She waited in the shop, eager for a first sight of Sean's boat. When it did pull into its stall, she was terrified of her own plan to have Sean. But she would. Because she was the new Hallie, and she loved Sean.

In a flash, she saw his child at her breast. She saw Timmy's black head of hair amid others of blond curls. She saw Sean come to their marriage bed.

Ewan leaped up onto the dock and tethered the boat. He stood, hands on hips, looking at Three Ravens Island, while Sean helped Cyd and the two couples of honeymooners to the dock.

Hand in hand, Cyd and Ewan started walking, obviously in deep discussion, their heads bent. They looked so close, so intimate, that Hallie decided whatever they shared was not for her to interrupt.

Sean loaded the honeymooners' bags onto a cart and pushed it to the parking lot. After saying good-bye to the couples, he came striding up from the docks, his blond hair gleaming, wearing his healthy, weathered Viking look. . . . And Vikings needed women who could match them. Hallie felt as if she could not only match Sean's hunger, but she could— Shock him? Yes, he'd be perfect!

Hallie came out of the shop to meet him. "What's wrong with Cyd and Ewan?"

Sean shook his head. "Something happened between them. I heard Cyd scream. She had nightmares, and we let her sleep in this morning. They've both been pretty quiet. Ewan seems stunned—I guess it would hit a man that way, to listen to a woman cry out like that."

Hallie looked at Cyd and Ewan walking along the sand, talking to each other. "They seem intent."

Sean grinned widely and placed his big hand on her head, waggling it as if she were his sister. "They shared a room. Quite shocking, isn't it?"

The new Hallie was all woman and strong and she'd just met her demons and Sean was standing beside her and—Hallie stood on tiptoe and opened her lips upon his, flicking them with her tongue. They'd kissed before, but Sean was very careful with her—too careful. "No, I'm not shocked in the least. They were bound to each other long ago, just like you and I. It's simmered between them, and they each fought, but time decides matters such as that. Are you shocked?"

He blinked and she enjoyed his struggling-for-words expression. Then he tugged her close to him, held her as she wanted, and bent to kiss her hungrily. Sean shook with his need, the same as hers, his hands open and pressing her so tightly that they were almost one—almost.

"Come inside . . . upstairs to my bedroom. To my bed?" she whispered.

# Chapter 18

"I've got to tell Hallie."

"Ewan, you're in pieces," Cyd stated. "You can't go to her this way."

"The truth isn't going to get any easier to take. After all these years of believing he was dead, my father has been living at Three Ravens Island."

At Cyd's house, with the day sliding into evening's shadows, Ewan sat in his father's chair. The decision not to return to the boat shop had been Cyd's. Her reasoning was that the shop held too many memories of his father—capable, happy, loving—working there. Unused to letting anyone else make his decisions, Ewan had agreed without an argument.

The man Ewan had encountered only bore faint traces of Tom Lochlain, and he didn't recognize his own son!

His throat tight with emotion, Ewan's fingertip cruised over the delicate carved wings of a tiny fairy. "I didn't know my father carved."

"It's been twenty-one years since the accident, Ewan. I don't remember him gardening either."

"Mother enjoyed that task and kept it for herself. She said he had two left feet and trampled more than he grew. When they went to dances, he was happy just watching her dance with other men. When she did force him to dance, it was an odd sort of sway-thing, holding each other close."

Cyd eased onto the arm of the chair, holding the box of gnomes and fairies. "They've been coming less frequently."

"He can't remember his tools or their purpose. He used to—now he hoes rows in the garden."

With her free hand, Cyd stroked Ewan's taut, broad shoulders. "It's almost dark now. Hallie's call said she was with Sean and from the sound of it, she doesn't want to be disturbed. When we were on the beach, I saw her flip the door's sign to CLOSED the minute Sean was inside. You can tell her in the morning."

At times furious, then silently brooding, Ewan leaned his head back and closed his eyes.

The lines on his face had deepened since the discovery of his father. Distracted, Ewan had silently walked beside Cyd to her home. "At least you know who's been looking into your windows and leaving these."

"He remembered me, after all those years."

"And not his son."

"Ewan . . ."

Ewan was on his feet, pacing. He tossed the fairy to her as if it was something he didn't want near him. "How could he not come back? Cyd, the man had two children. He is responsible for what happened to us. To Hallie."

"It's a lot to take in one day, Ewan. Try to understand. At first, Tom wanted to die. He felt guilty."

" '*Guilty!*' " Ewan exploded. "He is. He is guilty. Maybe he did—"

This time, Cyd's tone was sharp. "He didn't. Don't think for a moment he did."

"There's no way in hell that I can tell my sister that our father is still alive. That he deserted us, living in his—his fantasy life."

Cyd stood to her feet and faced Ewan. "You're definitely not going to talk to Hallie tonight. Not until you've calmed down."

"Don't tell me how to handle my own sister. I know what she's been through, and that guilt doesn't leave me for a minute."

"Then you know what guilt can do," Cyd stated firmly.

"He was responsible for two children. He should have come back." Ewan's hand slashed out, ripping the box from her hands, and the fairies and gnomes tumbled onto the floor. His boot lifted and before it could come down to crush a fairy, Cyd lunged at Ewan, her shoulder catching him in the stomach.

With a grunt, he fell backward, his hands catching her. Taking control of the fall, he landed on the small sofa with Cyd on top of him. "You still know how to tackle, do you? I should have never taught you that. What's it supposed to prove?"

"It proves that you'd better stop and think. Those are gifts to me, from someone who made me feel safe for the first time in my life. You're not destroying them." Cyd held on to Ewan when he would have pushed her aside, rising over him, her fists in his shirt. "You are not going anywhere. Got that. Not now, not in this mood. And you are not talking to Hallie."

"I'm not? And who's going to stop me? You?"

"Absolutely."

Ewan looked down at her fists, gripping his shirt, tugging at it. "What are you doing?"

"Shaking you."

With a disgusted grunt, Ewan easily lifted Cyd aside and stood, staring at the carvings still on the carpeting.

Cyd moved between Ewan and the carvings. "Don't you dare tromp on my fairies. That may be all I'll have of him. Or that Hallie will have. Everything else is gone—except the locket. She's going to marry Sean, and their children will have something of Tom Lochlain, one of the finest men who ever lived!"

She was shimmering with anger, not at Ewan, but at her own life, the nightmares that hadn't stopped. Tears spilled down her cheeks as she stooped to gather up the carvings. She'd put Ewan's stunned fury that his father had been alive all these years before her own dissection of the past. Now, reaction to the discovery of Tom Lochlain, the man who had fought for her mother, and herself, had moved past stunned and into absorbing the reality of what had happened. . . .

When she stood, Cyd hugged the box close to her. She'd held her emotions together, putting her own trauma secondary while dealing with Ewan's unsteady mood. But now, the memories crushed her, refreshed by Peter's description of the night Tom Lochlain protected her and her mother.

"It's because you look like Tom," she whispered, her mind flashing with bits of scenes. "The morning you came back and I found you in the boat, I was terrified and didn't understand why. You look so much like your father as I remembered him from that night. Somehow, in my mind, the man who wanted me, who terrified me, mixed with Tom's face. They were two very different men, all the time, and I put them together as one man in my nightmares. *They were two men . . . two men.*"

She was shaking now, easing into Tom's chair and the safety it gave her. "Two men. And all the time, I thought it was one man. The man who wanted to hurt me is dead. Your father is alive. My mother knew then how dangerous Angela could be—suspected that she might want to hurt your parents. . . . Linda knew something all the time—that ate her. She turned to drugs heavily the year I was six. I've been having nightmares since then."

Ewan stood with his hands shoved deep in his pockets. "Linda was protecting you and herself. Not the right way, but she probably convinced my father—"

Cyd was on her feet again, shaking in anger. "Tom Lochlain was—is—a kindhearted man. He would want mother and child to stay together. We were in danger, so was he, and what would happen to me, and to you and Hallie. If he had been put in prison, do you honestly think your mother could have thwarted Angela? They did the best they could."

" 'The best that they could.' Not quite good enough was it? Your mother is in a home, and my father is losing his memory. My mother was gentle, but she would have fought to defend her family. We could have made it."

Cyd stood her ground, facing him. "Don't you dare talk to Hallie with that bitter tone. Don't you dare."

Ewan's jaw tightened beneath the evening's stubble, and he eyed her. "I've never liked taking orders," he warned in a growling tone.

"Someone has to stop you. And I'm elected." Cyd plopped down onto the sofa, clutching the box. Whatever was locked in Tom's mind might never be released—including her father's identity.

Beside her the cushions depressed, the sofa creaking with Ewan's weight. His arm went around her, tugging her to him.

Cyd huddled against him, and they sat in silence. Ewan held her, his head leaning to rest against hers. After a time, he picked a gnome from the box, studied it, then lined up the carvings on a small table.

"Hallie will like these," he said quietly. "I'll be careful how I tell her, but she's going to be mad as hell at you—for not telling her about him looking in your windows and leaving these. She thought your nightmares came from the Night Man stories, and there it stopped."

"At least that will take some of the pressure off you then, won't it?"

"No. Because I went over the weather reports that day. My father never made a boat that wouldn't hold, that would come apart in a light wind. He was right. He should have

been able to make it either to Three Ravens Island, or to
Fairy Cove. . . . He's been motoring across in storms
through the years—without the capacities he once had. In
full control, he knew the waves, the storms, and the boat.
That boat did not just 'come apart.' "

"Peter said they were both drowsy after eating. Maybe—"

"There are plenty of maybes. Peter's little oddity, like
how my parents were probably sailing out in the open lake,
not in the water between Fairy Cove's harbor and the island.
Including that roar. A roar of wind. Strange expression for a
light summer squall, isn't it?"

Ewan tipped Cyd's face up to his. He stroked her damp
cheek with his thumb, and his light kiss said he understood
and cared. "You look exhausted. Where are we staying the
night? Here, or at my place?"

"I don't care. Ewan, I feel it now. As if someone has been
in my house, prowling through my life. As if someone is
waiting for me still . . . I guess it will take time for that feeling to go away."

Before dawn, Ewan eased from the arm Cyd had kept
firmly around him. In the darkness of her bedroom, he stood
to look down at her. After a restless night in which he held
her as she cried, Cyd slept deeply. She shifted slightly and
settled again as he tucked the sheet over her. "Go back to
sleep, Cyd."

"Are you coming back? You won't go to Hallie without
me, will you?" she asked drowsily.

"You'll be with me when I tell her. She'll need you."

Ewan moved through the shadows on his way to the bathroom. Her bedroom was scented of her, splashed with red
cabbage rose designs and ruffles. The bathroom was tiny and
perfect, contrasting Ewan's rugged face, his harsh expression, the black stubble covering his jaw. He stared at his reflection, recognizing Tom Lochlain's mark and how Cyd
could have been frightened of him—

The shower roused him slightly, enough to recognize the flower-scented shampoo and body soap he'd just used.

Standing in front of the mirror later, preparing to shave with Cyd's tiny razor, he remembered his father's haunted, vacant expression. *You're not my son. . . .*

Cyd was right; he had to be very careful in giving the news to Hallie.

Ewan rubbed his hands together, creating a lather from Cyd's feminine liquid dispenser. The foam reminded him of the life jackets—emptied of their lifesaving fillers, the straps torn away. The facts ran through Ewan's mind: the weather reports, the wave action, the small perfect sailboat that had come apart so easily. With the foam still on his hands, he drew his fingertip over the steam-clouded mirror. The outline of his father's sailboat appeared. "There is no way that boat just 'came apart.' My father was a good hand-crafter, and he kept that boat in solid repair . . . and a wind is not an ocean squall, the flapping of a sail is not a roar . . ."

Distracted and restless in the predawn, Ewan skipped shaving and made coffee. In his jeans, he stood on the back porch. He left the door open, the better to hear Cyd if she called for him. Layers of fog clung stubbornly to Cyd's backyard, the flower bed was only a blur of color, the brush at the back of the lot shadowy.

His mind on his father, and on how to tell Hallie, Ewan slowly sipped his coffee. There were legalities, deep ones with repercussions that could mean trials and sentences. The tangled web included Norma and Peter, who had done their best to help a friend, and even Sean, who did not know about Tom's residence on his property. And Tom would be the focus of any investigation, his mind weaving in and out of the past, a man who had loved his wife so deeply and who was so torn by guilt that he had wanted to die.

On the surface, it might look as if Tom Lochlain didn't

want the burdens of a family and had planned his escape from fatherhood.

And the sailboat had just "come apart."

Ewan locked on to that tidbit, turning it with the rest . . . his parents had been sailing on the open lake, past the island. . . .

As the dawn slid through the shadows, the lawn, heavy with dew, seemed almost gray—

Ewan placed his cup aside. The dawn was beginning to skip through the tops of the trees and lighten the shadows. There, straight from the bushes at the back of the lot to Cyd's windows and porch, was a path—only a lighter trail in the grass where someone had walked through the dew. . . .

His father? Disturbed by their visit, had Tom Lochlain come again to see Cyd?

Ewan closed the door to the house very carefully, testing the lock and keeping Cyd safe. In his bare feet, he crossed the backyard, keeping his path separate from the visitor's. Ewan followed the trail slowly, to the bushes, looking for the man who had visited Cyd before dawn.

He pushed aside a shielding branch and stopped.

Because the path was well traveled and worn. Bits of the lawn's grass lay upon the bare dirt path. This trail hadn't been worn by Tom's infrequent visits, but by someone who knew the path well and had traveled it many times. Turning, Ewan looked back at the house. The view took in the windows on the back of Cyd's house. Even with the windows shuttered and locked, a prowler could tell which rooms were being used by tracing the flow of activity within the house, by listening at the windows. . . .

Hurrying, Ewan followed the almost hidden path toward Fairy Cove's Main Street. It led across an unused, weed-covered lot and into an alley, filled with shadows. It was the alley that passed by Hallie's back door!

The alley's pavement yielded nothing, and Ewan quickly retraced his path. He studied Cyd's back porch before stepping onto it. Bits of grass marked someone's passing, and the trail stopped at the door. Someone had come directly to the door as if he or she knew how to enter Cyd's home.

The path circled to the bedroom window. Ewan, used to sleeping with fresh air, had opened the window slightly—their voices could have been heard easily. . . .

Ewan punched in the security system's code and entered the house, closing the door quietly. Cyd was still sleeping, and Ewan settled into his father's chair, studying the row of carved fairies and gnomes. Cyd had said she'd felt the presence of someone in her home, her office, her rental houses—and her senses were probably right.

A gnome with a bulbous nose and pointed ears leered at Ewan, who asked, "I wonder what you have to tell me. Who's been here? Who's been inside and how they did it? Or if they did?"

Ewan dialed his message machine and frowned as he listened. Angela's shrill tone demanded that he call. She had evidence, she said, that she would trade for his files. Her intimidation of a blackmailer's penalties indicated that she was panicked, giving away too much in a recorded message.

Hallie's call finished the messages. Her voice was happy and light. "Sean is here. Come for breakfast."

Ewan leaned his head back and closed his eyes. He heard Cyd rise and move through the living room to stand beside him. "Stop pretending," she said as she eased to straddle him. "You're not asleep."

With his eyes closed, Ewan sighed, as her kisses trailed over his face. "I haven't shaved."

"I know. I saw the sailboat you drew on the mirror."

"I don't believe it was an accident. But there's no proof now." His open hands skimmed Cyd's thighs and roamed up her sides to cup her breasts. "You're not wearing any clothes, darling-mine."

"The better to distract you. It's going to be a very long day, dealing with what we know. Do you think we could have this time—just for us?"

With her breath curling in his ear, her tongue flicking the lobe, then gently biting it, Ewan managed, "You need me then. But what if I'm that one wrong man?"

It was a small commitment, a tiny piece of softness that he desperately needed—Cyd's confirmation that he had some portion of her thoughts and her heart.

"That goddess statement went a long way. Flatter me some more."

"I'll work on it. Right now, I'm needing inspiration—"

She lifted slightly as Ewan's hand prowled between her thighs, stroking that moist, fragrant cleft. His other was busy with his jeans, lowering them. With a sigh, Cyd lowered herself slowly upon him, her hips lifting and easing down again as Ewan looked up at her. "This time, I'm going to watch you," she whispered unevenly against his lips.

"Are you? I don't think you can manage that, the way you go inside yourself."

"Want to bet?"

Ewan shifted and eased slightly away, enough to remove his jeans and kick them aside. "I'd like to try that fluffy flower of a bed you have. We didn't last night."

She laughed knowingly against his throat. "There isn't much room."

"For what I've got in mind, a single bed would do."

The day could wait, Ewan decided as he stood with Cyd, carrying her back to bed. He needed this softness, the gentle claiming, the feeling of homecoming mixed with sensual pleasure that he'd had with no other woman.

And just maybe Cyd needed him, too.

Ewan let his body take over, and let himself float in love-making there in the shadows with Cyd's fragrance wrapped around him . . . just a little buffer, he told himself—before delivering the blow to his sister. First things first, and right then Cyd was his priority. . . .

"Exactly what is *he* doing here?" Sean demanded.

With Sean growling and pressed against her back, and Allan on her back porch, Hallie had only glanced at her brother and Cyd making their way down the alley from the empty lot—not up from Main Street.

If Hallie had time, she would wonder why Cyd and Ewan approached from that direction, one leading back up to the residential district.

But she didn't have time. It was only seven in the morning, way past her usual rising time. She had been lying next to Sean, feeling his heart slow as she dozed after lovemaking. Bothered by the way Ewan and Cyd had walked together along the beach, Hallie had slid to answer the knock at her back door.

Sean had stretched out on her bed, his hands behind his head. His well-pleased with himself and life expression was almost boyish. "Tell your brother to get his breakfast someplace else, honey. I've got another present for you."

The playful lift of his body beneath the sheet had proved that statement. "Keep that confidence," Hallie had returned with what she thought was a pretty good sexy leer. "And I invited them when you were in the shower earlier."

"Uninvite them." The movement beneath the sheet at Sean's hips had caused Hallie to smile.

She had still been wearing that smile and a well-worn robe, tied at the waist and had called, "Okay, Ewan. Just a minute. I'm coming—"

She had opened the door and above the massive bouquet of roses was Allan's contrite expression. "I do love you," he'd just begun when tears shimmered in his eyes. "Please forgive me. I want to make it up to you. I'll do anything you say. I just want you back."

"Allan, you shouldn't be here. You know that's not possible—" The sound of two big feet had pounded the floor in her bedroom and had headed toward her on a steady path.

Now Sean pressed against her back, and Allan wasn't budging. Instead, his tears started to drip down his cheeks.

Sean's sound of manly disgust didn't discourage Allan. "You don't understand, Hallie. I wanted to be a good husband, you've got to believe me. I'll take those classes you wanted me to take. I'll learn how to be a good husband. If you'll just listen to me, see me once more."

Hallie's soft heart quivered just that bit. She had known Allan's upbringing had been rough, a dominant "do-as-I-say" male as his father figure. Maybe she could help him, and he could go on to love someone else.

Another disgusted sound, this time feminine, drew Hallie's eyes to Cyd, standing with her arms crossed in the alley. She was wearing a black silk blouse and belted jeans, and Cyd's total Ninja look usually meant she was determined to do a job. From the brace of her body back against Ewan's, she was keeping him at bay. Ewan's savage expression said that Allan might not escape him this time.

Hallie did not want to start a beautiful day with a brawl in the alley. "Not now, Allan. Please go away."

Sean reached past Hallie to snatch the bouquet and toss it to the pavement. "Yes, Allan. I suggest that you do exactly that. Forever."

Allan backed down the stairs and turned to Cyd, whose scowl matched Ewan's. "I do love Hallie."

"Sure." Cyd's tone was disbelieving, then she said, "Get lost. But first I want to feel your pants."

Allan's expression changed from shock to comical horror as he backed away from Cyd. She advanced on him. He pressed back against the alley wall and Cyd quickly bent to feel the hem of his slacks. She stood, looked at Ewan, and shook her head. "They're dry. He didn't come across the lawn, the path, or that lot, or they'd be wet. I'd leave now, Allan," she said quietly, turning to him. "Ewan isn't in a forgiving mood this morning. Neither am I."

With a last beseeching look at Hallie, Allan slumped as he walked toward Main Street and turned the corner. Ewan was already brushing past Cyd, who quickly leaped on Ewan's back. She wrapped her arms around his neck, and her legs around his waist. He stopped instantly, a man struggling with a situation, torn between needing revenge and hauling a woman around on his back. "I want to talk with him, Cyd. He could be the one using the path."

"What path?" Hallie asked.

"His pants were dry, Ewan. It wasn't him, and I do not like being undignified," Cyd stated fiercely, ignoring Hallie's question. "What if someone sees me like this? I'm a businesswoman, for gosh sakes, not a kid riding piggyback. Ewan, I haven't had breakfast, and you've got to talk with Hallie. Don't use Allan as a distraction for what needs to be done."

"Then get off."

Sean began to chuckle, and Ewan shook his head. He reached behind his body and linked his hands beneath Cyd's bottom. He turned, and grimly carried her back to Hallie's porch. At the steps, he turned and ordered, "Off."

She bit his ear gently. "If I let you go, will you come inside?"

His tone was sarcastic. "Oh, I'd just love to do that, dear."

"Promise?"

When Ewan nodded, Cyd kissed his ear and slid down to stand on Hallie's porch. "Inside. After you."

"Ladies first."

"Oh, no. I don't trust you. You'll go after Allan."

Ewan's show of teeth said he intended to do just that, and Cyd gripped his belt.

Sean's arms were around Hallie's waist, his face nuzzling her hot cheek. "Do you suppose you two could, just this once, have breakfast at the Blue Moon?"

Cyd's serious look at Hallie equaled her quiet, "No."

Angela replaced the telephone in its cradle. "My sources tell me that Hallie is going back to Three Ravens Island with Sean, Cyd, and that Ewan. Do you know what's going on there, Fred? Allan has just called and said that they were all at Hallie's earlier. I don't like this at all. Fred, stop reading the morning paper and see what you can find out."

Fred slowly closed his morning paper and looked over his glasses to Angela. "Maybe Three Ravens Resort is having a picnic for the guests and invited Hallie and Ewan. Cyd and Ewan are an item, you know."

"Linda Callahan's tramp daughter," Angela hissed. "She's up to no good."

"Perhaps now that Hallie isn't on Allan's priority list, he might try to get into Cyd's good favor. The girl is energetic. I hear she's already ordered carpet for the Elfindale house and plans to do the wall coverings herself. A plumber is at work now, and a gardener—an English garden in the back, they say, with a clipped hedge maze. She plans to open in July, but the whole of the remodeling will be done next year. It should be a lovely bed-and-breakfast—"

"I do not want to hear one more word about Cyd Callahan and her plans. I should have run her out of town a long time ago."

"But she wouldn't let you, would she? Molly Claire seems to have a strength Linda did not have."

Angela turned on him, hissing in fury. "You just called her 'Molly Claire.'"

"That was her name, dear. Before she changed it and her life, remember? She pulled herself up from nowhere, just like your ancestors—shanty Irish, weren't they? Before I added those neat little touches to make them upper-crust?"

"You leave my ancestors out of this. I only gave you that idea, and you did it for Mary. But she didn't notice your attempts to win her favor, did she? Don't tell me you like that girl. That you have anything to do with her. I forbid it, Fred."

"Yes, dear." Fred stood slowly, his shoulders slumped. "I have work to do."

When Angela's fingers sought Tom's ring, Fred said, "Mary's ring isn't there, is it? Oh, yes, I remember it on her finger. She was saving it for her daughter. And Ewan remembered, didn't he? He isn't like Tom was. Ewan has a bitter edge to him, sharpened by you."

"He has to be stopped, Fred. He has papers that could put you and me in jail. He's been blackmailing me."

"I know."

"You know? He's got some attorney holding those copies for him. Deal with that, Fred. Get those copies."

"I'm sorry. There's nothing I can do. Ewan was too smart for you."

Fred left her struggling for words, and finally, as she heard him walk toward the front door, Angela screamed, "Fred, do not test me."

She controlled her fury until the house door closed quietly behind him.

Then Angela hurried to her desk and took out an envelope of bills, tucking it in her pocket. It was the help's day off, and Angela went into the kitchen. She quickly packed a picnic basket.

Paddy O'Connor's demands increased by the day, and Angela detested carrying his whiskey to him—not the cheap sort either, she brooded, but Irish in nature and hefty in price. She'd seen his grimace, the slight doubling over after he drank, and was careful about the bottles she gave him, only half-full.

But she'd play his servant, only until her need for him was finished, then Paddy just might not come back from one of his Chicago jaunts into the dark side. She'd simply give him a wad of money and he'd head straight for whiskey and drink himself to death—or someone in a back alley would aid that journey.

She pushed through the brush to the shack where Ewan had lived. A brisk knock on the door, and Paddy jerked it open, taking the food from her. "About time."

He set the basket on the cot and opened it, lunging into the food and drink. Paddy's piglike eyes watched her as bits of food tumbled from his overstuffed mouth.

Angela both feared and detested him. "Cyd, Ewan, and Hallie have gone to Three Ravens Island again, a picnic probably. I don't care to know how you do it, just get rid of Cyd, and soon."

She tossed the payment envelope onto the bed, and Paddy grabbed it, tearing it open. "That's only a bit."

"The rest when the job is finished. Remember, it has to be an accident, Paddy."

She straightened and tried to keep fear from her face as she asked, "Do you know anything about the deaths of my friends?"

"Not a thing, except the old biddies should have been done in a long time ago—high noses, all of them, like they had no stinks. It would have been easy to do them in though, making it look like an accident."

When Angela returned to the house, she hurried up to the attic, where she could gather Tom around her—the man she should have married.

"Cyd will pay for challenging me, for trying to usurp me in my own town. If she wants to play games, then she has to pay the penalty. Elfindale House is not the start—it is the end, for her."

Angela opened the trunk quickly, took out a shirt Tom

Lochlain had worn, and wrapped it around her, nuzzling the cloth, remembering how safe she'd felt in his arms—until he'd become aware that she wasn't seeking comfort or giving a sister-in-law's affectionate hug.

"Tom . . ." she crooned, longing for the only man she'd ever admired and loved.

# Chapter 19

Did he have time to end his work, to tie up the neat ends of his cowardly life?

Was his deadly disease caused by his self-disgust and bitterness?

Fred's disease was progressing quickly, devouring him, and yet he hadn't killed Angela—enjoying too long the little torments that put fear into her eyes.

She had reacted perfectly, he decided, satisfied that he'd scored with that tidbit about Cyd's wrangling, her intelligence and ability to battle Angela.

Pain sent its tentacles knifing through Fred. He'd delayed using the heavier drugs that could ease him—they would also dull his mind. He needed his wits for murder, but then he'd been successful in that, hadn't he?

He'd been having a quite civilized tea with Bertha Linnea last October, when suddenly she gasped. With several heart repair operations behind her, Bertha clutched her chest and had been in obvious pain.

He'd just learned of his own terminal disease, debating how to keep himself safe once Angela discovered his infirmity. She wouldn't tolerate his illness. Fred had calmly dissected his own chances for survival, if Angela knew, while watching Bertha thrash and beg for help.

Fred had found himself enjoying the sight, watching Bertha's almost graceful tumble to the floor. Clinically interested in how someone so evil might die, he'd ignored her plea for her pills, for help. Instead, he'd carried his teacup and saucer into the kitchen. Her death had taken only a few moments, then he had removed the brooch—Mary's brooch—from Bertha's throat.

With one of Angela's harpies dead on the floor, his life had taken a new purpose: first, to kill the rest and restore Ewan's and Hallie's mementoes to them.

Secondly, he began another set of books: one false, for Angela, and one to start transferring her assets to the Lochlain children. He knew when she was most distracted and would automatically sign the necessary paperwork.

He knew exactly how to take away everything that, in his greed, he had once helped Angela amass.

Cyd's office and Hallie's Fairy Bin were perfect examples of what a good attorney could do in finding loopholes. The house on Elfindale was going to be gorgeous. He'd done that much, at least—helping Hallie and Cyd.

Patricia Erland's asthma-induced death was easy enough to manage. On a late-night visit, he simply concealed his real purpose—to kill her—with the fabricated need of going over legal papers with her. He'd merely stuffed his pockets with an assortment of pollen, small bags of animal hairs—mostly from a long-haired cat—and he'd carried a sachet liberally dosed with a heavy flowery perfume, a scent easily removed.

Patricia's asthma had instantly kicked into gear. When she reached for her inhaler, it was necessary for Fred to withhold it. He'd enjoyed the words, "You're going to die, Patricia. But you'll be with Bertha, and, soon, Thelma and Angela. You've ruined too many lives to live."

While Patricia struggled to get to her extra oxygen tank in the closet, Fred simply waited until she had opened the door, then he'd pulled the rug from her feet. She'd been almost comical, wallowing amid a tangle of her deceased husband's golf clubs, wheezing and pleading. He'd promised to help her—if she'd tell him where she'd put Angela's cross.

But once it was in his pocket, Fred simply came back to watch Patricia's last struggles.

At Thelma Brit's, he'd noticed the locket lying amid a pile of tin can lids. A known pack rat and eccentric, she hadn't noticed him slipping the locket—Mary's locket—into his pocket. He routinely stayed quite late, pretending to let himself out of the cluttered house, but instead went to her bedroom. He'd studied her apnea machine's adjustments and a small series of pinpricks in the hoses caused the machine to malfunction. He added her telephone number to every advertisement, and salesmen had called her several times a day. On the same pretense of handling Thelma's legal documents, he'd visited her late at night and asked for coffee. Thelma, a coffee addict, had, of course, been unable to withstand the aroma.

Without rest, Thelma Brit had fallen asleep while driving, and her accident had been fatal.

His pain hummed steadily through him, but Fred maintained a casual appearance as he walked down Main Street. Though a late-morning breeze came from the lake, a fine sheen of sweat covered Fred's face. Struggling to stay ahead of his pain, not to reveal it, cost him minute by minute.

Ewan should now have the brooch, the cross, and the locket in his keeping. Would he understand that someone watched him, understood his life, his struggles?

Hatred slashed through Fred, deeper than the pain.

He had to kill Angela and soon. He had to make certain Angela died—before his disease made him incapable—or, he took his own life. . . .

He had to die—because he hated himself most of all, for

his cowardice, for his weakness, for Linda, the Lochlain family, and Cyd.

But first, he had work to do, priorities that had to be met in his list to rectify his wrongdoings. He had to find Paddy—because Fred knew Angela's look. She had set Paddy to kill Cyd.

Hallie looked down at the brooch and the cross that Tom Lochlain had placed in her hands. His mind was temporarily clear, and his face filled with pleasure as he studied his daughter. "They were your mother's. You look like Mary."

Tom straightened slightly to stare at Ewan. "You look like me, Ewan. You've grown into a fine man. Peter tells me you're opening up the boat shop, making kits, is it? That's a good idea."

He frowned, his puzzled expression turning to panic as he tried to leap through the years. "But you were just children, you and Hallie."

"Yes, we were." Ewan didn't hide the bitterness of a son whose father was alive and did not come back for his children.

"Angela and Fred took good care of you, and there should have been money from the sale of our house and the boat shop to do well by you. How are your aunt and uncle?"

Peter shook his head, and Cyd's fingers bit into Ewan's arm, warning him of Tom's fragile mind. Hallie, always sensitive, placed her hand on Ewan's cheek, her eyes telling him that she understood.

Then Hallie turned to Tom and took his hand. "They were wonderful. I love fairies."

He looked down at her, his eyes filled with tears that he dashed away. "I'm ill, you know. Peter and Norma take good care of me. Norma used to be a nurse, you know, and Peter researches how to help me. A man never had two dearer friends. I . . . I get confused and I wander. Eventually . . . I don't know what will happen eventually. This disease has unpredictable twists and turns. Sometimes I go to Fairy Cove at night. Sometimes it is to bring Cyd a little gift—I didn't know you were doing so well, Hallie, that you have your own shop. I thought you'd moved away, or I would have—"

"Yes—would have," Ewan stated, and wanted to say more, to damn his father for not coming back.

Ewan struggled with reality—and the emotions churning within him, the past that wasn't pleasant, because Tom hadn't come back for his children.

Aware of Ewan's bitterness, Cyd gripped his hand, reminding him of the necessity to keep Tom calm. "I love the carvings, Tom. I'll give them to Hallie."

"Sweethearts . . . my little fairy-girls, the both of you," Tom said in his old lilting tone. "Shall we have a tea party? Coming, boys?"

"A tea party. He . . . Dad . . . sat there in the clearing, having tea and laughing as though the years had been perfect—for him, maybe." At nine o'clock, the wind howled around the boat shop, the waves as dark and tempestuous as Ewan's emotions. He stood at his apartment window, watching the low clouds churn in the rising wind.

After a long, emotional day, Cyd had slipped from her clothes into one of his shirts and boxer shorts. Ewan turned to see her smooth a blanket on the floor. "That makes about as much sense as what happened today."

"My exercises," she said briskly, as she lay on the blanket. "My hamstrings are tight, to say nothing of my nerves. If I'm going to handle you, I've got to get myself up to par. You should try it. You're not going to solve anything overnight, and Hallie is with Sean. You wouldn't let me go back to my place, because of whoever is stalking me, so I'm doing the best I can—watching you brood and hurt isn't easy, you know."

On her back now, Cyd bent one knee with her hands, then drew it to her chest. "You're complicated, Ewan. You love Tom, and you know it. You're eventually going to wade through all past garbage and come to the one conclusion possible—that Tom needs help. Peter and Norma do, too, and probably Sean. Then you're going to settle down and figure out how we can help them all."

Ewan shook his head and walked to the cabinet, taking out Finlay's bottle of whiskey. He poured the amber liquid into a shot glass and sat to watch Cyd. "It's a mess, you know. Legalities that need to be faced. Insurance fraud for one thing. Money paid on my parents' death—but then, only one of them died. Using someone else's identity is illegal, and there's that little matter of hiding Tom for twenty-one years. My father could be prosecuted, assuming he's found fit, for any number of things. Norma and Peter are right in the thick of it. The courts and attorneys would have a field day tearing them apart, let alone the news media, raking up more muck about them and the Donovan family."

Cyd finished stretching the other leg and lifted her legs off the floor and her head, and with her arms out straight pumped them up and down. "Can't be untangled overnight, or in a week. I'll ask Fred what to do. For right now, you need to resolve how you feel so that you're not upsetting Tom and tipping him further into his disease. And then there's Hallie. She's got enough to deal with."

"Like that jerk, Allan. I'm not done with him."

"Don't you dare. Hallie has changed, and part of her independence and strength now is dealing with her past. It's a priority, and she'll take care of Allan. But Hallie has a soft heart, Ewan, and she forgives easily. Maybe that's something for us to learn. Don't make her choose between you and Tom."

Ewan settled in to watch Cyd. "You could hurt yourself doing that. What do you mean, you'll 'ask Fred'?"

Cyd turned on her side to him, braced her head on her

hand, and began scissoring her legs. "Just that. We've had an ongoing relationship through the years. I give him a 'suppose this happened,' or 'what would you do if,' or 'this will probably never happen, but how would I protect whatever.' He's always helped me. He helped me find a good place for Linda, and Angela never knew about his endowment to that facility, lowering the price for me, of course. He even helped me against Angela. On the sly, of course. If she knew, she'd make his life even more miserable."

She rotated one foot from the ankle. "When I was stewing about Angela owning everything on Main Street, I passed him on the street one day. He gave me a daffodil from the bouquet he was carrying and casually asked me if I'd read the leases for the two empty shops. I found the loophole he intended me to find. Basically, I paid the owners what they needed to pay off that rent-to-own, and they paid off Angela. According to the loophole, they owned the property. We simply deducted that money from a purchase price, and I bought them out. I would never have thought of that. I think he feels sorry for me. Poor man."

"That poor man did nothing to help Hallie and me."

"Hallie has a strong affection for Fred, Ewan. She hasn't told you yet of the good things that he's done, because she doesn't want to argue with you. I'll leave that to Hallie, but take my word for it, Fred did help people anonymously. And he helped pay the tab for my mother at first. I wasn't able to do it all then. 'An anonymous person just paid your mother's bill in advance' my foot. That information came the day after Fred asked about my mother, and I mentioned the cost of her care."

Ewan sipped his drink while Cyd completed the cycle of rotating her other foot. She stood and dragged the blanket to where he sat, then bent to kiss him quickly and take away his drink. "You don't need that."

She pushed his feet apart and lay down, looking up at him

from between his legs. She gripped his calves with her hands, and said, "Hold these. I've got to stretch my spine more."

"Fred deserves sympathy, is that what you're saying? After what we went through, and he didn't help us?"

"Hallie is not going to let you go after Fred. You'll be fighting your sister, Ewan, and she's not a pushover now. How long are you going to hold on to that? Forever? Think of the life he's led, of what he's had to put up with. Don't you think that might be punishment enough?"

Ewan gripped the ankles she had raised to him and looked down at her face on the floor between his feet. "No," he stated firmly.

Cyd looked up at him and smiled softly. "You'll work this out, Ewan. All of us will, but not tonight or tomorrow. Let Hallie deal with discovering that your father is alive. It's waited twenty-one years. It can wait a little longer. Don't push Tom. You're both handcrafters and know boats, the weather here, and the wave action. If you don't think that boat could come apart or they weren't where he thought they were on the lake, in his clear moments, Tom might be able to help you. Give it time. Let go of my ankles now."

Ewan held them, and, in his frustration with life that could not be changed, said, "All that is easy for you to say. You're not living it."

"Not this particular problem. In a way, I think it might be worse to know that your father is alive—under the circumstances, than not knowing who your father is at all."

Reminded that Cyd had met and borne her share of pain, Ewan released her ankles. "I'm sorry, Cyd."

She gracefully came to her feet. She sat on his lap and smoothed back the hair from his forehead, studying his face. "No, it isn't easy," she said softly, unevenly. "It isn't easy watching you and Hallie, my best friend, being torn to pieces. But I love both of you, and I'm doing what I know how to do—deal with life. But I feel so helpless watching this—I love you, Ewan. I always have."

Emotion strangling him, Ewan tried to speak and failed. This softness from Cyd, now when he hurt the worst, gave him more than he could bear. He knew he wanted her, as a woman and as a companion. He knew he enjoyed Cyd, fascinated by each look, each straightforward mood, nothing held back. Ewan knew he might not be capable of giving a woman love like his parents'.

So he simply wrapped his arms around what he needed and pulled her tight, his face against her throat. "Molly Claire . . ."

Whatever storms and rage fought within him, she gave him ease.

Cyd stroked his hair and held him tight. "It's all right, Ewan. I understand. You don't have to say anything."

"I want to. But I want to say the right thing. . . . It's a bad one, Cyd. You should have better." Ewan wanted to say more, but instead he rested against her, held the one safe thing in his life—Cyd. His heart had been too barren for too long, and now emotions squeezed it tightly, little fissures spreading through the shell he'd placed around him.

"I make my own choices," Cyd whispered, and lifted his face for his kiss. "Come to bed, Ewan. You've had a long day. Come and rest. . . ."

In the night, Cyd awoke to an empty bed, the storm howling like a banshee outside the shop. She lay still, listening to the fearful beat of her heart, the waves punishing the pier.

Lovemaking hadn't been important, only holding Ewan safely from his pain, if just for a few hours. He had lain quietly beside her, staring into the night. His silence was worse than his earlier anguish, and when Cyd awoke from a restless sleep, Ewan only gathered her closer. But now she was alone, a storm crashing outside. . . .

"Ewan?" On her feet, she rushed from the empty apartment out to the shop. The front access door was closed, but opened easily under Cyd's hand.

Ewan stood at the edge of the pier, the wind tossing his hair, dressed only in his jeans, his shoulders slick with rain. The wind pushed her back, but Cyd reached him. "Ewan?"

When he turned, his expression was savage, as furious as the storm tearing at the pier, the waves roaring like a hungry beast beneath the rough boards. "Get back," he ordered roughly. "You've got no business being out here."

"And you do?" Cyd wrapped her arms around him, keeping him from the darkness that threatened to swallow him.

Slowly, as if drawing back to himself, Ewan said, "I do." His arms tugged her to him. "It's a stormy night."

"You thought he'd come, didn't you?"

"Your Night Man? Yes. I thought my father might try it tonight. I thought if that's what he needed, to search with what time he has left, I would help him."

"He wants your mother, Ewan, and there's only one place he can find her. I think we can help him, if he sees how perfect her grave has been kept— You're soaking wet. Come inside. We'll watch together."

But Ewan turned to watch the furious waves. "The summer squall my mother died in wasn't this rough. It was only a wind, really, and a little bit of rain. They should have made it. Get inside."

"I am not leaving you."

Ewan searched her face and a slash of lightning lit his wet rugged one. "You're tough, Cyd. But not enough to—"

She tried a distraction, rising on tiptoe to open her lips upon his cold hard ones.

The rough sound that entered her mouth told her of his surprise. Then with his arms still wrapped around her, Ewan walked into the shop, his kiss devouring her, heating her. His kick slammed the door behind them. "Is this what you want?"

She wanted to give him everything, anything, to keep him from his pain, from what he must face. Yet she had her own pride and pulled back from him. "Tell me that you want me. Tell me that you need me. Even if it's only for this way, it's what I want, too. I love you, you idiot. But do you think I'm going to let you run all over me? Tell me what to do? Well, you've got another—mmft . . ."

This time, Ewan's kiss was softer, searching, lush, hungry. He eased Cyd to her feet, his big hands open and pressing her close. His tone was deep and raw, and the words seemed to be dragged from him. "I need you too much. I'm not certain I like it."

Cyd knew how to fight for what she wanted—and just then, it was peace for Ewan— Even if she had to tear it out from him. "Because someone you loved deeply was ripped away from you, you're afraid to put yourself on the line. I'm not. I said I love you, and I meant it. That's the bottom line, no matter what. But I'm no rag rug. I can hold my own with you, and that's what really terrifies you, doesn't it? That we've got more between us than sex. Good sex. But hey, you can get that anywhere, can't you?"

Ewan's fierce expression had shifted into amusement. "Sure," he admitted too easily.

"Jerk. I'm not standing in line."

"But it's better with you. Because you love me, right?"

Cyd sensed a vulnerability beneath the teasing tone, the curve of Ewan's lips. Instead of a retort, she framed his hard face with her hands and gave him the truth, "I do, Ewan."

She ached for the sadness in his eyes, for the way his body shuddered, fighting the past and reality and the future. Cyd followed her instincts and stood on tiptoe to trail kisses over his face. She didn't know where it came from, because she'd always been protective of herself, but she knew how to soothe this one man. She knew how to ease him, if only temporarily, to keep him moving forward, step by step, away from the past. "I'm starved," she said simply. "You need to feed me."

Ewan smiled and studied the way her tumbled hair flowed through his fingers. "And then?"

When Ewan came to her, it was fierce with heat, hunger, and need. This time was different, a branding, a claiming that said she was his. Cyd gave herself to him, allowing the possession, her body moving beneath his hands, his open mouth on her, the suckle of it, and stroke of his fingers.

Then she took, hoarding him, determined to get her share of the muscle and hot skin and raw sounds that she could tear from him. Skin against skin, slick and hot, curving and meeting, a mix of battle and surrender and tenderness.

Poised over Cyd, Ewan watched her, his eyes only slits of silver, his cheekbones gleaming, his nostrils flaring. This was her lover, the man of her heart, the only one whose body had ever pulsed with need, pressing bluntly, intimately against her. His hand ran down her sides, caught the back of her knees, and drew them high as he slowly filled her.

She smoothed his taut shoulders, his chest, and rose to nip his bottom lip, her fingers raking down his back.

Ewan's body jerked hard against hers, locking them. Then he lifted slightly and studied her. "I could be that one wrong man your mother warned you about. . . . I am probably."

"But you're what I've got." She wasn't giving an escape, not now. "If you want a way out, you're going to have to fight for it."

The incredible tenderness in his expression changed the mood, and Ewan moved gently within her. He brought her hand to his lips, kissed her palm, then linked his fingers with hers. He lowered his face to gently nuzzle her cheek, then the other and against her throat.

Cyd lay very still, aware that Ewan was giving her what he could, if not the words, the tenderness he felt for her, perhaps deeper than the sexual need that would soon take them flying. She smoothed his hair, loving the warm strong texture, and drew him down for a long, smooth kiss.

When he moved again, it was slowly, deeply, his lips brushing, teasing hers. The gentle fire rose and bloomed, and Cyd slid safely down to hold Ewan close, to smooth his shoulders, to meet his light kisses.

"I love you," she heard herself whisper before she slid into sleep.

But the man holding her remained awake long after.

*No light summer wind would tear apart a good boat made for sailing.* That fact nagged at Ewan. He shoved away the idea that his father had planned the trip for insurance money. Step by step, Ewan focused on exactly how a sailboat would just "come apart" and how life preservers could be emptied of their filling.

Both answers came back the same: Someone had tampered with the boat. But who?

By agreement, Hallie and Ewan, Sean and Cyd, decided not to do anything until emotions cooled, and thought and steps were clear.

At two o'clock in the afternoon, Sean had taken Hallie back to Three Ravens Island. Hallie wanted to spend as much time with Tom as she could, loving him and becoming a part of his life, and probably, later, his caretaker.

Ewan had thrown himself into his craft, measuring and sawing and tormenting himself. He'd pulled away from Cyd, despite the love she had admitted for him.

It was a slight pain, while Ewan's was much more, Cyd told herself. If he needed time to adjust, she might as well make use of her own—if only for a few hours, before she dragged him into whatever lair she could find.

He'd get his rest and plenty of love, Cyd decided, firmly digging into cleaning out the one-bedroom rental house on

Brownie Lane. Paddy O'Connor's bad check had bounced for the last time, and she had given him warning enough.

The small, tidy house would be lovely for summer people, but not with the stench of Paddy in it. Cyd waded through the trash on her way to a window and jerked it open. She soon opened every window and both doors, admitting sunlight and fresh air while she worked.

She nudged aside garbage with her boot, providing enough room to set a standing oscillating fan. It hummed, propelling the odors toward the windows. Cyd studied the room and, with a nod, walked back out to her pickup. She stripped her cell phone from its belt holster and tossed it onto the seat; losing it amid the trash wouldn't do.

With experience, she placed two boxes in the middle of the living room floor, one for things that the thrift shop could use, the other for the Dumpster. Experienced at cleaning— although never this bad—Cyd immediately dosed the rooms with air freshener from her bucket of cleaning supplies.

"Cleaning? I doubt it," she said to herself. "The place will have to be emptied first. There is no way you're getting your deposit against damages and cleaning back from me."

In an hour, she'd tugged those boxes out to the front porch, swept, and used a shop vacuum on the room. The kitchen took another hour, the refrigerator and the stove layered with food residue. The appliances would take a good day's cleaning themselves, but Cyd did what she could, and trash bags piled up behind the kitchen door. The bathroom needed more than she could give it just then.

Working with a fan and rubber gloves, Cyd could no longer delay cleaning the bedroom—a room that at first glance looked more like a cave than a room. At least she could make a good start. She moved the fan into position.

Pornographic posters covered the walls, and matching magazines littered the bed. Cyd almost gagged at the sight of the overflowing trash bucket beside the bed. From the look of tissues and the lubricating jelly tubes, Paddy had serviced himself.

Cyd decided to gut the room. The thrift shop wouldn't want the clothing, and she began stuffing it into trash bags, careful not to let it touch her.

She stripped the bedding, and noted a corner of paper beneath the bare mattress. Thinking it to be a magazine, Cyd tugged it free.

About to toss it into a waiting garbage can lined with a bag, Cyd noted the neat hand printing.

*Angela's!*

Spotted, dirty, and blurry, the instructions were to Paddy—

Intent upon reading the note, Cyd didn't hear the creaking of the floor as it protested the passage of a big man—until it was too late.

Paddy hurled her onto the bare mattress. "Snooping, are you, Ms. Callahan? Naughty, naughty."

When she pushed herself upward, Paddy shook his finger at her. "Bad girls need to be punished. Old Paddy has a little something for you before you—well, have that little accident I promised Angela. Who's to know if I enjoy you first—make you scream a little? My pleasure, of course."

She refused to give way to the panic nudging her. Paddy O'Connor was beefy and mean; the large well-honed knife he'd just drawn from its sheath gleamed in the dim light. "Give me what I want, and you'll last longer, girlie."

Cyd managed to stand and face him. Paddy blocked the route to the door. The room was too small to maneuver, to escape. He'd have her before she could slide through the window. She had to play for time—and an opening. She would do what was necessary to survive. . . .

"Of course, Paddy. What do you want?"

The knife lifted threateningly; the order came fast and guttural. "Strip. I want to see what Ewan Lochlain has been poking."

Cyd forced back her fear. She slowly removed her rubber gloves, then unbuckled her watch, noting the time. She prayed that Ewan would miss her— Ewan . . . Ewan . . . I need you. . . . Please . . .

She held up her watch. "This is worth something."

"You're not buying me off. I've waited for this."

"It was a gift, Paddy." It was four-thirty in the afternoon. How long would it take before Ewan—distracted by the discovery of his father—missed her? Ewan . . . come to me. . . .

Paddy moved close, his breath foul upon her face. "More."

She unbuckled her jeans belt and slid it slowly away, wondering if she could use it somehow—but Paddy jerked it away and lifted the knife point to beneath her chin. "Take off your clothes," he ordered roughly.

Cyd fought the terror that leaped within her. Paddy would kill her—she had to play for time. Ewan!

She sat on the bed and propped up her boot, slowly unlacing it. Eager for her, Paddy moved closer, and Cyd saw her chance—she suddenly reared back, braced her hands, and kicked him in the genitals.

Paddy doubled, but still crouched and obviously in pain, he raised the knife. "You'll pay for that, girlie."

But Cyd was looking past him at Ewan. "Ewan—"

"That old trick won't work," Paddy sneered.

"Won't it?" Ewan asked coldly, before he grasped the back of Paddy's shirt and hauled him backward. Off-balance, Paddy stumbled against a wall. With a roar, he was back on his feet, charging at Ewan.

Faster and lighter, Ewan chopped Paddy's wrist with his hand, and the knife fell to the floor. "I thought we went through this dance once, Paddy," Ewan said too quietly as he scooped up the knife and hurled it point first to the wall.

Instinctively, Cyd knew—she knew that Ewan meant to kill the other man. "Ewan, don't. I'm not hurt."

"You'd protect him?" Ewan looked down at the man he'd just felled with a flurry of belly punches.

Cyd knew that Paddy could serve as a momentary release for what Ewan could not undo, for his pain. "I know how your mother died," she said slowly, carefully, and tossed a roll of duct tape to him. "I know how the boat came apart. But take care of Paddy first."

# Chapter 20

The door to Greer House was slightly ajar, and Ewan didn't wait to use the doorbell. Furious with his aunt, he stepped inside, followed closely by Cyd. Her fingers locked on his arm.

Determined to face Angela with her note to Paddy, Ewan shook Cyd's hand away. Out of breath from running after him, Cyd reached for his shirt, clutching it. "Be careful, Ewan. I'm not losing you to a murder charge."

"I want to see her face when I tell her about the note you found. You're not saving her from this one, Cyd. Back off."

He followed the sound of the music—a waltz, coming from the stairway. Hurling himself up the stairs, two at a time, to the landing of the second floor, Ewan paused and listened.

The opulent sitting room and bedroom doors lining the hallway were heavy with silence. The music sounded from above, coming from a small open door; the next narrow flight of stairs took Ewan and Cyd to the attic.

When Ewan stepped into the wide, shadowy space lit only by the dormer windows, he stopped suddenly. Cyd, hurrying behind him, bumped into his back and almost toppled down the stairs. He reached for her arm and pulled her up close to him. They stood, stunned by what they saw.

When the music stopped, Cyd's gasp echoed like a shout in the silence. Seated on an old rocker, Fred turned to smile warmly at them as if they were expected and welcome guests. He placed his china teacup on its saucer; the elegant silver service sat on a low stool beside him.

At odds with his calm behavior was a woman about to be hanged, her eyes begging for help, her hair mussed.

Fred placed one foot on the floor and the other on the small chair in front of him.

Angela stood on that chair. The noose from the ceiling wrapped tautly around her throat and her hands apparently tied behind her. Her elegant dress was torn at the sleeve and her hair disheveled; her lips had been taped. Above them, her eyes were wide and bright with terror.

Fred's foot pushed the chair slightly, just enough to make it wobble.

Instantly, Angela's muffled scream tore through the shadows, and Fred smiled, clearly enjoying himself. His voice was cheerful when he greeted Cyd and Ewan. "Oh, hello, Ewan. And Cyd. I'm delighted to see you. Angela and I were just enjoying the music, weren't we, dear? Do sit down—on the trunk, if you will—and let's chat, shall we?"

The old camelback trunk stood between Ewan and Fred.

Angela's eyes followed Ewan and Cyd as they made their way around the trunk to sit on it.

"What's this about, Fred?" Ewan asked softly as he held Cyd's hand tightly in his own. Despite the fury and revenge burning him, he didn't want to see Angela killed.

"I'm sorry there aren't more cups. And there isn't time to get more. I need that large glass of water for the pills that I'm going to take when my work is done with Angela. My disease won't wait any longer. I'm going to die, but I must make certain that Angela can't do any more damage. And I was going to call—I must warn you that she set Paddy on Cyd . . . to kill her."

"We've taken care of Paddy. He's not going anywhere until we call the police."

"He's a murderer, you know. And sadly, his maneuvers cost your parents their lives."

Ewan chose his words carefully, because unknown to Fred, Tom Lochlain was alive. "I know. Cyd found Angela's note directing Paddy to tamper with the boat. He was probably saving it for blackmail. Only an experienced seaman would know how to weaken the stress points of a boat so that it couldn't withstand a good wind. Or to weaken the stitches in a life jacket and the ties."

Ewan looked at Angela. "They were drugged, weren't they? The picnic lunch you so thoughtfully sent?"

Fred nudged the chair, a gesture for Angela to answer, and a shudder rippled through her. Slowly, she nodded.

He smiled briefly. "That's a good girl, Angela. I discovered Angela's plot only recently. Her memory is sliding a bit, and I found a notation about Paddy—to kill Cyd—left like an instruction to a servant. Angela also told Paddy to destroy any evidence, any note, she might have given him about the day your parents died. She wanted them both dead, because she couldn't have Tom Lochlain. He would never have her. He loved Mary so."

Fred looked around the attic. "This is where Angela came to be with him—Tom Lochlain. That trunk you're sitting on holds mementoes of your family, hoarded by her, Ewan. I did remove the little music box and place it where a sweet little girl could find it."

"And you placed Mother's jewelry in the boat shop, didn't you?"

Fred nodded slowly. "The women—Bertha Linnea, Patricia Erland, and Thelma Brit—had them. Angela would have kept anything very expensive, but she did give these small sentimental pieces to her friends—as tokens for helping her ruin lives and the good name of the Lochlain family. As for their deaths, I merely withheld what they needed—until they died. I'm not really a hands-on, physical man, though I did manage my wife into her current state."

The room was suddenly too still, the shadows shifting, as Ewan adjusted to this new fact: The women had been murdered, and Fred was about to do the same to his wife. While his emotions were churning with too many new and painful discoveries, anger battling the need to think clearly and appear calm, Ewan settled in to talk casually—to prevent Fred from killing once again. "Was that necessary, Fred?"

"Looking back, here at the end of my life—and Angela's—probably not," he admitted sadly. " 'Murderer' is a sad label to leave to my daughter. But I simply could take no more—of Angela's schemes, the pain they had caused. It seemed like a whole storeroom of condemning evidence, and for once I was in power—judging them guilty. Retribution was mine. Cyd is shocked, isn't she? Poor girl, I'm afraid there is more bad news to come. I fear I must do this before ending my life."

Then as though too tired to go on, Fred slowly removed his glasses and folded them meticulously. "As our beneficiaries, you and Hallie will receive everything, as is your due . . . except for those things that I want Cyd to have, my little Molly Claire."

When he turned to face them, a shaft of light caught the emerald green of his eyes. "Linda Callahan loved waltzing. I came to her first because I needed her body, then I came because I loved her. She gave me love and understanding and you, Molly Claire. You see, you're my daughter. Angela thought I loved Mary, and I did, but not as a man loves a woman. Linda was that love for me. I was so wrong and foolish then, and not very brave, not brave at all."

The muffled sound from Angela was that of surprise.

"Oh, yes, not even my dear wife knew that you're my

daughter. She only hated you because you were Linda's child. Angela knew I went to Linda for comfort—our marriage bed was cold—and I think my wife was pleased at first that I used discretion, excusing her from wifely duties. But my visits to Linda lasted—until you were six or so, and she drastically declined. Did I help her? No. I was too weak and fearful of how I could lose everything—material things that I no longer care about. I only watched, and for that I am eternally regretful. Later, Angela hated you for your strength and intelligence and the challenge you presented to her."

Fred removed a handkerchief from his suit pocket and polished his lenses methodically. "The body found at Linda Callahan's place was that of a man who had started her on heavy drugs and alcohol. I'm quite certain that Angela had something to do with that connection. Linda was too far gone to listen to reason, sliding deeper into her addictions, and I did nothing—still fearing to ruin what I had built. I will regret that until I die—which will be shortly."

Ewan put his arm around Cyd, who was staring at Fred. "Your eyes are green. You waltzed with my mother. To this music . . . it's the same music that she hums. . . ."

She seemed to freeze, putting facts together and coming up with an answer that when spoken so quietly, shook the room. "Fred? You're my father? *You're my father?*"

"You're angry now, aren't you? I don't blame you." He smiled sadly. "I disgust even myself. Since you were born, I've hung on every word of you, and then I began visiting your house—"

"The path behind my house. You let yourself in, didn't you?"

"Locks have never been a problem for me, especially cheap ones. I've been in Elfindale House, your rental property, and your office at times. I'm so proud of what you've done. I cherished each triumph. There is no excuse for me, for how I managed to mire myself so deeply in Angela's designs—until I could not struggle free. To protect you, Linda would tell no one, not even you—about your father. She protected me, too, you see."

Fred breathed deeply, tiredly. "I desperately wanted Tom Lochlain's strength, but it would not come. He came to me, just shortly before the boating accident. Somehow, he'd talked with Linda about your care and, on drugs heavily then, she named me. He wanted me to take responsibility for you, and I . . . I just never could face condemnation or Angela's wrath. And I knew what she would do—or cause done—to you."

Cyd placed her face against Ewan's throat, as if seeking safe shelter. Her skin was cold, her body shaking.

"I've sickened you, haven't I, my dear, dear child? I can only tell you that I helped Linda as much as I could—I knew I should have broken free, but the disgrace Angela could have caused . . . Pride is a false god, and I regret serving it now."

Fred stood slowly, and placed his arms around Angela's waist. "Weight, you know. I've studied this technique, weighting the body, an old hangman's trick. I don't care what happens to me. Please tell Hallie that I didn't know about Angela's scheme involving Allan."

Angela's muffled, wild protests begged for help, her body shivering, her eyes desperately pleading.

"Wait. Fred, I have to know," Ewan said calmly, so as not to startle him. "Why didn't you stop Angela from abusing us?"

He glanced at Cyd, who was shaking and pale, her arms wrapped around herself as she stared at Fred. "Cyd, are you all right?"

She shook her head and continued staring at Fred. "I'm trying to understand. The strange thing is that I am not angry. I just think he did the best that he could—just like my mother—and sometimes guilt is the hardest burden of all.

He's probably had more punishment than all of us, and I don't think he could bear more."

Ewan didn't want to reason with Cyd now—that Fred could have taken her and her mother away, that their lives could have been much better. There would be time for that later—Angela could lose her life. . . .

And why should he care?

But he did. His mother had loved Angela, blind to her faults, and Angela looked like her—and Hallie. Apparently family ties went deeper than revenge, he decided, mocking himself. "Fred, I asked you why you didn't stop Angela?"

"Bargains made are bargains served. You and Hallie paid the price for keeping my Molly Claire safe, if you can call it that. While Angela focused on the two of you, Molly Claire was free of danger. I begged Linda to leave, tried to give her money for a new start. But she loved me, you see, and she wanted to be near me—she begged me. And I ruined her life. A single woman, alone with a child, was an easy mark. I tried to stop the drugs and drinking, but when the body was discovered, I knew why Linda had drastically turned her course—another secret, this time a death, was too much."

Cyd stood to her feet. She stood between Ewan and Fred, slightly aside. Her words, softly spoken, cut through the shadows. "You gave her more than she ever had. She'd never been loved by anyone, until you."

Ewan tensed, because he needed a chance to restrain Fred, and Cyd had just placed her body in the way. Was it possible that she could forgive him, that she could protect a man who had ignored his responsibilities, a man who had killed?

Fred's face jerked with emotion, tears shimmering in his eyes. "You have your mother's compassion and heart. She was the only good thing I've ever— I . . . Here at the end of my life, I can finally tell you: I love you, Molly Claire. If you only knew how proud I am of you. How very strong and fine you are, much better than your father."

She placed her hand on his shoulder. "Then help me. You have before. You did what you could. Help my mother. It isn't too late. She's kept silent all these years to protect you and me, and it's killing her. Please ease her mind. We need you."

He shook his head, gripping Angela tighter as Ewan started to stand. Cyd turned slightly and placed her hand on his shoulder, staying him. With a solemn look and a gentle pressure, she eased him back down to sit. She held Ewan's hand as she spoke to Fred. "My mother said she loved a green-eyed man . . . one who made her feel like she was in heaven when they waltzed. I can understand how a person can be pushed so hard, until they break. I really do. I saw it with my mother, how Angela relentlessly pushed her."

Cyd's voice softened as she continued. "There is something that needs doing now, after all these years. I have sworn that Angela would apologize to my mother. And I need you to help with a legal matter that is really involved. It could hurt Ewan and Hallie badly. You could help and give them the thing they need most now. It would take a fine mind like yours."

"I could? But my dear daughter, I would do anything— anything to help you, please tell me."

"Cyd . . ." Ewan tensed; decisions about his father hadn't been made. Fred seemed calm, but he'd had years of Angela's tangled plots. His mind was evidently unsteady—and he was a murderer of three women. The futures of Norma Johnson, Peter Hedwig, and Sean were all at stake.

Cyd seemed to understand Ewan's doubts; she moved in to protect Fred. "That's exactly why *my* father will be very good at the job we need. He knows details and the law. He can do it, Ewan. I know he can."

She moved closer to Fred. She placed her hand on his cheek, and said fiercely, "I need you more than I've ever needed anyone—right now. Please don't do this. Please help Hallie and Ewan. Do you know what it would mean to my mother to have Angela humbled before her? Let's do that, shall we? Let's take Angela downstairs and make her comfortable, so that we can talk privately."

But Fred had turned to look up at Angela, his expression hard. "You would like that, wouldn't you, my dear? To apologize to Linda? To beg for her forgiveness?"

His voice lowered and demanded. "I would like that very much. To see you grovel before Linda. You need to please me now, Angela. My disease has made me brave, because I am going to die anyway."

Angela quickly bobbed her head in agreement, and Fred smiled coldly. As if he had just taken on a new, exciting job, he replaced his eyeglasses. "Ewan, please make your aunt comfortable. She might enjoy a lie-down. Cyd and I will be in the kitchen."


"My father is a genius," Cyd stated firmly, when Ewan entered the kitchen.

Fred smiled, obviously delighted. "Just a rough idea that needs smoothing, but I think it will work. I'm so glad your father is alive, Ewan. All we have to do is to change his identity—I can do that easily. As a long-lost relative of your father's, needing care, he will resemble Tom. Tom—we may as well keep the Lochlain name, families usually repeat given names—will naturally come to Fairy Cove, seeking help as the disease progresses. He will, of course, find friendship with Peter and Norma. With a tight circle of family and friends around him as his mind shifts and dims, he'll be quite protected. They can smooth over any rough spots that might arise. I am quite capable of creating an identity and a transition. I thought I might escape once and studied the technique—however, I wanted to stay and watch my daughter."

He took the pill bottle that Ewan placed on the table. "Unfortunately, I do need these. The pain is extreme. Angela

never knew. She would have finished the job somehow, and I
had much to do, to try to untangle what we created. Nor does
she know that I've transferred funds into separate accounts
for my use. Angela's fate is in your hands, as it should be.
Now about Paddy—who remains tied up at Cyd's rental.
Paddy is a direct link to Angela, and he is the most dangerous to the safety of Tom, Norma and Peter. He could tear any
protective plan apart and he must be dealt with. He must be
silenced. Since he actually committed the crime, responsible
for the death of your mother—and the note from Angela is
incriminating—how do you want to handle this, Ewan?"

Ewan sat at the table, and Cyd came to sit on his lap, her
arm around his shoulder. "Ewan?"

He took her hand and smoothed her skin, the fine, strong
bones beneath it. "I'd like Angela to burn in hell. But Hallie
is forgiving, and Angela is Mother's twin."

"She's too dangerous to let go free," Fred said quietly.
"The doctor says I will be gone in six months. But right now,
I can help you. A little later, heavier drugs will be necessary
for the pain. I am a murderer. As a lifetime coward, I suppose I remain that, when I ask that you let me do this for
you—then take my own life. It will simply appear to be an
accidental overdose."

"I want to spend time with you," Cyd stated firmly. "Don't
you dare take that away from me. There are things I need to
know. I want to take care of you."

Fred seemed to wilt, clearly battling deep emotion with
tears filling his eyes. He wiped them with his folded handkerchief and struggled for composure. "Dear child, I am
humbled."

"I want to know you," she repeated. "Ewan, please, help
me. I've hunted for my father all my life, and I can't let him
go now. Say something."

Cyd smoothed Ewan's hair, her eyes pleading with him
and yet filled with understanding.

"Three women have died, Cyd. We can't erase that."

"And we can't bring them back either. It doesn't make it right, but that's where we are. He'll be gone soon enough as it is. I think the pain and years of abuse and guilt caused him to . . ." Cyd looked at Fred. "I have to have this last bit of time with him, Ewan."

Ewan shook his head and sifted through the facts: Angela and Ewan had clashed, and he had possession of a handwritten note that would send her to prison. Others were involved if the whole tale became public. Fred had helped three women die, and he had only a few months remaining that Cyd desperately wanted to share. To protect Tom, Norma and Peter had committed a number of crimes, any one of which was serious and punishable by prison—but given the choice, they would probably act the same again. And then there was Tom Lochlain, a man whose mind had been affected by undeserved guilt.

Ewan weighed Cyd's silent plea against any plan to keep them all safe. "What are the options? Do you see a way out of this?"

Fred tapped his finger on his cheek. "Angela must be punished and restrained from causing more pain. Money and power can be taken away—without that, she is helpless, and that could be her punishment. She's started to rave in private, and it will not be long before her mental infirmity is exposed. Her friends, if you can call them that, are gone. Ewan, I understand that you are holding evidence that proves fraud . . . in how your parents' funds were misused. I'm afraid I was a part of that, and somehow I thought it would increase your benefits later. With you and Hallie as our beneficiaries, it will."

"This isn't about money now, Fred," Ewan stated darkly. "It's about lives being torn apart."

"I know, but the most natural and unquestionable beneficiaries of our estate would be you and Hallie. This transfer would be seamless, while anything else might raise questions. There is quite a bit of money here, and later, you may do with it as you wish. A charity, perhaps?"

Fred turned to Cyd and smiled, his green eyes warm with affection. "A portion and several mementoes of my family will go to you. I'm so very proud of you. It won't do to have Angela committed to the home where Linda is, but perhaps another. Angela will simply decide that she's been distracted lately, that she's tired and needs a good rest. She has always used my intelligence. This time I'll use it against her. It's too late now; but now I do think I can help, do something for everyone, and I feel fearless and energized with a creativity that I thought had died years ago. I can wait until Angela's safely put away. Except that I do fear prison—and the pain."

Cyd covered his hand with hers and spoke urgently. "But Angela must apologize to my mother. Can you arrange that?"

Fred brought her hand to his lips. "Most certainly," he said humbly. "Give me some time with my wife. Her options are limited—a quiet assisted-living home in which she'll have good care . . . or in prison, in which she will not. Paddy is going to jail, of course. The good thing about keeping fastidious records is that you know where the bodies lie, so to speak.

He smiled apologetically. "I am not a criminal attorney, and would have to research particulars. But Paddy once had mob associations, and if it were to be known that he'd let go of certain information about their dealings and connections—oh, yes, I have that, too—he wouldn't live long, either in prison or out. His death wouldn't be pleasant, I'm sure. Paddy will have a sudden burst of conscience and admit to certain wrongdoings—oh, yes, I've kept quite the list of them, here and away. He won't admit to his part in Mary Lochlain's death, which would tie him to Angela. I'm

very good at negotiations. I'll see to that—if that is agree-
able, Ewan. But that part—about Paddy—must be done very
quickly—within hours."

"He caused my mother's death. I'd like to dump him in
the lake. But I won't." Ewan stood, his hands in his pockets.
His instincts told him that Angela had to pay. His heart told
him to consider the others involved, primarily Hallie.

He looked at Cyd and shook his head. "We're all taking a
big chance. It's dangerous."

"Ewan, prison is the place for Paddy. He needs to face
what he's done," Cyd said softly, reaching out to touch his
arm. "With Fred's help we can do this. You see how good he
is at details. Hallie will not want Angela in prison."

"Neither do I. My mother loved her. Make the arrangements, Fred."

"After he does, he's not going to be alone, and he's not
going to take an overdose," Cyd stated fiercely. "Can you
manage Angela until she is—retired? I don't want you staying here. You're staying with me. You'd like that, wouldn't
you?"

Visibly emotional and at a loss for words, Fred nodded
slowly. "My dear, you have your mother's forgiving heart. I
will stay here, until Angela is safely away and the loose ends
tidied. Then I'd like to be with Linda."

When Cyd placed her arms around Fred, he looked up at
Ewan, and let the tears flow freely down his cheeks. Then he
closed his eyes and held Cyd tight, as he wished he'd done
through the years. . . .

When Hallie could finally speak, she said, "All this time . . .
you hoarded things of my parents, Angela. What you put
Ewan through . . ."

At eleven o'clock that night, Hallie sat in the kitchen of
the Greer House, staring at her aunt. Visibly shaken and
fearful, Angela was unusually quiet and obedient. Her eyes

darted around the table, to Ewan's hard, unrelenting expression, to Fred's determined one, to Cyd, who stared back.

According to Fred, Paddy had performed well as he turned himself in to the police, citing his crimes away from Fairy Cove, "unable to stand my sins any longer." And according to plan, Paddy had asked that Fred be at his side.

Hallie glanced at the crumpled note in her hand—evidence that Angela had instructed Paddy to cause her parents' deaths. "I do not want our parents' things in this house one minute longer. I'd like to call Sean. You'll help him get the trunk to my place, won't you, Ewan?"

When Hallie had finished her call, she stood and walked to where the tea service and good china was kept. Methodically, she lifted the elegant teacups and saucers from their moorings and dropped them one by one to break on the floor.

Then she turned to Angela. "I dislike being angry. But I am now. I'm afraid that you'll have to clean that up, Angela."

Angela hurried to get the broom and dust pan, bending to clean the broken china. Whatever "negotiation" Fred had delivered privately had terrified her.

Hallie walked to Ewan, who was standing with his arms crossed, and looked up at him. "You'll do," she said unevenly, tears brimming in her eyes, "until Sean comes."

Ewan gathered her to him. "It's not enough, but it's the best we can do, Hallie."

"Because I want to spend time with our father, I understand Cyd's deep need to be with hers—for whatever time Uncle Fred has left. We have to keep Dad and Norma and Peter safe. I know that what he did was wrong, but I've suffered from abuse, too—though this is the first time I've said it aloud. I know the damage that can be done, and mine was just a short taste of it—Fred, Uncle Fred, has had years of it," she whispered against his cheek. "We can do this, Ewan. But I want nothing from this house, just what was our parents'. I don't want to remember our time here."

"Fairy-girl . . ." he returned. "I'm sorry."

She clutched him tighter, then with an uneven sigh that said she was close to sobbing, Hallie turned to Fred. "Well, Uncle Fred. I'm certain you'll do a fine job. We're counting on you, Ewan and I."

Ewan watched his sister hug Fred and kiss the tears on his cheek. "I don't know that I can be that forgiving, Hallie," he said slowly.

Hallie turned to her brother. No longer a victim, or a child needing her big brother to make her decisions, she spoke her mind firmly. "We have people we love, and we have to protect them. Is it so wrong to give Dad some peace now? To give Cyd the little bit of time she has with Fred? Ewan, if I am blessed enough to marry Sean, I intend to have children. I am going to teach them what Mother taught us—to love and help those around us, to cherish family. I will not have bitterness in my heart for what is past when so much future waits for the both of us."

Then Hallie kissed his cheek and returned to hug Fred once more. She smoothed his thinning hair. "You're welcome to stay at my apartment when you want. I'm a pretty good cook, too."

"Fred?" Angela's whine echoed in the kitchen.

As if bracing himself for a mission, Fred eased Hallie away. His voice was hard and commanding as he spoke to Angela. "I'm sorry, dear. You'll just have to make the best of it and do as you're told."

As Cyd dozed, Ewan lay awake beside her. He stared at the water's reflection upon the ceiling of his apartment.

Hours of churning the details that had emerged during the last two days, with the lives that had been lost, had made sleep impossible.

Cyd stirred, and, fearing that she was entering a nightmare, Ewan drew her closer, rocking her against him. With a sigh, the tenseness left her body, and her hand came to smooth his chest, her head on his shoulder. He nuzzled her hair, taking the fragrance into him.

"You have to sleep, Ewan. You're tight as a bowstring," she whispered sleepily.

Suddenly, the torrent of emotions in him burst, and Ewan shot off the bed. He stood to look out at the lake, the night, the past. Cyd came to stand behind him, her arms around him, her head against his back.

"It's not right that she doesn't pay." Ewan's anger and frustration burst savagely before he meant to speak. "Paddy came back just long enough to murder my parents, to ram that cruiser straight into them. The roar Dad heard was a motor with enough horsepower to kill. Yes, a good boat would come apart when it was rammed, let alone one that had been tampered with. The picnic lunch Angela so thoughtfully sent was drugged. No wonder Dad was off course. . . . I don't like protecting her."

"You made the right decision today—yesterday. There are others involved."

Ewan rubbed her hands, locked over his stomach. "It doesn't go down easy. What Hallie went through . . . Allan, the whole mess. Angela needs to pay."

"But others would, too, and we don't want that. Fred is concentrating on legal loose ends now, but he said that Angela really should be cleaning toilet bowls for the rest of her life. She's cracking, muttering to herself. I suspect he's gotten in a few nudges now and then, through the years, to whittle away at her insecurities. No one will believe her ravings—even if they are true."

"It won't be enough. I don't see how you can forgive Fred so easily. Everything could have been so different for you."

"What good would it do to taint the time I have left with him? None. And thank you, Ewan, for considering that I really need time with my father. I need that closure. Hallie needs it, too, and so do you—by spending whatever time remains for Tom with him. I know how much it cost you to put aside your own needs for revenge, but I also know what a good man you are. Don't you deny it, Ewan. You put everyone else's needs above your own. You won't regret it. You're angry and hurt now, and you're brooding, but you'll see that we all needed this soft closure—all of us."

"Says who?"

Cyd kissed Ewan's shoulder. "Says me. Sean is at Hallie's. Tomorrow you and she will go through that old trunk, and Sean will comfort her when she cries. You'll be brooding and furious for a while, and you can show that side to me—I'm not afraid of facing it with you. Look at the facts. Most of them are positive. You came back and untangled this whole terrible mess. It's never going to be right, or perfect, but we can settle, we always have. It's not going to be easy. But neither of us have had 'easy.' We can do this, Ewan. This is a time-will-heal situation. Sean and Hallie will be getting married. You'll be an uncle changing diapers in no time. Let's go for a walk."

"Cyd, it's two o'clock in the morning." But Ewan noted that Cyd wasn't afraid of the dark, of the Night Man, any longer.

"I know, and neither of us are sleeping. And then you can cook me something, then we'll make love and life will go on. You're going to be a success at the boat kit business. You'll make the Lochlain Boat Shop famous. Of course, I'm already a superior businesswoman. We'll deal with this," she stated confidently.

Ewan had to smile at her arrogance. " 'A superior businesswoman.' Sure of that, are you?"

"I've never been good at modesty. Facts are facts."

Ewan tugged Cyd in front of him, holding her tightly. A survivor, Cyd knew how to take care of priorities. With more restless, emotional nights ahead of them, at least one problem seemed resolved. "No more Night Man?"

She smoothed his face and smiled. Cyd reached around him and patted his bottom. "Just you, bud. Deal with it."

Ewan cradled her face for his kiss. "I'm thinking about doing just that, right now . . . dealing with you."

They came together gently, tenderly, each caress a new bond.

With their hands linked beside Cyd's head, their bodies locked and flowing together upon the bed, Ewan looked down at her. "There's more than this between us."

"Yes, I know. Now get busy."

"Demanding lady." Despite the highly emotional hours behind them, they needed the comfort of lovemaking, of teasing, and Ewan understood perfectly. Cyd's order was meant to ease that taut, restless, and, if the truth be known, helpless feelings for a past that couldn't be corrected. They could only work through the moments together now, doing the best they could for those they loved. . . .

Her hips rose to take him deeper, and Ewan bent to tend her breasts, peaking them with his lips, his tongue.

She arched, giving her body to his care, and when Ewan raised his head, their eyes met as pleasure wound into a tight knot that held them bound together, all else placed aside.

When the tightening could wait no longer, Ewan gave himself to her, and with her breath indrawn and holding, her body clenching his, Cyd still held his eyes.

"Come here," she whispered as he held her, still bound by the aftershocks of their gentle lovemaking.

Ewan eased carefully down, protecting Cyd from his weight. Without a word, she gathered him closer, smoothing the taut muscles of his back, meeting his light, seeking kisses.

"I love this," she whispered sleepily. "The feeling you give me. Like I'm home port and you need me."

He smiled against Cyd's throat. Because it was true. Whatever else would pass, they had each other.

\* \* \*

A week later, Linda sat staring at the mid-June flowers, bowing with the light summer breeze. For the first time in over twenty-one years, her eyes were untroubled as she looked at her daughter.

"The charade is finally ended. Angela and Fred came to see me yesterday," Linda said quietly, her hands folded over her lap. "She apologized, prompted by Fred. He says you know everything. I've had a good rest now. And it's time for me to talk."

Cyd kneeled beside her mother's lawn chair. "I know that he's your green-eyed man, the one who treated you like a lady, who waltzed with you—my father. Tell me why you fought to stay in Fairy Cove."

As though a weight had been lifted, Linda lovingly smoothed Cyd's cheek and looked up at Ewan. She smiled softly and eased Cyd's head upon her lap, smoothing the curls. "My hair was like this once— I fought to stay because I loved whatever I could have of Fred. I knew what he was, that he struggled with life, and that he loved me. I knew when he first held you in his arms and cried so humbly that I'd never leave. He's coming here for care, so we can be together. I don't know if Angela ever knew that you were his daughter—but she hated you, because of me, then because you were smart and young, filled with heart and passion that she didn't have."

Her hand stopped smoothing Cyd's hair, and she looked across the flower beds, toward Lake Michigan. "I'm glad Tom is alive. I won't tell. I've kept secrets for years. One of them is how I saw Peter bring Mary's body back, wrapped in that sail, arranging her carefully so that she would be found. I had heard Paddy talking about a sailboat accident, and making certain no one knew he was in Fairy Cove when it happened."

Linda took a deep uneven breath, and her hand started stroking her Cyd's hair again. "I was so afraid for you, Molly Claire, and maybe for myself, because then I knew Angela was capable of murder. That was why I desperately wanted those pieces of the boat . . . because someday Ewan would come after the truth. . . . Only too late, I discovered that she had sent that man—the one I killed—to get me started on drugs. I hated him, that one wrong man. I like to think that I could have managed my life if I hadn't—I'm so sorry."

Linda eased Cyd's head from her lap and gently pushed her away. "You have a man who loves you. I see it in his face, how he's aching for you. Leave me now and heal. Take her away, Ewan, and build a sweet new life for my Molly Claire."

# Epilogue

Cyd couldn't hide her grief that she'd only discovered her father and had so little time to share with him before he died. In the month since they'd unraveled so many secrets, Ewan had done enough to comfort her.

She stepped into the oversized bathtub he'd installed, with the excuse that if she wanted to spend so much time in the bathroom alone, she might as well do it in comfort.

But Ewan had wanted to do something visible for Cyd, to let her know that he understood what she had lost—a father she barely knew only now.

The boat shop was quiet. Ewan was visiting Tom Lochlain, and most likely they were sitting on the beach, silently watching the waves.

Outside, the mid-July heat was stifling, and Cyd had needed the quiet cool scented water of the huge four-legged tub. She leaned back and closed her eyes, exhausted by the restless, brooding nights in which she ached for Ewan and Hallie, and for herself.

Ewan hadn't wasted time moving her clothing and desk into his one-room apartment. She'd simply come to the boat shop after checking on a rental to find Ewan, leaning against the apartment door, and staring at her. "You won't like this. But this is how it is," he'd said briskly, and swung open the door. But as she entered, he added a little uncertainly, "It's okay, isn't it, Molly Claire? You and me together, not running back and forth for the clothes you need, but more of a—a permanent arrangement?"

"It will need a few homey touches," she'd said, startled and pleased by Ewan's adamant need of her.

"You want me, and I want you—there's no arguing, Cyd. We can work out the details of— What? It's okay with you?" He'd tugged her roughly into his arms, his body shaking. "We'll make it, Cyd. You and I. Just don't leave me."

Cyd smiled softly, reached for pins to bind up her hair, then sank lower into the massive tub. She wiped a tear from her cheek and settled in for a good private cry before Ewan returned—

A sound at the bathroom door signaled its being unlocked—from the outside.

The door swung open, and Ewan leaned against the doorframe, his arms crossed. "Having a private cry, are we, darling-mine?"

"Women do, you know. Let me have at it—alone," she returned a little too briskly.

"It's not exactly sweet, considering our living arrangement, for you to hoard what you feel, you know. I've got a part to play in this. You're supposed to come to me."

"You've got enough to do, dealing with—"

He lifted that one disbelieving eyebrow. "Time for changes. Now. I don't like doors locked between us."

Ewan turned and left the doorway. Cyd shook her head, feeling as soft and vulnerable as the bar of lavender soap, as fragile as the bubbles floating on the bathwater.

He returned and stood naked at the door, his hands and arms loaded with the scale model boats. "I had to put the Closed sign on the door and lock up."

Ewan placed the small boats of different designs, his father's work, in the water. His hands on his hips, he studied them for a minute, then eased into the opposite end of the tub. He gently pushed a skiff to Cyd. She pushed it back, and Ewan gave her one of his heart-stopping boyish smiles when he slid it to her again and it came to nestle between her breasts. "What nice islands you have, darling-mine."

The boats went back and forth between them in the tub, just as their lives had coursed through the years. "How's Tom?" Cyd asked.

Ewan frowned slightly. "Struggling. No more crying by yourself in here, Cyd. No more waiting until I've left to crawl inside yourself. It tears me apart."

"Women cry, hot shot."

Ewan ignored the brassy defense she'd always used, and said softly, "Then do it with me holding you. Here or wherever and whenever you need. Come to me, Cyd."

And so she did.

*Ten months later*

Brooding and watching the woman on the bulldozer, Ewan sat at the end of Cyd's pickup bed. She was methodically ramming the metal monster into the brush, reversing and charging again, forming a pile that would be burned.

At five o'clock on a beautiful warm May evening, Cyd was determined to finish the job of tearing up the old Callahan lot, of leveling it. Wildflower and wildlife habitat seeds stood ready for planting.

In a dirty T-shirt and jeans, Cyd wore a hard hat and gloves and steel-toed boots at Ewan's insistence . . . because she was set to methodically level the lot and partially erase her past. Already the house had been burned and leveled, with mounds of topsoil spread over it. And of course, to Ewan's frustration, she didn't want his help.

In the difficult, emotional year since Angela's plots had
been unraveled, Ewan could only watch Cyd deal with her
pain—her way. And love her.

On second thought, Ewan decided, there was something
he could do. He tramped across the leveled brush and dirt to
the bulldozer; now it was wheeling around the grove's trees,
pushing them into a pile to be burned. Cyd had already given
permission for anyone who wanted firewood to use their
chain saws and haul off what they wanted. All that remained
were stumps and brush, which would be burned.        .

Ewan stood in front of the big yellow machine and
grinned up at Cyd's scowl beneath her hard hat. The motor
hummed, and Cyd revved it, reversing away from Ewan.

He walked toward her, and Cyd pointed away, her mouth
moving to shape the words, "Get out of the way."

Ewan shook his head and walked to swing up onto the
bulldozer. He reached to shift and then cut the motor.
Sweaty and dirty, Cyd scowled up at him. She tore off her
hard hat. "Get off my rig, Lochlain. I'm busy."

He bent to kiss her. "You've been working here since
eight o'clock this morning—"

She frowned at him. "I would have been here earlier, but I
had a little diversion this morning, remember?"

Ewan didn't hide his grin; when a man's woman woke
him up as Cyd had, he could only give equal treatment—
long, slow, luxurious lovemaking that left them dozing and
turning to each other again. But with a mission in mind,
Ewan said, "Darling-mine, I've got a problem. What should
I cook for supper? And did I ever tell you that I love you?"

Ewan enjoyed Cyd's blank look. He ran a finger down her
grimy nose. He'd told her with his body, because some part
of him told Ewan to save the words until the time was ripe—
when Cyd had put away her past torment and eased into her
new life with him. His "I love you" weren't words to give casually, but needed the right timing and setting.

And just maybe, he couldn't say them until the bitterness that had been in his heart was gone. Love for Cyd had left no room for the darkness that had almost consumed his life.

Cyd, on a bulldozer, determined and sweaty, seemed perfect. It was the very first time he'd said the words in his heart, and Cyd's reaction fascinated him. "Oh, yes, I do, Molly Claire. I love you. Deal with it."

Then he eased off the bulldozer and started to walk away. "Ewan!"

He grinned and continued walking. It was a good day for walking, he decided, swinging along the road that would bring him to Fairy Cove.

Cyd's pickup was soon pulling up beside him. "Get in," she called. "You're embarrassing me."

Ewan kept walking, taking a shortcut down to the pier and the boat shop. In the apartment they shared, he noted Cyd storming by—straight into the shower.

When she turned to look at Ewan, he pretended to study a bottle of Michigan's best wine.

Joining her in the shower would be too simple. He gave her an innocent smile that he knew would set her off and grinned when she slammed the door.

Ewan decided to play out the game he enjoyed most of all, making Cyd come after him.

She'd be playing her game, of course, taking a long slow shower and making erotic sounds that could undo a man, and expecting him to join her.

Ewan hefted the filled picnic basic and carried it out onto the pier, down the ladder to their personal skiff, his first attempt at a fourteen-footer and very dear to his heart.

He settled into the boat to wait for Cyd, the woman he loved. Waves bumped the boat gently against a pier, as he looked at Fairy Cove's Main Street.

His sister's bedroom window above the shop was dark. She was at Three Ravens Island with Sean and Timmy and

Tom. The Donovan women were only too happy to see to the
shop when the Sean Donovans, plus the baby that was due in
September, were at the island.

Little could be done about clearing Tom Lochlain of Angela's rumors, without publicly unraveling the entire plot
and disclosing that Ewan's father was alive. Fred had done a
very neat job at sewing up the legal loose ends, and for a
short time Linda and Fred had stayed at Cyd's house.

Gossip circled them, but nothing touched the quiet peace
they'd found. Incredibly as Fred weakened, Linda grew
stronger, caring for him.

Cyd had spent every minute possible with Fred, learning
about him and her paternal grandparents. With care and love,
Fred had lived longer than the doctor had predicted.

Paddy had died soon after entering prison. He'd been un-
wise enough to challenge a younger, stronger bully.

Hallie visited her aunt, and, sensing that her niece was her
only tie to anyone who might love and visit her, Angela had
settled quietly into the assisted-living home.

With a long sigh, Ewan made himself comfortable in the
skiff. At peace, he leaned back to study the sky, the sun setting on the lake's horizon.

Cyd had been right: He didn't regret protecting all of his
loved ones and giving in to their gentler hearts. He'd come
back for revenge. He'd found more.

Including the woman with the long wet hair, wearing a
long white towelling robe, and glaring down at him from the
pier. Ewan smiled up at her. "Oh, hello."

In her bare feet, Cyd climbed down the ladder and took
the hand he extended to her, stepping daintily into the boat.

He admired the length of her smooth legs, the cleavage of
her breasts, both revealed by the robe.

"I can see you're going to be difficult. You know what I
want."

Ewan ran his hand up that smooth exposed leg and his

other hand eased her down to sit. He untied the rope and began rowing slowly along the pier toward the lake. "I thought
we'd have a picnic."

She took the towel from around her shoulders and rubbed
it over her head. "You know what I want," she repeated, as
she turbaned the towel over her hair.

Ewan rowed to the end of the pier and tied the rope again.
The boat rode the waves while he placed a rolled blanket between his feet. He held Cyd's hand to draw her to sit between
his legs, facing the sunset with him.

"You're taking your time," she prodded darkly, as she
leaned back to look up at him.

He kissed her nose. "All in good time, love."

"I hate waiting. Even for this. And you know it. You're deliberately baiting me to see if I'll come after you."

"But I love when you do." Ewan removed her damp towel
and eased his fingers through the thick, damp curls. He took
his time, drawing a little brush from his back pocket and
working through the tangles, just as he had done for little
Molly Claire.

He kissed the side of Cyd's throat. "Get used to it. You've
tormented me often enough. You know that towelling robe is
a killer and that I'm having trouble keeping my hands off
you."

He didn't have to see Cyd's pleased smirk to know it existed. "I know what it does to you. You're probably just a little uncomfortable, hmm?"

Ewan reached into the picnic basket and handed the wine
bottle to Cyd. "Waiting is everything."

He bent to kiss her forehead, to smooth his hands over the
face he loved so much, to enjoy those dark blue eyes, the
love in them. "Happy?"

Her long, pleased sigh told him everything. "Elfindale
House is booked for the summer. My rentals are full, no
problem people there. What about you?"

Ewan poured wine into two glasses and handed one to her. "On schedule. I think you may be right about actually making the kits somewhere else."

Cyd turned to him so quickly that a drop of wine spilled, sliding down her chest to even more interesting places. "You'd put the boat shop up for sale? I know just who might be interested—"

"Now, Cyd, that's not going to happen. The boat shop will be perfect for a showroom. I'll need a shop off Main Street and tourists everywhere to set up full production, in less than a year. I thought maybe you could—"

She turned back to the pink sunlit line running along the lake's horizon. "I'll find something suitable. You could make a bundle on the shop, though."

"And I thought while you were at it, maybe you could start looking for a place for us to build—a house, I mean, with a big backyard . . . fenced, of course."

Ewan held his breath as the idea he'd waited to serve Cyd seemed to hover in the air; and then she caught it, "For a tree house and a place for boys to run wild. And a front porch for little girls' tea parties. I don't think so, Ewan. Not if you mean children. I'm not likely to be a perfect mother."

He bent to kiss her cheek, to nuzzle her skin. The natural need for children rode him, but more importantly was what he shared with his love. "Just for us, Cyd. A real home for you and me, together."

She sipped her wine and leaned back against him, letting him rock her gently. "Feed me, and I'll think about properties you'll need—that we might need. There are commissions to be considered, you know."

"Oh, I know."

"You didn't buy those roses at the end of the boat, did you? They would have cost a pretty penny. Wait a minute. These are early bloomers, and I just—"

Ewan admired Cyd's curvy backside as she bent to retrieve a rose. She settled back between his legs as she studied the bloodred bloom. "You stole these. You're the thief who cut all the roses in the Elfindale House garden."

"Yes, but I did take the thorns off them, love." Ewan took the rose from her hand and tucked it into the fragrant, sexy hollow between her breasts. He handed her a plate filled with roast chicken and a pasta salad and refilled her wineglass.

They ate in silence and in peace, and when finished, repacked the picnic basket.

"Nice," Cyd said finally, and turned, kneeling in front of Ewan, her hands on his thighs. "Now tell me."

"Demanding lady."

"I'm sitting on a bulldozer today, minding my own business, when this smirking hunk of a lover comes up to me, and—"

Cyd smiled after Ewan's long tender kiss. "Told you so. Told you that you wouldn't regret working out life for us all, protecting those we love. So here we are, and words or not, you love me," she whispered huskily.

"Definitely," Ewan returned as he studied her face, the woman he loved.

Let your spring flower with the passion of these new romances coming soon from Avon Books.

### AN INVITATION TO SEDUCTION by Lorraine Heath
*An Avon Romantic Treasure*

Kitty Robertson is never more at home than when in an English parlor displaying her social graces. So she needs a husband who is just as comfortable with his lofty position. Yet she cannot ignore the attentions of an enigmatic duke, who is determined to convince Kitty that he would make a much better husband than his rakish reputation might suggest.

### LOVE: UNDERCOVER by Hailey North
*An Avon Contemporary Romance*

Eric, a "Love 'Em and Leave 'Em" investigator, has got a feeling that prim librarian Jenifer is responsible for the counterfeit money that's popping up all over town. As a trail of bogus bills leads nowhere, Jenifer shows she can let down her hair when she has to. And the wilder she gets, the more Eric starts to realize that a collar isn't the only thing he's after . . .

### THE SWEETEST SIN by Mary Reed McCall
*An Avon Romance*

Years after being sold to the English by his enemy, Duncan MacRae returns to Scotland to reclaim a protective amulet hidden by Aileana MacDonell. Though determined to recover what is rightfully his, Duncan's will is tested when he comes to know beautiful Aileana. Can he set aside his need for revenge for the chance of finding a once-in-a-lifetime love?

### IN YOUR ARMS AGAIN by Kathryn Smith
*An Avon Romance*

For Octavia, a marriage to one of society's wealthiest noblemen will provide her with a life unlike her impoverished childhood, and fulfill the promise she made to her grandfather. But when the Bow Street Runner who once possessed her heart bursts back into her world—at the request of her betrothed—she finds the fire she hoped was extinguished still burns hotly between them.

REL 0504

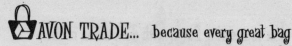

# AVON TRADE... because every great bag deserves a great book!

SARAH WEBB

*Always the* BRIDESMAID
*A Novel*

Paperback $13.95
ISBN 0-06-057166-7

BABE IN TOYLAND

Paperback $13.95
($21.95 Can.)
ISBN 0-06-057056-3

Miranda Blue Calling

*a novel by* Michelle Curry Wright

Paperback $13.95
($21.95 Can.)
ISBN 0-06-056143-2

THE NOT-SO-PERFECT MAN

VALERIE FRANKEL
*Author of* Smart vs. Pretty *and* The Accidental Virgin

Paperback $13.95
($21.95 Can.)
ISBN 0-06-053668-3

KiM WONG KELTNER

THE DiM SUM OF ALL THiNGS

Paperback $13.95
($21.95 Can.)
ISBN 0-06-056075-4

*Elegance*

KATHLEEN TESSARO

*True love never goes out of style*

Paperback $10.95
ISBN 0-06-052227-5

---

**Don't miss the next book by your favorite author.**
**Sign up for AuthorTracker by visiting www.AuthorTracker.com.**

Available wherever books are sold, or call 1-800-331-3761 to order.

ATP 0504